THE NEW SPRINGTIME

BY ROBERT SILVERBERG

THE NEW SPRINGTIME

Time is not succession and transition,
but the perpetual sound of the fixed present
in which all times, past and future,
are contained.

—*Octavio Paz*

For Malcolm Edwards

Book design: H. Roberts

Quality Printing and Binding By:
ARCATA GRAPHICS/KINGSPORT
Press and Roller Streets
Kingsport, TN 37662   U.S.A.

ROBERT SILVERBERG

THE NEW SPRINGTIME

WARNER BOOKS

A Warner Communications Company

T
he death-stars had come, and they had kept on coming for hundreds of thousands of years, falling upon the Earth, swept upon it by a vagrant star that had passed through the outer reaches of the solar system. They brought with them a time of unending darkness and cold. It was a thing that happened every twenty-six million years, and there was no turning it aside. But all that was done with now. At last the death-stars had ceased to fall, the sky had cleared of dust and cinders, the sun's warmth again was able to break through the clouds. The glaciers relinquished their hold on the land; the Long Winter ended; the New Springtime began. The world was born anew.

Now each year was warmer than the last. The fair seasons of spring and summer, long lost from the world, came again with increasing power. And the People, having survived the dark time in their sealed cocoons, were spreading rapidly across the fertile land.

But others were already there. The hjjks, the somber cold-eyed insect-folk, had never retreated, even at the time of greatest chill. The world had fallen to them by default, and they had been its sole masters for seven hundred thousand years. They were not likely to share it gladly now.

1

The Emissary

As he came over the knife-edge summit of the bare rock-strewn hill and turned to descend into the warm green valley that was his destination, Kundalimon felt the wind change. For weeks it had been at his back, hard and dry and biting, as he journeyed from the interior of the continent toward its southwestern coast. But it was blowing from the south, now: a sweet soft wind, almost a caress, carrying a host of strange fragrances toward him out of the city of the flesh-folk down below.

He could only guess at what those fragrances were.

One was a smell that he supposed might be like that of the lust of serpents, and another something like the scent of burning feathers, and there was a third that he imagined was the smell of sea-things that have been brought in nets, angrily thrashing, to the land. And then one that might almost have been the smell of the Nest—the flavor of black root-earth from the deepest passageways below the ground.

But he knew he was deceiving himself. Where he was now could not have been farther from the Nest, its familiar odors and textures.

With a hiss and a jab of his heels Kundalimon signaled his vermilion to halt, and paused a moment, breathing deeply, sucking the city's complex vapors deep down into his lungs in the hope that those strange fragrances would turn him to flesh again. He needed to be flesh, this day. He was hjjk now, in soul if not in body. But today he had to put aside all that was hjjk about himself, and meet these flesh-folk as if he truly were one of them. Which he had been once, long ago.

He would need to speak their language, such few scraps of it as he remembered from his childhood. Eat their foods, however much they nauseated him. And find a way to touch their souls. On him, much depended. Kundalimon had come here to bring the flesh-folk the gift of Queen-love, the greatest gift he knew. To urge them to open their hearts to Her. Cry out to them to accept Her embrace. Beg them to let Her love flood their souls. Then, only then, could Queen-peace continue in the world. If his mission failed, the peace must end, and there would be warfare at last between flesh-folk and hjjk: strife, waste, needless death, interruption of Nest-plenty.

It was a war that the Queen did not want. War was never an integral and necessary aspect of Nest-plan except as a last resort. But the imperatives of Nest-plan were clear enough. If the flesh-folk refused to embrace the Queen in love, to allow Her joy to bring gladness to their souls, then war would be impossible to avert.

"Onward," he told the vermilion, and the ponderous scarlet beast went shambling forward, down the steep hillside, into the lushly vegetated valley.

In just a few hours now he would reach the City of Dawinno, the great southern capital, the mother-nest of the flesh-folk. Where that race's largest swarm—*his* race, once, but no more—had its home.

Kundalimon stared in mingled wonder and disdain at the scene before him. The richness of it all was awesome; and yet something in him scorned this soft place, felt a dark and potent contempt for its superabundance. Wherever he glanced, there was such lavishness as made his head throb. All that foliage, dewy and shining in the morning light! Those golden-green vines, madly profligate, climbing tremendous trees with lunatic energy! From the boughs of squat long-armed shrubs there dangled heavy red fruits that looked as though they could quench your thirst for a month. Thick, sultry bushes with furry blue-tinged leaves sprouted absurdly huge clusters of shimmering lavender berries. The grass, close-packed and succulent with bright scarlet blades, seemed to be offering itself eagerly for the delight of hungry wanderers.

And the gaudy flocks of plump noisy birds, pure white with startling bands of crimson on their huge beaks—the small clamorous big-eyed beasts scrambling in the underbrush—the little winged insects flashing wings of rainbow color—

Too much, Kundalimon thought, too much, too much, much much too much. He missed the austerity of his northern homeland, the dry sparse plains where a patch of withered grass was cause for song, and one met one's food with proper reverence, knowing how lucky one was to have this pouchful of hard gray seeds, this strip of dried brown meat.

A land like this, where all manner of provender lay everywhere about for the mere taking, seemed undisciplined and overloving. A sloppy easy place that had the look of a paradise: but in the final truth it must surely do harm to its unsuspecting inhabitants in the guise of benefit. Where the nourishment is too easy, soul-injury is the inevitable result. In a place like this, one can starve faster with a full gut than an empty one.

And yet this very valley was the place where he had been born. But it had had little time to place its imprint on him. He had been taken from it too young. This was Kundalimon's seventeenth summer, and for thirteen of those years he had dwelled among the servants of the Queen in the far north. He was of the Nest now. Nothing was flesh about him except his flesh itself. His thoughts were Nest-thoughts. His soul was a Nest-soul. When he spoke, the sounds that came most readily to his tongue were the harsh clicks and whispers of hjjk speech. Still, much as he would deny it, Kundalimon knew that beneath all that lay the inescapable truth of the flesh. His soul might be of the Nest but his arm was flesh; his heart was flesh; his loins were flesh. And now at last he was returning to this place of flesh where his life had begun.

The flesh-folk city was a maze of white walls and towers, cradled in rounded hills beside an immense ocean, just as Nest-thinker had said. It soared and swooped like some bizarre giant sprawling organism over the high green ridges that flanked the great curving bay.

How strange to live above the ground in that exposed way, in such a dizzying host of separate structures all tangled together. All of them so rigid and hard, so little like the supple corridors of the Nest. And those strange gaping areas of open space between them.

What an alien and repellent place! And yet beautiful, in its fashion. How was that possible, repellent and beautiful both at once? For a moment his courage wavered. He knew himself to be neither flesh nor Nest and he felt suddenly lost, a creature of the indeterminate mid-haze, belonging to neither world.

Only for a moment. His fears passed. Nest-strength reasserted itself in him. He was a true servant of the Queen; how then could he fail?

He threw back his head and filled his lungs with the warm aromatic breeze from the south. Laden as it was with city-smells, with flesh-folk smells, it stirred his body to quick hot response: flesh calling to flesh. That was all right, Kundalimon thought. I am flesh; and yet I am of the Nest.

I am the emissary of the Queen of Queens. I am the speaker of the Nest of Nests. I am the bridge between the worlds.

He made a joyous clicking sound. Calmly he rode forward. After a time he saw tiny figures in the distance, flesh-folk, looking his way, pointing, shouting. Kundalimon nodded and waved to them, and spurred his vermilion onward toward the place called Dawinno.

A day's ride to the south and east, in the swampy lakelands on the far side of the coastal hills that lay inland of the City of Dawinno, the hunters

Sipirod, Kaldo Tikret, and Vyrom moved warily through the fields of luminous yellow moss-flower. A heavy golden mist shimmered in the air. It was the pollen of the male moss-flower, rising in thick gusts to seek the female fields farther to the south. A string of long, narrow phosphorescent lakes, choked with stringy blue algae, stretched before them. The time was early morning. Already the day was stiflingly hot.

Old Hresh the chronicler had sent them out here. He wanted them to bring him a pair of caviandis, the lithe quick fish-hunting creatures that lived in watery districts like this.

Caviandis were harmless, inoffensive animals. But not much else in this region was harmless, and the three hunters moved with extreme caution. You could die quickly in these swamps. Hresh had had to promise a thick wad of exchange-units to get them to take on the task at all.

"Does he want to eat them, do you think?" Kaldo Tikret asked. He was stubby and coarse, a crossbreed, with sparse chocolate fur tinged with the gold of the Beng tribe, and dull amber eyes. "I hear that caviandi is tasty stuff."

"Oh, he'll eat them, all right," said Vyrom. "I can see it from here, the whole picture. He and his lady the chieftain, and their crazy daughter, sitting down at table together in their finest robes, yes. Feasting on roast caviandi, cramming it in with both their hands, swilling down the good wine." He laughed and made a broad, comfortably obscene gesture, switching his sensing-organ briskly from side to side. Vyrom was gap-toothed and squint-eyed, but his body was long and powerful. He was the son of the sturdy warrior Orbin, who had died the year before. He still wore a red mourning band on his arm. "That's how they live, those lucky rich ones. Eat and drink, eat and drink, and send poor fools like us out into the lakelands to snare their caviandis for them. We should catch an extra caviandi for ourselves, and roast it on our way back, as long as we've come all this way to get some for Hresh."

"Fools indeed is what you are," Sipirod said, and spat. Sipirod was Vyrom's mate, sinuous and quick-eyed, a better hunter than either of the others. She was of the Mortiril tribe, a small one long since swallowed up in the city. "The two of you. Didn't you hear the chronicler say that he wanted the caviandis for his science? He wants to study them. He wants to talk to them. He wants them to tell him their history."

Vyrom guffawed. "What kind of history can caviandis have? Animals, that's all they are."

"Hush," said Sipirod harshly. "There are other animals here who'd gladly eat your flesh today. Keep your wits on your work, friend. If we're smart, we'll come out of this all right."

"Smart and lucky," Vyrom said.

"I suppose. But smart makes lucky happen. Let's get moving."

She pointed ahead, into the steamy tropical wilderness. Diamond-eyed khut-flies half the size of a man's head buzzed through the yellow air, trapping small birds with lightning swoops of their sticky tendrils and sucking the juices from them. Coiling steptors dangled by their tails from the branches of oily-barked trees, harrowing the black waters of the swampy lakes for fish. A long-beaked round creature with mud-colored fur and eyes like green saucers, standing high on naked stalk-like legs like stilts, waded through the shallows, scooping up struggling gray mud-crawlers with clumsy pouncing grabs of surprising efficiency. Far away, something that must have been of terrible size bellowed again and again, an ominous low rumbling sound.

"Where are all these caviandis?" Vyrom asked.

"By fast-flowing streams," said Sipirod. "Such as feed these filthy sluggish lakes here. We'll see a few of them on the other side."

"I'd be glad to be done with this job in an hour," Kaldo Tikret said, "and get myself back to the city in one piece. What idiocy, risking our lives for a few stinking exchange-units—"

"Not so few," Vyrom said.

"Even so. It's not worth it." On the way out, they had talked of their chances of running into something ugly here. Did it make sense, dying for a few exchange-units? Of course not. But that was how it was: you liked to eat regularly, you went hunting where they told you to hunt, and you caught what they wanted you to catch. That was how it was. They tell us, we do. "Let's get it over with," Kaldo Tikret said.

"Right," said Sipirod. "But first we have to cross the swamp."

She led the way, tiptoeing as if she expected the spongy earth to swallow her if she gave it her full weight. The pollen became thicker as they moved southward toward the nearest of the lakes. It clung to their fur and blocked their nostrils. The air seemed tangible. The heat was oppressive. Even during the bleak days of the Long Winter this must have been a land of mild weather, and here, as the New Springtime surged yearly toward greater warmth, the lake country lay in the grip of an almost unbearable sultriness.

"You see any caviandis yet?" Vyrom asked.

Sipirod shook her head. "Not here. By the streams. The streams."

They went onward. The distant rumbling bellow grew louder.

"A gorynth, sounds like," Kaldo Tikret said moodily. "Maybe we ought to head in some other direction."

"There are caviandis here," said Sipirod.

Kaldo Tikret said, scowling, "And we're risking our lives so the chronicler will have his caviandis to study. By the Five, it must be their coupling he wants to study, don't you think?"

"Not him," said Vyrom, with a laugh. "I'll bet he doesn't care a hjjk's turd for coupling, that one."

"He must have, at least once," Kaldo Tikret said. "There's Nialli Apuilana, after all."

"That wild daughter of his, yes."

"On the other hand, did he have anything to do with the making of her? If you ask me, Nialli Apuilana sprouted in Taniane's womb without any help from Hresh. There's nothing about her that's his. They look like sisters, that pair, not mother and daughter."

"Be quiet," Sipirod said, giving the two men a louring look. "All this chatter does us no good here."

Kaldo Tikret said, "But they say Hresh is too deep in his studies and his spells to spare any time for coupling. What a waste! I tell you, if I could have either one in my bed for an hour, the mother or the daughter—"

"Enough," said Sipirod more sharply. "If you don't have any respect for the chieftain or her daughter, at least show some for your own neck Those are treasonous words. And we have work to do. See, there?"

"Is that a caviandi?" Vyrom murmured.

She nodded. A hundred paces ahead, where a swift narrow stream flowed into the stagnant algae-fouled lake, a creature the size of a half-grown child crouched by the water's edge, trolling for fish with quick sweeps of its large hands. Its purple body was slender, with a stiff mane of yellow hair standing up along its neck and spine. Sipirod beckoned to the men to be still and began to creep up silently behind it. At the last moment the caviandi, taken altogether by surprise, looked around. It made a soft sighing sound and huddled frozen where it was.

Then, rising on its haunches, the creature held up its hands in what might have been a gesture of submission. The caviandi's arms were short and plump, and its outstretched fingers seemed not very different from those of the hunters. Its eyes were violet-hued and had an unexpected gleam of intelligence in them.

No one moved.

After a long moment the caviandi bolted suddenly and attempted to run for it. But it made the mistake of trying to enter the forest behind it instead of going into the lake, and Sipirod was too quick. She rushed forward, diving and sliding along the muddy ground, leaving a track behind her. Catching the animal by the throat and midsection, she swung it upward, holding it aloft. It squealed and kicked in anguish until Vyrom came up behind her and popped it into a sack. Kaldo Tikret tied the sack shut.

"That's one," said Sipirod with satisfaction. "Female."

"You stay here and guard it," Vyrom said to Kaldo Tikret. "We'll go find us another one. Then we can get out of this place."

Kaldo Tikret wiped a clot of yellow moss-pollen from his shaggy muzzle, "Be quick about it. I don't like standing here by myself."

"No," said Vyrom, jeering. "Some hjjks might sneak up on you and carry you away."

"Hjjks? You think I'm worried about hjjks?" Kaldo Tikret laughed. In quick bold hand-movements he drew the stark outline of one of the insect-men in the air, the towering elongated body, the sharp constrictions between head and thorax, thorax and abdomen, the long narrow head, the jutting beak, the jointed limbs. "I'd tear the legs right off any hjjk who tried to give me trouble," he said, acting it out in fierce pantomime, "and stuff them into its bunghole. What would hjjks be doing in country this hot, though? But there are dangers enough. Make it quick, will you?"

"Quick as we can," said Sipirod.

But their luck had changed. An hour and a half she and Vyrom trudged futilely through the swamps, until their fur was miserably soggy and stained a bright yellow everywhere. The moss-flowers, tirelessly pumping forth their pollen, turned the sky dark with it, and everything that was phosphorescent or luminescent in the jungle began to glow and pulsate. Some lantern-trees lit up like beacons and the moss itself gleamed brightly and somber bluish radiance came from the lakes. Of other caviandis they found none at all.

After a time they turned back. As they neared the place where they had left Kaldo Tikret, they heard a sudden hoarse cry for help, strange and strangled-sounding.

"Hurry!" Vyrom cried. "He's in trouble."

Sipirod caught her mate by the wrist. "Wait."

"Wait?"

"If something's wrong, no sense both of us plunging into it together. Let me go up ahead and see what's happening."

She slipped through the underbrush and stepped out into the clearing. Out of the lake rose a gorynth's black shining neck, perhaps that of the same monster they had heard hooting earlier. The huge creature's body lay submerged. Only its curving upper surface was visible, like a row of sunken barrels; but its neck, five times the length of a man and ornamented by triple rows of blunt black spines, arched up and outward and down again, and at the end of it was Kaldo Tikret, caught in its powerful jaws. He was still calling for help, but more feebly, now. In another moment he would be under the water.

"Vyrom!" she shouted.

He came running, brandishing his spear. But where to hurl it? What little of the gorynth's body could be seen was heavily armored with thick overlapping scales that would send his spear bouncing aside. The long neck was more vulnerable, but a difficult target. Then even that disappeared, and Kaldo Tikret with it, down into the dark turbid water. Black bubbles came upward.

The water churned for a time. They watched in silence, uneasily grooming their fur.

Abruptly Sipirod said, "Look. Another caviandi, over there by the sack. Probably trying to free its mate."

"Aren't we going to try to do anything for Kaldo Tikret?"

She made a chopping gesture. "What? Jump in after him? He's done for. Don't you understand that? Forget him. We have caviandis to catch. That's what we're paid for. Faster we find the second one, faster we can start getting ourselves out of this wretched place and back to Dawinno." The black surface of the lake began just then to grow still. "Done for, yes. Just as you said before: smart and lucky, that's what you have to be."

Vyrom shivered. "Kaldo Tikret wasn't lucky."

"Not very smart, either. Now, if I slip around to the side, while you come up behind me with the other sack—"

In central Dawinno, the official sector, a workroom on the second sublevel of the House of Knowledge: bright lights, cluttered laboratory benches, fragments of ancient civilizations scattered around everywhere. Plor Killivash delicately presses the firing-stud on the small cutting tool in his hand. A beam of pale light descends and bathes the foul-smelling, misshapen lump of he-knew-not-what, big as a bushel and tapered like an egg, that he has been brooding over all week. He focuses it and makes a quick shallow cut, and another, and another, slicing a fine line in its outer surface.

A fisherman had brought the thing in the week before, insisting that it was a Great World relic, a treasure-chest of the ancient sea-lord folk. Anything that might be sea-lord material was Plor Killivash's responsibility. Its surface was slimy with a thick accretion of sponges and coral and soft pink algae, and sour dirty sea-water dripped constantly from its interior. When he rapped it with a wrench it gave off a hollow thudding sound. He had no hope for it at all.

Perhaps if Hresh had been around he might have felt less disheartened. But the chronicler was away from the House of Knowledge this day, calling at the villa of his half-brother Thu-Kimnibol. Thu-Kimnibol's mate, the lady Naarinta, was seriously ill; and Plor Killivash, who was one of three assistant chroniclers, was as usual finding it hard to take his work seriously in Hresh's absence. Somehow when he was on the premises Hresh managed to infuse everyone's labors with a sense of important purpose. But the moment he left the building, all this pushing about of the sad shards and scraps of history became a mere absurdity, an empty pointless grubbing in the rubble of a deservedly forgotten antiquity. The study of the ancient days began to seem a meaningless pastime, a miserable airless quest into sealed vaults containing nothing but the stink of death.

Plor Killivash was a sturdy burly man of Koshmar descent. He had been to the University, and was very proud of that. Once he had had some hope of becoming head chronicler himself some day. He was sure he had the inside track, because he was the only Koshmar among the assistants. Io Sangrais was Beng, and Chupitain Stuld belonged to the little Stadrain tribe.

They were University people too, of course; but there were good political reasons for keeping the chroniclership away from a Beng, and nobody imagined that it would ever go to anyone from so trifling a group as the Stadrains. But far as Plor Killivash cared these days, they could have it, either one of them. Let someone else be head chronicler after Hresh, that was how Plor Killivash felt nowadays. Let someone else supervise the task of hacking through these millennia-thick accumulations of rubble.

Once, like Hresh before him, he had felt himself possessed by an almost uncontrollable passion for penetrating and comprehending the mysteries of the vast pedestal of Earthly history atop which this newborn civilization that the People had created sat, like a pea atop a pyramid. Had longed to mine deep, digging beyond the icy barrenness of the Long Winter period into the luxurious wonder of the Great World. Or even—why set limits? why any limits at all?—even into the deepest layers of all, into those wholly unknown empires of the almost infinitely remote era of the humans, who had ruled the Earth before the Great World itself had arisen. Surely there must be human ruins left down there, somewhere far below the debris of the civilizations that had followed theirs.

It had seemed so wonderfully appealing. To live billions of lives extending across millions of years. To stand upon old Earth and feel that you had been present when it was the crossroads of the stars. Flood your mind with strange sights, strange languages, the thoughts of other minds of unspeakable brilliance. Absorb and comprehend everything that had ever been, on this great planet that had seen so very much in its long span, realm piled upon realm back to the dawn of history.

But he had been a boy then. Those were a boy's thoughts, unfettered by practical considerations. Now Plor Killivash was twenty and he knew just how difficult it was to make the lost and buried past come alive. Under the harsh pressures of reality, that fiery passion to uncover ancient secrets was slipping from him, just as you could see it going even from Hresh himself, year by year. Hresh, though, had had the help of miraculous Great World devices, now no longer usable, to give him visions of the worlds that had existed before this world. For one who had never had the advantage of such wondrous things, the work of a chronicler was coming to seem nothing but doleful dreary slogging, carrying with it much frustration, precious little reward.

Somber thoughts on a somber day. And somberly Plor Killivash made ready to cut open the artifact from the sea.

The slim figure of Chupitain Stuld appeared in the doorway. She was smiling, and her dark violet eyes were merry.

"Still drilling? I was sure you'd be inside that thing by now."

"Just another little bit to go. Stick around for the great revelation." He tried to sound lighthearted about it. It wouldn't do to let his gloom show through.

She had her own frustrations, he knew. She too felt increasingly adrift amidst the mounded-up fragments of crumbled and eroded antiquity that the House of Knowledge contained.

Glancing at her, he said, "What's happening with those artifacts you've been playing with? The ones the farmers found in Senufit Gorge."

Chupitain Stuld laughed darkly. "That box of junk? It's all so much sand and rust."

"I thought you said it was from a pre–Great World level seven or eight million years old."

"Then it's sand and rust seven or eight million years old. I was hoping you were having better luck."

"Some chance."

"You never can tell," Chupitain Stuld said. She came up beside the workbench. "Can I help?"

"Sure. Those tractor clamps over there: bring them into position. I've just about sawed through the last of it now, and then we can lift the top half."

Chupitain Stuld swung the clamps downward and fastened them. Plor Killivash made the final intensity adjustment on his cutter. His fingers felt thick and coarse and clumsy. He found himself wishing Chupitain Stuld had stayed in her own work area. She was lovely to behold, small and delicate and extremely beautiful, with the soft lime-green fur that was common in her tribe. Today she wore a yellow sash and a mantle of royal blue, very elegant. They had been coupling-partners for some months now and even had twined once or twice. But all the same he didn't want her here now. He was convinced that he was going to bungle things as he made the last incision and he hated the idea that she'd be watching as he did.

Well. No more stalling, he tells himself. Checks his calibrations one last time. Draws his breath in sharply. At last forces himself to press the trigger. The beam licks out, bites into the artifact's shell-like wall. One quick nibble. He cuts the beam off. A dark line of severance has appeared. The upper half of the object moves minutely away from the lower half.

"You want me to pull up on the tractor harness?" Chupitain Stuld asked.

"Yes. Just a little."

"It's giving, Plor Killivash! It's going to lift!"

"Easy, now—easy—"

"Wouldn't it be wonderful if this thing's full of sea-lord amulets and jewels! And maybe a book of history of the Great World. Written on imperishable plates of golden metal."

Plor Killivash chuckled. "Why not a sea-lord himself, fast asleep, waiting to be awakened so he can tell us all about himself? Eh?"

The halves were separating. The weighty upper one rose a finger's-breadth's distance, another, another. A burst of sea-water came cascading out as the last inner seal broke.

For an instant Plor Killivash felt a flicker of the excitement he had felt when he was new here, five or six years before, and it had seemed every day that they were making wondrous new inroads into the mysteries of the past. But the odds were that this thing was worthless. There was very little of the Great World left to find, seven thousand centuries after its downfall. The glaciers grinding back and forth across the face of the land had done their work all too well.

"Can you see?" Chupitain Stuld asked, trying to peer over the top of the opened container.

"It's full of amulets and jewels, all right. And a whole bunch of fantastic machines in perfect preservation."

"Oh, stop it!"

He sighed. "All right. Here—look."

He scooped her up to perch on his arm, and they looked in together.

Inside were nine leathery-looking translucent purplish globes, each the size of a man's head, glued to the wall of the container by taut bands of a rubbery integument. Dim shapes were visible within them. Organs of some kind, looking shrunken and decayed. A fierce stench of rot came forth. Otherwise nothing. Nothing but a coating of moist white sand along the sides of the container, and a shallow layer of opaque water at the bottom.

"Not sea-lord artifacts, I'm afraid," Plor Killivash said.

"No."

"The fisherman thought he saw the broken stone columns of a ruined city sticking out of the sand at the bottom of the bay in the place where he dredged this thing up. He must have had a little too much wine with his lunch that day."

Chupitain Stuld stared into the opened container and shuddered. "What are they? Some kind of eggs?"

Plor Killivash shrugged.

"This whole thing was probably one gigantic egg, and I'd hate to meet the creature that laid it. Those things in there are little sea-monster embryos, I suppose. Dead ones. I'd better make a record of this and get them out of here. They'll begin to reek pretty soon."

There was a sound behind him. Io Sangrais peered in from the hallway. His brilliant red Beng eyes were glittering with amusement. Io Sangrais was sly and playful, a quick easy-spirited young man. Even the tribal helmet that he wore was playful, a close-fitting cap of dark blue metal with three absurd corkscrew spirals of lacquered red reed-stems rising wildly from it.

"Hola! Finally got it open, I see."

"Yes, and it's a wonderful treasure-house, just as I was expecting," Plor Killivash said dourly. "A lot of rotten little unhatched sea-monsters. One more great triumph for the bold investigators of the past. You come to gloat?"

"Why would I want to do that?" Io Sangrais asked. His voice was ripe with mock innocence. "No, I came down here to tell you about the great triumph *I've* just pulled off."

"Ah. Yes. You've finally finished translating that old Beng chronicle of yours, and it's full of spells and enchantments that turn water into wine, or wine into water, whichever you happen to prefer at the moment. Right?"

"Save your sarcasm. It turns out not to be a Beng chronicle, just one from some ninth-rate little tribe that the Bengs swallowed long ago. And what it is is a full and thorough descriptive catalogue of the tribe's collection of sacred pebbles. The pebbles themselves vanished ten thousand years ago, you understand."

Chupitain Stuld giggled. "Much rejoicing in the land. The unraveling of the mysteries of the past by the skilled operatives of the House of Knowledge goes on and on at the customary stupendous pace."

In the Basilica that afternoon it was Husathirn Mueri's turn to have throne-duty under the great central cupola, a task he shared in daily rotation with the princes Thu-Kimnibol and Puit Kjai. He was wearily hearing the petitions of two vociferous grain-merchants seeking redress from a third, who perhaps had cheated them and perhaps had not, when word came to him of the strange visitor who had arrived in the city.

No less a person than the captain of the city guard, Curabayn Bangkea, brought the news: a man of hearty stature and swaggering style, who generally affected a colossal gleaming golden helmet half again the size of his head, bristling with preposterous horns and blades. He was wearing it today. Husathirn Mueri found it both amusing and irritating.

There was nothing wrong with Curabayn Bangkea's wearing a helmet, of course. Most citizens wore them nowadays, whether or not they traced their descent from the old helmet-wearing Beng tribe. And Curabayn Bangkea was pure Beng. But it seemed to Husathirn Mueri, who was Beng himself on his father's side, though his mother had been of the Koshmars, that the captain of the guards carried the concept a little too far.

He wasn't one to put much stock in high formality. It was a trait he owed, perhaps, to his mother, a gentle and easygoing woman. Nor was he greatly impressed by men like the guardsman, who strutted boisterously through life making a way for themselves by virtue of their size and bluster. He himself was lightly built, with a narrow waist and sloping shoulders. His fur was black and dense, striped a startling white in places and nearly as sleek as a woman's. But his slightness was deceptive: he was quick and agile, with tricky whip-like strength in his body, and in his soul as well.

"Nakhaba favor you," Curabayn Bangkea declared grandly, dipping his head in respect as he approached the throne. For good measure he made the signs of Yissou the Protector and Dawinno the Destroyer. A couple of the Koshmar gods: always useful when dealing with crossbreeds.

Husathirn Mueri, who privately thought that too much of everyone's time was taken up by these benedictions and gesticulations, replied with a perfunctory sign of Yissou and said, "What is it, Curabayn Bangkea? I've got these angry bean-peddlers to deal with, and I'm not looking for more nuisances this afternoon."

"Your pardon, throne-grace. There's a stranger been taken, just outside the city walls."

"A stranger? What kind of stranger?"

"Your guess is as good as mine," said Curabayn Bangkea, shrugging so broadly he nearly sent his vast helmet clattering to the ground. "A very strange stranger, is what he is. A boy, sixteen, seventeen, skinny as a rail. Looks like he's been starved all his life. Came riding down out of the north on top of the biggest vermilion you ever saw. Some farmers found him crashing around in their fields, out by Emakkis Valley."

"Just now, you say?"

"Two days ago, or thereabouts. Two and a half, actually."

"And he was riding a *vermilion?*"

"A vermilion the size of a house and a half," Curabayn Bangkea said, stretching his arms wide. "But wait. It gets better. The vermilion's got a hjjk banner around its neck and hjjk emblems stitched to its ears. And the boy sits up there and makes noises at you just like a hjjk." Curabayn Bangkea put both his hands to his throat and uttered dry, throttled rattling sounds: *"Khkhkh. Sjsjsjssss. Gggggggggjjjjjk.* You know what kind of ghastly sounds they make. We've been interrogating him ever since the farmers brought him in, and that's about all that comes out of him. Now and then he says a word we can more or less understand. 'Peace,' he says. 'Love,' he says. 'The Queen,' he says."

Husathirn Mueri frowned. "What about his sash? Any tribe we know?"

"He doesn't wear a sash. Or a helmet. Or anything that might indicate he's from the City of Yissou, either. Of course, he might have come from one of the eastern cities, but I doubt that very much. I think it's pretty obvious what he is, sir."

"And what is that?"

"A runaway from the hjjks."

"A runaway," Husathirn Mueri said, musing. "An escaped captive? Is that what you're saying?"

"Why, it stands to reason, sir! There's hjjk all over him! Not just the sounds he makes. He's got a bracelet on that looks like it's made of polished hjjk-shell—bright yellow, it is, one black stripe—and a breastplate of the same stuff. That's all he's wearing, just these pieces of hjjk-shell. What else can he be, your grace, if not a runaway?"

Husathirn Mueri narrowed his eyes, which were amber, a sign of his mixed ancestry, and very keen.

Now and then a wandering band of hjjks came upon some child who had strayed into a place where he should not have gone, and ran off with him, no one knew why. It was a parent's greatest fear, to have a child taken by the hjjks. Most of these children were never seen again, but from time to time one did manage to escape and return, after an absence of days or weeks or even months. When they did come back they seemed profoundly shaken, and changed in some indescribable way, as though their time in captivity had been a horror beyond contemplation. None of them had ever been willing to speak so much as a word about their experiences among the insect-folk. It was considered an unkindness to ask.

To Husathirn Mueri the very thought of hjjks was distasteful. To be forced to live among them was the most miserable torture he could imagine.

He had seen them only once in his life, when he was a small boy growing up among the Bengs in Vengiboneeza, the ancient capital of the sapphire-eyes folk where some tribes of the People had taken up residence at the end of the Long Winter. But that one time had been enough. He would never forget them: gaunt towering insect-creatures larger than any man, strange, frightful, repulsive. Such great swarms of them had come to infest Vengiboneeza that the whole Beng tribe, which had settled there amid the ruined Great World buildings after years of wandering, finally had had to flee. Under great difficulties in a wet and stormy time they had crossed the endless coastal plains and valleys. Eventually they reached Dawinno, the great new city far to the south that the Koshmar tribe had built under Hresh's leadership after making its own exodus from Vengiboneeza; and there they found refuge.

That hard journey still blazed in his memory. He had been five, then, and his sister Catiriil a year younger.

"Why do we have to leave Vengiboneeza?" he had asked, over and over. And from his patient gentle mother Torlyri had come the same answer each time:

"Because the hjjks have decided that they want it for themselves."

He would turn then to his father in fury. "Why don't you and your friends kill them, then?"

And Trei Husathirn would reply: "We would if we could, boy. But there are ten hjjks in Vengiboneeza for every hair on your head. And plenty more where those came from, in the north."

During the interminable weeks of the journey south to Dawinno, Husathirn Mueri had awakened every night from terrible dreams of hjjk encroachment. He saw them standing over him in the dark as he slept, their bristly claws moving, their great beaks clacking, their huge gleaming eyes aglow with malevolence.

That had been twenty-five years ago. Sometimes he dreamed of them even now.

They were an ancient race—the only one of the Six Peoples that had inhabited the world in the blissful days before the Long Winter which had managed to survive that harrowing eon of darkness and cold. Their seniority offended him, coming as he did from so young a stock, from a people whose ancestors had been mere simple animals in the time of the Great World. It reminded him how fragile was the claim to supremacy that the People had attempted to assert; it reminded him that the People held their present territories by mere default, simply because the hjjks appeared to have no use for those places and the other elder peoples of the Great world—the sapphire-eyes, the sea-lords, the vegetals, the mechanicals, the humans— were long gone from the scene.

The hjjks, who had not let the Long Winter of the death-stars displace them, still had possession of most of the world. The entire northland was theirs, and maybe much of the east as well, though tribes of the People had built at least five cities there, places known only by name and rumor to those who lived in Dawinno. Those cities—Gharb, Ghajnsielem, Cignoi, Bornigrayal, Thisthissima—were so far away that contact with them was all but impossible. The hjjks held everything else. They were the chief barrier to the People's further expansion in these constantly warming days of the New Springtime. To Husathirn Mueri they were the enemy, and always would be. He would, if he could, wipe them all from the face of the Earth.

But he knew, as his father Trei Husathirn had known, that that was impossible. The best that the People could hope for against the hjjks was to hold their own with them: to maintain the security and integrity of the territories they already held, to keep the hjjks from encroaching in any way. Perhaps the People might even be able to push them back a little gradually and reach outward a short distance into some of the hjjk-controlled regions that were suitable for their own use. To think the hjjks could be altogether defeated, though—as certain other princes of the city were known to believe—was nothing but folly, Husathirn Mueri realized. They were an invincible enemy. They never would be anything else.

"There's one other possibility," Curabayn Bangkea said.

"And what would that be?"

"That this boy is no simple runaway, but in fact some kind of emissary from the hjjks."

"A what?"

"Only a guess, throne-grace. There's no evidence, you understand. But something about him—the way he holds himself, so polite and quiet and, well, solemn, and the way he tries to tell us things, the way he comes out once in a while with a word like 'peace,' or 'love,' or 'queen'—well, sir, he doesn't seem like your ordinary kind of runaway to me. It came to me all at once that this could be some sort of ambassador, like, sent to us by the wonderful Queen of the bug-folk to bring us some kind of special message. Or so I think, throne-grace. If you pardon me for my presumption."

"An ambassador?" Husathirn Mueri said, shaking his head. "Why in the name of all the gods would they be sending us an ambassador?"

Curabayn Bangkea gazed blandly at him, offering no answer.

Glowering, Husathirn Mueri rose from the justiciary throne and walked to and fro with a sliding gait before it, hands clasped behind his back.

Curabayn Bangkea was no fool; his judgment, however tentatively put forth, was something to respect. And if the hjjks had sent an emissary, someone of People birth, one who had dwelled among the bugs so long that he had forgotten his own speech and spoke only in harsh grinding hjjk-clatter—

As he paced, one of the merchants, coming up beside him, tugged at his sash of office and begged his attention. Husathirn Mueri, eyes flashing furiously, raised his arm as if to strike the man. The merchant looked at him in astonishment.

At the last moment he checked himself. "Your suit is remanded for further study," he told the merchant. "Return to this court when I am next sitting the throne."

"And when will that be, lordship?"

"Do I know, fool? Watch the boards! Watch the boards!" Husathirn Mueri's fingers trembled. He was losing his poise, and was troubled by that. "It'll be next week, on Friit or Dawinno, I think," he said, more temperately. "Go. Go!"

The merchants fled. Husathirn Mueri turned to the guard-captain. "Where is this hjjk ambassador now?"

"Throne-grace, it was only a guess, calling him an ambassador. I can't say for sure that that's what he really is."

"Be that as it may, where is he?"

"Just outside, in the holding chamber."

"Bring him in."

He resumed his post on the throne. He felt irritated and perplexed and impatient. Some moments went by.

Husathirn Mueri did what he could to regain control of himself, making a calmness at the core of his spirit as his mother Torlyri had taught him to do. Rashness led only to miscalculation and error. She herself— the gods rest her soul, that warm and tender woman!—had not been nearly this high-strung. But Husathirn Mueri was a crossbreed, with a crossbreed's vigor and intensity and a crossbreed's drawbacks of disposition. In his birth he had foreshadowed the eventual union of the two tribes. Torlyri had been the Koshmar tribe's offering-woman and the indomitable Beng warrior Trei Husathirn had swept the Koshmar priestess up into unexpected love and an unlikely mating, long ago, when the Beng people and the Koshmars still dwelled uneasily side by side in Vengiboneeza.

He sat waiting, more calmly now. At length the shadow of Curabayn Bangkea's immense helmet entered the cupola, and then Curabayn Bangkea himself, leading the stranger at the end of a leash of plaited larret-withes. At the sight of him Husathirn Mueri sat to attention, hands tightly grasping the claw-and-ball armrests of the throne.

This was a very strange stranger indeed.

He was young, in late boyhood or early manhood, and painfully slender, with thin hunched shoulders and arms so frail they looked like dried stems. The ornaments he wore, the bracelet and the shining breastplate, did indeed seem to be polished fragments of a hjjk's hard carapace, a grisly touch. His fur was black, but not a deep, rich black, like that of Husathirn Mueri: there was a dull grayish tinge to it, and it was pitiful scruffy fur, thin in places, almost worn through. This young man has been poorly fed all his life, Husathirn Mueri realized. He has suffered.

And his eyes! Those pale, icy, unwavering eyes! They seemed to stare toward the judicial throne across a gulf many worlds wide. Frightful remorseless eyes, an enemy's eyes; but then, as Husathirn Mueri continued to study them, he began to see them more as sad compassionate eyes, the eyes of a prophet and healer.

How could that be? The contradiction bewildered him.

At any rate, whoever and whatever this boy might be, there seemed no reason to keep him tethered this way. "Unleash him," Husathirn Mueri ordered.

"But if he flees, throne-grace—!"

"He came here with a purpose. Fleeing won't serve it. Unleash him."

Curabayn Bangkea undid the knot. The stranger seemed to stand taller, but otherwise did not move.

Husathirn Mueri said, "I am the holder of throne-duty in this court for today. Husathirn Mueri is my name. Who are you, and why have you come to the City of Dawinno?"

The boy gestured, quick tense flutterings of his fingers, and made hoarse chittering hjjk-noises deep down in his chest, as if he meant to spit at Husathirn Mueri's feet.

Husathirn Mueri shivered and drew back. This was the nearest thing to having an actual hjjk here in the throne-room. He felt rising revulsion. "I speak no hjjk," he said icily.

"*Shhhtkkkk*," the boy said, or something like it. "*Gggk thhhhhsp shtgggk.*" And then he said, wresting the word from his throat as though it were some spiny thing within him that he must expel, "Peace."

"Peace."

The boy nodded. "Peace. Love."

"Love," said Husathirn Mueri, and shook his head slowly.

"It was like this when I interrogated him, too," Curabayn Bangkea murmured.

"Be still." To the boy Husathirn Mueri said, speaking very clearly and loudly, as though that would make any difference, "I ask you again: What is your name?"

"Peace. Love. *Ddddkdd ftshhh.*"

"Your *name*," Husathirn Mueri repeated. He tapped his chest, where the white swirling streaks that he had inherited from his mother cut diagonally across the deep black fur. "I am Husathirn Mueri. Husathirn Mueri is my name. My name. *His* name"—pointing—"is Curabayn Bangkea. Curabayn Bangkea. And your name—"

"*Shthhhjjk. Vtstsssth. Njnnnk!*" The boy seemed to be struggling in a terrible way to articulate something. Muscles writhed in his sunken cheeks; his eyes rolled; he clenched his fists and dug his elbows into his hollow sides. Suddenly a complete understandable sentence burst from him: "I come in peace and love, from the Queen."

"An emissary, do you see?" cried Curabayn Bangkea, grinning triumphantly.

Husathirn Mueri nodded. Curabayn Bangkea began to say something else, but Husathirn Mueri waved him impatiently to silence.

This must indeed be some child the hjjks had stolen in infancy, he thought. Who has lived among them ever since, in their impenetrable northland empire. And has been sent back now to the city of his birth, bearing Yissou only knew what demand from the insect queen.

The purposes of the hjjks were beyond all fathoming. Everyone knew that. But the message that this boy was trying so agonizingly to communicate might portend the opening of some new phase in the uneasy relationship between the People and the insect-folk. Husathirn Mueri, who was only one of several princes of the city and had reached that point in manhood when it was essential to begin thinking of rising to higher things, took it as a lucky omen that the stranger had arrived on a day when he happened to be holding the magistracy. There must be some good use to which all this could be put. First, though, he needed to figure out what the envoy was trying to say.

An obvious interpreter came to his mind. The most celebrated of all the returned captives of the city, the only highborn girl ever to be taken: Nialli Apuilana, daughter of Taniane and Hresh. She'd know some hjjk, if anyone did. Three months in captivity among them, a few years back. Grabbed just outside the city, she was, setting off a vast uproar, and why not, the only child of the chieftain and the chronicler stolen by the bugs! Loud lamentations, much frenzy. Tremendous search of the outlying territory. All to no avail. Then, months later, the girl suddenly reappearing as if she had dropped down from the sky. Looking dazed, but no visible signs of harm. Like all who returned from the hjjks she refused to speak of her captivity; like the others also, she had undergone some alteration of personality, far more moody and remote than she had been before. And she'd been moody enough before.

Was it safe to draw Nialli Apuilana into this? She was self-willed, unpredictable, a dangerous ally. From her powerful mother and mysterious visionary father had come a heritage of many volatile traits. No one could control her. She was some months past the age of sixteen, now, and ran wild in the city, free as a river: so far as Husathirn Mueri knew she had never let anyone couple with her, nor had she been known to twine, either, except of course on her twining-day, with the offering-woman Boldirinthe, but that was just the ritual to mark her coming into womanhood, when she turned thirteen. Everyone had to do that. The hjjks had taken her the very next day. Some people said she hadn't been taken at all, that she had simply run away, because she had found her first twining so upsetting. But Husathirn Mueri suspected not. She had come back too weird; she must really have been among the hjjks.

One other factor figured in Husathirn Mueri's considerations, which was that he desired Nialli Apuilana with a dark fervor that burned at his core like the fires at the heart of the world. He saw her as his key to power in the city, if only she would become his mate. He hadn't yet dared to say anything about that to her, or anyone. But perhaps drawing her into this event today would help him forge the bond that was his keenest hope.

He looked toward Curabayn Bangkea and said, "Tell one of those useless bailiffs lounging in the hallway to go and bring Nialli Apuilana here."

The House of Nakhaba was where Nialli Apuilana lived, in one of the small chambers on the uppermost floor of the north wing of that enormous, sprawling building of spires, towers, and intricately connected hallways. That it was a dormitory for priests and priestesses meant nothing to her. That they were priests and priestesses dedicated to a Beng god, whereas she was of the Koshmar tribe's blood, meant even less. Those old tribal distinctions were breaking down very fast.

When she first chose the House of Nakhaba as her lodging-place, Prince Thu-Kimnibol had wanted to know if she had done it simply as a way of shocking everyone. Smiling in his good-natured way to take the sting out of the question, yes. But it stung all the same.

"Why, are you shocked?" Nialli Apuilana had replied.

Thu-Kimnibol was her father's half-brother, as different from her father as the sun is from the moon. Both the huge, hulking, warlike Thu-Kimnibol and the frail, scholarly, retiring Hresh were the sons of the same mother, Minbain by name. Hresh had been born to her in the cocoon days, when a certain Samnibolon, long dead and forgotten now, had been her mate. Thu-Kimnibol was her child by a different mate of later years, the grim, violent, and quarrelsome warrior Harruel. He had inherited his father's size and strength and some of his intensity of ambition; but not, so Nialli Apuilana had been told, his brooding, troubled soul.

"Nothing you do shocks us," Thu-Kimnibol said. "Not since you came back from the hjjks. But why live with the Beng priests?"

Her eyes flashed with amusement and annoyance. "Kinsman, I live alone!"

"On the top floor of a huge building swarming with Beng acolytes who bow down to Nakhaba."

"I have to live somewhere. I'm a grown woman. There's privacy in the House of Nakhaba. The acolytes pray and chant all day long and half the night, but they leave me to myself."

"It must disturb your sleep."

"I sleep very well," she said. "The singing lulls me. As for their bowing down to Nakhaba, well, what affair is that of mine? Or that they're Bengs. Aren't we all Bengs these days? Look, kinsman, you wear a helmet yourself. And the language we speak—what is it, if it isn't Beng?"

"The language of the People is what it is."

"And is it the same language we spoke when we lived in the cocoon, during the Long Winter?"

Thu-Kimnibol tugged uneasily at the thick red fur, almost like a beard, that grew along his heavy cheeks. "I never lived in the cocoon," he said. "I was born after the Coming Forth."

"You know what I mean. What we speak is as much Beng as it is Koshmar, or more so. We pray to Yissou and we pray to Nakhaba, and there's no difference to us any more, the Koshmar god or the Beng god. A god is a god. Only a handful of the older people still remember that we were two tribes, originally. Or care. Another thirty years and only the chronicler will know. I like where I live, kinsman. I'm not trying to shock anyone, and you know it. I simply want to be off by myself."

That had been more than a year ago, almost two. And after that no one in her family had bothered her about her choice of a place to live. She was of age, after all: past sixteen, old enough to twine and to mate, even if she didn't choose to twine, and certainly not to mate. She could do as she pleased. Everyone accepted that.

But in fact Thu-Kimnibol had been close to the truth. Her going to the House of Nakhaba had been a protest of some sort: against what, she wasn't sure. Ever since her return from the hjjks there had been a great restlessness in her, an impatience with all the established ways of the city. It seemed to Nialli Apuilana that the People had wandered from the true path. Machines were what they loved now, and comfort, and this new idea called exchange-units, which allowed the rich to buy the poor. Things were wrong here, so she had begun to think; and, since she had no power to change the ways of the city, she often found herself making strange silent rebellions against them. Others thought she was willful and unruly. What they might think was unimportant to her. Her stay among the hjjks had transformed her soul in ways that no one else could comprehend, in ways that she herself was only now beginning to come to terms with.

There was a knock at the door. Nialli Apuilana opened it to a plump, panting official of the Court of Justice, who had obviously found the climb to the top of the House of Nakhaba on this warm afternoon a profound challenge. He was running with sweat. His fur was sticking together in thick bunches, and his nostrils flickered as he struggled to catch his breath. His sashes and badges of rank were soggy and askew.

"Nialli Apuilana?"

"You know that's who I am. What do you want with me?"

A gasp. A wheeze. "Summons to the Basilica." Another gasp. An attempt to smooth the sodden fur. A huff and a puff. "By request of Husathirn Mueri, court-captain of the day."

"To the Basilica? Why, have I done something wrong, then? Is that what his lordship Husathirn Mueri believes? Am I going to be put on trial?"

The bailiff didn't reply. He was peering open-mouthed past her shoulder into her room. Stark as a prisoner's cell: scarcely any furniture at all, just a tiny cot, a little stack of books on the floor, and a single ornament, a star-shaped amulet of woven grass that Nialli Apuilana had brought back from the hjjks, hanging on the whitewashed wall directly opposite the door like a conquest-sign placed there by the insect-folk themselves.

"I said, have I done something wrong?"

"Nothing, lady. Nothing."

"Then why am I summoned?"

"Because—because—"

"What are you *staring* at? Haven't you ever seen a hjjk star before?"

The bailiff looked guiltily away. He began to groom himself with quick uneasy strokes. "His lordship the court-captain wishes your help, that's all," he blurted. "As a translator. A stranger has been brought to the Basilica—a young man, who seems to speak only the language of the hjjks—"

There was a sudden roaring in Nialli Apuilana's soul. Her heart raced painfully, frighteningly.

So stupid. Waiting this long to let her know.

She seized the bailiff by a sash. "Why didn't you say so right away?"

"I had no chance, lady. You—"

"He must be a returning captive. You should have told me."

Images rose from the depths of her mind. Powerful memories, visions of that shattering day that had changed her life.

She saw her younger self, already long-legged and woman-sleek but with her breasts only barely sprouting yet, innocently gathering blue chilly-flowers in the hills beyond the city walls on the day after her first twining. Black-and-yellow six-limbed figures, weird and terrifying, taller than any man of the city, taller even than Thu-Kimnibol, emerging without warning from a deep cleft in the tawny rock. Terror. Disbelief. A sense of the world she had known for thirteen years crumbling to fragments about her. Monstrous sharp-beaked heads, huge many-faceted eyes, jointed arms tipped with horrid claws. The chittering noises of them, the clickings and buzzings. This is not happening to me, she tells herself. Not to me. Do you know whose daughter I am? The words won't leave her lips. They probably *do* know, anyway. All the better, getting someone like her. The pack of them surrounding her, seizing her, touching her. Then the terror unexpectedly disappearing. An eerie dreamlike calmness somehow taking possession of her soul. The hjjks carrying her away, then. A long march, an endless march, through unknown country. And then—the moist hot darkness of the Nest—the strangeness of that other life, which was like some different world, though it was right here on Earth—the power of the Queen impinging, surrounding, engulfing, transforming—

And ever since, the loneliness, the bitter sense that there was no one else at all like her anywhere in the world. But now, at last, another who had experienced what she had experienced. At last. Another who *knew*.

"Where is he?" she demanded. "I have to see him! Quick! Quick!"

"He is at the Basilica, lady. In the throne-chamber, with his lordship Husathirn Mueri."

"Quick, then! Let's go!"

She rushed from her room, not even bothering with her sash. Her nakedness mattered nothing to her. Let them stare, she thought. The bailiff came running along desperately behind her, huffing and wheezing, as she raced down the stairs of the House of Nakhaba. Astonished acolytes in priestly helmets, scattering before her onslaught, turned to glare and mutter, but she paid no attention to them.

On this day in late spring the sun was still high in the western sky, though the afternoon was well consumed. Soft tropic warmth wrapped the city like a cloak. The bailiff had a wagon waiting outside, with two docile gray xlendis in the harness. Nialli Apuilana jumped in beside him, and the placid beasts started down the winding streets toward the Basilica at a steady, unhurried trot.

"Can't you make them go faster?" she asked.

The bailiff shrugged and laid on the whip. It did no good: one of the xlendis twisted its long neck about and looked back over its shoulder with great solemn golden eyes, as if puzzled that anyone would expect more speed of it than it was providing. Nialli Apuilana forced herself to hold her impatience in check. The returnee, the escaper, whatever he was, the one who had come from the Nest, wasn't going anywhere. He would wait for her.

"Lady, we are here," the bailiff announced.

The wagon halted. The Basilica stood before them now, the high-vaulted five-domed court building on the east side of the city's central plaza. The westering sun lit the green-and-gold mosaics of its facade and kindled them to brilliant flame.

Within the building flickering glowglobes gleamed in dark metal sconces. Court functionaries stood stiffly in the hallway, performing no apparent function except to bow and nod as they went by.

The stranger was the first person whom Nialli Apuilana saw, sharply outlined in a cone of light entering through a triangular window far up near the summit of the lofty central cupola. He stood in a downcast way, shoulders slumped and eyes averted.

There was a Nest-bracelet on his wrist. There was a Nest-guardian hanging from a lanyard on his chest.

Nialli Apuilana's heart went out to him. If she had been alone, she would have run to him and embraced him, and tears of joy would have flowed from her eyes.

But she held herself back. She looked toward the judge's ornate throne under the network of interlaced bronze struts that formed the cupola, where Husathirn Mueri sat, and allowed herself to meet his keen, brooding stare.

Husathirn Mueri seemed rigid and tense. A perceptible odor, something like that of burning wood, came from him. The language of his body was explicit and not at all difficult to decode.

There was hunger for her in his gleaming amber eyes.

That was the only word she could find for it. Not lust, though no doubt lust was there; not the desire for her friendship, though he might well feel that; not anything tender that could readily be called love, either. No, it was *hunger*. Simple but not at all pure, and not so simple, either.

He seemed to want to fall upon her and devour her and make her flesh a part of his own. Every time he saw her, which was no more often than she could manage, it was the same thing. Now, as he gazed at her across the vast space of the courtroom, it was almost as though Husathirn Mueri had his face between her thighs, gnawing, consuming. What a strange man! And yet quite appealing physically: slim, elegant, graceful, even beautiful, if a man could be called beautiful. And intelligent, and gentle in his way. But strange. Nialli Apuilana had no liking for him at all.

To the right of the throne stood the great brawny guard-captain, Curabayn Bangkea, half entombed within his gigantic helmet. He was looking at her in a pretty lascivious way also, but she knew it was something much less complex that was on his mind. Nialli Apuilana was accustomed to being stared at by men of all sorts. She realized that she was attractive: everyone said that she was the image of her mother Tanianc when Taniane was young, with glossy, silken red-brown fur and long slender legs; and her mother had been the most beautiful woman of her day. Even now she still was splendid. So I am beautiful too, and so they stare at me. An automatic thing, for them. She had some notion also that the air of absolute unapproachability in which she usually wrapped herself might add to her appeal, for some.

Unctuously Husathirn Mueri said, "Dawinno guide you, Nialli Apuilana. Nakhaba preserve and cherish you."

"Spare me these hypocrisies," she said sharply. "You want my help as a translator, your bailiff says. Translating what?"

He indicated the stranger. "The guards have just brought him in. All he speaks is hjjk, and a few stray words of ours. I thought you might remember enough of the language of the bug-folk to tell me what he's trying to say."

She gave Husathirn Mueri a cool, hostile stare. "The language of the *bug-folk?*"

"Ah. Sorry. The hjjks, I should have said."

"I find the other term offensive."

"Your pardon, lady. I mean that. I used the term too lightly. I won't use it again." Husathirn Mueri seemed to squirm. He looked genuinely dismayed. "Will you speak with him, now? And see if you can learn why he's here."

"If I can," Nialli Apuilana said icily.

She went to the stranger, taking up a position facing him, so close that she too stood in the cone of light and the tips of her breasts came nearly within touching-distance of the Nest-guardian that dangled on his chest. He raised his eyes and looked into hers.

He was older than she had first thought. At a distance he seemed like no more than a boy, but that was because he was so flimsily built; in fact he must be at least her age, or even a year or two older. But there was no fat on him at all, and precious little muscle.

A diet of seeds and dried meat will do that to you, Nialli Apuilana knew. She had experienced it herself.

Very likely this stranger had lived among the hjjks for years. Long enough for his body to be shaped by the sparseness of their rations, at any rate. He even held himself in a hjjk's stiff, brittle way, as if the fur and flesh that he wore were only a cloak concealing the gaunt insect beneath.

"Go on. Speak with him."

"A moment. Give me a moment!"

She tried to collect herself. The sight of the hjjk talismans on his wrist and breast had stirred deep feelings in her. In her excitement she found herself unable to summon a single syllable of the hjjk language, what little of it she had learned years ago.

Hjjks communicated in many ways. They had a spoken language, the clicks and buzzes and hisses from which the People had coined a name for them. But also they were able to speak with each other—and with such of the People as they encountered—in a silent language of the mind, as if speaking by second sight. And then too they had an elaborate system of communicating by means of chemical secretions, a code of scented signals.

While in the Nest Nialli Apuilana had dealt with the hjjks mainly through the mental language. When they used that, they were able to make themselves perfectly understood to her, and also to understand what she said. She had managed to learn a few hundred words of their spoken language as well. But she had forgotten most of that by now. The language of the chemical secretions had always been altogether a closed book to her.

To break the interminable silence she raised her hand and lightly touched the stranger's Nest-guardian, leaning forward and smiling warmly at him as she did.

He seemed almost to flinch. But he managed to hold his ground, and said something to her in harsh hjjk tones. His face was solemn. It didn't seem capable of changing expression. It was like something carved of wood.

She touched his Nest-guardian again, and then her own breast.

Some words of hjjk sprang into her mind, then, and she spoke them, shaping them with some difficulty in her throat, as if she were gargling. They were the words for Nest, and Queen, and Nest-plenty.

He drew back his lips in a grimace that was almost a smile. Or perhaps it was a smile that could not help becoming a grimace.

"Love," he said, in the language of the People. "Peace."

A start, at least.

From somewhere more hjjk words came to her, the ones for Nest-strength, for Queen-touch, for Thinker-thoughts.

He brightened.

"Love," he said again. "Queen—love."

He lifted his clenched fists, as if straining to find other words of People-speech long lost in the deeper reaches of his mind. There was anguish on his narrow face.

At length he brought out another hjjk word, which Nialli Apuilana recognized as the one that could be translated as "flesh-folk." It was the term the hjjks used for the People.

"What are you two saying?" Husathirn Mueri asked.

"Nothing very significant. Just making preliminary contact."

"Has he told you his name yet?"

Nialli Apuilana gave Husathirn Mueri a scornful look. "The hjjk language doesn't have a word for *name*. They don't have names themselves."

"Can you ask him why he's here, then?"

"I'm trying," she said. "Can't you see that?"

But it was hopeless. For ten minutes she worked in a steady dogged way at breaking through, without getting anywhere.

She had expected so much of this meeting. She was desperately eager to relive with this stranger her time in the Nest. To speak with him of Queen-love and Egg-plan and Nest-strength and all those other things that she had barely had a chance to experience during her too-brief captivity: things which had shaped her soul as surely as the austere food of the hjjks had shaped this stranger's lean body. But the barriers between them were a maddening obstacle.

There seemed no way to breach them. All they could do was stammer random words at each other, and fragments of ideas. Sometimes they seemed close to a meeting of minds, and the stranger's eyes would grow bright and the ghost of a smile, even, appeared on his face; but then they reached the limits of their understanding, and the walls descended between them once again.

"Are you getting anywhere?" Husathirn Mueri asked, after a while.

"Nowhere. Nowhere at all."

"You can't even guess at what he's saying? Or why he's here?"

"He's here as some sort of an ambassador. That much seems certain."

"Do you have anything to go by, or are you just guessing?"

"You see those pieces of hjjk shell he's wearing? They're tokens of high authority," she said. "The thing on his chest is called a Nest-guardian, and it's made out of the shell of a dead hjjk warrior. They wouldn't have let him take it out of the Nest except as a sign that he's on a special mission. It's something like a chieftain's mask would be among us. The other one, the bracelet, was probably a gift from his Nest-thinker, to help him focus his thoughts. Poor lost soul, it hasn't done him much good, has it?"

"Nest-thinker?"

"His mentor. His teacher. Don't ask me to explain it all now. They're only bug-folk to you, anyway."

"I told you that I regretted—"

"Yes," Nialli Apuilana said. "You told me that you regretted. Anyway, he's surely here with some special message, not just the usual hazy stuff that returnees tell us, if they say anything at all. But he can't speak. He must have lived in the Nest since he was three or four years old, and he can barely remember a word of our language."

Husathirn Mueri moodily stroked his cheek-fur.

"Can you suggest anything?" he asked, after a time.

"Only the obvious. Send for my father."

"Ah," Husathirn Mueri said. "Of course!"

"Does the chronicler speak hjjk?" Curabayn Bangkea asked.

"The chronicler has the Wonderstone, idiot," said Husathirn Mueri. "The Barak Dayir, the Barak Dayir! Of course! One touch of it and all mysteries are solved!"

He clapped his hands. The fat bailiff appeared.

"Find Hresh. Summon him here." He looked around. "Adjourned until Hresh comes."

The chronicler just then was in his garden of natural history, in the western quadrant of the city, supervising the arrival of his caviandis.

Many years earlier, Hresh in a vision of the Vengiboneeza of Great World times had entered a place called the Tree of Life. Here the sapphire-eyes folk had gathered all sorts of wild creatures and placed them in chambers that duplicated their natural surroundings. The dreaming Hresh, to his terrible shame and chagrin, had even found his own ancestors among the animals housed there; and so he had learned beyond question that day that his People, who once had thought of themselves as humans, were no such lofty thing, and in the days of the Great World had been regarded as nothing more than beasts fit for collecting and keeping in cages.

Most of the creatures Hresh had seen on that day of wandering in the remote past had perished in the Long Winter, and their kind was forever gone from the Earth. The Tree of Life itself had long ago crumbled to dust. But Hresh had built a Tree of Life of his own in the City of Dawinno, overlooking the tranquil bay: a maze-like garden where creatures from all parts of the continent had been assembled for him to study. He had water-striders there, and drum-bellies, and dancerhorns, and hosts of the other creatures whom the People had encountered in their migrations across the face of the land since leaving the ancestral cocoon. He had blue-furred long-legged stinchitoles, whose minds were linked in a way he had not begun to fathom. He had bevies of plump-legged red scantrins. He had the pink ropy long-fanged worms, longer than a man was tall, who lived in the steaming mud of the lakelands. He had the kmurs, and crispalls, and stanimanders. He had gabools. He had steptors. He had a band of the mocking green monkey-like tree-dwelling beasts who had pelted the People raucously with wads of dung when first they entered Vengiboneeza.

And now too he had a pair of caviandis, newly brought to him from the lakelands.

He would make a comfortable habitat for them along the stream that ran through the garden, and the stream would be stocked with the fish they most preferred, and they would have room to dig the burrows in which they liked to live. And once they had grown accustomed to life in captivity he would try to reach their minds through second sight, through use of the Wonderstone if necessary. He would touch their souls, if souls they had, and see what depths were to be found in them.

The caviandis, trembling, sat side by side in their carrier, giving him a saucer-eyed look of misery and fear.

Hresh returned that sorry stare with a deep look of curiosity and fascination. They were graceful, elegant beasts, unquestionably intelligent. Just how intelligent was what he meant to find out. The lesson of the ancient Tree of Life, of the Great World itself, was that intelligence was to be found in creatures of many sorts.

There were those among the People, Hresh knew, who hunted caviandis for their flesh. They were said to be tasty things. But that would have to stop, if the brightness of the caviandis' eyes turned out to be matched by a corresponding richness of intellect. Some sort of protective legislation, maybe—unpopular, but necessary—

He was tempted to take a quick peek into their minds now. A bit of preliminary probing. Just to get some general idea.

He smiled at the trembling animals, and lifted his sensing-organ, thinking to summon his second sight, only for a moment, only for a quick look.

"Lordship? Lord chronicler?"

The interruption was as jarring as a blow in the small of the back. Hresh whirled and saw one of his deputies behind him, and a coarse-looking man with him in the sash of a bailiff of the court of justice.

"What is it?"

The bailiff stumbled forward. "Your pardon, lord chronicler, but I bring a message from the court, from Husathirn Mueri, who sits in judgment today at the Basilica. A stranger has been found, a young man who appears to be returned from captivity among the hjjks, and who speaks no language except the noises of the bug-folk. And Prince Husathirn Mueri respectfully requests—if you could assist him—if you could come to the Basilica to aid in the interrogation—"

They had sent her off to wait in a holding chamber during the adjournment, a sweaty little room, nothing very much different from the cells where criminals were kept while awaiting the attention of the justiciary prince; and they had put the hjjk emissary in a different room of the same sort on the far side of the cupola. Nialli Apuilana had thought it might have been useful for them both to wait for Hresh in the same room, so that they could try to make some further attempts at communication, but no, no, take her to this room, take him to that one. She realized with some surprise that Husathirn Mueri must not trust the two of them together in any unsupervised situation. It was one more illustration of the pettiness and fretful suspiciousness of his soul, the small mean ignobility of it.

Can he possibly sense that there is Nest-bond between us? she wondered. Is he afraid that we'll flange up some sort of treacherous conspiracy, if he gives us a chance to spend an hour or so in the same cell? Or is what he's afraid of simply that we might pass the time with a little sweaty coupling? That was an odd idea. The stranger, all skin and bones, taking advantage of a bit of spare time to jump on her. She wasn't attracted by him at all. But she didn't put it past Husathirn Mueri to suspect such a thing. What does he think I am? she asked herself.

Furiously she paced the little wedge-shaped room until she had counted its measurements out fifty times over. Then she took a seat on a bench of black stone beneath a niche containing an ikon of Dawinno the Transformer, and leaned back, folding her arms across her breasts. A bit more tranquil now. Summoning a little patience. They might have a long wait coming before the bailiff managed to track her father down.

As she grew calmer she felt herself growing dreamy. Something strange arising within her, now. Visions come drifting into her mind. The Nest, is it? Yes. Yes. Increasing in clarity moment by moment, as if layers of filmy cloth are being stripped away. Old memories awaken now, after lying dormant so long. What has stirred them? The sight of those amulets on his wrist and chest, was it? The aura of the Nest that he carried about him, visible only to her?

She hears a rushing, a roaring, in her mind. And then she is there. That other world where she had passed the strangest three months of her life comes vividly to life for her.

They are all around her in the narrow tunnel, welcoming her back after her long absence, rubbing their claws gently against her fur by way of greeting: half a dozen Queen-attendants, and a pair of Egg-makers, and a Nest-thinker, and a couple of Militaries. The dry crisp scent of them tingles in her nostrils. The air is warm and close; the light is a dim pink glow, the familiar lovely Nest-light, faint but sufficient. She embraces them one by one, savoring the feel of their smooth two-toned carapaces and their black-bristled forearms. It is good to be back, she tells them. I have longed for this moment ever since I left here.

There is a commotion just then at the far end of the long passageway: a procession of young males, it is, jostling and crowding each other. They are on their way to the royal chamber to be aroused into fertility by Queen-touch. It is the last stage in their maturity. They will be allowed to mate, finally, once the Queen has done whatever it is that is done to bring the young to fertility. Nialli Apuilana envies them for that.

But she is ripe herself. Ready for mating, ready for life to be kindled within her, ready to play her proper part in Egg-plan. The Queen must know that. The Queen knows everything. Soon, she thinks, one of these days quite soon, it will be my turn to come before the Queen, and Her love will descend upon me, and my loins will be quickened to life by Her touch, and at long last I too will be—

I too will be—

"Lady, the court is reassembling," came a voice that cut through her like a dull rusty blade.

She opened her eyes. A bailiff stood before her, a different one from before. She glared at him in such rage that it was a wonder it didn't strip the fur from his skin. But he simply stood gaping like a clod. "Lady, they request that you return to—"

"Yes. Yes! Don't you think I heard you?"

Hresh did not appear to have arrived yet. Everything was as it had been before, more or less. The stranger stood in the absolute center of the room, wholly motionless, like a statue of himself. He seemed scarcely even to breathe. A hjjk trick, that was. They weren't ones for wasting energy. When they had no reason to be in motion, they didn't move at all.

Husathirn Mueri, though, was in constant motion. He crossed and uncrossed his legs; he shifted about uneasily as if the throne were growing icy cold beneath him, or fiery; he flicked his sensing-organ about, now curling it against his shins, now letting it arch upward behind him until the tip of it peered over his shoulder. His intense amber gaze flickered everywhere around the great room except in Nialli Apuilana's direction; but then suddenly she caught him staring at her again in that hungry fashion of his. As soon as their eyes met, he looked away.

She felt sorry for him, in an odd way. That he was so driven, so edgy. They said that his mother Torlyri had been a saintly loving person, and his father the most valiant of warriors. But Husathirn Mueri seemed not at all saintly, and Nialli Apuilana doubted that he would be of much use on a battlefield, either. Hardly a credit to his forebears. Perhaps it's true, she thought, the thing that the older people like to say, that in this modern era of city life we've become a race of confused, troubled folk, no clear sense of direction in our lives at all. Weaklings, in fact. Decadents.

But, she wondered, is it so? That we've gone from primitivism to decadence and weakness in a single generation? All that time pent up in the cocoon, scarcely changing in any way, and then we erupt and build ourselves a tremendous city, and practically overnight all the old virtues are lost, our godliness, our honor?

Husathirn Mueri may be a decadent, she thought. And probably so am I. But is he really a weakling? Am I?

"The chronicler! Hresh-of-the-answers! All rise for the chronicler Hresh!" came the braying voice of the bailiff who had gone to fetch him. She looked about and saw her father entering the throne-room.

How long it had been since she had last seen him, she wasn't sure: weeks, certainly, or possibly months. There had never been any formal estrangement between them; but her path and his simply tended rarely to cross, these days. He had his unending research into the world of the past to absorb him, while she, living her isolated and somehow suspended life in the upper reaches of the House of Nakhaba, felt little reason to come down into the central districts of the city.

The moment he entered the room Hresh turned to her, holding out his arms, as if she were the only person there. And Nialli Apuilana went quickly, eagerly to him.

"Father—"

"Nialli—my little Nialli—"

He had aged enormously in just these few months since they last had been together, as though each week had been a year for him. Of course he was at a point in his life when time galloped by. Some years past fifty now: old, as People life-spans went. His fur had long since grayed. Nialli Apuilana, his one child, born to him very late, could not remember a time when it had been any other color. His slender shoulders were bowed, his chest was hollow. Only his huge dark scarlet-flecked eyes, blazing like beacons beneath his wide forehead, still radiated the vitality that must have been his in those long-ago days when, still no more than a boy, he had led the People from the ancestral cocoon across the plains into Vengiboneeza.

They embraced quietly, almost solemnly. Then she stepped back from him and for a moment their eyes met.

Hresh-of-the-answers, the bailiff had called him. Well, that was his full formal name, yes. He had once told her that he had chosen it himself upon reaching his naming-day. Before that, when he was a boy, he had been called Hresh-full-of-questions. They were both good names for him. There was no mind like his anywhere, always probing, always seeking. Truly he must be the wisest man in the world, Nialli Apuilana thought. Everyone said so.

She felt herself drawn in, swallowed up, by those astonishing eyes of his, eyes that had looked upon such miracles and wonders as she could barely comprehend. Hresh had seen the Great World alive: he had held a device in his hand that brought it all back in visions, and showed him the mighty sapphire-eyes people and the sea-lords and the mechanicals and all the rest of those dead races—even the humans, whom the People had called by the name of Dream-Dreamers in the days when they lived in the cocoon—the baffling enigmatic humans, who had been masters of the Earth long before any of the others had come into being, so long ago that the mind was numbed merely to think of it.

Hresh seemed so mild, so ordinary, until you looked into his eyes. And then he became frightening. He had seen so much. He had achieved so much. Everything that the People had become since the Long Winter's end, they were because Hresh had shaped them that way.

He smiled. "I wasn't expecting to see you here, Nialli."

"Husathirn Mueri sent for me. He thought I still knew the language of the hjjks. But of course it's all gone from me now, all but a few words."

Hresh nodded. "You shouldn't be expected to remember. It's been two years, hasn't it?"

"Three, father. Almost four."

"Almost four. Of course." He chuckled indulgently at his own absentmindedness. "And who could blame you for blocking it from your mind? A nightmare like that."

She looked away from him. He had never understood the truth of her stay among the hjjks. No one had. Perhaps no one ever would. Except this silent stranger here, and she was unable to communicate in any useful way with him.

Husathirn Mueri, descending from the throne, led the stranger to Hresh's side. "He was found at midday, in Emakkis Valley, riding a vermilion. He makes hjjk-sounds, and speaks a few words of our language also. Nialli Apuilana says that these are hjjk-amulets on his wrist and breast."

"He looks half starved," Hresh said. "More than half. He's like a walking skeleton."

"Do you remember what I looked like, father, when I came back from the hjjks?" Nialli Apuilana asked. "They eat very little, the hjjks. Sparseness is what they prefer, in eating, in everything. That's their way. I was hungry all the time, when I was with them."

"And looked it when you returned," said Hresh. "I do remember. Well, perhaps we can find some way to talk with this boy. And then he ought to be given something to eat. Eh, Husathirn Mueri? Something to put a little meat on his bones. But let's see what we can do, first."

"Will you use the Wonderstone?" Husathirn Mueri asked.

"The Wonderstone, yes. The Barak Dayir." Hresh drew a worn velvet pouch from a pocket of his sash and tugged at its drawstring. Into the palm of his hand tumbled a tapered bit of polished stone, like a finely made spearhead. It was a mottled purple and brown in color, with a pattern of intricate fine lines inscribed along its edges. "No one must come near me," he said.

Nialli Apuilana trembled. She had seen the Wonderstone no more than five or six times in her life, and not in many years. It was the People's single most prized possession. No one, not even Hresh, knew what it was. They said it was made of star-stuff, whatever that meant. They said it was older even than the Great World, that it was a human-thing, an instrument out of that remote unknown world that had existed before the sapphire-eyes folk began to rule the Earth. Perhaps so. The only thing that was certain was that Hresh had learned how to work miracles with it.

He took it now in the curve of his sensing-organ, grasping it firmly. His expression grew distant and strange. He was summoning his second sight, now, unleashing all the formidable powers of his mind and focusing them through the strange device that was called the Barak Dayir.

The stranger, motionless, stood with his eyes fixed unblinkingly on Hresh. They were unusual eyes, a clear pale green, like the water in the shallows of Dawinno Bay, but much colder. The stranger too seemed to be locked in deep concentration; and once again that odd almost-smile had appeared on his face.

Hresh's eyes were closed. He appeared not even to be breathing. He was lost in his own spell, his mind given up entirely into the power of the Barak Dayir. But after an eternity he could be seen to return. The room was very still.

"His name is Kundalimon," Hresh said.

"Kundalimon," Husathirn Mueri repeated gravely, as though the name had some deep significance.

"At least, that's what he thinks it is. He isn't entirely sure. He isn't entirely sure even of what a name is. He doesn't have one among the hjjks. But the traces of the name *Kundalimon* are still in his mind, like the traces of ancient foundations in a ruined city. He knows that he was born here, seventeen years ago."

Husathirn Mueri said quietly to the bailiff, "Go to the House of Knowledge. See if there's any record of a lost child named Kundalimon."

Hresh shook his head. "No. Let it be. I'll take care of that myself, afterward." He turned to the stranger. "We have to teach you your own name. Everyone in this city has a name, a name that belongs only to himself." And in a clear high tone he said, pointing to the boy, *"Kundalimon."*

"Kundalimon," the stranger repeated, nodding, tapping his chest, smiling something that was close to being an actual smile.

Hresh touched his own breast. *"Hresh."*

"Hresh," said the stranger. "Hresh."

He looked toward Nialli Apuilana.

"He wants to know your name too," Hresh said. "Go on. Tell him."

Nialli Apuilana nodded. But to her horror her voice wasn't there when she called upon it. Nothing would come from her throat but a cough and a tight hoarse rasping that could almost have been a hjjk-sound. Dismayed, embarrassed, she clapped her hand over her mouth.

"Tell him your name," said Hresh again.

Silently Nialli Apuilana tapped her throat with her fingers and shook her head.

Hresh seemed to understand. He nodded to Kundalimon and pointed to her. *"Nialli Apuilana,"* he said, in the same clear high tone as before.

"Nialli—Apuilana," Kundalimon repeated carefully, staring at her. The supple vowels and liquid consonants did not seem to rise easily to his lips. "Nialli—Apuilana—"

She looked away, as if scalded by his gaze.

Hresh took the Barak Dayir and closed his eyes again, and disappeared once more into his trance. Kundalimon stood statue-still before him. There was utter silence in the room.

Shortly Hresh seemed to return, and after a time he said, "How strange his mind is! He's been with the hjjks since he was four. Living in the great main Nest, the Nest of Nests, far in the north."

The Nest of Nests! In the presence of the Queen of Queens Herself! Nialli Apuilana felt a surge of envy.

She found her voice and said softly, "And do you know why he's come here, father?"

In a curious muffled tone Hresh said, "The Queen wants to make a treaty with us."

"A *treaty?*" Husathirn Mueri said.

"A treaty, yes. A treaty of perpetual peace."

Husathirn Mueri looked stunned. "What are the terms? Do you know?"

"They want to draw a line across the continent, somewhere just north of the City of Yissou. Everything north of the line is to be considered hjjk, and everything south of it will remain the territory of the People. No one of either race will be allowed to enter territory belonging to the other."

"A treaty," Husathirn Mueri said again in wonder. "The Queen wants a treaty with us! I can't believe it."

"Nor can I," said Hresh. "Almost too good to be true, isn't it? Hard and fast boundaries. A no-trespass agreement. Everything clear, everything straightforward. In one stroke, an end to the fear of war with them that's been dangling over us all our lives."

"If we can trust them."

"If we can trust them, yes."

"Have they sent an emissary to the City of Yissou also, do you know?" Husathirn Mueri said.

"Yes. They've sent them to each of the Seven Cities, so it appears."

Husathirn Mueri laughed. "I'd like to see King Salaman's face. Out of nowhere, peace breaks out! Perpetual peace with the great insect enemy! What then becomes of the holy war of extermination that he's been aching to launch against them for the past ten or twenty years?"

"Do you think Salaman was ever serious about a war with the hjjks?" Nialli Apuilana asked.

Husathirn Mueri looked at her. "What?"

"It's all politics, isn't it? So he can go on building his great wall higher and higher and higher. He keeps saying the hjjks are about to invade his city, but in fact the last time they did was before most of us were born. When Harruel was king up there, and Yissou had just been founded."

He turned to Hresh. "She has a point. Despite all of Salaman's fretting, there haven't been any real hostilities between the hjjks and the People in years. They have their lands, and we have ours, and nothing worse than a few border skirmishes ever takes place. If all the treaty does is ratify the status quo, what meaning does it have? Or is it some kind of trap?"

"There are other conditions besides the one I spoke of," Hresh said quietly.

"What do you mean?"

"That had best be saved for discussion in the Presidium, I think," said Hresh. "Meanwhile we have a weary stranger here. Give the boy a place to stay, Husathirn Mueri. See if you can find something for him that he's willing to eat. And make sure that his vermilion is cared for, also. He's very worried about his vermilion."

Husathirn Mueri signaled to one of the bailiffs, who came lumbering forward.

"No," Nialli Apuilana said. Her voice was a harsh croak again, but she managed to make herself heard. "Not you." She held out her hand to the stranger. "I'll take charge of getting him his food. I know what kinds of things he eats, better than anyone else here. Don't forget I've been in the Nest myself." She glanced defiantly around the room. "Well? Any objections?" But no one spoke.

"Come," she said to Kundalimon. "I'll look after you."

As it should be, she thought.

How could I let anyone else? What do they know, any of them? But we are both of the Nest, you and I. We are both of the Nest.

2

Masks of Several Sorts

Afterward, when he is alone again, Hresh closes his eyes and lets his soul rove forth, imagining it soaring in a dream-vision beyond the bounds of the city, far across the windy northern plains, into that unknown distant realm where the hordes of insect-folk scurry about within their immense subterranean tunnels. They are a total enigma to him. They are the mystery of mysteries. He sees the Queen, or what he imagines to be the Queen, that immense remote inscrutable monarch, lying somnolent in Her heavily guarded chamber, stirring slowly while acolytes chant harsh clicking hjjk-songs of praise: the hjjk of hjjks, the great Queen. What hjjk-dreams of total world domination is She dreaming, even now? How will we ever learn, he wonders, what it is that those creatures want of us?

"Your abdication?" Minguil Komeilt cried, astonished. "Your *abdication*, lady? Who would dare? Let me take this paper to the captain of the guards! We'll find the one who's behind it and we'll see to it that—"

"Peace, woman," Taniane said. This fluttery outburst from her private secretary was more bothersome to her than the actual petition had been. "Do you think this is the first time I've had a note like this? Do you think it'll be the last? It means nothing. *Nothing.*"

"But to throw a stone at you in the streets, with a message like this attached to it—"

Taniane laughed. She glanced again at the scrap of paper in her hand. YOU STAY MUCH TOO LONG, it said, in huge crude lettering. IT'S TIME YOU STEPPED ASIDE AND LET RIGHTFUL FOLK RULE.

The words were Beng, the handwriting was Beng. The stone had come out of nowhere to land at her feet, as she was walking up Koshmar Way from the Chapel of the Interceder to her chambers in the House of Government, as she did almost every morning after she had prayed. It was the third such anonymous note she had received—no, the fourth, she thought—in the last six months. After nearly forty years of chieftainship.

"You want me to take no action at all?" Minguil Komeilt asked.

"I want you to file this wherever you file outbursts of this sort. And then forget about it. Do you understand me? Forget about it. It means nothing whatsoever."

"But—lady—"

"Nothing whatsoever," said Taniane again.

She entered her chambers. The masks of her predecessors stared down at her from its dark stippled walls.

They were fierce, vivid, strange, barbaric. They were emblems out of a former age. To Taniane they were reminders of how much had changed in the single life-span since the People had come forth from the cocoon.

"Time I stepped aside," she said to them, under her breath. "So I've been told." Rocks thrown at me in the street. Bengs who don't care for the Act of Union. After all this time. Restless fools, that's all they are. They still want one of their own to govern. As if they knew a better system. I should give them what they want, and see how they like it then.

There behind her desk was the Mask of Lirridon, which Koshmar had worn on that long-ago day when the tribe had made its Going Forth into the newly thawed world. It was a frightening thing, harsh and angular and repellent. Surely it was patterned after some old tribal memory of the hjjk-folk, some ancestral nightmare, for it was yellow and black in color, and outfitted with a terrible jutting sharp-edged beak.

Flanking it was Sismoil's mask, bland, enigmatic, with a flat unreadable face and tiny eye-slits. Thekmur's mask, very simple, hung beside it. Farther down the wall was the Mask of Nialli, a truly horrifying one, black and green with a dozen long spikes, red as blood, standing away from its sides at sharp angles. Koshmar had worn the Nialli mask on the day the invading force of Helmet People—Bengs—first had arrived and confronted the People in Vengiboneeza.

And there were Koshmar's own masks: the shining gray one with red eye-slits that she had worn in her lifetime, and the finer one carved in her honor by the craftsman Striinin after her death, with powerful features marked in burnished black wood. Taniane had worn that mask herself, on the day of departure from Vengiboneeza, when the People were setting out on their second migration, the one that would bring them eventually to the place where they would build the City of Dawinno.

Glimmers of a vanished past, the masks were. Spark-trails, leading backward through the muffled swaddlings of time to forgotten days of what now seemed a claustrophobic enclosure.

"Should I go?" Taniane asked, looking at the Koshmar masks. "Are they right? Have I ruled long enough? Is it time to step aside?"

Koshmar had been the last of the old chieftains—the last to rule over a tribe so small that the chieftain knew everyone by name, and adjudicated disputes as though they were mere bickerings between friends.

How much simpler an age that had been! How guileless, how naive!

"Perhaps I should," Taniane said. "Eh? Eh? What do you say? Do the gods require me to spend every remaining minute of my life doing this? Or is it out of pride that I hang on year after year? Or because I wouldn't know what else to do with myself?"

From Koshmar's masks no answers came.

The People had been just a little band, in Koshmar's time, a mere tribe. But now the People were civilized; now they were city-dwellers; now they numbered in the thousands instead of in the handfuls, and they had been compelled to invent one new concept after another, a dizzying profusion of things, in order to be able to function at all in this new and expanded order. They had come to use the thing known as exchange-units instead of simply sharing alike, and they fretted over profits, possessions, the size of their living quarters, the number of workers they employed, tactics of competition in the marketplace, and other such strangenesses. They had begun to divide into classes: rulers, owners, workers, poor. Nor were the old tribal lines completely erased. They were fading, yes. But Koshmars and Bengs had not yet entirely forgotten that they had been Koshmars and Bengs; and then there were all the others, the Hombelions and Debethins and Stadrains and Mortirils and the rest, the proud little tribes gradually disappearing into the bigger ones but still struggling to retain some shred of their old identities.

Each of these things brought new problems, and all of them fell ultimately to the chieftain to solve. And everything had happened so rapidly. The city, powered by Hresh's unceasing inventiveness and his researches into the archives of antiquity, had sprung up like a mushroom in a single generation, in unabashed and hopeful imitation of the Great World cities of the past.

Taniane looked at the masks.

"You never had to worry about census figures and tax rolls, did you? Or minutes of the Presidium, or statistics on the number of exchange-units in current circulation." She riffled through the mound of papers on her desk: petitions of merchants seeking licenses to import goods from the City of Yissou, studies of sanitation problems in outlying neighborhoods, a report on the poor condition of the Thaggoran Bridge on the south side of town. On and on and on. And, right on top, Hresh's little memorandum: *A Report on the Proposed Treaty with the Hjjks.*

"If only you were down here," Taniane said fervently to the masks, "and I were up there on the wall!"

She had never had a mask of her own. At first she was content to wear Koshmar's, on those occasions when wearing a mask was appropriate. And then, after the Bengs had come to Dawinno to merge with the People under the Act of Union, the political compromise that provided for a chieftain of Koshmar blood but a Beng majority on the Presidium, and the city had entered the most spectacular phase of its growth, mask-wearing had begun to seem antiquated to her, a mere foolish custom of the earlier days. It was years now since she had worn one.

Even so, she kept them around her in her office. Partly as decorations, partly as reminders of that darker and more primitive time when ice had covered the land and the People were nothing more than a little band of naked furry creatures huddling in a sealed chamber cut into the side of a mountain. The harsh shapes and bright, slashing colors of those masks were her only link to that other era now.

Seating herself behind the curving block of black onyx, rising on a pedestal of polished pink granite, that was her desk, Taniane scooped up a handful of the papers that Minguil Komeilt had left there for her and shuffled somberly through them again and again. Words swam before her eyes. *Census . . . taxes . . . Thaggoran Bridge . . . hjjk treaty . . . hjjk treaty . . . hjjk treaty . . .*

She glanced up at Lirridon's mask, the hjjk-faced one with the great hideous beak.

"Would *you* sign a treaty with them?" she asked. "Would you deal with them at all?"

The hjjks! How she despised and dreaded them! From childhood on you were taught to loathe them. They were hideous; they were gigantic frightful nightmare bugs, cold and evil; they were capable of committing any sort of monstrous thing.

There were rumors of them all the time, roving bands of them said to lurk in the open country everywhere to the east and north. In truth there turned out to be no substance behind most of those tales. But all the same they had stolen her only child from her, just outside the city walls; and the fact that Nialli Apuilana had returned after a few months had done nothing to ease Taniane's hatred for them, for the Nialli Apuilana who had returned was something mysteriously different from the girl they had taken. The hjjks were the menace. They were the enemy against whom the People would one day have to contend for supremacy in the world.

And this treaty—these purported messages of love from their ghastly Queen—

Taniane pushed Hresh's report aside.

I've been chieftain so long, she thought. Ever since I was a girl. My whole life, so it seems—nearly forty years—

She had taken the chieftainship when the tribe was tiny, and she just a short time beyond her girlhood. Koshmar was dying, and Taniane the most vigorous and far-seeing of the younger women. They had all acclaimed her. She hadn't hesitated. She knew she was made for the chieftainship, and the chieftainship for her. But she had had no way of seeing as far as *this*, these reports and studies and petitions for import licenses. And ambassadors from the hjjks. No one could have foreseen that. Perhaps not even Hresh.

She picked up another paper, the one on the cracks in the roadbed of the Thaggoran Bridge. That seemed more urgent just now. You are evading the real issue, she told herself. And other words floated before her eyes.

YOU STAY MUCH TOO LONG
IT'S TIME YOU STEPPED ASIDE
LET RIGHTFUL FOLK RULE

"Your abdication, lady? Your *abdication*?"
"It's nothing—nothing whatsoever—"

YOU STAY MUCH TOO LONG

A Report on the Proposed Treaty with the Hjjks
"Your abdication, lady?"
"Would *you* sign a treaty with them?"
"Mother? Mother, are you all right?"
"Your *abdication*?"
"Can you hear me, mother?"

IT'S TIME YOU STEPPED ASIDE

"Mother? Mother?"

Taniane looked up. There was a figure at the door of her chambers. That door was always open to any of the citizens of Dawinno, though few of them dared to come to it. Taniane struggled to focus her eyes. She had been in some sort of haze, she realized. Minguil Komeilt? No, no, Minguil Komeilt was a soft, round, timid little woman, and this one was tall and athletic, strong and restless.

"Nialli?" she said, after a moment.
"You sent for me."
"Yes. Yes. Of course. Come in, girl!"

But she hovered in the doorway. She wore a green mantle casually over one shoulder and the orange sash of the highborn at her waist. "You look so strange," she said, staring. "I've never seen you look this way. Mother, what's the matter? You aren't ill, are you?"

"No. And nothing is the matter."

"They told me a rock was thrown at you in the street this morning."

"You know about it?"

"Everyone knows. A hundred people saw it, and everyone's talking about it. It makes me so furious, mother! That anyone should dare—should dare—"

"So big a city is bound to have a great many fools," Taniane said.

"But to throw a rock, mother—to try to injure you—"

"You have it wrong," Taniane said. "The rock fell well in front of me. It wasn't meant to hit me at all. It was simply carrying a message. Some Beng agitator thinks I ought to abdicate. I've stayed much too long, is what he said. It's time I stepped aside. In favor of a Beng chieftain, I suppose."

"Would anyone really presume to suggest such a thing?"

"People presume to suggest anything and everything, Nialli. What happened this morning is meaningless. Some crank, nothing more. Some agitator. I can tell the difference between an isolated crank letter and the outbreak of a revolution." She shook her head. "Enough of this. There are other things to discuss."

"You dismiss it so lightly, mother."

"Shall I let myself take it seriously? I'd be a fool if I did."

"No," Nialli Apuilana said, and there was heat in her tone. "I don't agree at all. Who knows how far this will spread, if it's not stopped right away? You should find the person who threw that rock and have him nailed to the city wall."

They stared tensely at each other. A pounding began behind Taniane's eyes, and she felt a tightness in her stomach. Congealing juices roiled there. With anyone else, she thought, this would merely be a discussion; with Nialli it was a battle. They were always at war. Why is that? she wondered. Hresh had said something about their being so similar, that like repels like. He had been doing something with little metal bars then, studying how one of them would attract the other at one end, but nothing would happen at the other. You and Nialli are too much like each other, Hresh had said. And that is why you will never be able to exert any real force over her. Your magnetism won't work on her.

Perhaps so, although Taniane suspected that something else was at work too, some transformation which she had undergone while she was among the hjjks, that made her so difficult. But there was no denying her daughter's likeness to her. The two of them were cast in the same image. It was an eerie and sometimes troubling thing. Looking at Nialli was like looking at a mirror that reflected through time. They could almost have been twins, mysteriously born some three and a half decades apart. Nialli was her one child, the child of her middle years, conceived almost miraculously after she and Hresh had long since given up hope of bringing any into the world; and there seemed to be no imprint of Hresh anywhere upon the girl, except, perhaps, her stubborn, independent mind. In all other ways she was Taniane reborn. Those elegant legs, those strong shoulders and high breasts, that splendid silken red-brown fur—yes, Taniane thought. She looked regal. She carried herself like a chieftain. There was a glory about her. Not always a comforting thing, that. Sometimes, when she saw Nialli, Taniane was all too painfully reminded of her own aging body. She felt herself already drifting downward into the earth, beckoned by the powers of decay, too soon dragged under by the mass of corroding flesh and softening bones. She heard the flutter of moth-wings, she saw trails of gray dust along stone floors. There were days when there was death in the air.

After a long silence Taniane said, "Must we quarrel, Nialli? If I thought there was something to worry about here, I'd take action. But if someone really wanted to overthrow me, it wouldn't be done with rocks tossed in the street. Do you understand that?"

"Yes," said Nialli Apuilana. It was barely more than a whisper. "I understand."

"Good." Taniane closed her eyes a moment. She struggled to cast off fatigue and strain. "Now: if we can get down to the matter I called you here to discuss. Which is this supposed ambassador who has come to us from the hjjks, and the supposed treaty that he supposedly invites us to sign."

"Why all these supposeds, mother?"

"Because everything that we really know about this comes by way of Hresh and the Barak Dayir. The boy himself hasn't said anything coherent at all, has he?"

"Not yet, no."

"You think he will?"

"As our language comes back to him, he may. He's been in the Nest for thirteen years, mother."

"What about your talking to him in *his* language?"

Nialli Apuilana seemed uneasy. "I'm not able to do that."

"You can't speak any hjjk?"

"Only a handful of words, mother. It was years ago—I was with them just a few months—"

"You're the one who brings him his food, aren't you?"

Nialli Apuilana nodded.

"What if you used those occasions to refresh your memories of the hjjk language? Or to teach him a little of ours."

"I suppose I could," Nialli Apuilana said grudgingly.

The obvious reluctance in her tone was maddening. Taniane felt her resistance. The girl is innately contrary, she thought. She said, perhaps a little too sharply, "You're the only person in this city who can serve as an interpreter for us. Your help is essential, Nialli. The Presidium will meet soon to take up this entire treaty thing. I can't rely on Wonderstone trances alone. The Wonderstone is all well and good; but we need to hear actual words from the boy. You'll have to find some way of communicating verbally with him and learn from him what this is all about. And then give me a full report. I want to know everything that he says to you."

Something was wrong. Nialli Apuilana's jaw was set. There was a cold, hard look in the girl's eyes. She stared without speaking, and the silence stretched across too many ticking moments.

"Is there some problem here?" Taniane asked.

Nialli Apuilana glared sullenly. "I don't like acting as a spy, mother."

A spy? Taniane thought. That was unexpected. It hadn't occurred to her that serving as an interpreter on behalf of one's own people could be construed as spying.

Is it because of the hjjks? she wondered.

Yes. Yes. It is because the hjjks are involved in this. And she sat stunned, appalled. For the first time she understood that her daughter might feel an actual conflict of loyalty.

Since Nialli Apuilana's return from captivity she had never said a word to anyone about her experiences among the hjjks: nothing of what they had done to her, nothing of what they had said, not a scrap of information about what life in the Nest was like. She had steadfastly deflected all inquiries, meeting every query with an odd mix of distress and steely ferocity, until the inquiries had ceased altogether. Up till this moment Taniane had assumed that the girl had simply been shielding her privacy, protecting herself against the awakening of painful memories. But if she saw a request to report on her conversations with Kundalimon in terms of spying, then it might well be that it was the privacy of the hjjks, not her own, that she felt a powerful desire to protect. That was worth some further investigation.

Just now, though, such ambiguities of attitude were a luxury the city was unable to afford. An actual hjjk ambassador, tongue-tied and uncommunicative though he might be, was here. Guessing at his message, or relying on Hresh's Wonderstone-assisted ability to read his mind, was insufficient. He had to be made to state his errand in words. Nialli would simply have to yield. Her assistance in this thing was too important.

Brusquely Taniane said, "What kind of foolishness is this? There's no spying involved here. We're talking about service to your city. A stranger comes, bearing news that the Queen wants to negotiate with us. But he can't speak our language and nobody here can speak his, except for one young woman who happens to be the chieftain's daughter, but who also seems to think that there's something unethical about helping us to find out what an ambassador from another race is trying to say."

"You're turning everything your own way, mother. I simply don't want to feel that if I do manage to open some sort of communication with Kundalimon, I'm obliged to report whatever he says to me to you."

Taniane felt the beginnings of despair. Once she had thought Nialli Apuilana would succeed her one day as chieftain; but plainly that could never be. The girl was impossible. She was baffling: volatile, headstrong, unstable. It was clear now that the long line of the chieftainship, which could be traced back into the remote days of cocoon life, was destined to be broken. It was the hjjks that did this to her, Taniane thought. One more reason to despise them. But all the same Nialli Apuilana could not be allowed to win this battle.

Summoning all the force that was within her, she said, "You *have* to do it. It's vital to our security that we understand what this is all about."

"Have to?"

"I want you to. You have to, yes."

There was silence. Inner rebellion knotted Nialli Apuilana's forehead. Taniane stared at her coldly, pitilessly, matching the hardness of her daughter's glare with an even fiercer look, one meant to overpower. To enhance it she allowed her second sight to arise, and Nialli Apuilana looked at her in amazement. Taniane maintained the pressure.

Nialli Apuilana, though, continued to resist.

Then at last she gave ground: or appeared to. Coolly, almost contemptuously, she said, "Well, then. As you wish. I'll do what I can."

Nialli Apuilana's face, so wondrously a reflection of Taniane's own refracted through decades of time, was expressionless, unreadable, a mask void of all feeling. Taniane felt the temptation to reach out at the most intimate level of second sight, to reach with forbidden force and penetrate that sullen mask for once. Was it anger that Nialli Apuilana was hiding, or mere resentment, or something else, some wild rebellious flare?

"Are we finished?" Nialli Apuilana asked. "Do I have permission to leave now?"

Taniane gave her a bleak look. This had all gone so very badly. She had won this little battle, perhaps. But she sensed that she had lost a war.

She had hoped to reach out to Nialli in love and friendship. Instead she had snapped and snarled, and had made use of the blunt strength of her position, and had coldly issued orders, as though Nialli were nothing more than some minor functionary of her staff. She wished she could rise, walk around the desk to her, take her in her arms. But that was beyond her, somehow. Often it seemed to her that a wall higher than King Salaman's stood between her and her daughter.

"Yes," she said. "You can go."

Nialli Apuilana went briskly toward the door. When she reached the hallway, though, she turned and looked back.

"Don't worry," she said, and, to Taniane's surprise, there seemed to be a conciliatory tone in her voice. It sounded almost gentle. "I'll do things the right way. I'll find out everything you need to know, and tell you. And I'll tell it to the Presidium too."

Then she was gone.

Taniane swung around and looked at the masks behind her on the wall. They seemed to be laughing at her. Their faces were implacable.

"What do you know?" she muttered. "None of you ever had mates, or children, did you? Did you?"

"Lady?" a voice called from outside. It was Minguil Komeilt. "Lady, may I come in?"

"What is it?"

"A delegation, lady. From the Guild of Tanners and Dyers of the Northern District, concerning repairs to their main water conduit, which they say has become blocked by sewage that is being illegally released by members of the Guild of Weavers and Wool-Carders, and is causing—"

Taniane groaned.

"Oh, send them to Boldirinthe," she said, half to herself. "This is something the offering woman can handle as well as the chieftain can."

"Lady?"

"Boldirinthe can pray for them. She can ask the gods to unplug the water line. Or bring down vengeance on the Guild of Weavers and—"

"Lady?" Minguil Komeilt said again, with alarm in her voice. "Do I understand you rightly, lady? This is a joke, is it not? This is only a joke?"

"Only a joke, yes," said Taniane. "You mustn't take me seriously." She pressed her fingers against her eyes, and drew three quick deep breaths. "All right. Send in the delegation from the Guild of Tanners and Dyers—"

A veil of hazy heat shrouded the sky as Nialli Apuilana stepped into the street outside the House of Government. She hailed a passing xlendi-wagon.

"The House of Nakhaba," she told the driver. "I'll be there just five minutes or so. Then I'll want you to take me somewhere else."

That would be Mueri House, where the hjjk emissary had been lodged: a hostelry used mostly by strangers to the city, where he could be kept under close watch. Now it was time to bring him his midday meal. She went to Kundalimon twice a day, at noon and twilight. He had a small one-windowed room—it was more like a cell—on the third floor, facing backward into a blind plaza.

Her confrontation with her mother had left her drained and numb. Love warred with fear in her whenever she had to deal with Taniane. There was never any telling, with Taniane, when her powerful sense of the needs of the city was going to override all other considerations, all thought of the messy little private needs and problems of private individuals, whether they happened to be her daughter or some absolute stranger. For her the city always came first. No doubt you got that way, Nialli Apuilana supposed, when you held the chieftainship for forty years: time made you hard, narrow, singleminded. Maybe the Beng who had hurled the rock was right: maybe it *was* time for Taniane to step aside.

Nialli Apuilana wondered whether she really was going to spy for Taniane, as she had so abruptly found herself agreeing to do.

It had been a mistake, perhaps, to put the whole thing in terms of spying. She was, after all, a citizen of Dawinno and the daughter of the chieftain and the chronicler. And she did, after all, have at least a little knowledge of the hjjk language, which was more than anyone else here could claim. Why *not* serve as interpreter, and do it gladly, with pride in being of service? It didn't mean that she'd have to repeat every single word of her conversations with Kundalimon to Taniane and the Presidium, or to open up her whole experience of the hjjks to their probing. She could pick and choose: she could easily enough limit what she reported to them to the basic matters of the negotiation. But it had been so frightening, the thought that they might grill her on everything she knew about the Nest and its ruler. That horrified her, that they would break through the shield of privacy which she had held in place around herself for nearly four years. She meant to cast off that shield herself, when and if she felt it was the proper time. The idea that they might in some way strip her of it before she was ready filled her with terror, though. An overreaction, perhaps. Perhaps.

She stopped off at the House of Nakhaba only long enough to pick up the food for Kundalimon's midday meal. Today she had a stewed loin of vimbor for him. Hjjk-food, mostly, was what she brought him: seeds and nuts and baked meats, nothing moist with sauces, nothing at all rich—but also she tempted him carefully now and then with the heartier fare of the People, a morsel or two at a time. Food could be a language too. The meals they took together were one means they had of learning to communicate with each other.

There was one time—it was the third or fourth time she had brought him his meal—when he spent a long time thoughtfully chewing a mouthful of nuts and fruits without swallowing, and finally spat out a quantity into his hand. This he held out to her. Nialli Apuilana's first response was surprise and disgust. But he continued to press the handful of moist pulp upon her, pointing and nodding.

"What is it?" she asked, bewildered. "Is there something wrong with it?"

"No—food—you—Nialli Apuilana—"

She stared, still not comprehending.

"Take—take—"

Then it came back to her. In the Nest the hjjks shared partly digested food all the time. A mark of solidarity, of Nest-bond; and something more than that, perhaps, having to do with the way the hjjks' bodies processed their food, that she could not understand. She remembered now the sight of her nestmates pressing chewed food on one another. It was a common thing among them, this sharing of food.

Hesitantly she had taken what Kundalimon offered. He smiled and nodded. She forced herself to nibble at it, though all her instincts recoiled. "Yes," he said. "Oh, yes!"

She got it down somehow, struggling against nausea. He seemed pleased.

By pantomime he had indicated then that she should take some of the People-food she had brought and do the same with it for him. She picked up a haunch of roast gilandrin and bit into it, and when she had chewed it for a time she pulled the whole wad of it from her mouth, taking care to conceal her queasiness, and gave it to him.

He tasted it cautiously. He looked uncertain about the meat itself; but obviously he was gladdened by her having had it in her mouth first. She could feel a flood of warmth and gratitude coming from him. It was almost like feeling Nest-bond once again.

"More," he said.

And so, gradually, because she was willing to adopt the hjjk custom with him, he was able to expand his range of foods. Once it became apparent to him that the things Nialli Apuilana brought him were doing him no harm, he ate them with gusto. There was new flesh on his bones, and his dark fur was thickening and had acquired a little sheen. Those strange green eyes of his no longer seemed so hard and icy.

Communication, of a sort.

He was shy and remote, but he seemed to welcome her visits. Had he figured out yet that she too had been in the Nest? Sometimes it seemed that way; but she wasn't yet sure. Verbal contact between them was still very uncertain. He had picked up a dozen or so words of the language of the city, and she was starting to reconstruct her knowledge of hjjk. But vocabulary was one thing and comprehension was another.

Learn his language, or teach him to speak ours. Those were Taniane's orders, and no maybes about them. *Do it quickly, too. And tell us what you find out.*

The first part, at least, was exactly what Nialli Apuilana intended to achieve. And when she and Kundalimon were able to communicate easily with each another, and had come to know each other better, and he had begun to trust her, perhaps he would talk with her of Nest-matters: of Queen-love, of Thinker-thoughts, of Egg-plan, and all the other things of that nature that lay at the heart of her soul. Taniane didn't need to be told anything about that. The rest, this proposed treaty, the diplomatic negotiations: oh, yes, I'll let her know whatever I might learn about all that, Nialli Apuilana thought. But nothing about the deeper things. Nothing about the things that really matter.

The xlendi-wagon was waiting. She got in.

"Mueri House, now," she told the driver.

In Prince Thu-Kimnibol's grand villa in the southwestern quadrant of the city the healers had gathered once again by the bedside of the lady Naarinta. This was the fifth night running that they had come. She had been ill for many months, slipping gradually downward from weakness to weakness. But now she was passing into the critical phase.

Tonight Thu-Kimnibol was keeping watch in the narrow antechamber just outside the sickroom. The healers had refused to let him get any closer. This night only women might enter Naarinta's room. The smell of medicines and aromatic herbs was in the air. The smell of impending death was in it, too.

His sensing-organ trembled with the awareness of the great loss that was rushing toward him.

In the sickroom the offering-woman Boldirinthe sat beside Naarinta. Whenever spells and potions were needed and the aid of the Five Heavenly Ones had to be invoked, fat old Boldirinthe heaved her vast body into a wagon and obligingly came to be of service. Old Fashinatanda, godmother to the chieftain—there was another one, blind and feeble though she was, who rarely missed an opportunity to minister to the gravely ill. Some Beng herb-doctor was there, too, a little shriveled woman wearing a dark feather-trimmed helmet flecked with rust, and two or three others whom Thu-Kimnibol could not recognize. They were murmuring to one another, chanting in low lilting voices.

Thu-Kimnibol turned away. He couldn't bear to listen. It sounded like a chant for the dead.

Outside, in the hallway, bundles of purple flowers with dark red stalks were stacked like temple offerings. The richness of their perfume made Thu-Kimnibol sputter and cough. He walked quickly past, into the huge high-vaulted room that was his audience-chamber. A little group of men waited there in the dimness: Maliton Diveri, Staip, Si-Belimnion, Kartafirain, Chomrik Hamadel. Gaming partners, hunting companions, friends of many years. They clustered round him, smiling, joking, passing a huge flagon of wine back and forth. This was no time for long faces.

"To happier times," Si-Belimnion said, swirling the wine in his mug. "Happier times past, happier times to come."

"Happier times," Chomrik Hamadel echoed. He was of Beng royal blood, a short blunt-featured man with a piercing scarlet gaze. He drank deep, throwing back his head so vehemently that he came close to sending his helmet flying.

Maliton Diveri and Kartafirain joined the toast, grinning, noisily clinking mugs: two robustly built men, one short, the other tall. Only Staip was quiet. He was older than the others, which accounted in part for his restraint; but also he was Boldirinthe's mate, and no doubt Boldirinthe had told him how little hope there was for Naarinta's life. Staip had never been one for dissembling: a warrior's simplicity, that was his style.

Thu-Kimnibol said, picking up a mug and offering it to Maliton Diveri to be filled, "Happier times, yes. Joy and prosperity to us all, and a swift recovery for my lady."

"Joy and prosperity! A swift recovery!"

It was fifteen years since Thu-Kimnibol had begun to share his life with Naarinta. He had met her not long after he had come from the north to settle in the city that his half-brother Hresh had built; and they had been inseparable ever since. She was of the Debethin tribe, the chieftain's daughter—not a great distinction, perhaps, there having been only fourteen Debethins still alive when the last survivors of that tribe's unhappy wanderings had come marching out of the east to ask for citizenship in Dawinno, but a chieftain was a chieftain nonetheless. She was tall and graceful, with an air of quiet strength about her. They were splendid together: majestic, even, the towering Thu-Kimnibol and his stately lady. The gods had given them no children, which was his greatest regret; but he had been content with Naarinta alone, the partner of his labors, the companion of his days. And then this wasting disease had come upon her, this terrible incomprehensible decree of the Heavenly Ones, against which there seemed to be no appeal.

Chomrik Hamadel said, "Is there news, Thu-Kimnibol?"

"She's very weak. What can I say?"

"News of the envoy from the hjjks, I mean," said Chomrik Hamadel hastily. "They keep him locked up in Mueri House, I hear, and Taniane's daughter runs to him every day. But what's happening? What is this all about, this visitation from the bug-folk?"

"They want a peace treaty, so I understand it," Kartafirain said, and laughed. He was a tall silver-furred man of Koshmar ancestry, nearly shoulder-high to Thu-Kimnibol himself, jovial and belligerent by nature. The warrior Thhrouk had been his father. "Peace! Who are they to talk of peace? They don't know what the word means."

"Perhaps Hresh misunderstood," Si-Belimnion said, and rubbed the rolls of fat beneath his thick blue-gray fur. He was a wealthy man, and well fed. "Perhaps it's a declaration of war that the boy carries, and not a message of peace. Hresh is getting old, I think."

"So are we all," said Chomrik Hamadel. "But do you think Hresh no longer knows the difference between peace and war? He used the Wonderstone to look into the boy's mind, Curabayn Bangkea tells me. You have to trust what the Wonderstone says."

"A treaty of peace," Maliton Diveri said, and shook his head in wonderment. "With the hjjks! What will we do? Fall down on our faces and thank the gods for such mercies, I suppose!"

"Of course," said Thu-Kimnibol gruffly. "And then scurry up and put our signatures on the treaty. I'll be the first, if they'll permit me. We have to show our deep gratitude. The kindness of the bug-folk! They'll condescend to let us keep our city, I hear. And maybe even a little of the farmland outside it."

"Are those the terms?" Si-Belimnion asked. "What I had heard was much more favorable to us: the hjjks will stay back of Vengiboneeza, is what I heard, provided we don't attempt to expand beyond—"

"Whatever it is," said Kartafirain flatly, "we'll be the losers. You can bet your ears on that, and your sensing-organ too. When the Presidium meets, we've got to argue for rejection of this thing."

"And when will that be?" asked Chomrik Hamadel.

"A week, ten days, maybe sooner. While Taniane's daughter is tending this Kundalimon, she's supposed to question him about the details of the treaty in his own language. She can speak it, you know. She picked it up while she was living with the bugs herself. She'll tell Taniane what she finds out and then it all goes to the Presidium for general discussion, after which—"

Just then Staip, who had not said a word all the time, went suddenly from the room, holding his sensing-organ high. It was as though the old warrior had been called by some summons that no one else could hear. A strained silence fell.

Kartafirain ponderously got the conversation going again after a moment. "I don't see the sense of involving Nialli Apuilana in this at all." He looked toward Thu-Kimnibol. "What help can she possibly be?"

"Why do you say that?"

"Because she's so strange. Friend, you know better than any of us what sort of creature she is. Do you think she's likely to find out anything worthwhile? Or tell us if she does? Has that girl ever been willing to cooperate with anyone? Has she revealed so much as one syllable of whatever took place between her and the hjjks while she was their prisoner?"

Thu-Kimnibol said, "Be a little more charitable. She's intelligent and serious. And she's not a girl any more. She's capable of changing.

Perhaps the arrival of the envoy will help her start to develop a bit of a sense of responsibility to her city, or at least to her own family. If anyone can get any information out of this stranger from the north, she's the one. And—"

He halted abruptly. Staip had come back into the room. He held himself stiffly and his expression was grim.

To Thu-Kimnibol he said quietly, "Boldirinthe wants a word with you."

The offering-woman had left the sickroom and was sitting in the antechamber. Boldirinthe's huge fleshy form overflowed a wickerwork chair that seemed hard pressed to sustain her. She gestured as if to rise, but it was only a gesture, and she subsided the instant Thu-Kimnibol signaled her to remain where she was. She seemed subdued of mood, uncharacteristically so, for she was one who bubbled with life and jollity at even the darkest of times.

"Is this the end, then?" Thu-Kimnibol asked bluntly.

"It will be very soon. The gods are calling her."

"There's nothing you can do?"

"Everything has been done. You know that. Against the will of the Five we are helpless."

"Yes. So we are." Thu-Kimnibol took the offering-woman's hand in his. Now that the news had come he was calm. He felt an obscure desire to console Boldirinthe for having failed in her lifesaving task, even as she was seeking to give consolation to him. For a moment they both were silent. Then he asked, "How much longer?"

"You should make your farewells to her now," said Boldirinthe. "There'll be no chance later."

He nodded and went past her, into the room where Naarinta lay. She seemed tranquil, and very beautiful, strangely so, as though the long struggle had burned all fleshly impurities from her. Her eyes were closed and she was breathing very faintly, but she was still conscious. Old blind Fashinatanda sat beside her, chanting. As Thu-Kimnibol entered she broke off her chant and, without a word, rose and left the room.

For a little while he talked quietly with Naarinta, though her words were cloudy and disconnected and he couldn't be sure that she understood anything he said. Then they fell silent. She seemed to have traveled more than half the distance into the next world. After a time Thu-Kimnibol saw that the unearthly beauty was beginning to go from her as the final moments approached. Softly he spoke to her again, telling her what she had meant to him; and he took her hand, and held it until everything was over. He kissed her cheek. The fur of it already seemed strangely changed, less soft than it had been. One sob, only one, broke from him. He was surprised his reaction was no more vehement. But the pain was real and strong all the same.

He left then and returned to the audience-chamber, where his friends stood in a little knotted group, no one speaking. He loomed over them like a wall, feeling suddenly cut off from them, set apart by the loss that he had suffered and the new solitude that was descending on him, falling so unexpectedly into a life that until this time had been marked only by happiness and accomplishment and the favor of the gods. He felt hollow, and knew that this strange calmness that possessed him now was that of exhaustion. A powerful sense came over him then that the life that had been his until today had ended with Naarinta, that he must now undergo transformation and rebirth. But into what? What?

He put such thoughts aside for now. Time enough later to let the new life begin to enter the drained vessel that was his soul.

"She's gone," he said simply. "Kartafirain, pour me more wine. And then let us sit for a while, and talk of politics, or hunting, or the benevolence of the hjjks. But first the wine, Kartafirain. If you please."

At the service Hresh spoke first, words he had spoken often enough before, the words of the Consolation of Dawinno: that death and life are two halves of one thing, for everything that lives arises out of all that once had lived but lives no longer, and in time must yield up its life so that new life may come forth. Boldirinthe then spoke the words of the service for the dead; Taniane spoke also, just a quiet sentence or two, and then Thu-Kimnibol, holding the body of Naarinta in his arms as though it were a doll, laid her cloth-wrapped form at the edge of the pyre. The flames engulfed her and in that fierce brightness she was lost to sight.

Time now for the mourners to return to the city from the Place of the Dead. Taniane and Hresh rode together in the chieftain's ornate wagon. "I've decreed seven days of public mourning," she told him. "That gives us a little time to think about this scheme of the hjjks, before we have to take it to the Presidium."

"The hjjks, yes," said Hresh softly. "The Presidium."

His spirit was still with Thu-Kimnibol and Naarinta. Taniane's words seemed to him at first like mere empty sounds, tinny and meaningless. They seemed to be coming to him across a vast distance. Presidium? Hjjks? Yes. *This scheme of the hjjks*, she had said. What was that? The hjjks, the hjjks, the hjjks. He felt strangeness whispering at his mind, as it so often did when the thought of the hjjks came into it. The rustling of bristly claws. The clicking of great beaks.

She said, breaking in on him sharply, "Where have you gone, Hresh?"

"What?"

"You seem to be on the far side of the moon, all of a sudden."

"Ah. You were saying—" He looked at her vaguely.

"I was speaking of the hjjks. Of the offer of a treaty. I need to know what you make of it, Hresh. Can we possibly abide by it? To let the hjjks isolate us in our own little province? To cut ourselves off from everything else in the world?"

"That is unthinkable, yes," he said.

"So it is. But you seem to take it very calmly. It hardly seems to matter to you at all."

"Must we talk about these things now? It's a sad day, Taniane. I've just seen my brother's beloved mate lowered into the fire."

She seemed to stiffen. "By the Five, Hresh, we'll see everyone we know lowered into that fire. And then someday our turns will come, and it won't be as pretty as it is in that little sermon you always preach! But the dead are dead, and we're still here, with plenty of trouble to cope with. This request for a peace treaty, Hresh: there's nothing innocent or friendly about it. It has to be a maneuver in some larger game that we aren't able at this time to comprehend. For us to sign it—"

"Please, Taniane."

She ignored him. "—would indeed be unthinkable, just as you say. Hresh, they want to take three-quarters of the world away from us under the guise of a treaty of friendship, and you won't even raise your voice?"

He said, after a while, "You know I won't ever give my support to a surrender to the hjjks. But before I take a public position there's more I need to learn. The hjjks are complete mysteries to me. To everyone. Our ignorance affects our dealings with them. What are they, really? Nothing more than oversized ants? A vast swarm of soulless bugs? If that's all that they are, how could they have been part of the Great World? There may be much more to them than we think. I want to know."

"You always want to know! But how will you find out? You've spent your whole life studying everything that there ever was in this world and the worlds that went before it, and the best you can say after all that is that the hjjks are total mysteries to you!"

"Perhaps Nialli—"

"Nialli, yes. I've ordered her to speak with the envoy and bring me whatever she can discover. But will she? Will she, do you think? Who can say? She wears a mask, that girl. That girl is more mysterious than the hjjks themselves!"

"Nialli's difficult, yes. But I think she'll be of great help to us in this."

"Perhaps so," said Taniane. But there wasn't much conviction in her voice.

The center of the city: the familiar confines of the House of Knowledge. A good place of refuge on a difficult day. Hresh found his assistants Chupitain Stuld and Plor Killivash there, huddling over some bits of rubble in one of the ground-floor offices. They seemed surprised to see him. "Will you be working today?" Plor Killivash asked. "We thought—"

"No, not working," he said. "I simply want to be here. I'll be upstairs. I won't want to be disturbed."

The House of Knowledge was a white slender spear of a tower, hardly a stone's throw wide but many stories high—the tallest building in the city, in fact. Its narrow circular galleries, in which Hresh had stored the fruits of a lifetime of inquiry, coiled around and around, narrowing as they rose, like a great serpent coiled within the tower's walls. At the summit of the whole structure was a parapet completely encircling the tip of the building to form a lofty balcony. From there Hresh could see virtually the whole of the great city that he had envisioned and laid out and brought into being.

A warm sultry wind was blowing. In his right hand he held a small silvery sphere that he had found long ago in the ruins of Vengiboneeza. With it, once, he had been able to conjure visions of the ancient magnificent epochs of the Great World. In his left lay a similar metal ball, golden bronze in color. It was the master control instrument that governed the Great World construction machines he had used to build Dawinno, in a place where nothing at all had existed but marshes and swamps and tropical forests.

Both these globes, the silver one and the golden bronze one, had long since burned out. They were of no value to him, or anyone, now. Within its translucent skin Hresh could see the master control's core of shining quicksilver stained and blackened by corrosion.

As he hefted the two dead instruments thoughts of the Great World came into his mind. He was swept by powerful envy for the people of that vanished era. How stable their world had been, how tranquil, how serene! The various parts of that grand civilization had meshed like the gears of some instrument designed by the gods. Sapphire-eyes and humans, hjjks and sea-lords, vegetals and mechanicals, they all had lived together in harmony and unity, and discord was unknown. Surely it was the happiest time the world had ever known.

But there was something paradoxical about that; for the Great World had been doomed, and its people had lived under the knowledge of that impending doom for a million years. How then could they have been happy?

Still, he thought, a million years is a long time. For the people of the Great World there must have been much joy along the way to the inevitable end. Whereas our world has the precariousness of a newly born thing. Nothing is secure yet, nothing has real solidity, and we have no assurance that our fledgling civilization will last so much as a million hours, or even a million minutes.

Somber thoughts. He tries to brush them aside.

From the parapet's edge he looked out over Dawinno. Night was beginning to descend. The last swirling purples and greens of sunset were fading in the west. The lights of the city were coming on. It was very grand, yes, as cities of the New Springtime went. But yet tonight everything about it seemed dreamlike and insubstantial. The buildings that he had long thought were so majestic appeared to him suddenly to be nothing more than hollow facades made of molded paper and held up by wooden struts. It was all only the mere pretense of a city, he thought dismally. They had improvised everything, making it look as they thought it should. But had they done it the right way? Had they done anything at all that was right?

Stop this, he tells himself.

He closed his eyes and almost at once he saw Vengiboneeza once again, Vengiboneeza as it had been when it was the living capital of the Great World. Those great shining towers of many colors, the swarming docks, the busy markets, the peoples of six vastly different races existing peacefully side by side, the shimmering vessels arriving from the far stars with their cargoes of strange beings and strange produce—the grandeur of it all, the richness, the complexity, the torrent of profound ideas, the poetry, the philosophy, the dreams and schemes, the immense vitality—

For a moment its beauty delighted him, as it always had. But only for a moment; and then he was lost in gloom again.

How small we are, Hresh thinks bitterly.

What a pathetic imitation of the lost greatness we've created here! And we're so proud of what we have done. But in truth we've done so little—only to copy, like the monkeys that we are. What we have copied is the appearance, not the substance. And we could lose it all, such as it is, in the twinkling of an eye.

A dark night, this. The darkest of the dark. Moon and stars, yes, shining as they always had. But very dark within, eh, Hresh? You've thrown a cloak over your soul. Stumbling around in unyielding blackness, are you, Hresh?

For a moment he thought of tossing the useless globes over the side of the parapet. But no. No. Dead as they were, they were still able to summon lost worlds of life in his mind. Talismans, they were. They would lead him out of this bleakness. He caresses their silken-smooth surfaces and the endless past opens to him. And at last he begins to extract himself a little way from this smothering weight of clamoring misery that has engulfed him. Some perspective returns. Today, yesterday, the day before the day before yesterday: what do they matter, against the vast sweep of time? He has a sense of millions of years of history behind him: not only the Great World but a world even older than that, lost empires, lost kings, lost creatures, a world that had had no People in it, nor even the hjjks and sapphire-eyes, but only humans. And there might have been a world even before that, though his mind swims to think of it. World upon world, each arising and thriving and declining and vanishing: it is the way of the gods, that nothing can be perfect and nothing will last forever. What had all his studies of the past taught him, if not that? And there is powerful consolation in that.

He had been devouring the world all his life, hungrily gobbling its perplexing wonders. Hresh-full-of-questions: that was what they had called him when he was a boy. Cockily he had renamed himself Hresh-of-the-answers, once. He was that too. But the earlier name was truer. Every answer holds the next question, throbbing impatiently within it.

His thoughts wander back to the day when he was eight years old, in the time before the Time of Going Forth, when he had bolted through the hatch of the cocoon to see what lay outside.

Where was that boy now? Still here, a little worn and frayed. Hresh-full-of-questions. Dear Torlyri had grabbed him then, the gentle offering-woman, long since dead. It was almost fifty years ago, now. But for her, he too would have been long since dead, and long forgotten too, trapped outside when she closed the hatch after her morning prayers, and before nightfall eaten by rat-wolves, or carried off by hjjks, or simply perished of the chill of that forlorn era.

But Torlyri had caught him by the leg and yanked him back as he tried to scramble down the ledge into the open world. And when the chieftain Koshmar had sentenced him to death for his impiety, it was Torlyri who had successfully interceded on his behalf.

Long ago, long long ago. In what seems to him now like some other life. Or some other world.

But there was a continuity all the same. That unending desire to see, to do, to learn, had never left him. *You always want to know*, Taniane had said.

He shrugged. And went inside, and set the two globes down on his desk. The darkness was threatening to invade him again.

This was his private chamber. No one else was permitted to enter it. Here Hresh kept the Barak Dayir and the other instruments of divination handed down to him by his predecessors. His manuscripts, too: his essays on the past, thoughts on the meaning of life and the destiny of the People. He had told the story of the greatness and the downfall of the sapphire-eyes folk, as well as he understood it. He had written of the humans, who were even greater mysteries to him. He had speculated on the nature of the gods.

He had never shown any of these writings to anyone. Sometimes he feared that they were nothing but a jumble of lofty-minded nonsense. Often he thought of burning them. Why not? Give these dead pages to the flames, as Thu-Kimnibol had given Naarinta to them a few hours before.

"You will burn nothing," said a voice out of the shadows. "You have no right to destroy knowledge."

In the darkest of the dark moments visions often came to him—

Thaggoran, sometimes, long-dead old Thaggoran who had been chronicler before him, or sometimes the wise man Noum om Beng of the Helmet People, or even one of the gods. Hresh never doubted these visions. Figments they might be; but he knew they spoke only truth.

To Thaggoran now he says, "But is it knowledge? What if I've assembled nothing but a compilation of lies here?"

"You don't know what it is to lie, boy. Errors, maybe: lies, never. Spare your books. Write other ones. Preserve the past for those who follow after."

"The past! What good is preserving the past? The past is only a burden!"

"What are you saying, boy?"

"There's no point in looking back. The past is lost. The past is beyond preserving. The past slips away from us every hour of our lives, and good riddance to it. The future is what we need to think about."

"No," Thaggoran says. "The past is the mirror in which we see that which is to come. You know that. You have always known that. What ails you today, boy?"

"I've been at the Place of the Dead today. I've seen my brother's mate become ashes and dust."

Thaggoran laughs. "Whole worlds have become ashes and dust. New worlds come forth from them. Why should I have to remind you of such things? You were telling the others that only this day, at the Place of the Dead."

"Yes," Hresh says, in sudden shame. "Yes, I was."

"Is it not the will of the gods that death should come from life, and life from death?"

"Yes. But—"

"But nothing. The gods decree, and we obey."

"The gods are mockers," Hresh says.

"Are they, do you think?" says Thaggoran coolly.

"The gods gave the Great World happiness beyond all understanding, and then dropped the death-stars down on them. Wouldn't you call that mockery? And then the gods brought us forth out of the Long Winter to inherit the world, though we are nothing at all. Isn't that mockery also?"

"The gods never mock," says Thaggoran. "The gods are beyond our understanding, but I tell you this: what they decree, they decree for reasons that are true and deep. They are mysterious in their ways, but they are never merely whimsical."

"Ah, but can I believe that?"

"Ah," says Thaggoran, "what else is there to believe?"

Faith, yes. The last refuge of the desperate. Hresh is willing to accept that. He is almost pacified now. But even in matters of faith he still clings to logic. Not yet fully comfortable with what the old man is trying to get him to see, he says:

"But tell me this, then—if we are to be the masters of the world, as our ancient books promise us, then why have the gods left the hjjks here to stand against us? Suppose the hjjks cut us off before we've barely begun to grow. What becomes of the plan of the gods then, Thaggoran? Tell me that!"

There was no answer. Thaggoran was gone, if indeed he had ever been there.

Hresh slipped into his worn familiar chair, and put his hands to the smooth wood of his desk. The vision had not carried him quite as far as he had needed to go, but it had done its work nevertheless. Somehow his mood had shifted. The past, the future: both of them darkness, all darkness, he thought. And under cover of darkness despair finds a good place to hide. But then he asked himself: Is it all truly so bad? What else can the future be, but unknowable, a darkness? And the past: we cast our little lights backward into it and illuminate it, after a fashion, and what we learn guides us onward into the other great unknown. Our knowledge is our comfort and our shield.

Yet I know so little, Hresh thought. I need to know so much more.

You always want to know, Taniane had said.

Yes. Yes. Yes, I do.

Even now. Although I am so tired. Even now.

"We've looked up your name in the records at the House of Knowledge," Nialli Apuilana told Kundalimon. "You were born here, all right. In Year 30. That makes you seventeen, now. I was born in 31. Do you understand?"

"I understand," he said, smiling. Perhaps he did, a little.

"Your mother was Marsalforn and your father was Ramla."

"Marsalforn. Ramla."

"You were taken by the hjjks in 35. It's in the city records. Captured by a raiding party outside the walls, just like me. Marsalforn disappeared while searching for you in the hills. Her body was never found. Your father left the city soon afterward and no one knows where he is now."

"Marsalforn," he said again. "Ramla." The rest of what she had said seemed lost on him.

"Do you follow what I'm telling you? Those are the names of your mother and father."

"Mother. Father." Blankly. Her words didn't seem to hold meaning for him at all.

"Do you know what I want to do with you?" she said in a low, urgent voice, with her face close to his. "I want to talk about life in the Nest. I want you to make it come alive for me again. The smell of it, the colors, the sounds. The things that Nest-thinker says. Whether you ever went marching with the Militaries, or had to stay behind with the Egg-makers.

Whether they let you go near the Queen. I want to hear all about it. Everything."

"Marsalforn," he said again. "Mother. Father. Ramla. Marsalforn is Ramla. Mother is Father."

"You aren't really getting much of what I'm saying, are you? Are you, Kundalimon?"

He smiled, the warmest smile she had seen from him yet. It was like the sun emerging from behind a cloud. But he shook his head.

She had to try something else. This was too slow.

Her heart began to pound.

"What we ought to do is twine," Nialli Apuilana said, suddenly audacious.

Did he know what she meant? No. He made no response, simply maintained the same fixed smile.

"Twine. I want to twine with you, Kundalimon. You don't know what that is, either, do you? *Twine*. It's something that People do with their sensing-organs. Do you even know what a sensing-organ is? This thing here, hanging down behind you like a tail. It is a tail, I suppose. But much more than that. It's full of perceptors that run up into your spine and connect right to your brain."

He was still smiling, smiling, obviously comprehending nothing.

She persisted. "One of the things we use the sensing-organ for is to make contact with other people. Deep, intense, intimate contact, mind to mind. We aren't even allowed to try it until we're thirteen, and then the offering-woman shows us how, and after that we can go looking for twining-partners."

He looked at her blankly. Shook his head.

She took his hand. "Any two people can be twining-partners—a man and a woman, a man and a man, a woman and a woman, anyone. It's not like coupling or mating, you see. It's a union of souls. You twine with anyone whose soul you want to share."

"Twine," he said, and smiled even harder.

"Twine, yes. I've done it only once. On my twining-day—when I was thirteen, you know—with Boldirinthe the offering-woman. Since then, never. Nobody here interests me that way. But if I could twine with you, Kundalimon—"

"Twine?"

"We'd make contact such as we've never known in our lives. We could share Nest-truths and we wouldn't need even to try to speak each other's languages, because there's a language of twining that goes beyond any mere words." She looked around to see if the door was latched. Yes. A kind of fever was on her now. Her fur was damp, her breasts were rising and falling swiftly. Her own scent was rank and musky in her nostrils, an animal reek.

He might be beginning to comprehend.

Gingerly she lifted her sensing-organ and brought it forward, and let it slide lightly across his.

For an instant there was contact. It was like a shock of lightning. She felt his soul with astonishing clarity: a smooth pale parchment, on which strange inscriptions had been written in a dark, bold, alien hand. There was great sweetness in it, and tenderness, and also strangeness. The dark cloistered mystery of the Nest was everywhere in it. He was open to her, entirely vulnerable, and there would be no difficulty about completing the twining and linking their spirits in the keenest of intimacies. Relief, joy, even something that might have been love, flooded her soul.

But then, after that first stunning moment, he whipped his sensing-organ back out of her reach, breaking the contact with jarring suddenness. Uttering a hoarse ragged sound, midway between a growl and a hjjk's chittering insect-noise, he beat frantically at her for a moment using both his arms at once, the way a hjjk would. His eyes flared wildly with fright. Then he hopped backward and crouched in a defensive stance in the corner, pressed tight up against the walls of the room, panting in terror. His face was a frozen mask of fear and shock, nostrils wide, lips drawn back rigidly, both rows of teeth bared.

Nialli Apuilana looked at him wide-eyed, horror-stricken at what she had done.

"Kundalimon?"

"No! Away! No!"

"I didn't mean to frighten you. I only—"

"No. *No!*"

He began to tremble. He muttered incomprehensibly in hjjk. Nialli Apuilana held out her arms to him, but he turned away from her, huddling close to the wall. In shame and anguish she fled from him.

"Are you making any progress?" Taniane asked.

Nialli Apuilana gave her a quick uneasy look. "A little. Not as much as I'd like."

"Can he speak our language yet?"

"He's learning."

"And the hjjk words? Are they coming back to you?"

"We don't use the hjjk words," Nialli Apuilana said in a low, husky tone. "He's trying to put the Nest behind him. He wants to be flesh again."

"Flesh," Taniane said. Her daughter's strange choice of words sent a chill through her. "You mean, to be part of the People?"

"That's what I mean, yes."

Taniane peered close. As always she wished she could see behind the mask that hid her daughter's soul from her. For the millionth time she wondered what had happened to Nialli Apuilana during the months she had spent below the surface of the Earth in the dark mysterious labyrinth of the Nest.

She said, "What about the treaty?"

"Not a word. Not yet. We don't understand each other well enough to talk about anything but the simplest things."

"The Presidium will be meeting next week."

"I'm going as fast as I can, mother. As fast as he'll let me. I've tried to go more quickly, but there are—problems.

"What sort of problems?"

"Problems," Nialli Apuilana repeated, looking away. "Oh, mother, let me be! Do you think this is easy?"

For three days she couldn't bring herself to see him. A guardsman had been sent with his food in her place. Then she went, bringing a tray of edible seeds and the small reddish insects known as rubies, which she had gathered that morning in the torrid drylands on the northeastern slope of the hills. These she offered timidly, without a word. He took the tray from her just as wordlessly, and fell upon the rubies as if he had not eaten in weeks, sweeping the little ruddy carcasses into his mouth with broad avid motions of his hand.

He looked up afterward and smiled. But he kept a wary distance from her throughout that day's visit.

So the damage wasn't irreparable. Still, the breach would be some time in healing. She knew that her attempt at twining with him had been too hasty, too bold. Perhaps his sensing-organ itself was something he barely understood. Perhaps the fleeting touch of intimacy he had shared with her had been too powerful a sensation for him, raised as he had been among a species that had emotions of quite a different kind; perhaps it had begun to undermine his already uncertain sense of which race he belonged to.

He must regard himself as a hjjk in flesh-folk flesh, Nialli Apuilana thought. Such intimacy with a flesh-folk person would seem a disgusting obscenity to him, then. And yet some part of him had reached out eagerly and lovingly to her. Some part of him had yearned to let their souls rush together and become one. She was sure of that. But it had terrified him even while it tempted him; and he had pulled back in agonizing confusion.

That day she remained with him only a little while, and spent the time trying to break through the linguistic barrier. She ran through her short list of hjjk words, and told him the People equivalents, using pantomime and sketches to aid her. Kundalimon seemed to make progress. She sensed that he was deeply frustrated by his inability to make himself understood. There were things he wanted to say, amplifications of the message that Hresh had extracted from him by means of the Barak Dayir. But he had no way of expressing them.

Briefly she considered attempting to reach him by second sight. That was the next best thing to twining. She could send her soul's vision forth and try to touch his soul with it.

But most likely Kundalimon would become aware of what she was doing and see it as another intrusion, another violation of his soul's inner space: as offensive, or as frightening, as her attempt to twine with him had been. She couldn't risk it. The relationship would have to be rebuilt more slowly.

"What can you tell us?" Taniane asked her that evening. Brusquely getting right to it, all business as usual. Chieftain-mode, not mother-mode. Almost never mother-mode. "Have you started to talk about the treaty with him?"

"He still doesn't have the vocabulary." She saw the suspicion in Taniane's eyes, and in distress she said, "Don't you believe that I've been trying, mother?"

"Yes. I do believe it, Nialli."

"But I can't do miracles. I'm not like father."

"No," said Taniane. "Of course not."

On the evening of the meeting of the Presidium, at the sixth hour after midday, the leaders of Dawinno began to assemble in their noble meeting-room of dark arching beams and rough granite walls.

Taniane took her place at the high table of mirror-bright red ksutwood, beneath the great spiral that represented Nakhaba of the Bengs and the five gods of the Koshmar tribe entwined in divine unity. Hresh sat at her left. The various princes of the city were arrayed along the curving rows of benches before them.

In the front row, the three princes of the justiciary: the dapper, elegant Husathirn Mueri, with the massive figure of Thu-Kimnibol looming beside him, still clad in his flame-red mantle and sash of mourning, and Puit Kjai, the Beng, sitting upright and rigid. Next to them Chomrik Hamadel, the son of the last independent Beng chieftain before the Union. In the row behind them the old warrior Staip, and his mate Boldirinthe the offering-woman, and Simthala Honginda, their eldest son, with his mate Catiriil, who was Husathirn Mueri's sister. Around them, half a dozen of the wealthy merchants and manufacturers who held seats on the Presidium, and various members of the nobility, the heads of some of the founding families of the city: Si-Belimnion, Maliton Diveri, Kartafirain, Lespar Thone. Lesser figures—representatives of the smaller tribes, and of the craftsmen's guilds—were in the row to the rear.

Everyone was mantled and robed in finest cloth. And all were grandly

helmeted also, in accordance with the formal custom of the day, a congregation of intricate, lofty headpieces everywhere in the great room.
Chomrik Hamadel's helmet was easily the most conspicuous, a towering
agglomeration of metal and sparkling gems that rose above him to an
improbable height; but Puit Kjai, wearing one of red bronze with huge
silver projections flaring fore and aft, was scarcely to be outdone.

That these Beng princes would be so splendidly outfitted was no surprise. The Bengs were the original helmet-wearers. Nor was it startling
that Husathirn Mueri, who was half Beng, should have donned a grand
golden dome with crimson spikes.

But even those of pure Koshmar birth—Thu-Kimnibol, Kartafirain,
Staip, Boldirinthe—were wearing their most magnificent headgear. More
unusual still, Hresh, who wore a helmet perhaps once every five years, had
one on now: a small one, some cleverly interwoven strips of dark bristly
fiber bound by a single golden band, but a helmet nevertheless.

Only Taniane wore no helmet. But one of the bizarre old masks of
the former chieftains that usually hung on her office wall was resting on
the high table beside her.

Husathirn Mueri said, as the hour called for starting the meeting came
and went, "What are we waiting for?"

Thu-Kimnibol seemed amused. "Are you in such a hurry, cousin?"

"We've been sitting here for hours."

"It only seems that way," Thu-Kimnibol said. "We waited much longer
than this in the cocoon before we were allowed to make the Coming Forth.
Seven hundred thousand years, wasn't it? This is only the flicker of an eye."

Husathirn Mueri grinned sourly and turned away.

Then, astonishingly, Nialli Apuilana came bursting into the chamber,
breathless, her sash and mantle in disarray.

She seemed amazed to find herself here. Blinking, fighting to catch
her breath, she stood for a moment staring at the assembled notables in
unconcealed awe. Then she scurried into a vacant place in the front row,
next to Puit Kjai.

"Her?" Husathirn Mueri said. "We've been waiting for *her* all this
time? I don't understand this."

"Hush, cousin."

"But—"

"Hush," said Thu-Kimnibol more sharply.

Taniane, rising, brushed her hands lightly across the chieftain's mask
on the high table before her. "We are ready now to begin. This is the final
session of deliberations on the proposal of a treaty of mutual territorial
respect that the hjjks have made. I call upon Hresh the chronicler."

The chronicler got slowly to his feet.

Hresh cleared his throat, looked around the room, let his keen, piercing gaze rest on this highborn one and that. And said, finally, "I'll begin by recapitulating the terms of the hjjk offer, as I received it by way of the Barak Dayir from the mind of the hjjk emissary Kundalimon." He held up a broad sheet of sleek yellow parchment on which a map had been sketched in bold brown lines. "This is the City of Dawinno down here, where the edge of the continent curves out to meet the sea. Here is the City of Yissou, to our north. Here, beyond Yissou, is Vengiboneeza. Everything from Vengiboneeza northward is undisputed hjjk territory."

Hresh paused. Looked around again, as if taking the roll.

Then he continued. "The Queen proposes that we set a line passing between Vengiboneeza and the City of Yissou, extending from the seacoast across the northern half of the continent, past the great central river once known as the Hallimalla, and onward to the coast of the other sea that we believe touches the land at the eastern edge of the continent. Can you all see the line?"

"We know where the line goes, Hresh," said Thu-Kimnibol.

The chronicler's scarlet-flecked eyes brightened with annoyance. "Of course. Of course. Pardon me, brother." A quick smile, pro forma. "To continue: the line is drawn in such a way as to confirm the present territorial division of the land. What the hjjks now hold is to be forever theirs, without dispute. What is ours will remain ours. The Queen promises to prohibit all hjjks under Her control—and as I understand it She controls all the hjjks in the world—from entering the territory of the People except by our specific invitation and consent. And no member of the People is to go north of the City of Yissou into hjjk territory without permission of the Queen. That's the first condition.

"There are others.

"First, the Queen offers us spiritual guidance, that is, instruction in the concepts loosely known as Nest-truth and Queen-love. These seem to be hjjk philosophical or religious ideas. Why the Queen thinks they'd be of interest to us, I can't imagine. But it's proposed that instructors in Nest-truth and Queen-love will take up residence in our city—in each of the Seven Cities—to teach us their meaning."

"Some sort of joke?" Kartafirain boomed. "Hjjk missionaries living right here among us, spouting their lunatic mumbo-jumbo? Hjjk spies, I should say. Right in the middle of our city! Does the Queen think we're that foolish?"

"There's more," Hresh said calmly, raising a hand to signal for silence. "A third proviso. The Queen further stipulates that we must also agree to confine ourselves to the territories we now hold. That is, permanently to relinquish our right to venture into any other continent, whether simply to explore or for actual settlement."

"What?" This time it was Si-Belimnion who cried out in disbelief. "Absurd," said Maliton Diveri, rising, shaking his arms in fury. Lespar Thone let forth peals of ringing laughter.

Hresh looked flustered. Taniane rapped for order. When the noise subsided she looked toward the chronicler and said, "Hresh, you still have the floor. Is that the complete report on the treaty terms?"

"Yes."

"Well, what do you make of it all?"

"I'm of two minds," he said. "On the one hand, we'll be given undisputed possession of the warmest and most fertile half of the continent. And be freed forever from the danger and destructiveness of war."

"Provided the hjjks honor their treaty!" Thu-Kimnibol said.

"Provided they honor it, yes. But I think they will. They have much more to gain from it than we do," said Hresh. "I mean by keeping us away from the other continents. Of course we don't have any idea of what's on those continents. Nor do we have any way at present of getting across the tremendous oceans that separate us from them. But I do know this: there could be ruined Great World cities out there, and some of them may be as full of treasure as Vengiboneeza was." Again his eyes scanned the room. "Back when we were still living in Vengiboneeza," he said, "I came upon an instrument that let me see a vision of all the four continents of the world, and all the cities that once existed on them: cities with names like Mikkimord, and Tham, and Steenizale. Very likely the ruins of those cities are waiting for us, even as Vengiboneeza was. Maybe they're buried under hundreds of thousands of years of debris, or perhaps, as in Vengiboneeza, repair machines have kept them almost intact. You all know how useful the tools we found in Vengiboneeza were to us. These other ancient cities—and I don't doubt that they're there—might hold things that are even more valuable. If we sign this treaty, we sign away forever our right to go searching for them."

"What if we stand no more chance of getting to these places than we do of swimming to the Moon?" Puit Kjai asked. "Or if we do reach them somehow, at the cost of the gods only know how many lives, and they turn out not to hold anything worthwhile? I say give them to the hjjks, wonders and all. This treaty lets us keep the lands that are already ours without risk of challenge. That seems more important."

"You're speaking out of turn," said Taniane briskly. "The chronicler still has the floor." Looking toward Hresh, she said, "Is it the chronicler's opinion, then, that we should reject the hjjk treaty outright?"

Hresh stared at her as though answering so direct a question gave him keen pain.

At length he said, "The first clause of the treaty, the setting of boundaries, is acceptable to me. The second, the one sending us teachers of Nest-truth, I don't understand at all. But the third—" He shook his head. "The thought of surrendering those treasure-troves to the hjjks forever isn't to my liking at all."

Taniane said, "Should we ratify the treaty or not, Hresh?"

He shrugged. "That's for the Presidium to decide. I've stated my views." And he sat down.

There was hubbub again. Everyone talking at once, helmets waggling, arms waving about.

"Let me speak!" Taniane cried, once more rapping the high table.

Over the diminishing voices of the unruly assembly she said, "If the chronicler won't take a clear stand on this issue, the chieftain will!"

She leaned forward, staring fiercely down at the front rows. Casually, almost as though unaware of what she was doing, she scooped up the chieftain's mask that lay beside her, and held it clasped against her breast, face outward. It was a monstrous glossy yellow mask tipped with black, with a great savage beak and jagged swooping projections along its periphery: almost a hjjk-face mask. The effect was much as if a hjjk were gnawing its way out of her from within and had burst forth suddenly, face foremost, upon her breast.

She stood in silence just a moment too long. There was more murmuring and then louder disputes began.

"Will you allow me to speak?" Taniane cried. And then, with anger in her voice: "Let me speak! Let me speak!"

"Gods! Will you let her speak?" Thu-Kimnibol roared ferociously, rising halfway to his full great height, and in moments the hall grew silent.

"Thank you," said Taniane, looking furious. Her fingers ran busily over the rim of the mask that she held clutched to her bosom. "There is only one question that we need to address," she said. "What do we actually gain from this treaty, at the price of handing away our claim to three-quarters of the world?"

"Peace," said Puit Kjai.

"Peace? We *have* peace. The hjjks are no threat to us. The one time they made war on us, we slaughtered them. Have you forgotten? It was when they attacked the City of Yissou, which Harruel had only just founded then, and we all came to his aid. You were there, Staip, and you, Boldirinthe. And Thu-Kimnibol—you were just a boy, but I saw you killing hjjks by the dozen that day, fighting by the side of your father Harruel. At the end of the day the field was covered with the corpses of the hjjks, and the city was saved."

"It was Hresh that killed them," Staip said. "With that magic of his, that he found in the Great World city. It swallowed them up. I was there. I saw it."

"That was part of it, yes," said Taniane. "But only a part. They were unable to stand before our warriors. We had nothing to fear from them that day. We have nothing to fear from them now. They hover up north like angry buzzing bees, but we know that they have no real power over us. They are hateful, yes. They are foul and repellent creatures. But they no longer go raiding in any number. The occasional small scouting party does go forth, and these"—she glanced significantly at Nialli Apuilana— "do cause us some distress. But such occasions, Yissou be thanked, have become very rare. If we encounter three hjjks in our province in a single year, that's unusual. So we mustn't cringe in terror before them. They are our enemy, but we can withstand them if ever they dare to challenge us. If they descend upon us, we can and will drive them back. So why allow them to dictate to us? Now they grandly offer to let us keep our own lands, if we'll simply turn the rest of the world over to them. What kind of offer is that? Which of you sees merit in it? Which of you sees advantage for us?"

"I do," said Puit Kjai.

Taniane beckoned, and Puit Kjai arose and came to the speaker's podium. He was a lean, angular man of more than middle years, with the lustrous golden fur and brilliant sunset-red eyes of a pure Beng. He had succeeded his father, wizened old Noum om Beng, as keeper of the Beng chronicles. But after the union of the tribes he had turned that responsibility over to Hresh, taking a post on the justiciary in return. He was a proud and stubborn man, with passionately held opinions.

"I am not one to advocate cowardly surrender or timid withdrawal," he began, turning slightly so that his majestic bronze-and-silver helmet caught the light from above to best effect. "I believe, as most of you do, that it is our destiny someday to rule all the world. And, like Hresh, I would not casually sign away our right to explore the Great World cities of the other continents. But I believe in reason, too. I believe in prudence." He glanced toward Taniane. "You say the hjjks are no danger to us. You say that the warriors of the Koshmar tribe slew them easily at the battle of the City of Yissou. Well, I was not at that battle. But I've studied it, and I know it well. I know that many hjjks died that day—but also that there were casualties among the People, too, that King Harruel of Yissou himself was one of those who fell. And I know that Staip tells the truth when he says that it was the magical Great World device that Hresh employed against the hjjks which carried the day for the People. But for that they would have destroyed you all. But for that there would be no City of Dawinno, today."

"These are lies," Thu-Kimnibol muttered hoarsely. "By the Five, I was there! There was no magic in our victory. We fought like heroes. I killed more hjjks that day than he's ever seen, and I was only a child. Samnibolon was my name then, my child-name. Who will deny that Samnibolon son of Harruel was at that battle?"

Puit Kjai brushed the outburst aside with a grand sweep of his arm. "The hjjks number in the millions. We are only thousands, even now. And I have experienced more of hjjk aggression than most of you. I am Beng, you know. I was among those who lived in Vengiboneeza after the Koshmar folk left it. I ask you to recall that we had the city to ourselves ten years, and then the hjjks came in, first fifty, then a hundred and fifty, and then many hundreds. And then we couldn't count them at all, there were so many. There were hjjks everywhere we turned. They never raised a hand against us, but they pushed us out all the same, by sheer force of numbers. So it is when the hjjks are peaceful. And when they aren't . . . Well, you who fought at Yissou saw the hjjks in more warlike mode. You drove them off, yes. But the next time they choose to make war against us, we may not have Hresh's Great World weapons to serve us."

"What are you saying?" Taniane asked. "That we should beg them to let us keep our own lands?"

"I say that we should sign this treaty, and bide our time," said Puit Kjai. "By signing it we win ourselves a guarantee against hjjk interference in the territories we presently have, until we are stronger, strong enough to defend ourselves against any hjjk army, no matter how large. We can always think about expanding our territory at that time. We can give some thought then to these other continents and the wonders they may hold, which at present we have no means of reaching in any case. Treaties can always be broken, you know. We aren't signing anything away forever. This treaty buys time for us—it keeps the hjjks away from our frontier—"

"Pah!" Thu-Kimnibol bellowed. "Let me have the floor, will you? Let me say a thing or two!"

"Are you done, Puit Kjai?" Taniane asked. "Will you yield?"

Puit Kjai shrugged and gave Thu-Kimnibol a contemptuous look. "I may as well. I relinquish my place to the God of War."

"Let me get by," said Thu-Kimnibol, pushing brusquely toward the aisle and nearly stumbling over Husathirn Mueri's legs as he went past. He advanced in quick angry strides to the front of the room and stood hunched over the podium, grasping it with both his hands. So huge was he that he made it seem to be no more than a child's toy table.

His mourning mantle encompassed his great shoulders like a corona of fire. This was his first appearance in public since Naarinta's death. He seemed vastly changed, more aloof, more somber, much less the easy lighthearted warrior. Many that day had remarked on it. He visibly bore the weight of his position as one of the princes of the city. His eyes seemed darker and more deeply set now, and he studied the assembly with a slow, searching gaze.

When he began to speak it was in a ponderously sardonic manner.

"Puit Kjai says he is no coward. Puit Kjai says that what he advocates is mere prudence. But who can believe that? We all know what Puit Kjai is really saying: that he shivers with dread at the very thought of the hjjks. That he imagines them lurking outside our walls in enormous swarms, poised to burst into the city and tear him—*him*, the unique and irreplaceable Puit Kjai, never mind the rest of us—to tiny shreds. He awakens in cold sweats, seeing hjjk warriors hovering above his bed eager to rip chunks of his flesh loose from his body and devour them. That's all that matters to Puit Kjai. To sign a paper, any paper, that will keep the terrible hjjks at a safe distance while he is still alive. Is that not so? I ask you? Is that not so?"

Thu-Kimnibol's voice echoed resonantly through the hall. He leaned across the podium and looked around with a swaggering, defiant glare.

"This treaty," he continued after a moment, "is nothing but a trap. This treaty is a measure of the contempt with which the hjjks regard us. And Puit Kjai urges us to sign it! Puit Kjai pines for peace! Break the treaty some other time when it is more convenient for us, the honorable Puit Kjai tells us! But for now, let us crawl on our bellies before the hjjks, because they are many and we are few, and peace is more important than anything else. Is this not so, Puit Kjai? Am I not stating your point of view fairly?"

Around the room there were murmurs again: of surprise, this time, for this was a new Thu-Kimnibol they were hearing. He had never spoken in the Presidium with such eloquence before, such flash and fury. Of course Thu-Kimnibol was a great warrior, almost godlike in his size and energy, a fiery giant, warlike, flamboyantly belligerent. His name itself proclaimed it: for although, as he had just said, he had been born Samnibolon, on his naming-day at the age of nine when the time came under Koshmar custom to choose his adult name, he had renamed himself Thu-Kimnibol, which meant "Sword of the Gods." Other men flocked around him, eager for his advice and approval. But some—like Husathirn Mueri, who saw Thu-Kimnibol as his great rival for power in the city—tended to credit his powers of leadership to his immense physical strength alone, thinking there was no wit or subtlety to his soul. Now they found themselves unexpectedly forced to revise that appraisal.

"Let me tell you what I believe, now," Thu-Kimnibol said. "I believe the world is rightfully ours—the *entire* world—by virtue of our descent from the humans who once ruled it. I believe it is our destiny to go forth, ever farther afield, until we have mastered every horizon. And I think that the hjjks, those ghastly and hideous survivors from a former world, must be eradicated like the vermin that they are."

"Boldly spoken, Thu-Kimnibol," said Puit Kjai with deep contempt.

"We'll make rafts of their dead bodies, and paddle ourselves across the sea to the other continents."

Thu-Kimnibol shot him a murderous glance. "I hold the floor now, Puit Kjai."

Puit Kjai threw up his hands in a comic gesture of surrender.

"I yield. I yield."

"Here is what I say," Thu-Kimnibol went on. "Send the hjjk messenger back with our rejection of the treaty stitched to his hide. At the same time, send word to our cousin Salaman of Yissou that we will do what he has long implored us to do, which is to join forces with him and launch a war of extermination against the roving bands of hjjks who threaten his borders. Then let us send our army north, every able-bodied man and woman we have—you needn't trouble yourself to go, Puit Kjai—and together with King Salaman we'll smash our way into the great Nest of Nests before the hjjks understand what is happening to them, and slay their Queen of Queens like the loathsome thing She is, and scatter their forces on the winds. That is how I say we should reply to this offer of love and peace from the hjjks."

And with those words Thu-Kimnibol resumed his seat.

There was a stunned silence in the chamber.

Then, as though in a dream, Husathirn Mueri found himself rising and making his way toward the podium. He was not at all sure what he meant to say. He had not prepared a clear position. But he knew that if he failed to speak now, in the aftermath of Thu-Kimnibol's astonishing outburst, he would spend all the rest of his days in the shadow of the other man, and it would be Thu-Kimnibol and not Husathirn Mueri who came to rule the city when Taniane's time was done.

As he took his stance before the Presidium he asked the gods in whom he did not believe to give him words; and the gods were generous with him, and the words were there.

Quietly he said, looking out at the still astounded faces before him, "Prince Thu-Kimnibol has spoken just now with great force and vision. Permit me to say that I share his view of the ultimate destiny of our race. And I tell you also that I agree with Prince Thu-Kimnibol's belief that we cannot avoid, sooner or later, an apocalyptic confrontation with the hjjks. It is the warrior within me who responds to Thu-Kimnibol's stirring words, for I am Trei Husathirn's son, whom some of you remember. But my mother Torlyri, whom you may also remember, and who was beloved by all, instilled in me a hatred of strife where strife was not needed. And in this instance I think strife is not only uncalled for, but profoundly dangerous to our purposes."

Husathirn Mueri took a deep breath. His mind was suddenly awhirl with ideas.

"I offer you a position midway between those of Puit Kjai and Prince Thu-Kimnibol. Let us accept this treaty with the hjjks, as Puit Kjai suggests, in order to buy ourselves some time. But let us also send an envoy to King Salaman of Yissou, yes, and enter into an alliance with him, so that we will be all the stronger when the time to make war against the hjjks finally is at hand."

"And when will that time be?" Thu-Kimnibol demanded.

Husathirn Mueri smiled. "The hjjks fight with swords and spears and beaks and claws," he said. "Although they are an ancient race, actual survivors of the Great World, that is the best they can do. They have fallen away from whatever greatness must have been theirs in those ancient times, because the sapphire-eyes and the humans are no longer here to teach them what to do. Today they have no science. They have no machinery. They have only the most primitive of weapons. And why is that? Because they are nothing but insects! Because they are mere mindless soulless *bugs!*"

He heard an angry intake of breath from somewhere directly in front of him. Nialli Apuilana, of course.

"We are different," he said. "We are discovering—or rediscovering," he amended, with a diplomatic glance toward Hresh—"new things every day, new devices, new secrets of the ancient world. You have already seen, those of you who remember the battle of the City of Yissou, how vulnerable the hjjks are to such scientific weapons. There will be others. We will bide our time, yes; and in that time, we will devise some means of slaying a thousand hjjks at a single stroke—ten thousand, a hundred thousand! And then at last we will carry the war to them. When that day finally comes, we will hold the lightning in our hands. And how then can they stand against us, no matter how much greater than ours their numbers may be? Sign the treaty now, I say—and make war later!"

There was another uproar. Everyone was standing, shouting, gesticulating.

"A vote!" Husathirn Mueri shouted. "I call for a vote!"

"A vote, yes!" This from Thu-Kimnibol. And Puit Kjai, too, was calling out for a decision.

"There will be one more speaker, first," said Taniane, her voice cutting through the clamor like a blade.

Husathirn Mueri stared at her, amazed. Somewhere in the last few moments Taniane had actually placed the Mask of Lirridon over her head; and now the chieftain stood beside him at the high table like some figure out of nightmare, stiff and solemn and erect, with that appalling hjjk-face commanding the attention of everyone. She looked both foolish and frightening, all at once: but rather more frightening than foolish, a weary aging woman no longer but now some supernal being of tremendous imperious force.

For a moment, though he had no more to say, Husathirn Mueri held his place at the podium as though he were rooted to the floor. Then Taniane gestured commandingly, a gesture that could hardly be disobeyed. With that mask on, she was unanswerable, a fount of power. He went numbly from the speaker's platform to resume his seat beside Thu-Kimnibol.

Nialli Apuilana came forward to take his place.

She stood stock-still, staring at the blur of faces before her. At first everyone was indistinct; but then a few individual figures stood out. She looked toward Taniane, hidden behind the startling mask. Toward Hresh. Toward the stolid massive figure of Thu-Kimnibol, sitting front and center, odious little Husathirn Mueri beside him. A swirl of conflicting thoughts ran through her head.

That morning she had gone to Taniane to confess failure: she hadn't been able to find out any more about the hjjk treaty than Hresh had already learned with the Barak Dayir. Not that she was holding anything back: communicating with Kundalimon had proven more difficult than she—or Taniane—had expected. And so she had been a poor spy. On the subject of the treaty, she had nothing useful to report. It was the truth. And Taniane seemed to accept it as the truth.

That should have been the end of it, her vital mission fizzling away in anticlimax. But instead of dismissing her, Taniane had waited, as though expecting something more. And then there was something more. Nialli Apuilana listened, astonished, as words broke loose inside her and leaped unexpectedly to her own tongue.

Let me speak to the Presidium anyway, mother. Let me tell them about the hjjks. About the Queen, about the Nest. Things I've never been able to say. Things I can't keep to myself any longer.

Bewilderment. *You want to speak to the Presidium?*

The Presidium, yes. During the debate over the treaty.

She could see the turmoil in Taniane. It was craziness, what she was proposing. Send a girl like her up to the podium? Allow her to contaminate the high legislative body of the city with her capricious, erratic, impulsive flights of fantasy? But it was tempting. The moody Nialli Apuilana finally breaks her silence. Speaks at last, reveals the mysteries of the Nest. Pours forth the awful details. In Taniane's eyes temptation gleams. To know, at last, a little of what's in her daughter's mind. Even if it has to be spilled forth in the Presidium itself. *Let me, mother. Let me, let me, please let me.* And the chieftain nods.

And, unreal as it may seem, here she is. At the high table, all eyes upon her. The real story at last. The great revelation, after nearly four years. Did she dare? How would they respond? For a moment she was unable to find her voice. They were waiting. She felt their impatience, their hostility. To most of them she was nothing but a freak. Would they laugh?

Would they jeer? She was the chieftain's daughter. That would restrain them, she hoped. But it was so very hard to begin. Turn and run? No. No. Speak to them. Get the show started, Nialli.

And at last she did, speaking quietly, so quietly that she wondered if she could be heard even in the front row.

"I thank you all for this privilege. I stand before you now because there are things you must know, which I alone can tell you, before you decide how to respond to the message of the Queen."

Her heart was racing. Her tongue was thick with fright. She forced herself to be calm.

"Unlike any of you," she went on, "I have actually lived among the hjjks. As you are aware. You haven't forgotten that I was a captive. Certainly I can never forget it. I know them at first hand—these vermin of which you speak, these hideous bugs, whom you think are fit only for extermination. And I tell you this: that they are nothing at all like the mindless hateful monsters you make them out to be."

"They came to kill us when we founded Yissou," Thu-Kimnibol burst in. "There were only eleven of us, and a few children. A scruffy little village, hundreds of leagues from their territory. Not exactly a serious threat. But they came by the thousands to destroy us. And would have wiped us out if we hadn't—"

Calmly Nialli Apuilana overrode his full resonant voice. "No. They hadn't come to kill you."

"It certainly looked that way to us, an army like that, screeching, waving their spears around. Well, anyone can make a mistake, I suppose. It was just a little social visit."

The great room echoed with laughter.

Nialli Apuilana gripped the edge of the podium. In a crackling voice she said, "Yes, kinsman, it was a mistake. But how could you have known what they were doing there? Do you have the slightest understanding of why they do the things they do? Do you have the least bit of insight into their minds?"

"Their *minds?*" said Puit Kjai, with heavy scorn.

"Their minds, yes. Their thoughts. Their wisdom. No, let me finish! Let me finish!" All fear was gone from her. Nialli Apuilana was defiant now. There was passion burning in her. "You know me, I think. You think of me as a rebel, a godless one, a wild child. Maybe you're right. Certainly I've been unconventional. I won't deny that I have no feeling for the Five Heavenly Ones, or for Nakhaba, or for the Five and the One, or any other combination of those gods you might want to name. To me they are nothing at all, they are only—"

"Blasphemy! Blasphemy!"

She scowled, smacked the podium, shot fierce glances here and there. This was her moment: she wouldn't let them deprive her of it. This must be what Taniane feels like when she's being grand and chieftainly, Nialli Apuilana thought.

Grandly and buoyantly she said, "Spare me these outcries, if you please. I am speaking now. The Five Names are just that to me: names. Our own inventions, to comfort us in our difficult times. Forgive me, father, mother, all of you. This is what I believe. Once I believed other things, the same as you. But when I went among the hjjks—when they took me—I shared their lives, I shared their thoughts. And I came to understand, as I could never have understood when I lived here, the true meaning of the Divine."

"Do we need to listen to your daughter's nonsense much longer, Taniane?" someone called from the rear. "Are you going let her mock the gods right to our faces?"

But the masked chieftain made no reply.

Inexorably Nialli Apuilana said, "This Queen, whom Thu-Kimnibol wants to chop in pieces—you know nothing of Her greatness and wisdom, none of you. You have no inkling of it. The Nest-thinkers—have you ever even heard the term?" She was hitting her stride, and loving it. "What can you tell me of the philosophies of the Nest? What can you say of Queen-love, of Nest-bond? You know nothing! Nothing! And I tell you that these vermin of yours, these bugs, are far from deserving of your contempt. They are not vermin at all, not monsters, not hateful, not repellent, none of those things. What they are, in fact, is a great civilization of human beings!"

"What? What? The hjjks human? She's lost her mind!"

Into the incredulous outcry that came from all sides Nialli Apuilana retorted, shouting now, almost bellowing, "Yes, human! Human!"

"What is she saying?" old Staip asked muddledly. "The hjjks are insects, not humans! The Dream-Dreamers were the humans. The hairless pink ones, with no sensing-organs."

"The Dream-Dreamers were one kind of human, yes! But not the only kind. Listen to me! Listen!" She gripped the podium and sent her words surging out to them with the force of second sight. The full spate now, the whole pent-up surge coming out all at once. "The truth is," she declared in a high, ringing tone, "that all the Six Peoples of the Great World must be considered humans, whatever shape their bodies might have had. The Dream-Dreamers, and the sapphire-eyes, and the vegetals, and the mechanicals, and the sea-lords. And the hjjks! Yes, the hjjks! They were all human: six civilized peoples, able to live together in peace, and learn, and grow, and build. That is what it means to be human. My father taught me that when I was a child, and he should have taught you that too. And I learned it again in the Nest."

"What about us?" someone called. "You say the hjjks are human. Do you think we are? Is everything that lives and thinks human?"

"We weren't human in the time of the Great World, no. We were only animals then. But now we're beginning finally to become human ourselves, now that we've left the cocoon. The hjjks, though—they crossed the threshold of humanity a million years ago. Or more. How can we think of making war on them? They aren't our enemies! The only enemies we have are ourselves!"

"The girl's insane," she heard Thu-Kimnibol murmur, and saw him sadly shake his head.

"If you don't like the treaty," Nialli Apuilana cried, "then reject the treaty! Reject it! But reject war, too. The Queen is sincere. She offers us love and peace. Her embrace is our greatest hope. She will wait for us all to grow up—to attain full humanity, to become worthy of Her people—and then we will be free to join with them in a new companionship, the way the Six Peoples of the Great World once were joined, before the deathstars fell! And then—and then—"

She was gasping and sobbing, suddenly. All strength left her in a moment. She had expended herself beyond her endurance. Her eyes were frantic, her body was racked by tremors.

"Get her down from there," said someone—Staip? Boldirinthe?—sitting behind Husathirn Mueri.

Everyone was shouting and calling out. Nialli Apuilana clung to the podium, shivering, trembling violently. She thought she might be at the edge of some sort of convulsion. She knew she had gone too far, much too far. She had said the unsayable, the thing she had held back from them all these years. They all thought she was mad, now. Perhaps she was.

The room swayed about her. Below her, Thu-Kimnibol's bright red mourning mantle seemed to be pulsing and throbbing like a sun gone berserk. At the high table Hresh appeared frozen, dazed. She looked toward Taniane, but the chieftain was unreadable behind her mask, standing motionless in the midst of the chaos that swept the room.

Nialli Apuilana felt herself beginning to topple.

A terrible scene, Husathirn Mueri thought. Shocking, frightening, pitiful.

He had listened to her with growing amazement and dismay. Her appearance here, young, mysterious, heartachingly beautiful, had had a tremendous impact on him. He had never imagined that Nialli Apuilana would address the Presidium. Certainly he hadn't expected her to say any of the things she had, or to say them so boldly. To hear her speak in such a fierce and powerful way had made her all the more desirable to him: had made her irresistible, in fact.

But then what she was saying had degenerated into chaotic babble, and Nialli Apuilana herself had veered toward hysteria and collapse before them all.

Now she was plainly about to fall.

Without hesitating, almost without thinking, Husathirn Mueri rushed forward, vaulted to the platform, and caught her by both elbows, lifting her, steadying her.

The girl shook her head wildly. "Let—go—"

"Please. Come down from here."

She glared at him—but was it in hatred, he wondered, or simple confusion? Gently he tugged, and she surrendered to him. Slowly he led her from the podium and with his arm around her protectively he drew her toward the side of the room. He eased her into a seat. She stared up at him out of eyes that seemed to be seeing nothing at all.

Taniane's voice rang out like a trumpet behind him.

"Here is our decision. There'll be no vote today. The treaty will be neither rejected nor accepted, and we will make no reply to the Queen. The entire matter of the treaty is tabled indefinitely. Meanwhile what we intend is to send an envoy to the City of Yissou, for the purpose of discussing with King Salaman the terms of an alliance of mutual defense."

"Against the hjjk-folk, do you mean?" someone called.

"Against the hjjks, yes. Against our enemy."

3

Salaman Receives
a Visitor

Early on a chill fog-bound midsummer morning King Salaman of Yissou, with Biterulve, his favorite of his many sons, came forth to make the circuit of the great and perpetually unfinished wall that enclosed the city.

The king went out each day without fail from his palace at the heart of the city to inspect the ongoing work of wall-building. Standing at the foot of the wall, he would stare toward the battlements and embrasures far overhead, measuring them against the burning need he felt within his soul. Then he would ascend the wall by one of the many staircases along its inner face, and prowl its upper course. The immense black rampart, lofty as it was, never quite seemed adequate to that great need of his. In feverish moments of fear he imagined hjjk scaling-ladders suddenly appearing at the top of the wall. He imagined furious hjjk legions swarming across the highest parapets and down into the city.

Ordinarily these prowling inspections of Salaman's were carried out at dawn, always in solitude. If a citizen happened to be awake at that hour, he would avert his eyes, not wishing to intrude on the king upon the walls. No one, not even his sons, would approach him at such a time. No one would dare.

But this morning Biterulve had asked to accompany him, and Salaman had acquiesced at once. There was nothing that Salaman would deny Biterulve. He was fourteen, the sixth of the eight princes Salaman had sired, Sinithista's only boy—a frail and gentle child so little like the others that Salaman once had doubted that Biterulve could be of his own engendering, though he had kept those doubts to himself and was glad of it now. Biterulve's frame was slender and long-boned, whereas Salaman and all his other sons were squat and stocky; and his fur was an eerie pale hue, the color of a snowy field by moonlight, where Salaman and the rest of his brood were dark. But Biterulve's cool gray eyes were the unmistakable eyes of the king; and his supple spirit, though its nature was less fierce than that of Salaman or any of his other sons, was one that the king recognized as kin to his.

In the hour before sunrise they rode out together from the palace. Salaman, out of the corner of his eye, watched the boy closely. He handled his xlendi well, keeping the loose-limbed beast on a tight rein as they moved through the narrow curving streets, pulling back capably when an early-morning workman with a dray-wagon came unexpectedly around a sharp corner.

One of Salaman's great fears was that this gentle son of his was too gentle: that there was nothing at all warlike about him, that Biterulve would be unable to play a proper role when the hjjks at last made the move he had so long expected, and the great cataclysmic time arrived. It was not so much the disgrace that Salaman feared, for he had a host of other sons who would be heroic enough. But he didn't want the boy to suffer when that dread host of unholy insects began their onslaught.

It may be that I have misjudged him, thought Salaman, as Biterulve proudly urged the clattering xlendi forward through the quiet streets.

The king spurred his own mount and caught up with him just as he emerged from the warren of inner streets into the wider outer avenues that led to the wall.

"You ride very well," Salaman called. "Better than I remember."

Biterulve glanced over his shoulder, grinning. "I've been going out with Bruikkos and Ganthiav practically every day. They've showed me a few tricks."

The king felt a stab of alarm.

"Outside the wall, you mean?

The boy giggled. "Father, we can't very well go riding inside the city, can we?"

"You have a point," said Salaman grudgingly.

And what harm, he thought, could come to him out there, really? Surely Bruikkos and Ganthiav had more sense than to stray very far into places where hjjks might roam. If the boy wants to go riding with his older brothers, I'll say nothing, Salaman told himself. I mustn't overprotect him, if I want him to be a proper prince, if I want him to be a true warrior.

They had reached the wall now. They jumped down from their xlendis and tied them to posts. The first gray strands of morning were coming into the sky. The fog was scattering.

Salaman felt an uncharacteristic sense of ease. Ordinarily his spirit was dark and tense; but this morning his mind was loose and unfocused, his body poised and calm. He had spent the night just past with Vladirilka, the fourth and newest of his mates. The aroma of her was still on his fur, the warmth of her still soothed his flesh.

He was certain that he had sired a son on her in this night's coupling. One is able to tell, Salaman believed, when a son is being made: and surely this had been a coupling for sons.

He had so many daughters that he had difficulty remembering all their names, and he needed no more of those. Women had ruled in the cocoon, and a woman still ruled, he knew, in Dawinno. But Yissou from the first had been a city for men. Salaman had respected old Koshmar and thought well of Taniane; but there would be no female kings here.

It was sons he wanted, and many of them, sons aplenty, so that the succession would be assured. A king, he thought, could never have too many sons. Building dynasties is like building walls: one must look beyond the immediate, and prepare for the worst of eventualities. Therefore Salaman had sired eight boys so far, and he hoped he had added a ninth tonight. If it wasn't Chham who followed him to the throne, then it would be Athimin; and if not Athimin, then Poukor, or Ganthiav, or Bruikkos, or one of the even younger princes. Perhaps even the one he had engendered on Vladirilka this very night would be the next king. Or some boy yet to be conceived, by some mate not yet chosen. Only one thing was certain, that he would not give Biterulve the kingship. The boy was too sensitive, too complex. Let him be a royal counselor, Salaman felt. Let someone like Chham or Athimin handle the hard choices a king must face.

But there was plenty of time for fixing the succession. Salaman had just reached his sixtieth year. There were those who thought of him as old, he knew, but that was not an opinion he shared. He regarded himself as in the full vigor, still, of his manhood. And he suspected that soft young Vladirilka, lying now asleep with his warmth still between her thighs, would back him up on that score.

Biterulve pointed to the nearest of the staircases that led to the top of the wall.

"Shall we go up, father?"

"A moment. Stand here by me." He liked to take it in from down here, first. To study it. To let its strength enter him and sustain his soul.

He looked up, and out, letting his gaze sweep along the wall as far as he could see. He had done this ten thousand times, and he never grew weary of it.

The immense wall that enclosed the City of Yissou was fashioned of cyclopean blocks of hard black stone, each one half the height of a man, and twice as wide as it was high, and deeper than a man's arm is long. For decades now, a phalanx of master stone-cutters had worked from dawn to twilight, every day of the year, slowly and patiently cutting those immense blocks in a mountain quarry in the steep ravine west of the city, trimming them, squaring them, dressing them smooth. Uncomplaining teams of vermilions hauled the massive blocks across the rough plateau to the edge of the wide, shallow crater in which the city lay sheltered. As each megalith reached its intended site along the constantly growing wall, Salaman's skillful stonemasons lifted it and swung it boldly into its place, using elaborate wooden engines, and harnesses of tightly woven larret-withes.

The king nodded toward the wall. "This is the place where a block was dropped, five years back. That was the only time such a thing ever happened."

Bitterness rose in his soul at the thought of it, as it always did when he was here. Three workmen had been crushed by the falling block, and two more were put to death for having dropped it, at Salaman's order. His own sons Chham and Athimin had objected to the cruelty of that. But the king was inflexible. The men had been taken off and sacrificed that very day in the name of Dawinno the Destroyer.

"I remember it," Biterulve said. "And that you had the men who dropped it killed. I often still think of those poor men, father."

Salaman shot him a startled glance. "Ah, do you, boy?"

"That they should have died for an accident—was that really right, do you think?"

Keeping his anger carefully in check, the king said, "How could we tolerate such clumsiness? The wall is our great sacred endeavor. Carelessness in its construction is a blasphemy against all the gods."

"Do you think so, father?" Biterulve said, and smiled. "If we were perfect in all things, we would be gods ourselves, so it seems to me."

"Spare me your cleverness," said Salaman, dealing him a light affectionate slap across the back of his head. "Three good men died because those masons were stupid. The foreman Augenthrin was killed. This wall had been his life's work. That hurt me, losing him. And who knows how many more might have died if I'd let such incompetents live? The next stone they dropped might have been on my own head. Or yours."

In truth he had wondered about the wisdom of his own harsh decree right in the moment of uttering it. Biterulve didn't need to know that. The words had simply escaped from his lips in his first red instant of fury when he saw that fallen block, so beautifully hewn and now cracked beyond repair, and those six bloody legs jutting out pathetically from beneath it.

But decrees once spoken may not be revoked. A king must be merciful and just, Salaman knew, but sometimes a king finds himself being unthinkingly cruel, for that is sometimes kingship's nature. And when he is cruel he must take care not to let himself be seen second-guessing his own cruelty, or the people will think he is that worst of all tyrants, a capricious one. The very injustice of that hastily uttered sentence had made it impossible for him to call it back. Thus had blood atoned for blood in the building of Salaman's great black wall. If the people were troubled by it, they kept their discontent to themselves.

"Come," Salaman said. "Let's go up on top."

At eighteen equidistant points around the perimeter, handsome stone staircases rising along the inner face gave access to the narrow brick footpath that ran along the wall's summit. When he had first had them built, some of Salaman's sons and counselors had found those staircases paradoxical and even perverse. "Father, we should never have built them," said Chham, with all the gravity that he affected as the eldest of the princes. "They'll make it all the easier for the hjjks to descend into the city if they scale the wall."

And Athimin, Chham's full brother, the king's only other son by his earliest mate Weiawala, chimed in, "We ought to rip them out. They scare me, father. Chham's right. They make us too vulnerable."

"The hjjks will never scale the wall," Salaman had retorted. "But we need the stairs ourselves, so we can get troops up there in a hurry if anyone ever does try to come over."

The princes dropped the issue then. They knew better than to tangle with their father in any sort of dispute. He had ruled the city with a sure and capable hand throughout their entire lives, but in his later years he had grown increasingly irascible and stark of soul. Everyone, even Salaman himself, understood that the wall was not a topic suited for reasonable discussion. The king had no interest in being reasonable where the Great Wall was concerned. His concern was in making it so high that the question of its being scaled would be beyond all consideration.

In his dawn perambulations he chose a different staircase every day, and invariably descended via the second staircase to the left of the one he had ascended, so that it took him six days to complete the full circuit of the rampart. It was a ritual from which he never deviated, winter or summer, rain or heat. It seemed to him that the safety of the city depended on it.

Biterulve went skipping up to the summit. Salaman followed at a more stately pace. At the top he stamped his feet against the solid brick of the footpath, which lay above the huge black stones like a tough layer of skin above a mighty musculature.

Salaman laughed. "Do you feel the strength of it, boy, beneath your legs? There's a wall for you! There's a wall to be proud of!"

He slipped his arm over the boy's shoulders and stared out into the misty lands beyond the city's bounds.

Yissou lay in a pleasant fertile vale. Dense forests and high ridges flanked it to the east and north, gentler hills rose to the south, and there was harsh broken country in the westlands leading off toward the distant sea.

The huge crater which the city itself occupied lay at the center of a broad shadow thickly carpeted with grasses, both the green and the red. It was perfectly circular, and surrounded by a high, sharply delineated rim. Salaman believed, though he had never been able to prove it, that the crater had been created by the force of a death-star's impact, plummeting into the breast of the Earth during the early dark days of the Long Winter.

The crater's rim, lofty as it was, offered little protection against invaders. And so the Great Wall of Yissou had been under continuous construction for the past thirty-five years.

Salaman had begun it in the sixth year of the city, the third of his own reign after the death of the turbulent dark-souled Harruel, Yissou's first king. During his long span of power he had seen the wall rise to a height of fifteen courses in most places, forming a gigantic fortification that completely encircled the city along the line of the crater's rim.

In Yissou's earliest days a simple wooden palisade had guarded that perimeter, not very effectively. But Salaman, who had been only a young warrior then but already was dreaming of succeeding Harruel as king, had vowed to replace it one day by an unconquerable wall of stone. And so he had.

If only it were high enough! But how high was high enough?

There had been no hjjk attacks thus far during his reign, for all his fears. They wandered through the outlying countryside, yes. Now and then some small band of them, ten or twenty of them straying for some unfathomable hjjk reason out of their outpost at Vengiboneeza, might approach the city. But they came no closer than the edge of visibility— nothing more than black-and-yellow specks, seemingly no larger than the ants who were their distant kin. Then they would turn and swing back toward the north, having satisfied whatever urge it was that had brought them this way in the first place. There is never any understanding hjjks, Salaman thought.

So what the hjjks called Queen-peace prevailed, year upon year. But Queen-peace might be no more than a trap, a lie, a hallucination, an accident of the moment. The hjjks could end it whenever they chose. War might come at any time. Sooner or later it certainly would.

How could he convince himself that a wall fifteen courses high was high enough? In his mind's eye he saw invading hjjks building longer ladders, and longer ones yet, topping his wall no matter how high he built it, even if it reached through the roof of the sky.

"We will take it higher, I think," Salaman often would say, with a sweeping gesture of both his hands. "Another three courses, or perhaps four."

And the builders and masons would sigh; for as Salaman's rampart continued to rise, all the battlements and parapets and guardhouses and watchtowers that existed presently along the highest level had to be ripped away to make room for the new rows of stone blocks, and rebuilt afterward, and then ripped away once more as Salaman's insatiable hungers led him to demand yet another course or two, and so on and so on.

But they were used it. The wall was Salaman's obsession, his cherished plaything, his monument. It would continue growing ever higher, everyone knew, so long as he was king. They wouldn't have known what to do or say, if Salaman were to tell them some afternoon, "The wall is finished now. We are safe against any conceivable enemy. Go to your homes, all of you, and take up some new employment tomorrow."

Small chance of that. The wall would never be finished.

The king stamped his feet again. He imagined the wall sending down deep massive roots and anchoring itself in the depths of the Earth. He laughed. To Biterulve he said, "Boy, do you know what I have done here? I've built a wall that will stand a million years. A million million, even. The world will grow old, and enter into a time of greatness someday beside which the Great World will seem like nothing at all, and people will say then, seeing the wall, 'That wall is Salaman's, who was king at Yissou when the world was young.' "

Biterulve said, with a sly look coming over his face, "And is the world young now, father? I thought it was very old, that we live in the latter days."

"So we do. But to those who come after us, these will seem like early times."

"Then how old is the world, do you think?"

The king smiled to himself. The boy reminded him of Hresh, sometimes, young Hresh, Hresh-full-of-questions. With a shrug he said, "The world is at least two million years old. Perhaps three."

"Is it, do you think? But if seven hundred thousand years have gone by since the Great World lived, and there was a time before the Great World when the humans ruled everything, and there must have been a time before that, when even the humans were simple folk—can that all have happened in only three million years?"

"Perhaps four, then," said Salaman. It amused him to be quibbled with in this way: but only by Biterulve. "Even five. The world is ever-renewing, boy. First it's young, and then it grows old, and then it becomes young again. And when it's old the next time, people look back and think of that early time barely remembered that came just before their time, and say that that was when it was young, not knowing that it had been old before that. Do you follow me, boy?"

"I think I do," said Biterulve, but there seemed to be more slyness in his tone. Salaman gave him a rough caress.

They moved southward along the wall, toward the domed pavilion of shining smooth-hewn gray stone that rose atop the wall above the southernmost of the eighteen staircases. The sky continued to brighten. The pavilion was for Salaman's use only, his private place. He often lingered there, sometimes for hours, during his dawn meditations and at other times as well.

The wall here—and only here—diverged from the route of the old crater rim. Here it extended some way out to the south, in order to climb a ridge so high that the distant western sea and the eastern forests could be seen from it, as well as the southern hills.

In the early days, when Harruel was king and even the wooden palisade was still incomplete and the city nothing more than seven lopsided wooden shacks held together by vines, Salaman had gone frequently to that high ridge, usually alone, sometimes with his mate Weiawala. There he would sit dreaming of glorious times to come. The same vision would come to him again and again: the City of Yissou grown to greatness and splendor, greater even than old Vengiboneeza of the sapphire-eyes folk: a mighty city, capital of a mighty empire spreading to the horizon and beyond, ruled not by the descendants of uncouth Harruel, but by the sons of the sons of Salaman.

Some of that had come to pass. Not all.

The city had expanded beyond its original bounds, though not exactly as far as the horizon. With the hjjks now in Vengiboneeza to cut off his dreams of empire to the north and east, and the sea forming an impassable barrier on the west, nothing but the south remained. New little farming villages had lately begun to spring up out there, but only those closest at hand acknowledged Salaman's sovereignty. The others maintained a hazy independence, or, in the farthest south, regarded themselves as tributaries to Taniane's Dawinno.

Salaman suspected and feared that his city was not as great by half as the City of Dawinno that Hresh and Taniane had built in the far south. But he had plenty of time left for empire-building. Still he would stand in the pavilion that he had caused to be constructed on the site of his dreaming-place of long ago, and he would look out over the land, imagining the grandeur of the realm that would someday be.

As they approached the pavilion now, Biterulve said abruptly, "I feel a strangeness, father."

"A strangeness? What sort of strangeness do you mean?"

"Coming from the south. Approaching us now: a force, a power. I felt it all night, and all through the dawn. And now it's stronger yet."

Salaman laughed. "I felt a strangeness in this place myself once, do you know? An afternoon of bright sunlight: I was here with Weiawala. Long ago, when I was just a few years older than you are now. And I felt the drumming sound of an army on the march, heading toward us. An onrushing force of hjjks it was, a vast company of them, driving herds of their shaggy vermilions before them, sweeping down out of the north. Is that what you feel, boy? An army of hjjks?"

"No, nothing like that, father. Not hjjks."

But Salaman was lost in reminiscence. "A great migration, it was, heading our way. A sound like thunder, the booming of a thousand thousand hooves. And then they came. But we beat them, we drove them away. You know that story, do you?"

"Who doesn't? It was the day Harruel was killed, and you became the king."

"Yes. Yes. That was the day." Salaman thought for a moment of Harruel, brilliant in battle but too brutish and brooding and violent to be a successful king, and how he had perished valiantly that day of a hundred wounds, during the battle with the hjjks. So long ago! When the world was young! He slipped his arm around Biterulve again. "Come with me. Into the pavilion."

"I thought you didn't ever allow anyone to—"

"Come," Salaman said again, a little roughly. "I ask you to stand by my side. Will you refuse me, when I invite you this way? Come, stand by my side, and we'll see what this strangeness is that you say you feel."

They moved quickly around the curve of the wall and entered the little pavilion. Side by side they stood by the long window, resting their hands on the beveled window-ledge. It was very odd, having someone in here with him. He couldn't remember ever having done this before. But he'd make an exception in anything, for Biterulve, only for Biterulve.

He looked outward, toward the south, and let his soul rise and rove. But he felt nothing out of the ordinary.

His mind began to wander, backward into the night. He thought of Vladirilka, lying asleep now in the palace with his newest son—he was sure of that—already growing in her womb. Only sixteen, she was, soft of flesh, lively of spirit. How lovely, how tender! Nor will she be the last mate I will take, thought Salaman. Kingship carries great burdens. Therefore there must be great rewards. Nowhere had it been decreed by the gods that a king could have only one mate. And therefore—

Your mind drifts foolishly, he told himself in annoyance.

To Biterulve he said, "Well? Do you feel it here?"

The boy was straining forward, nostrils flickering, head held high, like some trembling highbred beast restrained on a leash.

"Even stronger, father. In the south. Don't you?"

"No. No, nothing." Salaman focused his concentration more intently. Reaching out, probing into the lands beyond the wall. "No—wait!"

What was that?

Something had touched the periphery of his soul, just then. Something unexpected, something powerful. Gripping the window-ledge tightly, Salaman leaned far out, staring into the mists that still covered the southern plains.

Then, raising his sensing-organ, he sent forth his second sight.

Movement, far away. Only a hazy gray blur, a little ground-hugging cloud, a smudge on the horizon, near the place where the valley floor began to rise toward the southern hills. Gradually it grew larger, though he was still unable to make out detail.

"You feel it, father?"

"I feel it now, yes."

Hjjks? Not likely. Even at this distance Salaman was sure of that. He could detect no hint of their dry, bleak souls.

"I see wagons, father!" Biterulve cried.

Salaman grinned dourly. "Ah! Young eyes."

But then he saw them too, and gawky long-legged xlendis pulling them in their loose-jointed clip-clopping way. The hjjks didn't use xlendi-wagons. They traveled on foot, and when they had heavy loads to transport they used vermilions. No, these must be members of the People, coming out of the south. Merchants from Dawinno, were they?

No Dawinno caravan was due at this time of year. The caravan of early summer had already been here and gone; the one of autumn wasn't expected for another two months, nearly.

"Who are they, can you say?" Biterulve asked, excited.

"From Dawinno," Salaman said. "See, the red-and-gold banners flying from the roofposts? One, two, three, four, five wagons, coming up the Southern Highway. A real strangeness, boy—you spoke the truth!" But were they merchants, he wondered? Why would merchants come out of season, when there'd be no goods ready for them to buy?

Had the Dawinnans acquired a sudden whimsical liking for conquest? Hardly. Warfare wasn't Taniane's style, and certainly not Hresh's, and in any case those absurd xlendi-wagons didn't look like military vehicles.

"There's someone very powerful in that caravan," said Biterulve. "It's his spirit that I've felt getting closer, all this night past."

"This must be an embassy," Salaman murmured.

There's trouble somewhere, he thought, and they've come here to entangle me in it. Or if there's no trouble yet, there soon will be.

He signaled to Biterulve, and they descended from the wall. Quickly they rode back to the palace. The hour was still very early. The king went to awaken his sons.

The struggle to win appointment as Dawinno's ambassador to King Salaman had been much like the frenzy that occurs when a slab of tender meat is tossed into a cage of hungry stanimanders or gabools. The ambassador would be gone many months; he would have ample time to forge a close bond with the powerful Salaman; he would be one of the prime figures in whatever alliance of the two cities ultimately emerged. And so the great men of the city circled fiercely around, vying for the rich morsel: Puit Kjai, Chomrik Hamadel, Husathirn Mueri, Si-Belimnion, and others besides.

But in the end it was Thu-Kimnibol whom Taniane picked to make the journey northward.

It was a choice she made with no little uncertainty and hesitation, for Thu-Kimnibol and Salaman had quarreled famously, long ago, when Thu-Kimnibol still lived in the city that his father Harruel had founded and Salaman now ruled. Everyone knew that. They had angry words, an exchange of threats, even, and finally Thu-Kimnibol had fled, taking refuge in Hresh's new city in the south. There were many, Husathirn Mueri and Puit Kjai among them, who felt that sending Thu-Kimnibol on a diplomatic mission to his old enemy was a strange thing to do, and unwise.

But Thu-Kimnibol argued his case eloquently, saying that he understood the nature of the King of Yissou better than anyone, that he was the only plausible man for the task. As for the quarrel he had had with Salaman, he said, that was something ancient, an episode of his hotheaded youth, a matter of foolish pride, long put aside by him and certainly of no moment to Salaman after so many years. And also Thu-Kimnibol made it known with great force that he longed to serve his city now in some new and strenuous high capacity, to ease the grief that he still felt over the loss of his mate. Pouring his energies into this mission to Salaman would distract him from his pain.

Ultimately it was Hresh who tipped the decision toward his half-brother. "He's the right one," he told Taniane. "The only one who can stand face to face with Salaman. The others who've put themselves up for the job are small-spirited men. Nobody can say that of Thu-Kimnibol. And it seems to me he's grown even stronger since Naarinta's death. There's something about him now that I've never seen before—a kind of greatness growing in him, Taniane. I can feel it. He's the one to send."

"Perhaps so," said Taniane.

Thu-Kimnibol's journey began in prayers and fasting, and a lengthy consultation with Boldirinthe; for he was in his way a devout man, loyal to the Five Heavenly Ones. There were those who said he was simple for holding such faith in these modern times. What such people said mattered nothing at all to Thu-Kimnibol.

"I'll invoke Yissou for you, of course," Boldirinthe said, wheezing as she reached into her cupboard for the talismans. She was a broad sturdy woman, very old now: cocoon-born, in fact, one of the last ones left who had been alive at the time of the Coming Forth. Boldirinthe had gone heavily to fat in recent years: she looked like a barrel, now. "Yissou, for your protection," she said. "And Dawinno, to help you to smite any enemies you may encounter."

"And also Friit, to heal me if they do the smiting first," said Thu-Kimnibol, with a grin.

"Yes, Friit, of course, Friit." Boldirinthe laughed, setting the little stone figurines out on the table. "And the goddess Mueri to console you, if you grow homesick in the northland. And Emakkis to provide for you. We'll ask the benefits of all the Five for you, Thu-Kimnibol. It's the wisest course." Her eyes twinkled. "And should I invoke Nakhaba for you, too?"

"Am I a Beng, Boldirinthe?"

"But their god is a mighty one. And we accept him as our own, these days. We've become one tribe."

"I'll make my way without Nakhaba's help," said Thu-Kimnibol stolidly.

"As you wish. As you wish."

Boldirinthe lit her candles, sprinkled her incense. Her hands trembled a little. Age was lying more burdensomely on her these days. Thu-Kimnibol wondered if she might be ill. A kindly old woman, he thought. A little mischief in her, perhaps, but not of any malicious sort. Everyone loved her. He wasn't old enough to have clear memories of Torlyri, who had been offering-woman before her, but those who did said that Boldirinthe was a fitting successor, as warm and kind as Torlyri had been. Which was high praise, for even now, so many years later, the older people spoke of Torlyri with great love. Torlyri had been the offering-woman of the People in Koshmar's time, first in the cocoon and then in Vengiboneeza after the Coming Forth. But when the People had left Vengiboneeza to make their second migration she had stayed behind, for she had fallen in love with the Beng warrior Trei Husathirn, and hadn't wanted to leave him. That was when Boldirinthe had become the offering-woman in Torlyri's place.

Hard to understand, Thu-Kimnibol thought, how a woman as widely beloved as Torlyri had been could have brought forth a serpent like Husathirn Mueri as her son. It was the Beng blood in him, perhaps, that had made Husathirn Mueri what he was.

Boldirinthe said, "How long will the journey take you, do you think?"

"Until I get there. No more than that, but no less."

"I remember the City of Yissou. Seven miserable wooden huts is all the place was, every one of them very crudely made, even the one they called the royal palace."

"The city is somewhat bigger now," said Thu-Kimnibol.

"Yes. Yes. I suppose it is. But I remember it when it was next to nothing. I was there, you know, once. We passed through it, on our way from Vengiboneeza to here. I saw you there, then. You were a little boy.

Not so little, in truth. You were always large for your age, and warlike. You killed hjjks in a great battle that was fought at Yissou around that time."

"Yes," Thu-Kimnibol said indulgently. "I remember that too. Shall I kneel beside you, Mother Boldirinthe?"

She gave him a sly look. "Why is Taniane sending you to be the ambassador?"

"Why not?"

"It seems strange. There's bad blood between you and King Salaman, I understand. Isn't it true that you were his rival for the throne of Yissou? And now you come back to him as an envoy, but I wonder if he'll trust you. Won't he think you're still trying to push him aside?"

"All that was very long ago," Thu-Kimnibol said. "I don't want his throne. He knows that. And I couldn't take it from him even if I did. Taniane is sending me because I know Salaman better than anyone else, except perhaps Hresh and Taniane themselves, and they can hardly be the ones to go. Pray me a safe journey, Mother Boldirinthe, and pray with me also for my mate Naarinta, whose soul is on a journey of its own. And then let me be on my way."

"Yes. Yes."

She began the Yissou invocation. But after a moment she halted, and disappeared for a moment into a long silence, so that Thu-Kimnibol thought that she might have fallen asleep. Then she giggled.

"I coupled with Salaman once. It was in the cocoon. He was younger than I was, four or five years younger, just a boy, ten or eleven. But full of lust, even then, and he came to me—he was very quiet, then, a short dark boy, very broad through the shoulders, and so strong you wouldn't believe it. He came to me and took me by the breasts—"

"Mother Boldirinthe, please. If you would—"

"And we did it, Salaman and I, right on the floor of the growing-chamber. Rolling around and around under the velvetberry vines. He didn't say a word. Not before, not during, not after. He never said much in those days. It was the only time we coupled, the only time I had anything to do with him, really. Afterward it was all Weiawala for him, and I was with Staip, anyhow. If I had known Salaman was going to be a king some day—but of course how could I, we had no kings, the word itself meant nothing to us—"

"Mother Boldirinthe," said Thu-Kimnibol, more urgently.

He was afraid the old woman would go on to recount her entire life's history, every coupling and twining of the last fifty years. But she was done with her recollections. Her mind was on her work now. Lightly she touched him with her sensing-organ. She made the Five Signs, she uttered the words, she handled the talismans, she brought the gods into the room and opened Thu-Kimnibol's soul to them. They were vivid before him, so real that he knew them each by sight, even though they had no shapes, only auras. They were bright clouds of light, encircling him in the darkness. This was loving Mueri, this was fierce inexorable Dawinno, and this was Emakkis who provides, and this was Friit, and this was Yissou, who would protect him. In the sanctuary of Boldirinthe's offering-chamber he reached out to them and found them, the Five Heavenly Ones who ruled the world, and mantled his soul in their warm protective presences. It was a deeper communion than he had ever known, or so it seemed to him at that moment. A great satisfaction came over him, and a deep and abiding peace.

He felt ready to undertake his departure. The gods were with him, *his* gods, the ones he understood and loved. They would guide him and shelter him as he made his way north.

Thu-Kimnibol had no use for the more complex theologies that had sprung up among the People. There were some who worshiped the vanished humans—who believed that the humans were gods higher than the Five. Others knelt before the Beng god Nakhaba, saying that he too held a rank in heaven above that of the Five, that he was the Interceder who could speak with the humans on the People's behalf.

And then there were those—mostly University people, they were, old Hresh's crowd—who spoke of a god superior to all the rest, above the humans, and Nakhaba, and the Five. The Sixth, that one was called. The Creator-God. Of him, or it, nothing was known, and they said that nothing ever could be, that he was fundamentally unknowable.

Thu-Kimnibol had no idea what to make of any of this profusion of gods. It seemed needless to him to have any but the Five. But he could understand a willingness to pray to these others more easily than he did the position of those few, like his impossible niece Nialli Apuilana, who seemed not to believe in any gods at all. What a bleak existence, to walk godless beneath the unfriendly sky! How could they bear it? Weren't they paralyzed with fear, knowing that they had no protectors? To Thu-Kimnibol it seemed crazy. Nialli Apuilana, at least, had an excuse. Everyone knew that the hjjks had tampered with her mind.

Slowly he came up out of his communion, and found himself sitting slumped at Boldirinthe's rough wooden table, while she went puttering about, putting the gods back in her cupboard. She seemed pleased with herself. She must know the intensity of the communion she had created for him.

Silently he embraced her. His heart overflowed with love for her. Gradually the power of the communion faded, and he made ready to go.

"Be wary of King Salaman," Boldirinthe said, when Thu-Kimnibol was about to leave her chamber. "Salaman's a very clever man."

"I know that, Mother Boldirinthe."

"Cleverer than you."

Thu-Kimnibol smiled. "I'm not as stupid as is generally thought." "Cleverer than you, all the same. As clever as Hresh, Salaman is. Believe me. Watch out for him. He'll trick you somehow."

"I understand Salaman. We understand each other."

"They tell me he's grown wild and dangerous in his old age. That he's had power so long that he's gone mad from it."

"No," Thu-Kimnibol said. "Dangerous, yes. Wild, perhaps. But not a madman. I knew Salaman a long time, when I lived in Yissou. You can tell who has madness in him and who doesn't. He's a steady one."

"I coupled with him once," Boldirinthe said. "I know things about him that you'll never know. Fifty years, and I've never forgotten. Such a quiet boy, but there was fire inside him, and in fifty years the fire burns through to the surface. Be wary, Thu-Kimnibol."

"I thank you, Mother Boldirinthe."

He knelt and kissed her sash.

"Be wary," she said.

As Thu-Kimnibol descended from the offering-woman's cloister his path crossed that of Nialli Apuilana, who was coming toward him up steep cobblestoned Minbain Way. The day was bright and golden, with a perfumed wind blowing out of the west, where groves of yellow-leaved sthamis trees were blooming on the hills above the bay. Nialli Apuilana carried a tray of food and a flask of clear spicy wine for Kundalimon.

Her mood was brighter, though still not bright enough. After her startling breakdown at the Presidium she had gone into hiding, more or less, keeping out of sight for days, going out only for the sake of making her twice-daily journeys to Mueri House and hurrying back to her room as soon as Kundalimon had had his meal. Some days she hadn't gone at all, but left it up to the guardsmen to feed him. Yissou only knew what they brought him. Most of her time she spent alone, meditating, brooding, going over and over everything she had said there, wishing she could call half of it back, or more than half. And yet it had seemed so important finally to speak out: all that talk of the hjjks as bugs, the hjjks as cold-blooded killers, the hjjks as this, the hjjks as that. And they knew nothing. Nothing at all. So she had spoken. But she had felt edgy and exposed ever since. Only now was she starting to realize that scarcely anyone in the city had heard about her outburst at all, and most or perhaps all of those who had witnessed it had chosen to see it as nothing more than a little show of hysteria, the sort of thing that one would expect from someone like Nialli Apuilana. Not very flattering, really: but at least she didn't need to worry about being jeered at in the streets.

She was happy to see Thu-Kimnibol. She knew that she disagreed with him about practically everything, especially where the hjjks were concerned; but yet there was a strength about her imposing kinsman, a dignity, that she found steadying. And a certain warmth, too. Too many of these warrior princes liked to strike ostentatious poses. Thu-Kimnibol had a simpler style.

She said, "Are you coming from Boldirinthe, kinsman?"

"How can you tell that?"

With a toss of her head Nialli Apuilana indicated the offering-woman's cloister at the top of the hill. "Her house is right up there. And the light of the gods is still in your eyes."

"You can see that, can you?"

"Oh, yes. Yes, of course."

She felt a sharp pang of envy. There was such tranquility on his broad face, such a sense of self-assurance.

Thu-Kimnibol said, grinning down at her, "I thought you were godless, girl. What do you know about the light of the gods?"

"I don't need to believe in Yissou and the rest of them in order to see that you've touched another world just now. And I'm not as godless as you think. I tell you, the light of the gods is in your eyes. Shining as brightly as the light of a lantern-tree on a night without a moon."

"Not godless?" Thu-Kimnibol repeated, frowning. "You say you aren't godless, after all?"

"I have my own sort of worship," she said, feeling increasingly uncomfortable at this turn in the conversation. "After my own fashion, a kind of worship, yes. At least I look upon it as worship, though others around here might not. But I don't like talking of such things. Faith's an extremely private matter, don't you think?" She managed a dazzling smile. "I'm happy for you, that Boldirinthe was able to give you the comfort you needed."

"Boldirinthe!" he said, and laughed a little. "Boldirinthe lives now with one foot in the past and the other in the next world. It wasn't easy for me to keep her attention on the task. But finally she got to it, and I felt the presence of the gods, indeed. They were there right in front of me, the Five were. A great comfort they've been to me, too, in my time of mourning. A great comfort they've always been to me, and always will. I wish the joy of them upon you also some day, Nialli Apuilana." Thu-Kimnibol indicated the tray and flask she carried. "Going to visit your hjjk, are you? Bringing him some special treats?"

"Kinsman!" she cried, chiding him. "Don't call him a hjjk!"

"Well, if he isn't a hjjk, they say he sounds like one. He speaks only in gargles and spittings, or am I wrong?" In an amiable way Thu-Kimnibol made harsh rough noises far back in his throat, a crude parody of hjjk speech. "To me somebody's a hjjk if all he speaks is hjjk. And wears hjjk talismans around his neck and thinks hjjk thoughts and carries himself hjjk-style. You know, walking around as though he's got a long pole rammed up his rump."

"If living as a captive among the hjjks makes a person a hjjk, well, then I'm a hjjk too," Nialli Apuilana said, putting some severity into it. "Anyway, Kundalimon has started to learn our language very nicely indeed. The words come back to him. He's beginning to remember that he was once one of us. It's wrong of you to mock him. Or me, through him."

"Indeed."

"Thu-Kimnibol, why do you hate hjjks so much?"

"Do I?" Thu-Kimnibol said, as though the idea were new to him. "Perhaps I do. But why is that? Let me think." A look of irritation flickered in his eyes. "Could it be because they'd like to pen us down in a small part of the world, when we should have the whole thing? And that I resent this restraint that they put upon us? Perhaps that's it, eh? Or is it, maybe, a simpler matter, a personal thing, having to do with the fact that one day long ago a band of hjjks came to the place where I was living, in the north, the very place I'll be setting out for in just a little while, and fell upon the handful of innocent people who lived there, and killed some of them. My own father was one of those they killed, you know. Maybe that's it, eh, Nialli Apuilana? A petty little grudge of mine, a simple hankering for revenge?"

"Oh, no, Thu-Kimnibol. I didn't mean to say—"

Thu-Kimnibol shook his head. He reached down from his great height and let his hands rest tenderly on her shoulders for a moment. "I understand, Nialli. All that happened long before you were born. Why should you have given it a thought? But let's keep the peace between us, shall we? We oughtn't to bicker this way. Go to your friend, and bring him his wine and meat. And pray for me, will you? Pray to whatever god it is you pray to. I'm leaving for the northland tomorrow. I'd like to have your prayers go with me."

"They will," she said. "And my love also, kinsman. A safe journey to you."

If she hadn't been so laden with burdens she would have embraced him. That surprised her. She had never felt such warmth toward him before: until this moment he had been only her great robust mountain of a kinsman, half as big as a vermilion and scarcely any brighter; or so he had always seemed to her. Suddenly she saw Thu-Kimnibol now in a different way, as someone rather more complex than she had imagined, and more vulnerable. Suddenly now she feared for him and wished him well.

It must be the god-light flowing from him that does this to me, she thought. Perhaps I should go to Boldirinthe for a communion too. I might finally find the gods speaking even to me.

"A safe journey, yes," she said again. "And a happy outcome, and a swift return."

Thu-Kimnibol thanked her, and went on his way. Nialli Apuilana continued up the hill toward Mueri House.

The guard on duty at the gate was Curabayn Bangkea's youngest brother, Eluthayn, a meaty flat-faced man wearing a gaudy, preposterous helmet. As Nialli Apuilana approached him he said to her, "He's been waiting for you, the one from the hjjks. Been asking all morning why you're so late today. At least, I think that's what he's been saying. Not that I can make much sense out of that arglebargle way he speaks." Eluthayn Bangkea loomed toward her, so close that she could smell on his breath the sharp kharnigs he had had for his morning meal. Astonishingly, he leered at her in an offensively intimate way. "I can't say I blame him. I wouldn't mind being locked up in there all afternoon with you myself."

"And what could we possibly say to each other, if we had to spend a whole afternoon in each other's company?"

"It isn't what we'd *say*, Nialli Apuilana."

And he leered again, more exaggeratedly than before, rolling his eyes, whipping his sensing-organ about, thrusting his face practically into hers.

He was too much the fool to be taken seriously. This sort of ponderous unasked attention must be more of a joke than anything else. But if it was a joke, it was a coarse one. How dare he? He'd be grabbing her, next.

Her anger rose abruptly and she spat at him with sudden ferocity, leaving a gobbet between his wide-set eyes.

Eluthayn Bangkea gaped at her incredulously. Slowly he wiped his face. His forehead was furrowed with consternation and barely contained wrath.

"Why did you do that? You didn't need to do that!"

She drew herself up. "Your kind is tiresome to me."

"My *kind*? What do you mean, my kind? I'm me. The only me there is. And I meant you no harm. There was no call for your doing that." He lowered his voice. "Listen, would it be such a terrible thing if we went off and coupled for an hour, Lady Nialli? A guardsman can give pleasure even to a chieftain's daughter, you know. Or don't you think coupling's a pleasure? Could that be it? Too proud to couple, are you? Or too frightened? Which is it?"

"Please," she said in disbelief. It was as though she were dreaming this. How humiliating it all was! She was angry and stunned and close to tears, all at once. But it was important to remain strong in the face of this kind of thing. She glared at him. "Enough. What a vulgar clown you are."

"You'll have me punished, I know. Won't you? But I'll tell them you spat in my face. And I never laid a hand on you. I never did anything but wriggle my eyebrows at you."

"Get out of my way and let me go upstairs," Nialli Apuilana said fiercely. "And may I never see you again!"

Giving her a sullen bewildered stare, he opened the gate for her. She brushed past him, eyes averted, and passed within the building. Once she was safely beyond him she paused, shivering. She felt shaken, she felt soiled and violated, as though he had been the one to spit on her, and not the other way around. Her whole body was taut with fury and shock. She took a couple of deep breaths and felt her pulse begin to slow a little. In a calmer state, she ascended the stairs to Kundalimon's third-floor room and knocked.

Instantly the door opened. Kundalimon peered out. He smiled shyly. His green eyes, which often were so icy and remote, seemed bright and warm today; and Nialli Apuilana felt such a rush of innocence and sweetness coming from him that it went a long way in only a moment to wipe away the stain of that sorry encounter down below.

"So you come to me at last!" Kundalimon cried, with a tremor of joy in his voice. "Good. Very good. At last you come. I miss you, Nialli Apuilana. I miss you very much. I wait the hours all the time."

Slipping his hand around her wrist, he drew her gently into the room and closed the door. He took the tray of food from her, and the flask of wine, and knelt to set them on the floor. When he rose, he stood in silence a moment, his eyes trained steadily on hers. Once again he put his hand on her wrist.

There's something different about him today, she thought. Something new, something strange.

Hesitantly he said, "I am thinking. How I feel, you know? I am so much alone. Nest is—so far away. Nest-thinker. Queen. So far. Flesh-folk everywhere about me."

Compassion for his loneliness overflowed in her. Impulsively she told him, "You mustn't worry, Kundalimon. You'll be going back soon."

"I will? I will?"

He seemed thunderstruck by her words. She was surprised by them herself. Was there any plan to release him? She had no idea. Thu-Kimnibol had talked of sending him back to the Nest carrying a rejection of the treaty, true, but Taniane had given no indication that she'd go along with that. More likely she had it in mind that Kundalimon, his captivity ended, would now simply set about living a normal life in the city of his birth, as though he had been absent only a matter of weeks or months.

But he seemed so needy today. The consoling words had just popped from her mouth. Might as well follow through, Nialli Apuilana thought. Tell him the things he wants to hear.

"Of course you'll go back. You'll be carrying a message to the Queen, from our chieftain. They'll be sending you in just a little while. I'm sure of that."

Kundalimon's hand tightened on her wrist.

"You come with me, then?"

She hadn't been expecting that.

"I?"

"We go together. This no place for you. You have Nest-truth in you! I know this. You have felt Queen-love!" He was trembling. His sensing-organ was moving in slow arcs from side to side behind him, and his tongue flicked out again and again to moisten his lips. "You and I—you and I, Nialli Apuilana—we—we are of the Nest—oh, come close, come close—"

Mueri guide me, she thought desperately. Does he want to twine with me?

Perhaps so. Over the past weeks, as his command of the language had grown, they had begun to enter some new phase of rapport, which today suddenly seemed to be approaching a kind of culmination. Certainly he was far more outgoing than he had ever been with her before; certainly there was an imperative need in him today, an urgency, that was new. Everything about him, the way he stood, the expression of his eyes, the movements of his sensing-organ, even the sharp bitter scent that was rising from him, argued that.

But—twining?

She wondered. It had aroused such fear and even horror in him, that other time early in their friendship when she had touched her sensing-organ to his and begun to lead him into the first stage of the communion. As though he couldn't bear even the idea of the oneness that she was offering; as though the thought of such union with one who was not of the Nest was repugnant beyond any hope of acceptance.

On the other hand, they knew each other much better now. Apparently Kundalimon had come to realize that she was indeed of the Nest: not to the same degree that he was, but Nest-touched all the same, a Nest-soul within a flesh-body, just as he. And therefore no longer saw her as alien, a member of the enemy. And in that case—

He looked at her imploringly. She smiled and raised her sensing-organ, and brought it into the most grazing of contacts with his.

"No," he said at once, quickly whipping his sensing-organ beyond her reach. "Not—twine. No. Please—no."

"No?"

"Frightens. Still. It is too much, the twining." He shook his head. A deep quiver ran through him. He seemed to brood. But then his face grew sunny again. "You and I—you and I—oh, come close! Will you come close?"

"What do you want?" she asked, baffled.

He made an inarticulate sound, a hjjk-noise, not even a word: simply a noise, like that of a rusty gate resisting the pressure of a hand. A rush of emotions, nearly all of them unreadable, fluttered across his features in wild succession. Nialli Apuilana imagined that she saw sheer terror there, and embarrassment, and something that might have been Nest-love, and a kind of desperate yearning, and also something else, far more familiar, that she had seen only a little while before in the dull lust-ridden Beng-red eyes of Eluthayn Bangkea.

His hands went to her shoulders, her forearms, her breasts. He stroked her with frantic eagerness and pressed himself against her. His mating-rod was stiff.

Mueri and Dawinno and Yissou! she thought, in amazement and dismay. It's *coupling* that he wants!

No question of it. His breath was hot against her cheek. He was muttering to her, still inarticulately, in a muzzy mixture of hjjk-clicks and People-grunts. He seemed dazed, lost in a swelter of desire.

It was almost funny. But it was alarming, too. Nialli Apuilana had never coupled with anyone. She was as frightened of coupling as Kundalimon seemed to be of twining. To her it had always meant the breaching of a mysterious barrier that she dared not surrender.

Others, she knew, did it at the snap of a finger, some of them beginning when they were no older than nine or ten. They casually flung their bodies together for a quick sweaty joining and thought nothing of it. But Nialli Apuilana had held herself fastidiously aloof from all that when she was younger, and now that she was well on her way into womanhood she had begun to think that she had held back too long, that she had by her very denial raised coupling to an act of such significance that she would need the most overwhelming imaginable reason ever to do it all. That reason had never presented itself: certainly she hadn't seen it in the sniggering eye-rollings of an Eluthayn Bangkea, nor the subtler hungry stares of a Husathirn Mueri.

But now—now—

Kundalimon was all over her, pawing, snorting, just the way she had always thought men did. He could barely control himself. And yet she felt no revulsion, only compassion. Penned up here alone day after day in this little single-windowed cell, he must have been overwhelmed by his solitude, his separation from the Nest, until the anguish had reached flood level in his spirit, and now it was flowing over. Nialli Apuilana saw no way of holding him back.

"Wait," she said. "Please."

"I—want—"

"But—please, Kundalimon, please—" He paused, just a moment, as if he really understood what she was trying to say. Or perhaps he simply felt the fearful agitation of her unwilling body. But he was still eager to proceed. How to stop him? In sudden wild inspiration she said, "I must not. Coupling is forbidden to me." And in the hjjk language she told him, "I have yet to undergo Queen-touch."

There was a chance, just a chance, he might yield to that argument. In the Nest, there was no mating until the Queen had brought you to maturity and fertility, in a rite the nature of which Nialli Apuilana didn't know, but which marked the transition into adulthood for every hjjk.

Kundalimon, in the full grip of his own undeniable and no longer denied fleshhood, might not understand why a woman of the flesh-folk would not want to give herself up gladly to the powerful craving that now was sweeping through him. Shouldn't she feel the same desires that he did, since she too was of the flesh? Well, yes: but he wasn't able to comprehend her fears. Not even she could. But perhaps he might respond to that other argument for virginity that was unique to the Nest.

His fleshly aspect, though, was in the ascendant. No argument was going to sway him.

"I have not yet had Queen-touch either," he said. "But we are—not in the Nest now—" He sucked his breath in deeply, and a look of mingled torment and passion blazed in his eyes. He was as virgin as she was. Of course. Who would he have coupled with, in the Nest? But now he was swept by need, flesh-need, the need inborn in everyone of his true race.

And so, she understood suddenly, was she.

Almost without realizing what was happening, she was warming to his touch. As he stroked her, sensations were arising in her that she had never known before. She felt hot, she felt itchy, she felt eager. Muscles strained and throbbed along her thighs, her belly, her chest. Her breath came in gusts.

They were the sensations of pleasure. And somehow she knew that greater pleasure still was within her grasp. All she had to do was let it sweep over her.

It came upon her unanswerably that this was the moment, this the time, this the place, this the man. The barriers fell away. She smiled and nodded. He reached for her again, uttering hjjk-sounds, and she responded to them in hjjk and in inchoate wordless People-sounds, and together they slipped down to the floor, knocking over the flask of wine, scattering the tray of food she had brought. That didn't matter. His hands were everywhere on her. He seemed to have no real idea of what to do, only vague guesses and approximations, and she knew barely more than that herself; but somehow they found an alignment that was right, and she drew him to her and parted her thighs, and he slipped inside.

So this is what it is like, she thought.

So this is what it is, the great thing over which so much is made. The bodies fit together and they move. That's all there is to it. But how good it feels! How simple, how right!

And then she ceased thinking at all, except to wonder vaguely whether they had fastened the door securely. Even that thought went from her mind. They rolled about and about, laughing and crying out in both their languages, clutching at each other and nipping and clawing, and gasping in the strange excitement of it, until Nialli Apuilana heard him make a hoarse heavy sound that she had never heard from him before, and a kind of convulsion swept him. And, to her astonishment, she became aware of a warm welling-up of feeling within her, almost as if she would burst, and she heard a sound not unlike the one he had made erupting suddenly from her own lips a moment later. It was, she realized, the sound of joy, the sound of ecstasy, the sound of release from a self-imposed penance.

They lay in silence, in wonder, now and again looking at each other. Then he reached for her once more.

Afterward, long afterward, when they were calm again, passion giving way to quiet tenderness, Kundalimon said, "Is one other thing I want."

"Tell me. Tell me."

"Is too sad here, always in one room for me," he said, as he ran the tips of his fingers fondly across the fur of Nialli Apuilana's back. "You get them let me go outside? You get them let me walk in city like free man? You do that for me, Nialli Apuilana? You do that?"

Thu-Kimnibol had five handsome well-made wagons, each drawn by a pair of xlendis that he had selected personally for their spirit and vigor, and a quartet of equally fine animals as spares, in case any of the others fell by the wayside. He had no intention of making this journey the way a merchant would, plodding placidly along northward for month after month. No, he meant to race northward in one single furious burst, like a shooting star streaking across the heavens, halting only when he must, driving the xlendis and his companions to the limits of their capacity. He longed to hurl himself quickly into this enterprise, to come before King Salaman swiftly and sit down with him to bring into being the alliance that was so long overdue.

But for all his high resolve the trip went slowly, and he saw very quickly that there was little he could do to hasten things. Esperasagiot was his wagonmaster, a bright golden Beng of the pure blood who knew xlendis the way he knew the name of his own father; and Esperasagiot drove the animals to their limits, but he knew where those limits were.

"We should stop now and rest," he said on the first evening out from Dawinno, when the sun was still high in the west.

"So early? Half an hour more," said Thu-Kimnibol.

"The xlendis will die of it."

"Just half an hour."

"Prince, do you want to kill the beasts on our very first day?"

Something about the man's tone told Thu-Kimnibol to take him seriously. "Will they actually die, if we ask them to carry us just a little way farther?"

"If not today, then tomorrow. If not tomorrow, then the day after. This is where we must halt. I'll stake my helmet on it, that if we go any farther tonight, and try to do as much tomorrow, we'll have some dead xlendis within three days. There's delicacy behind their strength. These aren't lumber-wagon xlendis. You've chosen high-spirited beasts, that carry us swiftly enough when they're fresh. But when they've begun to weary—" Esperasagiot pulled off his helmet, an artful one with five plumes of a silvery metal sweeping straight back, and put it in Thu-Kimnibol's hands. "I stake my helmet on it, Prince Thu-Kimnibol. Against your sash. Two dead ones in three days, at this pace."

"No," Thu-Kimnibol said. "We'll stop when you say."

The summer was still high, and the air was thick and heavy. Rain fell often. This was fertile land, out here north of Dawinno, with many farms. Sometimes Thu-Kimnibol saw little knots of farmers standing uneasily by the borders of their property, perhaps wondering whether he meant to raid them.

Soon the caravan was climbing into the hill country, though. Here it was much drier, and there were no more farms. The land was brown and rocky and bleak and the wind came from the north, with an edge on it. Some wild beasts, which had become scarce closer to the settled territories, roamed here. Flights of beaky wide-winged carrion-birds passed ominously overhead. At night the great scarred silver eye that was the Moon, dark with the wounds the death-stars had inflicted on it, lit the bare terrain with a cold gleaming glare.

The xlendis, under Esperasagiot's expert handling, performed well. Each day they seemed to scamper with greater zeal. They were slender gray beasts, slender-flanked and proud-necked, with aristocratic round heads and flaring nostrils, and they snorted and pranced as they went.

Thu-Kimnibol understood now why Esperasagiot had been so sparing with the xlendis in the early days of the trip. These were city-trained animals, accustomed to pulling the chariots of princes, and they had no experience of long hauls in open country. If he wore them out at the beginning, when provender was easy to come by, what reserve of energy would they have in the harder days to come? Let them grow tough gradually, and be fully inured by the time the journey's most difficult work was upon them, that was Esperasagiot's theory.

"I owe you an apology," Thu-Kimnibol told the wagonmaster, when they had been on the road ten days. "Your way with the xlendis is the right one."

Esperasagiot only grunted. He had no use for apologies, or praise, or anything else but xlendis.

They were in the great windswept coastal plateau now that lay between Dawinno and Yissou. Small twisted gray plants grew here in pale pebbly soil. There were ruined Great World cities along the route. But all that remained of them were faint white lines in the ground, the merest sketchy traces of foundations and pavements. Hresh had sent crews of University students here to dig for more, but there was nothing more to find.

Thu-Kimnibol ordered a halt at the first of these ancient sites that they came to, and looked around. He imagined a host of sapphire-eyes living in this place once, great meaty long-jawed reptilian things with big heads and heavy thighs, strolling slowly about like philosophers with their huge tails propped behind them as a sort of crutch, and the light of genius ablaze in their bulging blue eyes.

At another time he would have made a point of searching such a site as this for a trinket or two of the Great World to bring back for Naarinta. Things of that sort had always cheered her, a bit of fossil bone, some snippet of a mysterious instrument. She had decorated the halls of their villa with an odd and haunting collection of gnarled and twisted fragments of antiquity, and spent many an hour contemplating them.

He poked at this ruin now for sad memory's sake, and, perhaps, to amuse himself. Thinking that he might stumble on some shining machine of the ancient days that could work miracles, something simply lying there for the taking in the ground that no one else had noticed. A weapon, perhaps, that might be used to obliterate the hjjks. Or even the bones of a sapphire-eyes. No one had ever found any of those. He scuffed at the chalky soil with his boot. But there was nothing.

On a whim he ordered a trench driven a short way into the ground. The diggers worked for an hour or more; but all they brought him was a clump of brown rust, which turned to loose powder in his hand. He shrugged and cast it aside.

A powerful sense of the ancientness of the world came over him, of former worlds that lay upon this one like a film, a crust.

There were echoing traces of history here, and of lost magics, and of magics that still lived, but were beyond his grasp. An abiding melancholy began to take hold of him. His mind dwelt on the Great World, on all that it had been. Why had it perished, for all its greatness? Why did great civilizations perish, even as living people did?

He was struck by the inadequacy of his knowledge: the inadequacy of his mind itself. Hresh knows these things, Thu-Kimnibol thought. We are of one flesh, or almost so, he and I, and yet he knows everything, and I— I know nothing at all. I am merely great strong Thu-Kimnibol, whom others wrongly think stupid, though I am not. Ignorant, yes. But not stupid.

I must speak with Hresh about these matters, when I return.

"I wonder why it is," Thu-Kimnibol said to Simthala Honginda, who was his lieutenant-ambassador, "that Vengiboneeza survived over the years, or at any rate a good deal of it, enough so that we were able to walk in and take up lodgings there. But there's nothing left of these cities except streaks of dust and rust."

Simthala Honginda was of Koshmar blood, a wiry, quick-tempered man of high family connections, the eldest son of Boldirinthe and Staip, linked also to the line of Torlyri by way of his mating with Husathirn Mueri's sister Catiriil. He kicked idly at the ground. "Vengiboneeza was a sapphire-eyes city. Those old crocodiles had clever machines to do all the work for them, my father tells me. And the machines stayed there, continuing to repair everything, thousands of years after the Long Winter killed off all the sapphire-eyes."

"They must have been miraculous things, if they could last so long."

"The sapphire-eyes had machines to repair the machines. And machines to repair the machines that repaired the machines. And so on and so on."

"Ah. I see." Thu-Kimnibol scratched a comic face in the dry soil with his heel. "And this place, it had no such machines, you think?"

"Maybe it was a city of the vegetals," Simthala Honginda suggested. "They must have been very delicate, the plant-people, and froze to death and dried up and blew away like flowers. And so did their cities, I suppose, when the cold weather came. Or a human city, maybe. The humans are beyond our understanding. They mightn't have cared to build cities as substantial as those of the sapphire-eyes. It could be that their cities were mere things of mist and film, and when the humans went away, nothing but the faint traces of their cities stayed behind. But how can I say? It was all so long ago, Thu-Kimnibol."

"Yes. I suppose it was." He knelt and scooped up a handful of dirt, and tossed it into the wind. "A miserable sad place. There's nothing for us in it. We waste our time stopping here."

He ordered the caravan onward. Staring morosely ahead across the dry tawny landscape, he felt himself sinking into an uncharacteristic mood of gloom and irritation.

Thu-Kimnibol had known since boyhood that there had been a world before the present one, when all the Earth had been a radiant paradise and six very different races lived together in splendor and magnificence. Great Vengiboneeza had been their capital then, the chronicles said. He had never seen it himself, but he had heard tales of it from his brother Hresh. The things that Hresh had told him of those sky-high towers of turquoise and pink and iridescent violet that had somehow survived out of distant antiquity, and all the wondrous machines that still could be found in them, had stayed vivid in Thu-Kimnibol's mind ever since. What marvels! What astonishments! In those ancient times when the world had belonged to the slow heavy bright-eyed crocodilian sapphire-eyes folk, whose minds were ablaze with such powerful intelligence, the People, or the creatures who would one day become the People, had been no more than frisky jungle beasts. And Vengiboneeza had been the hub of the cosmos, visited by travelers from many lands and even, magically, other stars.

In those days also had lived the delicate vegetals, beings with petaled faces and hard knotty stems. And the brown-furred flipper-limbed sea-lords, who dwelled in the oceans but could come up on land and move about in clever chariots. And the dome-headed mechanicals, an artificial race, but something more than mere machines.

And hjjks, of course: they had been part of the Great World too, their lineage went back that far. And lastly the humans, the high mystery, that sparse race of arrogant regal creatures not unlike the People in form, but hairless and without sensing-organs. They had been the masters of the world before the coming of the sapphire-eyes to greatness, so it was said. And had chosen to resign all power to them.

Thu-Kimnibol found that a hard thing to understand, the resigning of power. But stranger yet than that to him was the passive way that the entire Great World had allowed itself to die when it became known that the terrible death-stars would crash down out of the sky, raising such clouds of dust and smoke that the sun's light would be unable to reach the Earth, and all warmth would depart for a period of uncountable centuries.

Hresh said that the Great World had been aware for at least a million years that the death-stars were going to come. And yet its people had chosen to do nothing.

That willingness of the Great World to die without a struggle was infuriating to Thu-Kimnibol. It was irrational; it was incomprehensible. Thinking about it made his muscles grow taut and his soul begin to ache.

If they were as great as all that, he asked himself, why didn't they blast the death-stars from the sky as they fell? Or string some sort of net across the heavens? Instead of doing nothing. Instead of simply letting the death-stars come.

The sapphire-eyes and the vegetals had frozen to death in their cities; so too, probably, had the sea-lords, when the oceans turned icy; the mechanicals had allowed themselves to rust and decay; the humans had disappeared, no one knew where, though they had taken the trouble to help such simpler creatures as the People to save themselves, first, by leading them into the cocoons where they were to wait the Long Winter out.

Only the hjjks, who were untroubled by cold and ignored most other discomforts, had survived the cataclysm. But even they had slipped a long way back from the peak of greatness they had attained in the former age.

Simthala Honginda, riding beside Thu-Kimnibol in the lead wagon, noticed his mood after a time.

"What troubles you, prince?"

Thu-Kimnibol gestured toward the dry plain. "This place where we've just been."

"It's nothing but a ruin. Why should a ruin disturb you so?"

"The Great World disturbs me. The death of it. The way they made no attempt to protect themselves."

"Perhaps they had no choice," Simthala Honginda said.

"Hresh thinks that they did. They could have kept the death-stars from falling, if they'd wanted to. Hresh says that there's an explanation for why they didn't; but he won't say what it was. You must work it out for yourself, says Hresh. You won't understand, he says, if I simply tell it to you."

"Yes. I've heard him say something along the same lines when that question came up."

"What if he's lying? What if he simply doesn't know the answer himself?"

Simthala Honginda laughed. "There's very little that Hresh doesn't know, I think. But in my experience, when Hresh doesn't know something, he usually admits it, without pretending otherwise. Nor have I ever known him to lie. Of course, you know him far better than I do."

"He's no liar," said Thu-Kimnibol. "And you're right: he'll say straight out, 'I don't know,' if he doesn't know. Therefore there has to be an answer to the question, and Hresh must know it. And it ought to be easy enough to work out, if you give it a little thought." He was silent a time, kneading a sore place in the muscles of his neck. Then he turned to Simthala Honginda and said, smiling, "In truth, I think I know the answer myself."

"You do? What is it, then?"

"Suddenly it's all quite clear to me. You don't need to be one tenth so wise as Hresh to see it, either. Do you want me to tell you the reason the sapphire-eyes allowed themselves to die without a struggle? It's that they were a race of fools. Fools, that is all they were, without sense enough to try to save themselves. Do you see? Nothing more complicated than that, my friend."

Curabayn Bangkea was at his desk in the guard headquarters, shuffling documents about, when Nialli Apuilana appeared without warning, stepping through the doorway unannounced. He looked up in surprise, flustered at the sight of her. A host of excited fantasies blossomed instantly in his soul as his eyes traveled the length of her tall, slender figure, so supple, so regal in bearing.

He had always lusted after her, though he knew he was only one of many who felt that way.

She is as skittish as a xlendi, he thought, looking at her now. She eludes everyone who would harness her. But all she needs is the right hand to bring her into line. And why should that hand not be mine?

Curabayn Bangkea was well aware of how absurd these fantasies of his were. The chances that she would come here to offer herself in love-making to the captain of the city guard were very small. If he had any doubt of that, he only had to look at her face. Her expression was entirely businesslike, cold and formal.

He rose hastily. "Well, lady, to what do I owe the unexpected pleasure?"

"You have Kundalimon under what amounts to house arrest. Why is that, Curabayn Bangkea?"

"Ah, does it trouble you?"

"It troubles him," she said. "This is the city where he was born. Why should he be treated as a prisoner?"

"He comes to us from the hjjks, lady."

"As an ambassador. Entitled to diplomatic courtesies, in that case. Either he should have the run of the city because he's a citizen of this place, or else because he's a representative of a sovereign nation with whom we're not at war."

Her eyes were bright with anger, her nostrils flaring, her breasts agitated. Watching her, Curabayn Bangkea found himself growing agitated also. She wore nothing but a sash and some ornamental ribbons across her shoulders. Not an unusual costume in this season of warm weather, but scantier in general than was typical of unmated women nowadays. That kind of near-nakedness might have been acceptable in the cocoon era, Curabayn Bangkea thought, but we are more civilized now. Why did she have to be so provocative?

He said cautiously, "The rule is that all strangers are sent to Mueri House for a period of observation, until we know whether they're spies or not."

"He's no spy. He's an ambassador from the Queen."

"There are those who'd argue—your kinsman Prince Thu-Kimnibol is among them, let me say—that that's simply two ways of saying the same thing."

"Be that as it may," said Nialli Apuilana. "He's complained to me of being held in what amounts to captivity. He thinks it's unkind and unfair, and I do also. I remind you that his welfare is my responsibility. He was given into my particular charge, you know, by the chronicler himself."

Curabayn Bangkea's eyes widened a trifle at that. "If it were up to me, I'd release him from all restraint in a moment, lady. But Husathirn Mueri's the one who has jurisdiction over him. He was the holder of the judicial throne the day the stranger was remanded to custody. You ought to be addressing your request to him, not to me."

"I see. I thought it was a matter for the guard-captain."

"I don't have any authority in this. But if you like, I'll speak to Husathirn Mueri about it on your behalf."

"On Kundalimon's behalf, you mean."

"As you say. I'll try to get the order changed. You'll be sent word when I do, later today, I hope. You're still at the House of Nakhaba, right?"

"Yes. Thank you. I'm grateful for your help, Curabayn Bangkea."

She didn't sound particularly grateful. Her look was a flinty one, not the least flicker of warmth about it, and the anger was still there, too. Something was definitely wrong, and his offer of cooperation had not repaired it.

"Is there anything else I can do for you, lady?"

Nialli Apuilana was silent a moment. She allowed her eyes briefly to close. Then she said, "Yes, a very foolish one, which I'm almost unwilling to speak of, it was so offensive. There's a brother of yours, who is on guard duty at Mueri House—Eluthayn, I think that's his name—he is your brother, isn't he?"

"Eluthayn, yes. My youngest brother."

"Yes. A few days ago, when I was paying a regular call there, this brother of yours attempted to interfere with me. There was an ugly incident."

Curabayn Bangkea said, mystified, "To interfere with you, lady?"

Her nostrils flared again. "You know what I mean. He made a crude offer to me, this brother of yours. Without warning, without the slightest provocation, he approached me, he breathed his stinking breath in my face, he—he—"

She didn't go on. Curabayn Bangkea felt a surge of alarm. Had Eluthayn really been idiotic enough to do such a thing? There probably was provocation aplenty, he thought, staring at Nialli Apuilana's uncovered breasts, at her long silken thighs thickly thatched with sleek red-brown fur. But if Eluthayn had dared to put his hands on the chieftain's daughter uninvited—

"He *touched* you, lady? He made *overtures*?"

"Overtures, yes. In another moment he'd have been touching me too."

"Yissou!" Curabayn Bangkea exclaimed, throwing his hands out to his sides. "The stupidity of him! The effrontery!" The guard-captain bustled across the room toward Nialli Apuilana, so hastily that he came close to clanging his helmet into the lamp fixture dangling overhead. "I'll speak to him, let me assure you, lady. I'll investigate fully. He'll be disciplined. And I'll send him to you to apologize in a proper way. Overtures, you say? Overtures?"

The lightest of quivers crossed her shoulders, a disgusted shudder, making her breasts tremble. She looked away from him. In a softer voice than she had been using, as though distress and shame were gaining the upper hand over anger in her, she said, "Punish him any way you see fit. I don't want any apologies from him. I don't want to set eyes on him again."

"I assure you, lady—"

"Enough. I'd just as soon not discuss any of this further, Curabayn Bangkea."

"I understand, lady. I'll handle everything. I would not have you insulted in such a way, by my own brother or by anyone else."

Did she soften a little, then? For the first time since she had come in she smiled. A faint smile, but a smile all the same. It could be that her anger was going from her, now that she had said what she had come here to say. Curabayn Bangkea thought he even saw gratitude in her eyes and perhaps something more than that: that something had leaped across the gap that separated him from her. He had seen that look often in the eyes of other women to whom he had offered aid, or other things. He was sure that he had seen it just then. Curabayn Bangkea was a fundamentally self-confident man. A great swell of confidence overcame him now, verging on boldness. Where Eluthayn, young and raw and foolish, had failed, he himself might very well succeed. This could be the fulfillment of his wildest fantasy. Unhesitatingly he reached for Nialli Apuilana's hands and took them fondly in his.

"If I can venture to make amends, lady, for my brother's unfortunate boorishness—if perhaps you would do the courtesy of sharing dinner with me, and wine, this evening or the next, I'll endeavor to show you that not all the men of the house of Bangkea are such crass and unthinking—"

"What?" she cried, snatching her hands away from him as though his were covered with slime. "You too, Curabayn? Are you all insane? You denounce your brother for effrontery, and then you put your hands on me yourself? You invite me to *dinner?* You offer to prove to me that—oh, no, no, no, guard-captain, no!" She began to laugh.

Curabayn Bangkea stared at her in shock.

"Do I have to go around encased in armor? Must I assume that every soldier of the guards in this city will slobber and leer at me if I happen to come within his reach?" Her eyes were flinty again. She had become the image of her mother. Curabayn Bangkea shrank back before her fury as though he stood before the chieftain herself. Coldly Nialli Apuilana said, "Speak to Husathirn Mueri about the matter of the house arrest, if you will. As for your brother, I want him transferred to other duties far from Mueri House. Good day, Curabayn Bangkea."

She went storming from the room.

He sat frozen a long while, dumbfounded by the thing he had so brazenly dared to attempt.

How could I have been so foolish? he asked himself.

Even though she had come in here wearing only ribbons and a

sash. Even though she had given him that warm, melting smile of gratitude. Even though he had been overcome by the fragrance of her, and by the closeness, and by his own lunatic self-assurance. For all of that, he had ventured into territory he should never have permitted himself to enter. He wondered how much harm he had done to himself. He wondered if he had ruined himself. He trembled in unaccustomed fear.

Then anger, unfocused and wild, directed at the universe in general rather than at any specific target, welled up in him and swept the fear away. In a loud voice he called to his aide in the hall, "Get me my brother Eluthayn."

The young guardsman came in wearing a cheerful, jaunty expression, but it faded the moment he saw the look on his older brother's face.

Coldly Curabayn Bangkea said, "You moron, is it true you tried to rape the chieftain's daughter?"

"Rape? What are you talking about, man?"

"She was just in here, talking about your *interfering* with her. Making *overtures* to her. She was furious with me, you simpering little bastard. I tried to calm her, and perhaps I did. But maybe not. By the time she's done with this, she might bring me down as well as you. What in the name of Nakhaba did you try to do, anyway? Grab her rump? Stroke her breasts?"

"I made an innocent little suggestion, brother. Well, not so innocent, perhaps, but playful. There she was, just about naked, the way she goes around all the time, you know, getting ready to go upstairs to that boy who came from the hjjks, and I said something to the effect that I wouldn't mind being shut up in a room with her myself for a little while. That was all."

"That was all?"

"I swear to you by our mother. Just a little come-on, you understand, nothing serious—though I'd have become serious in a moment, let me tell you, if she'd gone for the bait. You never can tell, with these highborns. But instead she went crazy. She began to rant and scream. She spat at me, Curabayn."

"Spat?"

"In my face, right here. A good healthy wad of it it was, too, that left me feeling filthy for hours. You'd think I'd offended her to the depths of her soul, the way she was raging. To spit at me like I was an animal, or worse than an animal, brother! Who does she think she is?"

"She's the daughter of the chieftain, in fact. And of the chronicler," said Curabayn Bangkea heavily.

"I don't care whose daughter she is. She's just a spread-legged slut like all the rest of them, brother."

"Careful. It's risky to slander the highborn, Eluthayn."

"What slander? Is she such a model of virtue? She and that boy in Mueri House, they couple like rutting xlendis. The two of them go at it for hours at a time, brother!"

Curabayn Bangkea rose from his seat, grunting in surprise. "What's that? What are you saying?"

"Only the truth. That day she spat at me, I went upstairs and listened at the door, to see if she had any right being so high and mighty. And I could hear them thumping around. On the floor, they were, like animals. I'm sure of it. And there was no mistaking the sounds they were making. I've heard it since, other times. You think Hresh would be amused, knowing she's coupling with *him?* Or the chieftain, if she knew?"

His brother's words went through Curabayn Bangkea like a spear. The situation was transformed completely by this. Coupling with Kundalimon, was she? Was that what those cozy little visits were all about? He and Eluthayn were safe, then. Why shouldn't the captain of the guards, or even his stupid younger brother, also be able to offer himself for a little coupling to the highborn Nialli Apuilana, if she was willing to roll on the floor with something out of the hjjk Nest, who could speak only in clicks and clatters?

He said severely, "Are you absolutely certain of this?"

"On our mother's soul, I am."

"All right. All right. This is going to be very helpful, what you've just told me." Curabayn Bangkea dropped back into his chair and sat utterly still for a moment, letting the tension of the morning ease away from him. At length he said, "You understand I'll have to transfer you to guard duty somewhere else, to pacify her. You don't care a spider's ass about that, naturally. And if you happen to see her in the streets, for Yissou's sake be humble and full of respect. Bow to her, make holy signs to her, get down and kiss her toes, if necessary. No, not that. Don't kiss her anywhere. But show respect. You've mortally offended her, and she has power over us that has to be taken into account." Curabayn Bangkea grinned. "But I think I have some power over her now, too. Thanks to you, you lecherous idiot."

"Will you explain yourself, brother?"

"No. Just get yourself out of here. And be careful hereafter when you're around highborn women. Remember who and what you are."

"She had no call spitting in my face, brother," Eluthayn said sullenly.

"I know that. But she's highborn, and she thinks differently about such things." He waved his hands in his brother's face. "Go, now, Eluthayn. Go."

The landscape changed again and again as Thu-Kimnibol continued northward toward the City of Yissou. Now the caravan moved through broad plains open to the sea-breezes out of the west, and the air was moist and salty and blue-green beards of scalemoss shrouded every bush; and now the route traversed wide flat silent arid valleys walled off from the sea by stark bare mountain ridges, and the skulls of unknown beasts lay bleaching on the sandy ground; and now the travelers passed into forested highlands, where jagged leafless trees with pale spiral trunks clung to tortuous outcroppings of black earth, and strange howlings and whistlings came floating down from the even higher country that lay to the east.

He was struck by a deep awareness of the hugeness of the world, of the greatness and heaviness of the immense globe across whose face he was moving.

It seemed to him that every hand's-breadth of it that he covered was entering into him, becoming part of him: that he was engulfing it, devouring it, incorporating it within himself for all time to come. And it made him all the more eager to go onward, on and on and on across the face of it. He knew himself to be different in this way from those of the People who were old enough to have been born in the tribal cocoon, who still harbored some urge, he suspected, to crawl back into a small, warm, safe place and close the hatch behind them. Not him. Not him. More deeply, perhaps than ever before, he understood his brother Hresh's hunger to know, to discover, to experience.

Thu-Kimnibol had been through here once before: when he was eighteen, going southward then, in his flight from Yissou to the City of Dawinno. But he remembered very few details of that earlier journey. He had ridden all the way with his head down and his eyes veiled by anger and bitter sorrow, driving his xlendi at full gallop. That grim and fretful ride survived in his memory now, two decades and some years later, only as a hard encapsulated knot, still capable of giving pain when prodded, like the memory of some terrible loss, or of a mortal illness successfully weathered at great inner cost. He touched it no more often than he had to.

They were past the halfway point now, in territory subject to Salaman. Mostly his mood was dark these days. The turning point had come at that Great World ruin, summoning memories of Naarinta as it did, and bleak thoughts of the remote past. Now the bygone days of his own life had begun to press heavily on him: lost opportunities, false paths taken, the beloved mate snatched away.

He did what he could to conceal his state of mind. But as the caravan was descending from the hills into a fertile plain cut by a host of swift streams and rivers Simthala Honginda said abruptly, "Is it the thought of seeing Salaman again that troubles you so much, prince?"

Thu-Kimnibol looked up, startled. Was he that transparent?

"Why do you say that?"

"You and he were bitter enemies once. Everyone knows that."

"We were never friends, I suppose. And for a time things were bad between us. But that was long ago."

"You still hate him, I think."

"I've scarcely given him a thought in fifteen years. Salaman's ancient history to me."

"Yes. Yes, of course he must be." Then, delicately: "But the closer we get to Yissou, the deeper you drift into gloom."

"Gloom?" Thu-Kimnibol forced a laugh. "You think I've turned gloomy, Simthala Honginda?"

"A blind man could see it."

"Well, if I am, it has nothing to do with Salaman. I've suffered a great loss lately. Or have you forgotten?"

Simthala Honginda seemed abashed. "Yes, yes, of course. Forgive me, prince. The lady Naarinta, may the gods give her rest!" He made the sign of Mueri the consoler.

Thu-Kimnibol said, after a time, "It'll be strange, I suppose, seeing Salaman again after so long. But there'll be no problems. However angry we may have been at each other once, what does it matter now? What matters is the hjjks. And we think alike on that subject, Salaman and I. From the beginning we were destined to fight side by side against them, and soon we will. The alliance that we'll form is the thing that counts. Why would he want to dig up grievances decades old? Why would I?"

He turned again to the window, and let the conversation lapse into silence. After a time he reached out and signaled to Esperasagiot to halt the caravan. The xlendis would want watering here; and it was a good place to stop for the evening meal, besides.

The land before them was green and rich. A maze of streams, reflecting the late afternoon light, gleamed like channels of molten silver. Good productive country, this. With a little drainage work it could probably support a city the size of Dawinno. Thu-Kimnibol wondered why Salaman hadn't yet occupied this district and put it under cultivation. It wasn't that far south of Yissou.

How like Salaman it was, he thought in contempt, to let this rich land lie fallow. To turn inward this way, pulling back from expansion and holing up behind his preposterous wall.

Simthala Honginda's right, he told himself. You do still hate him, don't you?

No. No, *hate* was too strong a term. But despite all he had said to Simthala Honginda he suspected that the old resentments still were simmering somewhere within him.

The conventional notion in Dawinno was that he had tried to challenge Salaman somehow for the throne of Yissou. But that notion was wrong. Thu-Kimnibol had realized very early that he would never rule the city his father had founded in his father's place. He had been much too young, when Harruel had died in the battle with the hjjks, to take the kingship for himself. Salaman had been the only possible candidate then. And once he had tasted such power, it wasn't likely that out of the goodness of his heart he'd relinquish it when Thu-Kimnibol came of age. Everyone understood that. Thu-Kimnibol was willing from the start to recognize Salaman as king. All he wanted in return was a little respect, as was due him as the son of the city's first king: the proper precedence, a decent dwelling, a high seat by Salaman's side at the feasts of state.

Which Salaman had given him, for a time. Until the king in his middle years began to change, until he started to grow fretful and unquiet of soul, a new dark Salaman, harsh and suspicious.

It was then, only then, that Salaman had decided Thu-Kimnibol was scheming against him. Thu-Kimnibol had offered him no cause for thinking that. Perhaps some enemy of his had whispered fabrications in the king's ear. Whatever the reason, things quickly had begun going sour. Thu-Kimnibol hadn't minded Salaman's favoring his son Chham at his expense: that was only to be expected. But then the second son was placed above him at the royal table, and the third; and when Thu-Kimnibol asked to have one of the king's daughters as his mate he was refused; and after that came other slights. He was a king's son. He deserved better of Salaman. The last straw had been a minor point of precedence, so minor that Thu-Kimnibol could no longer remember what it was. They fell to shouting over it; Thu-Kimnibol threatened the king with his fist; he came close to striking him. He knew he was finished, then, in the City of Yissou. That night he left, and he had never been back.

To Simthala Honginda he said, "Look there, Dumanka's been hunting up something for our dinner."

The quartermaster had left his wagon. Down below, on the bank of a stream just south of the route, he had speared some animal and was casting for a second one.

Thu-Kimnibol was glad of the distraction. His conversation with Simthala Honginda had been an oppressive one, stirring up difficult old days, and impaling him in contradictions. He saw now that although he could put aside his quarrel with Salaman, forgiving and forgetting were harder, however he pretended otherwise.

Cupping his hand to his mouth, he called out, "What are you after there, Dumanka?"

"Caviandis, prince!" The quartermaster, a brawny, irreverent man of Koshmar ancestry who wore a battered and dented Beng-style helmet slung casually across his shoulders, had killed a second one, now. Proudly he held the pair of purple-and-yellow bodies up, one in each hand. They dangled limply, plump little arms lolling, trickles of crimson blood dripping through their sleek fur. "Fresh meat, for a change!"

At Thu-Kimnibol's side Pelithhrouk, a young highborn officer who was a protégé of Simthala Honginda, said, "Is it right for us to kill them, do you think, prince?"

"Why not? They're only animals. Meat, that's all they are."

"We were only animals once," Pelithhrouk said.

Thu-Kimnibol rounded on him in amazement. "What are you saying? That we're no better than caviandis?"

"Not at all," said Pelithhrouk. "I mean that caviandis may be more than we think they are."

"This is bold talk," said Simthala Honginda uneasily. "I don't much like it."

"Have you ever looked at a caviandi closely?" Pelithhrouk said, with a kind of desperate rash insistence. "I have. Their eyes have light in them. Their hands are as human as ours. I think if we touched the mind of one with second sight, we'd be surprised how much intelligence we'd find there."

Simthala Honginda snorted. "I'm with Thu-Kimnibol. They're only animals."

But Pelithhrouk was in too deep to retreat. "*Intelligent* animals, though! Waiting only for a touch, to be brought up to the next level, is what I think. Instead of hunting and eating them, we ought to be treating them with respect—teaching them to speak, maybe even to read and write if they're capable of it."

"Your mind is gone," said Simthala Honginda. "This is some madness you must have caught from Hresh." Turning to Thu-Kimnibol and looking up at him in dismay, as though such wild talk from one to whom he had been a mentor was a keen embarrassment to him, which probably it was, he said, "Until this morning I thought this young man was one of our finest officers. But now I see—"

"No," said Thu-Kimnibol, holding up his hand. "What he says is interesting. But the time's too soon for us to worry about raising up other creatures to read and write," he said to Pelithhrouk, laughing. "We have to make our own lives safer before we can go about teaching the creatures of the field how to be civilized. The caviandis will have to look after themselves, for the time being. For the time being, animals is what they are and have to remain. And if you tell me that we are animals too, well, so be it. We're animals too. But right now we are of the eaters, and they are of the eaten, and that makes all the difference."

Dumanka, who had come up to them during this discussion and stood listening blankfaced to it, now tossed the caviandis down at Thu-Kimnibol's feet. "I'll build a fire, prince. We'll be feasting in half an hour."

"Well done," Thu-Kimnibol said. "And an end to all this talk, thanks be to the Five."

The caviandi meat was tasty stuff, yes. Thu-Kimnibol ate his portion without regret, though for a moment the disturbing notion passed through his mind that Pelithhrouk might be right, that these agile little creatures who hunted fish by the fast-flowing streams might in truth have intelligence, and a society, and a language, and names, and gods, and even a history of their own, for all anyone knew. Who could tell which creatures were mere animals and which intelligent beings? Not he. He put the thought aside. He noticed, though, that Pelithhrouk left his portion of the meat untouched. He has the courage of his convictions, at least, Thu-Kimnibol thought. A point in his favor.

The next day they left the zone of streams and marshes behind, and entered a drier district of rich dark earth and grassy meadows. At nightfall they saw lantern-trees blazing like beacons to the north. That was a good sign. It meant the caravan was getting close to the city.

The lantern-trees were inhabited by thousands of small birds able to emit a cool but brilliant light from colored patches on their throats and chests. Tirelessly they flashed their dazzling signals in steady rhythmic pulses, visible for great distances, all the night long. By day the tiny dull-plumaged birds were quiescent, nestling quietly. Why they chose those particular trees to live in, no one knew. But once they took possession of one they appeared never to relinquish it. And so lantern-trees became valuable highway markers by night, dependable and familiar guides for travelers.

Beyond the lantern-tree groves lay the farms of Yissou. Here, as those other farmers had done on the outskirts of Dawinno many weeks before, the farmers of Yissou came out sullenly to stand by the boundary-stones of their properties, glaring at the strangers passing by.

Now the land began to rise toward the great ridge south of the city, beyond which was Yissou itself, snug within the crater that the death-star had made.

They went on, up the outer slope of the crater. A little way farther along they came to a halt before the vast black wall that protected the City of Yissou, a wall that seemed to block the entire horizon and rise to a height altogether beyond belief.

The sight of it took Thu-Kimnibol's breath away. It was one of the most astonishing things he had ever seen.

He remembered the wall of years past, four or five sturdy courses of solid square-cut stone: how proud Salaman had been, when that new wall finally circled the city on all sides and he could at last rip down the old wooden palisade! Thu-Kimnibol knew that Salaman had gone on enlarging his wall year by year. But he had never expected to be confronted by something like this. It loomed awesomely, a thing of overwhelming mass, a terrifying pile of dark rock that nearly blotted out the sky.

What sort of enemy did Salaman fear that he should feel the need of a wall like that? What demons had come to haunt Salaman's soul, Thu-Kimnibol wondered, in the years since their last meeting?

A file of perhaps a thousand spear-wielding warriors stood side by side atop it. Their spears bristled against the brightness of the sky. They held themselves stiffly, scarcely moving. The wall dwarfed them: they seemed hardly larger than ants.

Below them was a great metal-bound wooden gate. It opened with a loud creaking and groaning as the caravan came nearer to it, and half a dozen unarmed figures, no more, stepped through, advancing a hundred paces into the open fields outside the wall. The gate swung shut behind them. At the head of the group was a short, broad-shouldered man whom Thu-Kimnibol thought at first glance was Salaman himself; but then he realized that the man was much too young to be the king. One of his sons, no doubt. Chham, was it? Or Athimin, maybe? Thu-Kimnibol felt the old angers rising in himself at the sight of him, remembering how those sons of Salaman had displaced him long ago.

He dismounted and went forward, hand upraised in a gesture of peace.

"I am Thu-Kimnibol," he called. "Son of Harruel, and a prince of the City of Dawinno."

The broad-shouldered man nodded. Indeed he bore an uncanny resemblance to the Salaman Thu-Kimnibol remembered, the robust arms, the short stocky legs, the alert, inquisitive gray eyes set far apart in a round, strong-featured face. He was very young, too young even to be Chham or Athimin. "I am Ganthiav, son of Salaman. The king my father asks me to welcome you and conduct you into the city."

Some younger son, perhaps not even yet born at the time of Thu-Kimnibol's flight. Was the sending of this Ganthiav to greet him some sort of obscure insult?

Be calm, Thu-Kimnibol warned himself. No matter what, be calm.

"Will you follow me?" Ganthiav asked, as the gate began to open once again.

Thu-Kimnibol glanced once more toward the top of the wall, toward that astonishing horde of motionless armed men. There was a sort of pavilion up there also, a dome-shaped thing made of a smoother, grayer stone than the wall itself. A long window set in its face yielded a view of the plain. For a moment Thu-Kimnibol's gaze rested on that window. He caught sight of a shadowy figure standing beside it; and then the figure moved into the light, and Thu-Kimnibol saw the unmistakable gray eyes of Salaman, King of Yissou, looking back at him, somber and implacable and cold.

4

The Martyr

Kundalimon had the freedom of the city, now, by special order of Husathirn Mueri, who had been asked by Curabayn Bangkea to release him from house arrest. He could leave his little cell in Mueri House whenever he pleased, and roam into any quarter, even entering the holy buildings and the houses of government. Nialli Apuilana had made that clear to him. "No one will stop you," she said. "No one will harm you."

"Even if I go into the Queen-chamber?"

She laughed. "You know we have no queen."

"Your—mother? The woman who rules?"

"My mother, yes." Kundalimon still had trouble with such concepts as "mother" and "father." These flesh-folk matters were only slowly becoming clear to him. The mother was the Egg-maker. The father was the Life-kindler. Coupling, the thing he did so pleasurably with Nialli Apuilana, was the means they used to kindle eggs into life among the flesh-folk. It was something similar to what was done in the Nest, and yet all so different, so deeply different. "What about her?" Nialli Apuilana asked.

"Is she not queen of the city?"

"Taniane's title is chieftain, not queen," Nialli Apuilana said. "It's an old title, from when we were just a little tribe living in a hole in the side of a mountain. She rules the city—with the advice of my father and the offering-woman and the whole council of princes—but she's not our queen. Not as you and I understand Queen-nature. She's my mother, that's true. But not the mother of the entire city."

"Then if I go into her chamber, no one will stop me?"

"It depends on what she's doing. But ordinarily, yes, you can go in. You can go anywhere you like. They'll be watching you, I suppose."

"Who will?"

"The guards. They don't trust you, Curabayn Bangkea's whole crowd. They think you're a spy."

He didn't quite comprehend. Much of what Nialli Apuilana said was a mystery to him. Even now, after weeks of daily lessons, when his mind was flooded with the language of the flesh-folk and he even found himself at times thinking in their words and not with Nest-words, he often was puzzled by the substance of what she told him. But he listened, and tried to remember, and hoped that in time he would understand.

In any case he was achieving his purpose, here, and that was the important thing. He had come to bring Queen-love, and he was doing it. First to Nialli Apuilana, in whom Queen-love was already awake, for she had spent time in the Nest; and now, now that he was finally free to go out into the city, he was bringing it to all the others, those who were entirely without Nest-awareness.

He had expected that he would be frightened, the first time he went outside alone. Nialli Apuilana had taken him out a few times to show him the main thoroughfares and explain the pattern of the streets to him; but then one morning he had risked going out without her. It was a test, to see whether he'd be able to take more than a few timid steps without wanting to rush back into the safety of the building.

So huge a city, so many streets, such hordes of flesh-folk everywhere about! The thick clinging humid southern warmth, so different from what he had been accustomed to in the dry cool north. The strange sweet alien aromas of the place. The utter absence of Nest-bond. The possibility that the people of this place might look on him with hatred or disdain.

But he felt no fear at all. He walked down past the jeering, sour-faced guards and down cobbled Minbain Way, and turned left into an open-air marketplace on a side street he hadn't traveled with Nialli Apuilana, and moved from stall to stall, looking at the fruits and vegetables and the dangling slabs of meat. He was altogether calm. And when it seemed to him that the outing had lasted long enough, he found his way back to Mueri House without difficulty.

After that he went out almost every day. He had never known such excitement. Simply to stand at a streetcorner, listening to a ballad-singer or a preacher or a peddler of little toys—how different that was from the life of the Nest! To step into a restaurant and stare in wonder at the sizzling meat on the griddle, and then point and smile, and be smiled at in return, and be handed some strange tender bit of flesh-folk food to eat—how wonderful, how transfiguring that was! It was like moving through the most vivid of dreams.

A steady diet of the food of the flesh-folk was having a profound effect on him. His fur was much thicker, darker, now. His body was becoming almost plump: he could pinch his skin and there would be a thick strip of flesh between his fingers, as never before. And also this new rich nourishment was entering his soul. He felt a fresh access of vigor. He was restless, almost jumpy with unfamiliar energy. Sometimes, when Nialli Apuilana entered his room, he seized her almost before she had had a chance to say a word and drew her down with him to the floor or to his couch. In the streets, too, he moved in long forceful strides, enjoying the jolt of the pavement against his feet. That was new, too, to be walking on paved streets. Everything was new, everything was exciting.

They all seemed to know who he was. People pointed and whispered. A few spoke to him, courteously but with some uncertainty, as if they weren't sure how safe it was to approach him. With the children it was different. Platoons of them followed him about. There were children everywhere here; sometimes it seemed to Kundalimon that scarcely anyone but boys and girls lived in this city. They capered after him, shouting and whooping, calling out to him.

"Hjjk! Hjjk! There goes the hjjk!"

"Say something to us in hjjk-speak, hjjk!"

"Hey, hey, hjjk! Where's your beak?"

They meant no mockery. They were only children, after all. Their tone was light and playful.

He turned to them and beckoned. They were wary at first, the way the older ones tended to be, but then they came to him and stood close about him. Some of them shyly let him take their hands in his.

"Are you really a hjjk?"

"I am like you. I am flesh, like you."

"Then why do they say you're a hjjk?"

Kundalimon smiled. Gently he said, "The hjjks took me away when I was very young, and raised me in their Nest. But I was born here, you know. In this city."

"You were? Who's your mother? Who's your father?"

"Marsalforn," he said. "Ramla." He struggled to remember which was which. The mother, the Egg-maker, that was Marsalforn, Nialli Apuilana had said, and the father, he who had kindled, was Ramla. Or was it the other way around? He could never keep it straight. In the Nest it made no difference who your Egg-maker was, and who the Life-kindler. Everyone was really the child of the Queen, after all. Without Her touch there could be no new life. Makers, kindlers, they all served the Will of the Queen.

"Where do they live?" a little girl asked. "Do you ever visit them, your mother and your father?"

"They live somewhere else now. Or maybe they don't live anywhere any more. No one knows where they are."

"Oh. That's sad. Do you want to visit my mother and father, if you don't have any of your own?"

"I'd like that," said Kundalimon.

"How did you come here?" another girl said. "Did you fly like a bird?"

"I rode a vermilion." He made a sweeping gesture with his arms, indicating a beast of mountainous size. "Down out of the north, from the place of the Nest of Nests, traveling day after day, week after week. Riding my vermilion, heading for this city, this city Dawinno. The Queen sent me here. Go to Dawinno, She said. She sent me so that I could talk to you. So that I could get to know you, and you to know me. So that I could bring you Her love, and Her peace."

"Are you going to take us back with you to the Nest?" a boy in back called. "Did you come to steal us, like you were stolen?"

Kundalimon looked to him, amazed.

"Yes! Yes!" the children cried. "Are you here to take us to the hjjks?"

"Would you like that?"

"*No!*" they yelled, so loudly that his ears rang. "Don't take us! Please don't!"

"I was taken. You see that no harm came to me."

"But the hjjks are monsters! They're horrible and dangerous! Awful giant bug-creatures, is what they are!"

He shook his head. "It isn't so. You don't understand, because you don't know them. No one here does. They're kind. They're loving. If you only knew. If you only could feel Nest-bond, if you only could experience Queen-love."

"He sounds crazy," a small boy said. "What's he saying?"

"Shhh!"

"Come," Kundalimon said. "Sit down with me, here in the park. There's so much I want you to know. Let me tell you, first, what things are like, in the Nest—"

There was nothing left of the City of Yissou that Thu-Kimnibol remembered from his youth. Just as the first crude wooden shacks of Harruel's original Yissou had been swept away to be replaced by the early stone buildings of Salaman's city, so too by now had every vestige of that second city disappeared. A still newer and more powerful one had been superimposed on it, obliterating the other, which was gone without a trace, palaces and courts and houses and all.

Salaman said, "It looks good to you, does it? It looks like a real city, eh?"

"It doesn't look at all the way I expected it would."

"Speak up, speak up!" Salaman said sharply. "I have trouble understanding a lot of what you're saying."

"A thousand pardons," said Thu-Kimnibol, in a voice twice as loud. "Is this better?"

"You don't have to shout. There's nothing wrong with my hearing. It's all those damnable Beng words you use. You speak with helmets in your mouth. How am I supposed to make sense out of that? I suppose if I lived with Bengs in my lap the way you people do—"

"We are all one People now," Thu-Kimnibol said.

"Ah. Ah. Is that what you are? Well, try not to speak so much Beng, if you want me to know what you're saying. We're conservatives here. We still speak the pure speech, the language of Koshmar and Torlyri and Thaggoran. You remember Torlyri? You remember Thaggoran, do you? No, no, how could you? He was the chronicler before Hresh. The rat-wolves killed him, right after the Coming Forth, that time when we were crossing the plain. But you weren't even born then. You don't remember any of that. I should have realized. I'm turning into a forgetful old man. And very cantankerous, Thu-Kimnibol. Very cantankerous indeed."

Salaman grinned disarmingly, as though trying to deny his own words. But it was plain to see he was telling the truth. Cantankerous was what he had become, testy and sharp.

Time had brought changes to Salaman as well as to his city. Thu-Kimnibol remembered a Salaman from the early days who had been supple and resilient of mind, a clever and cunning planner, intelligent, far-seeing, a natural leader, an innately likable person. But then the changes had begun in him, that new Salaman emerging, darker, more crabbed of soul, a difficult and suspicious man. And now, twenty years later, the process was far along. The king seemed chilly and morose, gripped by some bitter malaise, or stained from within, perhaps, by the absolute power he had taken for himself here. You could see it in his face, drawn in upon itself, cheeks sunken, temples hollow, and in the taut, guarded way he carried himself. His fur had entirely whitened with age. There was a harsh wintry look about him.

The city he had created was like that too. Here were no broad sunny avenues, no brightly tiled towers against the blue of the sky, no green and leafy gardens, such as Thu-Kimnibol saw every day in airy Dawinno. The City of Yissou, penned within its crater-rim and its titanic rampart of heavy black stone, was a cramped, dismal place of narrow streets and low, thick-walled stone buildings with mere slits for windows. It looked more like a fortress than a city.

Was this what my father had in mind, Thu-Kimnibol wondered, when we left Vengiboneeza to found a city of our own? This dark, huddled, nasty town?

In the aftermath of the victory over the hjjks, on that sorry day when King Harruel had died fighting the insect hordes, Salaman had said, flushed with his new kingship, "We will call the city Harruel, in honor of him who was king before me." But later—by demand of the people, said Salaman, claiming that they preferred to honor the god who protected them rather than the man who had brought them to this place—he had restored the original name. Just as well, Thu-Kimnibol thought now. He wouldn't have wanted his father's name forever attached to so grim and cheerless a city as Salaman's City of Yissou.

Yet Salaman had managed to welcome him, at any rate, in an open-spirited and even cheerful way. He betrayed hardly a trace of recollection of the angry words that had passed between them long ago. Coming down from his walltop pavilion as Thu-Kimnibol's wagons passed through the great gate of the city, he had waited calmly with folded arms for Thu-Kimnibol to step forth, and then, his stern and rigid face softening un-expectedly into a smile, he strode forward, arms extended, hands reaching for Thu-Kimnibol's.

"Cousin! After so many years! What is this, do you return at last to take up your old life here, which was so suddenly interrupted?"

"No, king, I come only as an ambassador," Thu-Kimnibol replied evenly. "I have messages for you from Taniane, and other things to discuss with you. My place is in Dawinno, now." But he met Salaman's embrace with an embrace of his own, reaching down to encircle the king in his arms. There was some difficulty in it for him, but only because Salaman was so much shorter a man.

To Thu-Kimnibol's surprise, his heart did not resist the act of clasping Salaman to him, nor was there any insincerity in it. So it must be true, then: whatever grievance he had had against Salaman, or had thought he had, had burned away with time. The slights Salaman had visited upon him, or had seemed to visit upon him, when he was a young man, no longer mattered.

"We have our finest hostelry ready for you," said Salaman. "And after you're settled, a feast, eh? And then we'll talk. Not the official business, not so soon. Just a talk, between two who once were good friends. Eh, Thu-Kimnibol?"

Fair enough, and friendly enough, thought Thu-Kimnibol. He let them take him to his rooms. Esperasagiot went off to find stables for the xlendis, and Dumanka to see about housing for the ambassadorial entourage, and Simthala Honginda to meet with officials of the city and discuss the local rules of diplomatic courtesy.

It was only much later, in the huge dark stone-walled ceremonial hall of the palace, after the feasting and after too much wine, and after Thu-Kimnibol had presented the gifts he had brought with him for Salaman from Taniane, the fine white cloths and green-tinged porcelains, and the expensively bound volume of chronicles that Hresh had assembled, and also personal gifts of his own to the king, casks of wine from his own vineyards, pelts of rare animals from the far southlands, preserved fruits, and more—it was only then that tensions finally began to surface between Thu-Kimnibol and Salaman.

Perhaps it was the language problem, which had bothered him from the first, that caused him finally to flare up. Salaman, who spoke the pure Koshmar speech, seemed genuinely annoyed by the Beng words and intonations Thu-Kimnibol habitually used. Thu-Kimnibol hadn't realized how much the language of the People had changed in Dawinno since the union with the Bengs, how filled with Beng it had become. Salaman had never liked Bengs, ever since the golden-furred helmet-wearers had declined his invitation to settle in Yissou after being crowded out of Vengiboneeza by the Bengs, and had gone off to Hresh's new Dawinno instead. And apparently the grudge had never left him, if the mere sound of Beng phrases in Thu-Kimnibol's speech could so offend him.

Still, Thu-Kimnibol was taken by surprise, after an evening of drinking and entertainment, when Salaman suddenly said in a blunt way, as they lay comfortably sprawled side by side on ornate divans, "By the Five, I admire your gall! That you should come boldly dancing back to Yissou after the things you said to me the night you left."

Thu-Kimnibol stiffened. "They still rankle in you, do they? After all these years?"

"You said you'd throw me from the top of the wall. Eh? Eh? Have you forgotten that, Thu-Kimnibol? By the Five, I haven't! What do you think I made of your words, eh? Did I take them as pleasantries, do you think? Ah, no. No. The wall was much lower, then, but I took them to be a threat against my life. Which was correct, I think."

"I would never have done it."

"You *could* never have done it. Chham and Athimin were watching you the whole time. If you had laid a finger on me they'd have chopped you in pieces."

Thu-Kimnibol took a long drink of his wine: the sweet strong wine of the district, which he hadn't tasted in years. Over the top of the cup he glanced at the king. No one else was in the room but some of the evening's dancers, exhausted, who sprawled like discarded pillows along the far wall. Were Salaman's odious sons lurking behind the curtains, ready now to burst in and avenge the ancient slight he had given their father? Or would the dancers themselves suddenly come to life, with knives and strangling-cloths?

No. Salaman is simply playing games with him, he decided.

"You threatened me also," he said. "You told me I'd be stripped of all rank and perquisites, and sent to scrub slops in the marketplace."

"It was said in anger. If I'd had more of my brains about me, I'd have put a man of your size and strength to work on the wall, not in the market."

The king's eyes gleamed. He seemed immensely pleased by his own wit.

Best to ignore the insult. Thu-Kimnibol said only, "Why do you reawaken all this now, Salaman?"

Salaman smiled and stroked his chin. Long white tufts of hair sprouted from it now, giving him an oddly benign and almost comic appearance, probably not his intention. "We haven't spoken in—what, twenty years? Twenty-five? Shouldn't we at least try to clear the air between us?"

"Is that what you're doing? Clearing the air?"

"Of course. Do you think we can simply ignore what happened? Pretend it never took place?" Salaman refilled his wine glass, and Thu-Kimnibol's. He leaned across and stared at close range. In a low voice he asked, "Did you really want to be king in my place?"

"Never. I wanted only the honors due me as Harruel's son."

"They told me you meant to overthrow me."

"Who did?"

"What does that matter? They're all dead now. Ah, it was Bruikkos. Do you remember him? And Konya."

"Yes," Thu-Kimnibol said. "They came to resent me, when I was grown, because I had higher rank than they did. But what did they expect? They were only warriors. I was a king's son."

"And Minbain," Salaman said.

Thu-Kimnibol blinked. "My *mother*?"

"Ah, yes. She came to me, and said, 'Thu-Kimnibol is restless, Thu-Kimnibol is hungry for power.' She was afraid that you'd do something foolish and I would have to put you to death, which of course she would have regretted greatly. She said to me, 'Speak with him, Salaman, ease him, give him at least the pretense of what he wants, so that he'll do no harm to himself.' "

And the king smiled.

Thu-Kimnibol wondered how much of this was true, and how much simply some dark and devious amusement. Of course, Minbain might well have worried that her son would fatally overreach himself, and had taken steps to avert trouble. But that wouldn't have been much like her. She'd have spoken to me first, Thu-Kimnibol thought. Well, no way to ask her about it now.

"I'd never have tried to displace you, Salaman. Believe me. I took an oath to you: why would I break it? And I knew that I was too young and hotheaded to be a king, and you were too powerfully entrenched."

"I believe you."

"If you had given me the titles and honors I wanted, there'd never have been trouble between us. I tell you that truly, Salaman."

"Yes," the king said, in a suddenly altered voice, all anger and harshness gone from it. "It was a mistake, my treating you the way I did."

Instantly Thu-Kimnibol was on his guard.

"Are you serious?"

"I am always serious, Thu-Kimnibol."

"So you are. But do kings ever admit their mistakes?"

"This one sometimes does. Not often, but sometimes, yes. This is one such time." Salaman rose, stretched, laughed. "What I wanted was to goad you, to push you to your limit, to drive you out of Yissou. I thought you were too big for this city, too strong a rival, bound to grow even stronger as the years went on. That was my mistake. I should have cultivated you, honored you, disarmed you. And then put your strength to good use here. I saw that later, but it was too late. Well, you're welcome here again, cousin." Then an odd expression, half jovial, half suspicious, came into the king's eyes. "You haven't come here to seize my throne after all, have you?"

Thu-Kimnibol gave him a chilly look. But he managed a chuckle and a pale grin.

Salaman thrust out his hand. "Dear old friend. I should never have driven you off. I rejoice in your return, however brief it is." He yawned. "Shall we get some rest, now?"

"A good idea."

The king glanced at the sleeping dancers, who had not moved from their scattered places on the floor.

"Would you like one of these girls to warm your bed tonight?"

Again, a surprise. The thought of Naarinta, only a few weeks in the grave, came to him. But it was impolitic to refuse Salaman's hospitality. And what did it matter, one coupling more or less, this far from home? He was weary. He was on edge, after this strange conversation. A warm young body in his arms in the night, a bit of comfort before the real work began—well, why not? Why not? He didn't intend to remain chaste the rest of his life. "Yes," he said. "Yes, I think I would."

"What about this one?" Salaman prodded a girl with chestnut fur with his slippered toe. "Up, child. Up, up, wake up! You will be Prince Thu-Kimnibol's tonight!"

The king sauntered away, moving slowly, lurching just a little.

Without a word the girl gestured and led Thu-Kimnibol off to his draped and cushioned bedchamber in the rear of the palace. By the dim amber bedlight he studied her with interest. She was short, and looked strong, and was wide through the shoulders for a girl. Her chin was strong, her gray eyes were set far apart. It was a familiar face. A sudden wild suspicion grew in him.

"What's your name, girl?"

"Weiawala."

"Named for the king's mate, were you?"

"The king is my father, sir. He named me after the first of his mates, but actually I'm the daughter of his third. The lady Sinithista is my mother."

Yes. Yes. Salaman's daughter. That was what he thought. It was astounding. Salaman, who had refused him a daughter once to be his mate, giving him one now as a plaything for the night. A strangely casual gift; or did Salaman have some deep purpose in mind? Very likely the last merchant caravan from Dawinno had brought him word that Naarinta was close to death. But if he hoped to cement relations between Yissou and Dawinno by some sort of dynastic marriage, this was an odd way indeed of going about it. Then again, Salaman was odd. He must have many daughters by now: too many, perhaps.

No matter. The hour was late. The girl was here.

"Come closer, Weiawala," he said softly. "Beside me. Here. Yes. Here."

"He's preaching to the children," Curabayn Bangkea said. "My men follow him wherever he goes. They see what he does. He gathers the young ones to him, he answers all their questions, he tells them about life in the Nest. He says it's wrong to think of the hjjks as enemies. He spins fables for them about the Queen, and the great love She has for all creatures, not only creatures of Her own kind."

"And they swallow what he tells them?" Husathirn Mueri asked. "They believe him?"

"He's very persuasive."

They were in the reception-room of Husathirn Mueri's imposing house in the Koshmar district of the city, overlooking the bay. "Hard to imagine," Husathirn Mueri said. "That he's actually getting children to overcome their prejudice against hjjks. Children dread them. Always have. Great hideous hairy-legged bug-monsters, creeping stealthily around the countryside trying to grab little boys and girls—who wouldn't despise them? I did. You must have. I had nightmares about hjjks, when I was young. Sweats and screaming. Sometimes I still do."

"As do I," said Curabayn Bangkea.

"What's his secret, then?"

"He's very gentle. Very tender. They feel his innocence, and children respond to innocence. They like to be with him. He leads them in meditation, and little by little they join with him in chanting. I think he snares their minds somehow with the chanting. He does it so subtly they don't realize that what he's selling them is a pack of ugly monsters. When he talks of hjjks, they don't see real hjjks, I think. What they see is fairy-tale creatures, kindly and sweet. You can make any sort of monster seem sweet, your grace, if you tell the story the right way. And then the children are lost, once he's made them stop fearing and hating the hjjks. He's very clever, that boy. He reaches right into their minds and steals them from us."

"But he can barely speak our language!"

Curabayn Bangkea shook his head. "Not true. He isn't the uncouth wild man any more that he was when he first came here, not at all. Nialli Apuilana's done a tremendous job of teaching him. It's all come back to him. He must have known how to speak our language, you know, when he was young, before he was captured, and he's found it again, the words, everything. It never really goes from you, when you're born to it. He sits there—there's a park he likes to go to, and children meet him there—and he talks of Queen-love, Nest-bond, Thinker-thoughts, Queen-peace, all that filthy hjjk craziness. And they eat it up, your grace. At first they were disgusted by the thought that real people could live in the Nest and like it, that you could touch hjjks and they could touch you and it would somehow seem a loving thing. But by now they believe it. You should see them sitting there with their eyes shining as he pours out his spew."

"He's got to be stopped."

"I think so, yes."

"I'll talk with Hresh. No, with Taniane. For all I know, Hresh'll think it's utterly fascinating that Kundalimon's peddling stuff like Queen-love and Nest-bond to little boys and girls. He may applaud the idea. Probably he's interested in learning more about such things himself. But Taniane will know what to do. She'll want to find out what sort of creature it is that we've allowed into our midst, and what her daughter is spending so much time with, for that matter."

"There's another thing, your grace," said Curabayn Bangkea. "Perhaps you ought to know it before you talk with Taniane."

"And what is that?"

The guard-captain hesitated a moment. He looked unnerved. At length he said, quickly, with a flat intonation that twanged like an untuned lute, "Nialli Apuilana and the hjjk ambassador have become lovers."

It struck Husathirn Mueri with the force of a thunderbolt. He sat back, staggered, feeling a sudden ache in the pit of his stomach, a dryness in his throat, a harsh stabbing pain between his eyes.

"*What?* Coupling, are they?"

"Like monkeys in heat."

"You know this for a fact?"

"My brother Eluthayn was on guard duty at Mueri House until recently, you know. One day he passed outside the room of Kundalimon while she was with him. The sounds that he heard from in there—the thumpings, the gaspings, the passionate outcries—"

"And if she was teaching him kick-wrestling?"

"I don't think so, your grace."

"How can you be sure?"

"Because when Eluthayn reported this thing to me, your grace, I went to the door myself and listened. I tell you, I know the sounds of coupling from the sounds of kick-wrestling. I've done a little coupling myself, your grace. And some kick-wrestling too, for that matter."

"But she won't couple with anyone! That's well known all around town!"

"She's been in the Nest," Curabayn Bangkea said. "Perhaps she was only waiting for someone else with the flavor of hjjks all over his fur to come along."

Wild images leaped unbidden to Husathirn Mueri's mind, Kundalimon's hand between Nialli Apuilana's smooth thighs, Kundalimon's lips to her breasts, her eyes flickering with excitement and eagerness, their bodies coming together, their sensing-organs thrashing about, Nialli Apuilana turning to present her swollen sexual parts to him—

No. No. No. No.

"You're mistaken," he said, after a while. "They're doing something else in there. Whatever sounds you heard—"

"It wasn't the sounds, your grace."

"I don't understand."

"As you say, the evidence of the ears alone isn't enough. So I drilled a small observation hole in the wall of the room alongside his."

"You *spied* on her?"

"On him, your grace. On him. He was in my custody then, may I remind you. It was correct for me to ascertain the nature of his activities. I observed him. She was there. It wasn't kick-wrestling that they were doing, your grace. Not when he had his hands on her—"

"Enough."

"I can assure you—"

Husathirn Mueri held up his hand. "By Nakhaba, *enough, man!* I don't want to hear the sordid details." He struggled to calm himself. "I'll take it on faith," he said coldly, "that your report is accurate. Close your spy-hole and don't drill any new ones. Come to me daily with accounts of the ambassador's preachings among the young."

"And if I see him with Nialli Apuilana, your grace? In the street, I mean. Or in some public dining-hall. Or anywhere else, however innocent. Shall I tell you about that too?"

"Yes," said Husathirn Mueri. "Tell me about that too."

"I want to go into the Nest with you," Nialli Apuilana said. "To feel Nest-bond again. To speak Nest-truths."

"You will. When the time comes. When my work here is done."

"No. I mean here, today, now."

It was a quiet afternoon. The warm humid summer was over, and a strong autumn wind was blowing, hot but dry and crisp, out of the south. She and Kundalimon had coupled, and now they lay curled close together on his couch with limbs still entangled, grooming each other's rumpled fur.

He said, "Now? How can that be?"

She gave him a wary look. Had she misjudged the moment? Was twining, was any sort of soul-intimacy, still as frightening to him as it had been at the beginning? He had changed so much since he had begun going out by himself into the city. He seemed different now in so many ways, stronger, less tense, more assured of himself in his flesh-folk identity. But still she was uneasy about risking his trust by crossing the unspoken boundaries that had been established between them.

He seemed calm, though. He watched her with easy, gentle eyes.

Cautiously she said, "You can guide me through your Nest-memories. By the touching of minds."

"You mean the twining," he said.

She hesitated. "That would be one way. Or through using our second sight."

"You often speak of second sight. But I don't know what that is."

"A way of seeing—of perceiving the depths that lie beyond the surface of things—" Nialli Apuilana shook her head. "You've never felt yourself doing it? But everyone can do it. Young children, even. Although perhaps in the Nest, with no other flesh-folk minds around to show you what your own mind was capable of—"

"Show me now," he said.

"You won't be afraid when I touch you?"

"Show me."

He really has changed, she thought.

Still she was fearful of provoking fear in him, of forcing him away from her. But he had asked. He had asked. *Show me.* She summoned her second sight and sent it outward, expanding its field around him. He felt it. No doubt of that. She perceived his mind's instantaneous reaction, a startled drawing-back. And he was trembling. But he remained close beside her, open, accessible. There was no indication that he was putting up any of the usual defenses that one would put up against someone else's use of second sight. Was it simply that he didn't know how? No, no, he seemed to be accepting her probing willingly.

She took a deep breath and drove her expanded perceptions as deep into his mind as she dared.

And she saw the Nest.

Everything was blurred, indistinct, uncertain. Either his mental powers were still undeveloped, or he had learned some hjjk way of masking his mind. For what she saw in him she saw as though through many thicknesses of dark water.

It was the Nest, all right. She saw the dusky underground corridors, she saw the vaulted roofs. Dark figures moved about, hjjk-shaped, hjjk-rigid. But everything was vague. She couldn't distinguish castes. She couldn't even tell male from female, Military from Worker. And what was missing, above all else, was the spirit of the Nest, the dimension of soul-reality, the depth of Nest-bond that should envelop everything, the all-pervasive sweep of Queen-love flooding those dim subterranean aisles, the overriding imperative that was Egg-plan. There was no savor. There was no warmth. There was no nourishment. She was looking into the Nest and yet she remained cut off from it, an outsider, alone, lost in the cold realm of blackness that lies between the unfeeling stars.

In frustration, she probed a little deeper. No better. Then she felt a gentle push.

Kundalimon was trying to help her. Somehow he had discovered the font of his own second sight, which perhaps he had never used before, or had used without knowing what it was, and he was straining to amplify the vision for her. But even that couldn't entirely lift the veil. She saw more clearly, yes, but the new brightness merely brought new distortions.

Maddening. To come this close, and not get there—

A sob burst from her. She pulled her mind free of his and rolled away, to lie facing the wall.

"Nialli?"

"I'm sorry. I'll be all right in a moment." She wept silently. She felt more alone than ever before.

His hands caressed her back, her shoulders. "Did I do anything to upset you?"

"No. Nothing, Kundalimon."

"We went about it the wrong way, then?"

She shook her head. "I saw a little. Just a little. The edge of the outline of the Nest. It was all so shadowy. Unclear. Distant."

"I did it wrong. You will teach me the right way."

"It wasn't your fault. It—just didn't work."

There was silence for a while. He moved closer to her, covering her body with his. Then, suddenly, startlingly, he ran his sensing-organ along hers, a quick whispering touch that sent a shiver of keen sensation through her soul.

"We try the twining, you think?" he asked.

"Do you want to, Kundalimon?" She held her breath, waiting.

"You want to see the Nest."

"Yes. Yes, I do. So very much."

"Then maybe the twining."

"You were afraid, that other time."

"That was the other time." He laughed softly. "And there once was a time when you were afraid of coupling, I think."

She smiled. "Things change."

"Yes. Things change. Come. Show me the twining, and I'll show you the Nest. But you must turn toward me, first."

Nialli Apuilana nodded and swung around to face him. He was smiling, that wonderful open sunlit smile of his, a child's innocent smile in a man's face. His eyes gleamed into hers, bright, expectant, excited. He was beckoning to her in a way that he had never done before.

"I've twined only once," she said. "With Boldirinthe, almost four years ago. I may not be much better at it than you are."

"We will be fine," he said. "Show me what it is, this twining."

"First the sensing-organs, the contact. You focus everything, your entire being—" He began to look troubled. "No," she said. "Don't try to focus anything, don't even try to think. Just do as I do, and let things happen to you." She drew her sensing-organ close to his. He relaxed. He seemed completely trusting now.

They made contact. And held it.

Nialli Apuilana had never forgotten her hour of intimacy with Boldirinthe. The phases of it were clear in her mind, the way they had descended the ladder of perception that led to the deep realms of the soul where the communion took place. Kundalimon followed her readily. He seemed to know intuitively what to do, or else he discovered it as he went. In moments he was following her no longer, but was descending at her side, and even, at times, leading the way, down toward the dark mysterious depths where self was unknown and nothing existed but the unity of all souls.

They joined, then, in full twining.

His soul swept into hers, and hers into his, and at last she is back in the Nest.

The Nest of Nests, it is, the great one far in the north, not the subsidiary Nest where Nialli Apuilana had lived during her brief few months of captivity. In a sense all Nests were one, for Queen-presence infused them all; but she had known, even then, that her Nest was only a minor one in an outlying district of the hjjk domain, presided over by a subsidiary Queen. Where they are now is the heartspring of the nation, the core and hub of it, the great pivot, the axis of all. Here dwells the Queen of Queens.

Nothing about this place seems strange to Nialli Apuilana. It is where Kundalimon had spent most of the days of his life, flesh-folk boy among the hjjks, moving freely in their world, eating their food, breathing their air, thinking their thoughts, living as they lived. This was his home. And so it is her home also.

Hand in hand they float through it like wandering ghosts, unseen, undisturbed. She is Kundalimon, and he is Nialli Apuilana. He is she and she is he: no knowing where one leaves off and the other begins.

The great Nest is endless, a maze of warm dark galleries half hidden beneath the surface of the ground, stretching for leagues in all directions. The gentle glow of Nest-light comes from the walls, pink and soft, a dreamlight. On the easy currents of the air drifts the tingling sweet fragrance of Nest-breath, soft as fur, rich with the complex chemical messages that pass between the Nest's inhabitants. Here in these intricate labyrinths live millions of hjjks, and here too, in the deepest part, at the still point of this busy hive, at the center of everything, lies the quiescent immensity of the Queen of Queens, ancient, eternal, undying, vast, all-guiding, all-loving. Nialli Apuilana feels the presence of Her greatness now, rolling through every hall like the tolling of a giant gong. There is no escaping it. She encompasses all the Nest and all the subordinate Nests as well in Her overflowing outpouring of love. And then too over everything else there sweeps that even higher and more all-embracing force, which even the Queen Herself acknowledges as supreme, the great undeniable inescapable torrential energy that is Egg-plan, the fundamental power of life, the ineluctable universal femaleness that drives all existence endlessly forward.

Nialli Apuilana yields herself to that great song of perfection with utmost joy and ease. This is why she had yearned to come here: to feel once again the reassuring knowledge that the world has meaning and structure, to know once more that a shape, a design, an underlying purpose governs the bewildering workings of the cosmos.

"Here is Nest-truth," Kundalimon says to her, and she to him. "Here is Queen-light."

They drift onward, unhindered, here, there, everywhere.

Without a sound the myriad dwellers of the Nest go about their tasks. Each one knows its place, each its responsibility. That is Nest-bond: harmony, unity, pattern. Nothing like it exists in the chaotic random world outside; but nothing is chaotic or random here. A profound silence prevails in these corridors, and yet there is purposeful activity everywhere.

Here, bands of Militaries come trooping in from their latest forays, and Workers go to them to collect and clean their weapons, and to carry off for cleaning and storage the foodstuffs they have brought back. Here, in this place where the light is a dark purple, a smoldering smoky color, troops of Egg-layers rest in their stalls. Long lines of Life-kindlers move steadily past them, each pausing by this one or by that to perform the act of fertilization. Here, Nourishment-givers hover over eggs as they hatch, and bend to offer food to the newborn.

And here the Nest-thinkers hold forth, enclosed in gloomy narrow stalls, instructing the young who stand motionless before them in taut concentration. Here too are the Queen-attendants in their warm catacomb, preparing Her morning meal. Here are the Queen-guardians in close formation, arms linked tightly together, barring the way to the lower galleries where the royal chamber is. Here are processions of the young, males here, females there, awaiting their summons to the chamber, there to receive the gift of Queen-touch and be awakened to adulthood and fertility—or else to be set apart by a different designation, marked as a Warrior or a Worker or, perhaps, to become one of the chosen few, a Nest-thinker.

The royal chamber itself is the only area of the Nest that she and Kundalimon do not enter in this vision. They may not, not yet, for she was never granted First Audience in her earlier stay in the Nest, and Kundalimon cannot bring her before the Queen now, not even this way, in a vision, in a dream. That would have to wait until its proper time. When at last she would behold the Queen, vast and inscrutable, at rest in Her secret place at the heart of the Nest.

But everything else lies before them. Nialli Apuilana moves through it in wonder, in a rapture of Nest-love.

Nest-thinker says, "Here they are. The flesh-child, and the flesh-child's bride. Come, sit here with us, enter into Nest-truth with us."

So they aren't invisible to the Nest-dwellers after all. Of course not. How could they be?

She puts forth her hand, and a hard bristly claw takes it and holds it. Shining many-faceted blue-black eyes glow close by hers. Sweeping waves of force throb through her soul, the Nest-thinker's potent emanation.

Nest-thinker enters her spirit now and shows her the high Nest-truth, the one supreme unifying concept of the universe, the power that binds all things, which is Queen-peace. He shows her the great Pattern: the grandeur of Queen-love which embodies Egg-plan in order to bring Nest-plenty to all things. He fills her mind with it, as another Nest-thinker in another Nest had done once before, years ago.

And, as had happened before, the simplicity and force of what he tells her enters Nialli Apuilana's soul and takes possession of it, and she bows down to the unanswerable reality of it. She kneels there, sobbing in ecstasy, as the grand music of it roars through the channels and byways of her spirit. And gives herself up to it, in the fullest of surrenders.

She is in her true home again.

She will never leave it, now.

"Nialli?"

The sound of a voice, unexpected, numbingly intrusive. It fell upon her like a cascade of boulders roaring down an immeasurable slope.

"Nialli, are you all right?"

"No—yes—yes—"

"It's me, Kundalimon. Open your eyes. Open your eyes, Nialli!"

"They—are—open—"

"Please. Come back from the Nest. It's over, Nialli. Look: look, there's my window, there's the door, there's the courtyard down there."

She struggled. Why should she want to leave the place that was her home?

"Nest-thinker—Queen-presence—"

"Yes. I know."

He held her, stroked her, pulled her close against him. The warmth of him steadied her. She blinked a few times and her sight began to clear. She could make out the walls of his room, the little slit of a window, the clear, dazzling autumn light. She heard the sound of the dry rushing wind. Reluctantly she yielded to unanswerable reality. The Nest was gone. No Nest-light here, no Nest-scent. She could no longer feel the presence of the Queen. And yet, yet, the words of Nest-thinker still resonated through her spirit, and the powerful comfort she had taken from them still calmed and eased her soul.

She looked at him in sudden astonishment.

Kundalimon, she thought. I've twined with Kundalimon!

"Were you there with me?" Nialli Apuilana asked. "Did you feel it too?"

"All of it, yes."

"And we'll see it again, won't we? As often as we like."

"In visions, yes. And one day we'll see it as it really is. We will go to the Nest together, when the time comes. But for now, we have the visions."

"Yes," she said. She was trembling a little. "I knew we'd have to twine, if we wanted to see it together. And so we did. We did it very well."

"We are twining-partners now," he said.

"How do you know that term?"

"I learned it from you. Just now, while we lay twined together. I was in your soul while you were in mine." He smiled. "Twining-partners. Twining-partners. You and I."

"Yes." She looked at him tenderly. "Yes, we are."

"It is like coupling, but much deeper. Much closer."

Nialli Apuilana nodded. "Anyone can couple. But it's possible to achieve real twining only with a few. We're very lucky people."

"When we are in the Nest together, there will be much twining for us?"

"Yes. Oh, yes!"

"I will be ready to return to the Nest very soon now," he said.

"Yes."

"And you'll go with me when I leave here? We'll go together, you and I?"

She nodded eagerly. "Yes. I promise you that."

She looked toward the window. Out there all the city went about its varied occupations, her mother, her father, fat Boldirinthe, sly slippery Husathirn Mueri, filthy Curabayn Bangkea and his filthy brother, thousands of citizens moving along the hectic circles of their individual paths. And they were all blind to the truth. If they only knew, she thought. All of them, out there! But they had no idea what had happened in here. What sort of partnership had been forged in here, this day. What promises we have made. And will keep.

The first days of Thu-Kimnibol's visit had been the time for the entertainments, the dancers and the feastings and the lovemaking and the displays of kick-wrestling and fire-catching, and then the final exchange of gifts. Now it was time for business. Whatever thing it was that had brought him back to Yissou.

Salaman took his place on his great throne in the Hall of State. It was carved from a single immense teardrop-shaped block of glossy black obsidian streaked with flame-colored swirls, which he had unearthed long ago while digging in the heart of the original city. The Throne of Harruel, everyone called it: one of the few tributes the city paid to its first king. Salaman didn't mind that. A sop to the beloved founder's memory: why not? But Harruel had never so much as seen his supposed throne, let alone sat upon it.

People nowadays thought of Harruel, when they thought of him at all, as a great warrior, a wise far-seeing leader. A great warrior, certainly. But a leader? Wise? Salaman had his doubts about that. By now, though, scarcely anyone was still alive who remembered the true Harruel, that brooding drunkard, that beater and forcer of women, forever consumed by his own racking anguish of the spirit.

And here now was Harruel's son, come to Harruel's city to stand before the Throne of Harruel as Dawinno's ambassador to Harruel's successor. The great wheel turned, and in its turnings brought everything to everything. Why was he here? So far he had given no inkling. It had all gone smoothly up till now, at least. In the beginning Salaman had found Thu-Kimnibol's unexpected arrival ominous and oppressive: a mystery, a threat. But also it was an interesting challenge: can you still handle him, Salaman? Can you hold him in check?

The king said, gesturing amiably, "Will you be seated, Thu-Kimnibol?"

"If it pleases your majesty, I'm comfortable as I am."

"Whatever you prefer. Will you have wine?"

"After we speak, maybe. It's early in the day for me to be drinking."

Salaman wondered, not for the first time, whether Thu-Kimnibol was being shrewd or merely simple. The man was impossible to read. By choosing to remain standing, Thu-Kimnibol had, so it seemed, opted to dominate the room by sheer size and force; but had that been a deliberate choice, or, as he claimed, a matter of preference in comfort? And by refusing wine he had imposed a tension and a stiffness on the meeting that might work to his favor in any hard bargaining. Or was it just that drinking wasn't to his taste? The sons of drunkards often want to follow a different path.

The king felt the need of regaining the advantage that Thu-Kimnibol, by inadvertence or design, had taken from him so swiftly and easily. It was bad enough that he was so big. Salaman always felt uneasy in the presence of big men, not because he had any great regret at being short-legged himself, but because great slow lumbering fellows like Thu-Kimnibol made him feel overhasty and fevered in his motions, like some small scurrying animal. But aside from all that he could not allow Thu-Kimnibol the additional superiority of controlling the field of discussion.

"You know my sons?" Salaman asked, as the princes began to enter the hall and take their seats.

"I know Chham and Athimin, certainly. And Ganthiav I met when I arrived."

"This is Poukor. This is Biterulve. And these are Bruikkos and Char Mateh. My son Praheurt is too young to attend this meeting." The king spread his arms in a great curve, embracing them all. Let them surround Thu-Kimnibol. Let them engulf him. He may be big, but together we can outnumber him.

They lined the room, the seven princes, each of them a close copy of his father down to the cold gray eyes, the stockiness of frame—all but the one called Biterulve, rather less sturdy than the others, and pale of aspect, though he at least had the royal eyes. Salaman was pleased to see some shadow of dismay cross Thu-Kimnibol's face as these replicas of him assembled. An impressive phalanx, they were. They testified to the force of his spirit: when he coupled with a woman it was his seed that made the mark, his features and form that were born again. Anyone could see that in these sons of his. He was fiercely proud of it.

"A commendable legion you have here," Thu-Kimnibol said.

"Indeed. They are my great pride. Do you have sons, Thu-Kimnibol?"

"I was never blessed that way by Mueri. And am not likely to be, now. The lady Naarinta—" His voice trailed off. His face turned bleak.

Salaman felt a stab of shock. "Dead? No, cousin! Tell me it's not so!"

"You knew she was ill?"

"I heard something about it when the merchant caravan was last here. But they said there was some hope of her recovery."

Thu-Kimnibol shook his head. "She lingered all winter, and weakened in the spring. Not long before I set out for Yissou she died."

The somber words fell like stones into the room. Salaman was caught unprepared by them. They had managed so far this evening to be purely formal with each other, rigidly playing their official roles, king and ambassador, ambassador and king, like figures on a frieze, for the sake of keeping the troublesome past that lay between them from breaking through and disturbing the niceties of their diplomatic calculations. But now an unexpected moment of mortal reality had interposed itself. "A pity. A very great pity," Salaman said, after a moment, and sighed. "I prayed for her recovery, you know, when the merchants told me. And I grieve for you, cousin." He offered Thu-Kimnibol a look of genuine regret. Suddenly the tone of the meeting was altered. This man here, this looming giant, this ancient rival of his, this dangerous son of the dangerous Harruel: he was vulnerable, he had suffered. It became possible to see him as something other than a puzzling and annoying intruder, suddenly. He imagined Thu-Kimnibol at his lady's deathbed, imagined him clenching his fists and weeping, imagined him howling in rage as he himself had howled when his own first mate Weiawala had died. It made Thu-Kimnibol more real for him. And he remembered, then, how they had stood together, he and Thu-Kimnibol, at the battle against the hjjks, how Thu-Kimnibol, just a child then, still carrying his child-name, even, had fought like a hero that day. A great surge of liking and even love for this man, this man whom he had hated and had driven from his kingdom, flooded his soul. He leaned forward and said in a low hoarse tone, "No prince of your bearing should be without sons. You ought to choose another mate as soon as your mourning's over, cousin." Then, with a wink: "Or take two or three. That's how I've done it here."

"In Dawinno we still allow ourselves only one at a time, cousin," Thu-Kimnibol replied evenly. "We are very conservative that way." To Salaman it felt like a rebuke, and some of his good will toward Thu-Kimnibol evaporated as swiftly as it had come. Thu-Kimnibol shrugged and said, "For now the thought of choosing a new mate seems very strange to me. Time will take care of that, I suppose."

"Time takes care of everything," Salaman said elaborately, as though uttering oracular wisdom.

He could see that Thu-Kimnibol was growing impatient. Perhaps this talk of sons and mates was troubling to him. Or perhaps his impatience was yet another ploy. He had begun to pace about, stalking the vast room like some ponderous beast, striding past one row of princes, whirling, coming back past the other. Their eyes followed his every movement.

Abruptly Thu-Kimnibol settled on a divan close by the king and said, "Enough of this, cousin. Let me come to my business. Some months back a strange boy appeared in our city. A young man, rather. Riding out of the north, on a vermilion. Barely able to speak our language. Hjjk-noises were all he could manage, and maybe a People word or two. We couldn't figure out where he had come from or what he wanted or who he was, until Hresh, using the sort of tricks that only Hresh knows, went into his mind with the Wonderstone. And discovered that he was from our city in the first place: stolen, about thirteen years back. When he was just a child."

"Stolen by the hjjks, you mean?"

"Right. And raised by them in the Nest of Nests. And now they'd sent him back to us as an emissary, to offer us Queen-love and Queen-peace. So Hresh said."

"Ah," said Salaman. "We had one of those come to us a little time ago. A girl, she was. She'd spit and rant at us all day in hjjk. We couldn't make any sense out of it at all."

"She knew a few words of our language, father," Chham said.

"Yes. Yes, she did. She'd babble to us about the grandeur of the hjjk Queen, the high godly truth of Her ways. Or similar nonsense. We didn't pay much attention. How long ago was this, Chham?"

"It was Firstmonth, I think."

"Firstmonth, yes. And what finally happened? Ah: I remember. She tried to escape, wasn't it, and make her way back to the hjjks?"

"Yes," said Chham. "But Poukor caught up with her outside the wall and killed her."

"*Killed* her?" Thu-Kimnibol said, eyes wide, astonishment in his voice.

Thu-Kimnibol's show of seeming tenderness struck the king as amusing, even quaint in its sentimentality. Or did he mean it as another rebuke? Salaman wondered. He made a broad, imperiously sweeping gesture of his arms. "What else could we do? Obviously she was a spy. We couldn't let her go back to the Nest with everything she'd learned here."

"Why not simply bring her back into the city? Feed her, teach her how to speak the language. She'd have shed her hjjk ways sooner or later."

"Would she?" the king asked. "I doubt that very much. To look at her she was a girl of the People, but her soul was the soul of a hjjk. That wouldn't ever have changed. Once they get their poison into your head, you're never the same again. Especially when it happens young. No, cousin, before long she'd have escaped again and gotten back to them. Better to kill her than to let that happen. It's a terrible foulness, that a girl of the People should live in the Nest. Among those filthy creatures. The very thought of it sickens the gods themselves."

"So I'd say also. All the same, to butcher her that way—a girl, a young girl—" Thu-Kimnibol shrugged. "Well, it's no affair of mine. But I think she may not have been a spy. I think she was sent to you as an envoy, just as this Kundalimon—that's his name—was to us. Hresh says they were sent to all the Seven Cities, these envoys."

"Be that as it may. We're not interested in getting messages from the hjjks," said Salaman indifferently. "But of course Hresh would think otherwise. Does he happen to know why the Queen is sending these envoys around?"

"The Queen is offering us a treaty," Thu-Kimnibol said.

Salaman sat bolt upright. "A treaty? What kind of treaty?"

"A peace treaty, cousin. An imaginary line is to be drawn clear across the continent from Vengiboneeza to the eastern coast. The hjjks will promise never to come across that line into our territory without an invitation, provided, of course, that we don't go into any land of theirs. Our territory will be considered to be the region from the City of Yissou southward past Dawinno to the Southern Sea, or wherever it is that the land comes to its end. All the rest of the world is to be considered theirs, and is closed to us forever. Oh, yes, one other thing: we have to agree to let hjjk scholars live among us, so that they can teach us the truths of their religion and the wisdom of their way of life."

It sounded unreal. It was like something out of a dream.

Were they serious, the hjjks, proposing such an absurdity?

This was all so foolish that Salaman found himself suspecting some intricate trick on Taniane's part, or Thu-Kimnibol's. But no, no, that was just as foolish an idea.

"What a wonderful offer," he said, with a little laugh. "I assume that what you did was to have the ambassador skinned and send his hide back to the Queen with your answer written on it. That's what I would have done."

Thu-Kimnibol's eyes narrowed: that look of rebuke, again.

He thinks we're barbarians, Salaman thought.

"The boy's still in Dawinno. He's under guard, but being treated well. The chieftain's daughter herself brings him his food every day and is teaching him our language, which of course he's forgotten, having been a captive so many years."

"But this treaty? It's been rejected, naturally."

"Neither rejected nor accepted, cousin. Not yet. We've debated it in our high councils, but nothing's decided. Some of us are eager to sign it, because it would assure peace. These people believe you'd ratify it too, what with the hjjks of Vengiboneeza being so close to your northern boundary and you being so uneasy of the possibility of an invasion."

Amazed by that, Salaman said, with a snort of outrage, "They believe that? That I'd sign such a cowardly treaty?"

"Some do, cousin. I never imagined it myself."

"You're opposed to the treaty yourself."

"Of course. So is Hresh: he can't abide surrendering the unexplored parts of the world to the hjjks."

"And Taniane?"

"She hasn't said. But she despises the bugs. They grabbed her daughter a few years back, you know, and kept her for months. I thought Taniane would lose her mind. She's not likely to want to do business with the Queen. Especially if Hresh's already against the idea."

Salaman was silent. This was astounding stuff. He coiled himself back into the polished curving recesses of his throne, and let his eyes rove down the rows of his sons. Solemnly they returned his gaze, mirroring him in gravity and austere concern. Probably they didn't understand the half of what was at stake, he thought, but no matter. No matter. They'd grasp it soon enough.

It was hard for him to believe that Dawinno hadn't instantly flung the Queen's preposterous proposal back in Her face, if a face is what it could be called, without further ado. This so-called treaty was nothing more than a deed of perpetual surrender. And yet there were some down there who actually argued for signing it! Probably the Beng faction, Salaman supposed: the fat merchants, the comfortable politicians. Yes, appease the hjjks, go on living your own easy life in your own pleasant city of the balmy breezes, which in any case lies comfortably distant from the heart of the hjjk territory. They'd want that, yes. Regardless of the long-term risk. Regardless of the ultimate cost.

He said, after a bit, "What chance is there that the cowards will have their way and you'll sign the treaty?"

"That won't happen."

"No. I don't expect that it would. But I'll tell you what position I'll take if it did. If Dawinno wants to sign away its birthright to the hjjks, say I, well, so be it, but nothing that Dawinno signs is going to be binding on us. The City of Yissou will never recognize the authority of the hjjks in anything, so long as I live. Which goes for my sons as well."

"You needn't worry," said Thu-Kimnibol. "The hjjk treaty's a dead thing. That isn't what I came here to discuss with you."

"What is, then?"

"I'm here to propose an alliance, cousin. Dawinno and Yissou, joined together for a single purpose."

Salaman sat forward, grasping the sides of the throne. "And what would that purpose be, cousin?"

There was a strange new light in Thu-Kimnibol's dark chilly eyes. "To make war on the hjjks," he said, "and slaughter them like vermin."

The zoological garden, near sundown. It is the eve of the Festival of Dawinno, and everyone is getting ready for the games. All but Hresh, ever contrary. Alone he wanders among his animals, thinking that it's time to see what the minds of his caviandis are really like.

Sometimes, when he was younger, he would go about secretly trying to walk the way he imagined a sapphire-eyes would, slow and heavy, in an attempt to think like one. He remembers that now. Hold yourself like one, move like one, maybe you can make your mind work the way their minds worked. And also trying now and then to walk like a Dream-Dreamer, like a human, when no one was looking: pretending he was long and thin and skinny-shanked and had no sensing-organ. But the more he tried it, the more he felt like an ape. A monkey, even, just a jumped-up monkey. He would tell himself, then, that he was being too harsh on himself and on the People. We are much more than apes, very much more than monkeys. He still has to tell himself that once in a while. He's been telling himself that nearly all his life. Even believing it, most of the time. Look at the city, for example. Is Dawinno so trivial? Everything we've accomplished here: he knows it's a tremendous achievement. But sometimes when he sleeps Hresh dreams he's back in the cocoon, a scrawny boy again, kick-wrestling and cavern-soaring and hoping without much luck to sneak a peek at old Thaggoran's secret box of chronicles. That idle, empty, stagnant life. Living like animals, though we gave ourselves names, invented rites and ceremonies, even kept historical records. Why didn't we die of boredom? he often wonders. Spending seven hundred thousand years penned up in those little caverns, doing nothing in particular. No wonder we came erupting out building enormous cities and filling them with our young. All that lost time to make up. All those dark stifled years. Build, grow, discover, fight. Yes. And here we are. What good has it all done? All our ambitions. All our schemes. Our grand projects.

What good, the water-strider asked us once, when we wanted to know the way to Vengiboneeza? What good? What good? What good? All we are is furry monkeys playing at being human.

No. No. No. No.

We are the ones to whom the gods gave the world.

Time to walk like a caviandi, now. Time to find out what they're really like.

They've acclimated well to life in Hresh's little park. His workmen have diverted the stream that flowed through the garden so that it forks, and the left-hand branch of it now runs down the patch of sloping, uneven terrain that has become the caviandis' territory. Here, behind gossamer fences strong enough to hold back a vermilion, the two gentle beasts fish, sun themselves, patiently work at constructing a network of shallow subterranean tunnels flanking the stream on both sides. They seem to have recovered from the terror of their capture. Sometimes Hresh sees them sitting side by side on the great smooth pink rock above their nest, staring raptly at the rooftops and white walls of the residential district just beyond the park's boundaries, as though looking toward the palaces of some unattainable paradise.

He no longer doubts they're intelligent. It's the quality of that intelligence that he wants to measure. But first he has had to give them some time to get used to their captivity. They have to be calm, trusting, accessible, before he attempts any sort of deep contact with them.

He approaches them now. Entering their enclosure, he takes a seat on a rock next to the stream and waits for them to come close. The two sleek, slender, big-eyed purple beasts are at the other side, near the fence, standing upright as they often do. They seem curious about his presence. But still they hold back.

Gradually he activates his second sight at low level, letting the field of perception that it creates spread out in a sphere around him.

He feels the tingling warmth of contact. He senses the auras of their souls and perhaps the workings of their minds. But what he picks up is nothing more than a dull undercurrent, a vague uncertain throbbing of distant sentience.

Cautiously Hresh sharpens the focus.

This is nothing new to him, this experiencing of alien minds. Many of the creatures of the New Springtime are capable of thought, perhaps all of them. And could communicate with him, he suspects, if only he learned how to detect their emanations.

Over the years he has on occasions spoken, after a fashion, with goldentusks and xlendis and taggaboggas and vermilions. He remembers the clangorous mental voice of the water-strider, rising to its great height to mock the wandering folk of Koshmar's tribe as they searched for lost Vengiboneeza. And Young Hresh crouching behind a rock, listening by second sight to the bloodthirsty chanting of a pack of rat-wolves who spoke a dreadful howling language, the words of which were nevertheless unmistakably clear to him: *"Kill—kill—flesh—flesh!"*

He had even, once, when the tribe was only a few days out of the cocoon, heard with chilled fascination the dry buzzing silent mind-speech of a hjjk, greeting the tribe with cool scorn during a chance encounter in a bleak, chill meadow.

Everywhere in the world mind speaks to mind, creature hails creature in the voiceless speech of the spirit. It is not unusual. The world had long ago reached a time in the unfolding of its growth when such abilities were widespread. Virtually everything can speak, though some species have very little to say, and that little is often simple and dim.

But these caviandis now—standing there on their hind legs, their delicate hands outstretched, their whiskered snouts twitching thoughtfully, their dark luminous eyes warm and gleaming—Hresh suspects that they are extraordinary, that they are something more than mere beasts of the field—

He raises his sensing-organ, which intensifies the emanation that is coming from him. They don't draw back.

"I am Hresh," he says. "You have nothing to fear from me."

There is a stillness, an absence of contact. Then a whirling node of disturbance appears within the stillness, like a tiny red sun being born in the black shield of the heavens, and after a time the female caviandi says, in the silent voice of the mind, "I am She-Kanzi."

"I am He-Lokim," says the male.

Names! They have names! They have a sense of themselves as individual entities!

Hresh shivers with astonishment.

He has never found the concept of naming anywhere but among the People. The animals whose minds he has explored all seem to go nameless, as trees might, or rocks. Not even the hjjks use names, or so the story goes. They have no thought of themselves as individual beings separate from the mass of the Nest.

But here are She-Kanzi and He-Lokim proclaiming themselves to exist as their own selves. And the names, Hresh realizes almost at once, are more than mere labels. He comes to see that those two statements, "I am She-Kanzi," "I am He-Lokim," describe a whole cluster of complex things that he can barely comprehend, having to do with the two caviandis' relationship to each other, to the other creatures of their kind, to the world in general, and even, possibly, to the caviandi gods, if he understands the emanation rightly. He doubts that he does. He suspects that what he has taken from it is no more than a rough first approximation. But even that much is amazing.

The caviandis stand all but motionless, watching him. They seem tense. The elegant little fingers of their finely formed hands contract nervously and open again, over and over. Their whiskered snouts twitch. But their huge shining unblinking eyes are like deep pools of dark liquid, still, serene, unfathomable.

Hresh surrounds them now with his second sight, and they show their innerness to him more fully. Much is unclear. But he draws a vision from them of a peaceful, undemanding life, lived close to the fabric of nature.

They are not human, as he understands that concept: they have no wish to grow or expand in any way, to yearn, to reach outward, to achieve mastery over anything except their own little stream. Yet in their own way their minds are strong. To be aware of their own existence: that in itself puts them far beyond most of the animals of the wilderness. They have a sense of past and future. They have traditions. They have history.

And the scope of that history is surprising. The caviandis are aware of the ancientness of the world, the great long curving arc of time that lies behind all the beings of the New Springtime. They feel the pressure of the vanished epochs, the succession of the lost eras. They know that kings and emperors have come and gone, that great races have arisen and flourished and fallen and have been forgotten beyond hope of recall. They understand that these are the latter days upon a world that has suffered and been transformed and grown old, and now is young again.

Most keenly do they know of the Long Winter. It lives vividly in their souls. From their minds come images of the sky turning dark as the plummeting death-stars raise clouds of dust and smoke. Of snow, of hail of the burden of ice building up across the land. They show Hresh glimpses of ragged survivors of the early cataclysms trekking across the frozen land-scape, seeking places where they would be safe: caviandis, hjjks, even the People themselves, fleeing toward the cocoons where they will wait out the interminable eons of cold.

Hresh has long wondered how many of the wild creatures that he has collected to live in his garden have come down through the ages of the Long Winter. How could they have survived it unprotected? Surely most of the former species had perished with the Great World. There must have been a new creation as the Earth slowly turned warm again. Perhaps, he has thought, the rays of the returning sun engendered new creatures from the thawing soil—or, more likely, the gods had transformed the older, cold-resistant creatures into the new beasts of the Springtime. It was Da-winno's work.

But the caviandis are ancient, ancient as the People themselves.

The story is all there in the minds of these two, as though the memories are inborn, transmitted with the blood from mother to child. Cold winds sweeping across the Great World cities—the noble reptilian sapphire-eyes people waiting staunchly for their doom—the frail vegetal folk withering in the early blasts—the pale, hairless, mysterious humans now and again visible, moving calmly through the gathering chaos—

And the caviandis, adapting, burrowing into shallow tunnels, coming forth now and again to cut through the ice that covered their fishing-streams—

In wonder Hresh realizes that these creatures were able to survive the Long Winter outdoors, unprotected. While we hid ourselves away. While we cowered in holes in the rocks. And now, having lived on into the New Springtime, they find themselves hunted and slain and roasted for their meat by those who have come forth at long last from their hiding-places—or captured and put in pens, so that they could be studied—

Yet they hold no anger toward him, or toward his kind. That is, perhaps, the most amazing thing of all.

Hresh opens himself to them as fully as he can. He wants them to see his soul itself, and read it, and understand that there is no evil in it. He tries to make them realize that he has not brought them here to harm them, but only because he wishes to reach their spirits, which he could not have achieved in the wild lands where they lived. They can have their freedom whenever they want it, he tells them—this very day, even—now that he has learned what he had hoped to learn.

To this they are indifferent. They have their swift cool stream; they have their snug burrows; fish are plentiful here. They are content. How little they ask of life, really. And yet they have names. They know the history of the world. How strange they are, how simple, and yet so complex.

Now they seem to lose interest in him. Or else they are weary; for Hresh himself feels his energy running low, and knows he can't sustain the contact much longer. A grayness is sweeping over his mind. Fog enfolds him.

There is more he wants to learn from them, much more. But that will have to wait. This has been a fruitful enough beginning. He lets the contact slip away.

Dawn, now. The day of the Games of Dawinno, the annual celebration commemorating the founding of the city and honoring its tutelary god.

For the chieftain a busy day lay ahead. So were they all, all busy days; but this one would be busier than most, for today she faced a conflict of rituals. By coincidence the opening of the Festival and the Rite of the Hour of Nakhaba were both due to be celebrated this day, and she was required to be present at both of them, more or less simultaneously.

At sunrise she'd have to be at the Beng temple to light the candle marking the Hour of Nakhaba. Then she would have to make her way— on foot, no less, no palanquins allowed, humility before the gods!—all the way out to Koshmar Park to declare the Festival officially open. And then back to the Bengs by midday to make sure that Nakhaba had properly achieved his re-entry into the world, after his journey on high to see the Creator and discuss the problems of the world with Him. Off to the Festival of Dawinno again, then, to preside over the afternoon's round of athletic competitions.

All these gods! All these ceremonies!

In the simpler days long ago some of this would have fallen to Boldirinthe. But Boldirinthe was old and fat now, and turning a little silly, and in any event how could Boldirinthe preside over the Beng rite? To the Bengs she was nothing at all. Whatever authority the offering-woman had, it was confined entirely to those who still thought of themselves only as folk of the Koshmar tribe, and who clung to the old religion of the Five Heavenly Ones.

No, Taniane had to do the Hour of Nakhaba herself, not because she had a drop of Beng blood in her, or because she believed for a moment that Nakhaba existed or that he went on periodic trips to visit some still higher god far away, but because she was the head of the government here, who ruled over Koshmars and Bengs alike. Under the terms of the Act of Union she was in effect the successor to the whole long line of Beng chieftains. So Taniane would be there, at sunrise, to light the candle that sent the god of the Bengs on his way to the home of the Creator-god.

But first, there was this bothersome business with Husathirn Mueri—

He had sent a messenger to her late the night before, begging her for a private audience, telling her it couldn't be delayed even a single day. "A matter of the highest seriousness," he said. "Concerning the dangers to the city, and to herself, that certain activities of your daughter are creating. I can hardly underestimate the importance of these affairs."

Undoubtedly he couldn't. For Husathirn Mueri everything was a matter of the highest seriousness, especially if he saw something for himself in it. That was the way he was. All the same, Taniane didn't care to spurn him. He was too useful a man; and he had powerful connections with the Beng community on his father's side. If this concerned Nialli Apuilana—and if it really was serious, not just a ploy to enable him to get her attention—

She sent word that she would see him at her official residence, in the hour before dawn.

When she came downstairs in the morning Husathirn Mueri had already arrived and was pacing restlessly in the grand vestibule. The day was cool and overcast, with a light drizzle falling. He looked dapper and trim despite the rain. His thick black fur was impeccably groomed, and the white stripes that ran through it, so poignantly reminiscent of his mother Torlyri, stood out brilliantly.

He bowed elaborately as she entered, and made the sign of Dawinno at her, and for good measure wished her joy of Nakhaba's favor. That was bothersome, all that piety coming from him. It was no secret to her how little faith he had in any of the gods, be they Beng or Koshmar.

Impatiently she said, not troubling to make holy signs at him in return, "Well, what is it, Husathirn Mueri?"

"Shall we talk here? In the vestibule?"

"It's as good a place as any."

"I had hoped—someplace a little more secluded—"

Taniane cursed silently. "Come with me, then. Hresh has a little study just off this hallway."

A nervous look. "Will Hresh be there?"

"He gets up in the middle of the night and goes off to the House of Knowledge to play with his toys. Is this something Hresh isn't supposed to know?"

"I'll leave that to you to decide, lady," Husathirn Mueri said. "My sole interest is in sharing it with you, but if you think the chronicler should be informed, well—"

"All right," said Taniane. "Come." She was growing more annoyed by the moment. All this bowing and shuffling, and this making of signs to honor gods he didn't believe in, and these oily circumlocutions—

She led the way to the study and closed the door behind them. The place was a clutter of Hresh's pamphlets and manuscripts. Through the narrow window she saw that the drizzle was turning now to heavy rain. The Festival would be ruined. She could see herself standing up there in the chieftain's seat at the stadium, soaking wet, tossing down the smoldering sputtering torch that was supposed to inaugurate the races.

"So," she said. "Here we are. A secluded place."

"I have two things to report," said Husathirn Mueri. "The first comes to me from the guards of the justiciary, who have been keeping watch on the hjjk ambassador at my orders."

"You said this was about Nialli Apuilana."

"So it is. But I also said it concerns a danger to the city also. I'd prefer to tell you that part of it first, if I may."

"Well, go on, then."

"The ambassador, you know, wanders freely around the city every day. We were keeping him under house arrest, but at Nialli Apuilana's request it was lifted. And now he is corrupting the children, lady."

She stared at him. *"Corrupting?"*

"Spreading hjjk beliefs among them. He teaches them such concepts as Nest-truth, Queen-love, Nest-bond, Egg-plan. You know those terms?"

"I've heard them, yes. Everyone has. I don't really know what they mean."

"If you'd like to know, you could ask any child in the city. Especially the very young ones. Kundalimon preaches to them daily. Daily he fills their heads with this evil nonsense."

Taniane took a deep breath. "Are you sure of this?"

"He is very closely watched, lady."

"And the children—do they listen to him?"

"Lady, they listen and believe! Their whole attitude toward the hjjks is changing. They don't think of them the way the rest of us do, any longer. They don't see them as repulsive. They don't see them as evil. Talk to one of the children, lady, almost any child at all. You'll find out. Kundalimon's got them believing that the hjjks are deep and wise. Godlike, almost. Or at least creatures of some special high nature. He tells them how ancient the hjjks are, how important they were during the Great World days. You know how fascinated all children are by fables and tales of the Great World. And here he is, letting them know that people of one of the six Great World races still exist in our own time, and live in some fantastic underground castle far away, and want nothing more than to spread their loving wisdom among us—"

"Yes," Taniane said crisply. "I see the danger. But what does he mean to do? Lead all of our little ones out of the city like a piper playing a merry tune, and dance them across the hills and valleys to the Nest?"

"He might have that in mind, for all I know."

"And you say that Nialli Apuilana's involved in this? How?"

Husathirn Mueri leaned forward until his face was thrust practically into hers.

"Lady, she and the ambassador Kundalimon are lovers."

"Lovers?"

"You know that she goes to his room every day, lady. To bring him his food, to teach him our language."

"Yes. Yes, of course."

"Lady, sometimes she spends the entire night with him. My guards have heard sounds coming from the room that—forgive me, lady, forgive me!—can only be the sounds of coupling."

"Well, what of it?" Taniane flicked her hand through the air in an irritated gesture. "Coupling's a healthy thing. She's never been much interested in it. It's high time she developed a liking for it, and then some."

Husathirn Mueri's expression turned stark, as though Taniane had begun lopping off his fingers one by one.

"Lady—" he began feebly.

"Nialli's a grown woman. She can couple with anybody she pleases. Even the hjjk ambassador."

"Lady, they are twining also."

"What?" Taniane cried, caught by surprise. Twining was an altogether different matter. The thought of their souls fusing, of Kundalimon pouring feverish hjjk-fantasies into her daughter's mind, unstable as it was already from her experiences in captivity, stunned her. For a moment she felt herself swaying, as though her legs would give out beneath her and send her toppling to the pink marble floor. She fought to regain control of herself. "How could you possibly know that?" she asked.

"I have no proof, lady," said Husathirn Mueri huskily. "You understand that I have compunctions about spying on them. But the amount of time they spend together—the degree of intimacy—the fact that they have a common history of captivity among the hjjks—and also that they are unquestionably lovers already, and are of twining age—"

"You're only guessing, then."

"But guessing accurately, I think."

"Yes. Yes, I see what you mean."

Taniane glanced out the window. The rain was slackening again after the sudden severe downpour, and the sky was growing bright.

"Do you have instructions for me, lady?"

"Yes. Yes." Her throat was dry, her head was throbbing. Time to be on her way, time to appear at the Beng temple and perform the rite that would send Nakhaba off to the Creator's abode. The image of Nialli and Kundalimon twining blazed in her mind. She tried to push it away, and it would not go. Tautly she said, "Keep an eye on her, the way you've been doing. If you can find out what's actually going on between her and

Kundalimon, I want to know about it. But make sure she doesn't suspect she's being watched."

"Of course. And how should we handle the other part, the teaching of hjjk doctrines to small children?"

The chieftain turned to face him. "That has to be brought to a stop right away. We can't have him subverting the young. You understand what I'm saying? Brought to a stop."

"Yes, lady. I understand. I understand completely."

The drizzly dawn of the day of the Festival of Dawinno found Hresh at the House of Knowledge, making notes on his visit to the caviandis. Later in the day he would have to show himself at the Festival, take his seat beside Taniane in the place of honor, watch the city's young athletes go through their paces. To skip the games would be scandalous, and impious besides. The Festival had been his own invention, after all, many years ago, in homage to the clever and unpredictable god who was his special patron, and the city's. But he still had a few hours for getting some work done.

He heard sounds outside his half-open door. A light tapping, a gentle coughing.

"Father?"

"Nialli? Is it time to go to the games already?"

"It's still early. I wanted to talk to you before everything gets started." A pause. "I'm not alone."

Hresh squinted into the darkness. "Who's with you?"

"Kundalimon. We want to talk to you together."

"Ah." He pressed the palms of his hands against each other. "All right, come in, both of you."

They were damp from the rain, but the moisture, instead of soaking into their fur, seemed to cling in shining globules to the tips of it. And they were shining too. There was a radiance about them, a glow of rare joy. They stood before him holding hands like innocent children, brimming with evident happiness, overflowing with it.

Hresh felt an uneasy mixture of pleasure and anxious anticipation at the sight of them. He understood only too well that glow of inner fire that emanated from them both.

They giggled and glanced at each other, but neither spoke.

"Well?" Hresh said. "What have you two been up to?"

Nialli Apuilana turned away, sputtering smothered laughter into her shoulder. But Kundalimon stared levelly at him, smiling in that strange off-center way of his.

The boy no longer seemed like a wild creature. He had gained weight, and he looked far less unworldly, far less the eerie visitor from some unknown planet, more like any other young man of the city. There was new strength and assurance in him.

After a moment Nialli Apuilana said, "This isn't easy, father. I don't know where to begin."

"All right. Let me guess. I won't need the Barak Dayir for this. You and Kundalimon are lovers, eh?"

"Yes." Barely a whisper.

He felt no surprise at all. There had been something inevitable about it from the first, that these two should have come together.

She said, "And twining-partners too, father."

That too? He hadn't expected that, the deeper bond also. But he took it calmly enough. No wonder they were glowing!

"Twining-partners. Ah. Very good. Twining goes so far beyond coupling, you know. Surely you know that by now. Twining is the real communion."

"So we've found out, yes," Nialli Apuilana said. She moistened her lips. "Father—"

"Go on. Tell me the rest of it."

"Don't you know it already?"

"You want to become his mate?"

"More," she said.

He frowned. "More? What more is there?"

She made no reply. Instead she turned to Kundalimon, who said, "I will return to the Nest very soon. The Queen calls me. My work is done here. I ask Nialli Apuilana to go with me, to the Nest, to the Queen."

The quiet words went through Hresh like scythes.

"What?" he said. "The Nest?"

Earnestly Nialli Apuilana said, the words pouring out all in a rush, "You can't possibly know what it's like, father. No one does who hasn't been there. What sort of place it is, what sort of people they are. How rich their lives are, how deep. They live in an atmosphere of dreams, of magic, of wonder. You breathe the air of the Nest, and it fills your soul, and you can never be the same again, not after you've felt Nest-bond, not after you've understood Queen-love. It's so different from the way we live here. We lead such frightening *solitary* lives, father. Even with coupling. Even with twining. We're all alone, each of us, locked into our own heads, going through the meaningless round of our existences. But they see a vision of the world as a whole, as a unity, with purpose, and pattern, everything and everyone connected to everything else. Oh, father, everyone thinks of them as sinister evil bugs, as scurrying buzzing hateful machine-like things, but it isn't so, father, not at all, they aren't anything like what we imagine them to be! I want to go to them. I have to go to them. With Kundalimon. He and I belong together, and we belong . . . *there*."

Hresh stared at her, numb, stunned.

This too had probably been inevitable ever since her return from the Nest. He should have anticipated it. But he hadn't allowed himself to think about it. He hadn't allowed himself to see it.

"When?" he said, finally. "How soon?"

"A few days, a week, something like that. Kundalimon isn't quite finished here. He's teaching the children Nest-truth. Teaching them Queen-love. So that they'll understand, in a way that none of the older people possibly could. There's still more that he wants to tell them and show them. And then we'll go. But I didn't want simply to slip away without telling you. I can't tell Taniane—she'd never allow it, she'd clap me in prison to keep me from going—but you, well, you're different, you see everything so deeply, so profoundly—"

Hresh managed a smile, though shock waves still were rippling through him.

"What I see is that you've made me a co-conspirator in this, Nialli. If I speak of it to your mother, you'll never forgive me, is that correct?"

"But you won't speak of it to her, or anyone. I know that."

Hresh contemplated the pads of his fingers. Something cold and heavy was spreading within his chest. The full impact of Nialli's words only now was beginning to reach him: his daughter, his only child, was lost to him forever from this moment on, and there was nothing he could do about it, nothing at all.

"All right," he said, at length, hoping he could hide the sadness in his voice. "I'll keep quiet."

"I knew you would."

"But one thing you have to do for me before you go. Or else no deal, and Taniane finds out within the hour exactly what you two are up to."

Nialli was glowing again. "Anything you want, father. Just ask."

"I want you to tell me about the Nest. Describe the Queen to me, and tell me what Nest-bond is, and Queen-love, and all those other things. You've been keeping everything to yourself since you came back to live in the city. Do you know how eager I've been to know about them, Nialli? I couldn't force you, though. And you wouldn't open up, not for a moment. Now's the time. Tell me everything. I need to know. You're the only one who can teach me. And you will, as soon as the games are over today. That's the one thing I ask of you. Before you and Kundalimon go back to the Nest. Before you leave me forever."

Curabayn Bangkea was busily polishing his helmet in the little cell beside the Basilica that was his office when Husathirn Mueri appeared. The guard-captain's mood was somber, and had been for days. Nialli Apuilana haunted him, sleeping and waking. She danced for him in his dreams, naked, grinning, mocking him, hovering just out of reach. He longed for her in a way that he knew was an absurdity. She was beyond his reach in more ways than one, a woman of the city's highest nobility, and he nothing but an officer of the justiciary guard. He stood no chance. It was ridiculous. All the same, it was eating at his soul. There was a constant metallic taste in his throat, a pounding ache behind his rib cage, all from thinking of her. These idiotic fantasies, this miserable self-torment! And hopeless, absolutely hopeless. From time to time he would see her in the streets of the city, always at a distance, and she would glare balefully at him the way she might at some creature that had come wriggling up out of a sewer.

"There you are," Husathirn Mueri said, entering the room.

Curabayn Bangkea let his helmet fall clattering to the desk-top. "Your grace?" he said, almost barking it, coughing and blinking in surprise.

"Why such an ill-tempered look this morning, Curabayn Bangkea? Does the rain jangle you? Did you sleep poorly?"

"Very poorly, your grace. My dreams prick me awake, and then I lie there wishing I could sleep again; and when I sleep, the dreams return, no more soothing than before."

"You should go to a tavern," Husathirn Mueri said, with an amiable grin, "and drink yourself a good draught, and have yourself a good coupling or two, or three, and then another round of wine. And riot the night away without trying to sleep at all. That gets rid of sour dreams, I find. When the dawn comes you'll be a healthy man again. It'll be a long time before your dreams give you the soul-ache again."

"I thank your grace," said Curabayn Bangkea without warmth. "I'll put it under consideration."

He picked up his helmet and resumed buffing and glossing it, wondering if Husathirn Mueri had any true idea of what was troubling him. Everyone knew how hot Husathirn Mueri himself was for Nialli Apuilana—you had only to look at him when she was around, and you could tell—but did he realize that practically every man of the city felt the same way? Would it make him angry, knowing that a mere captain of the guards was just as obsessed with her as he was? Probably so. I'd do well to hide this from him, Curabayn Bangkea told himself.

Husathirn Mueri said, "You weren't at the temple for the Hour of Nakhaba this morning."

"No, sir. I'm on duty."

"Until when?"

"Midday, your grace."

"And then?"

"To the Festival, I thought. To watch the games."

Husathirn Mueri leaned close and smiled—an intimate, ingratiating sort of smile, a disturbing smile that signaled something unusual. In a soft voice he said, "I have a little work for you to do this afternoon."

"But the games, sir!"

"Don't worry. You'll get to go to the games afterward. But I need you, first. To do a little job for me, all right? Something that's vital to the security of the city. And you're the only one I'd trust to do it."

"Your grace?" Curabayn Bangkea said, mystified.

"The hjjk envoy," Husathirn Mueri said, perching himself casually on a corner of the guard-captain's desk. "Taniane knows now about his— activities. I mean his preaching, his corrupting of the children. She wants all that stopped as fast as possible."

"Stopped how, sir? By putting him back under house arrest?"

"More effectively than that."

"More effec—"

"You know what I'm saying."

Curabayn Bangkea stared. "I'm not sure I do. Let's be blunt, sir. Are you telling me to have him *killed?*"

Husathirn Mueri looked strangely serene. "The chieftain is deeply troubled by what's going on. She's ordered me to put an end to his sub-version of the children. To stop it right away, and to stop it for good. That should be clear enough."

"But to kill an ambassador—"

"There's no real need to keep using that word, is there?"

"But that's what you want. I'm right, aren't I? Aren't I?"

Husathirn Mueri said implacably, "The situation is critical. He's creating an enormous disturbance in the city. This is our responsibility, Curabayn Bangkea, and by all the gods we're going to deal with it responsibly."

Curabayn Bangkea nodded. He was beginning to feel like a leaf being swept along on a swiftly flowing stream.

Husathirn Mueri said, "You'll go to the games at the opening hour, and you'll make sure you're seen. Then you'll leave, and you'll make sure you *aren't* seen. You'll take care of the work that has to be done, and then you'll go back to the games, where I'll happen to run into you, and you'll come sit in my box where everyone can see you and we'll spend a little time together, just chatting, going over the highlights of the day's contests. No one will suspect you were mixed up in anything unusual while the games were going on."

He stared. "*I'll* take care of the work that has to be done, you say? You mean me, personally?"

"You and no one else. Taniane's explicit order. What's more, it's essential that we mustn't allow it to be traced back to her, or to me, for that matter. That would compromise the city leadership very seriously. Therefore you've got to do it, acting alone. Understand? And you have to forget it the moment it's done." Husathirn Mueri paused. "You'll be suitably rewarded, of course."

The only suitable reward, Curabayn Bangkea thought, would be the freedom to do as I please for a whole night with Nialli Apuilana. But they aren't going to give me that.

He felt a burst of anger. What did they think he was, an animal, a barbarian? He was the captain of the guards, the upholder of the law. Why pick him for this filthy business? Couldn't they have found some drifter in a tavern, who could be conveniently disposed of afterward?

I need you. You're the only one I'd trust to do it.

Well, maybe so. That softened it, the fact of being needed, of being specially chosen. A secret mission at the chieftain's specific request. Flattering, in a way. Unquestionably flattering. *The only one I'd trust.* A tavern drifter might bungle the job. Or might talk too much before getting it done. And this was official business, after all. Taniane's order: put an end to the subversion of the children. A critical situation, yes. A threat to law and order, the spreading of all this hjjk-love.

His annoyance subsided a little.

In any case he saw that he had no choice but to go along with it, like it or not. He was in this too deep already. He knew too much. Now he had to play the game out. Serve your masters loyally, rise to the top. Turn your back on them when they need you, and it'll be the finish for you.

"You aren't going to let us down, are you?" Husathirn Mueri asked, as if he had been using second sight on him.

"Not at all, your grace."

"What's troubling you, then?"

"I'd like to know a little more about the payment that's involved, if that's all right."

Smoothly Husathirn Mueri said, "This whole thing has come up so quickly that I haven't had time to work out the details. I'll be able to tell you that this afternoon, at the games. But one thing I promise you: it'll be suitable. More than suitable." The ingratiating smile again, soothing, conspiratorial: we're all in this together, and one hand washes the other. "You'll be well taken care of," Husathirn Mueri said. "You know you can trust me on that score. Can I count on you?"

I'd sooner trust in a rat-wolf, Curabayn Bangkea thought. But there was no turning back.

"Of course you can," he said.

Afterward, when Husathirn Mueri was gone, Curabayn Bangkea sat quietly for a time, letting the breath travel in and out of his body. He was past the first shock. His anger was gone, and he was beginning to see the benefits.

Not just the advantage that would accrue from carrying out a sensitive and secret mission for which he'd been specially selected, or the power that his part in the removal of Kundalimon would give him over Husathirn Mueri and even over Taniane. But also there was the killing itself, what it would accomplish. The clearing away of something infuriating, something unacceptable. If I can't have her, he thought, at least *he* won't either. It was pleasing to think about, the killing itself. To come up behind the man who had made himself Nialli Apuilana's lover—to seize him, to pull him into a dark corridor, to snuff the life from him—

That might just be the purgation he needed, freeing him from this torrent of impossible thoughts that tormented him. The obsession that had possessed him for so long. For days, now, nothing but Nialli Apuilana on his mind. Hardly any sleep, no rest at all. Nialli Apuilana and Kundalimon, Kundalimon and Nialli Apuilana. Feverish fantasies. Imagining her in that little room with the hjjk emissary, picturing him enfolding her in some weird caress he'd learned in the Nest, some bizarre scrabbling hjjk-like maneuver, vile and revolting. Bringing ecstatic gasps from her as she lay in his arms.

Very likely the reason why Husathirn Mueri wanted it done was connected with Nialli Apuilana, too—not the subversion of the children, why would Husathirn Mueri care a hjjk's turd about that, but the fact that the girl and Kundalimon were lovers. Doubtless Husathirn Mueri found that impossible to take. And had come to him, knowing that he'd be better able to manage the job than anyone else. Who'd suspect the guard-captain of such a crime? Who would even think of it?

He wondered what kind of payment he ought to ask for. He'd be in a strong negotiating position. One word from him and the city would explode with scandal: surely they realized that. He'd want exchange-units, certainly. A bushel of them. And a higher rank. And women—not Nialli Apuilana, of course, they could never deliver *her* to him, no one could, but there were other highborn women who were easier in their ways, and one of them—yes, they could let him have one of them, at least for a time.

Yes.

Everything took shape in Curabayn Bangkea's mind in a moment.

He rose, donned his helmet, finished his morning's chores. A wagon of the guard force took him to the stadium, then, and in a light downpour he watched the opening ceremonies and the first few competitions. Taniane presided, with Nialli Apuilana beside her. That made it much simpler for him, her being here instead of with Kundalimon. How beautiful she is, he thought. Her fur was soaked. Every curve of her body showed through. The chronicler Hresh was there with them in the chieftain's box, slumped down boredly as though he had no wish even to try to hide how bored he was. But Nialli Apuilana sat upright, bright-eyed, alert, chattering.

He stared at her as long as he could, and then he turned away. He couldn't stand to look at her for long. Too frustrating, too disturbing, all that unattainable beauty. The sight of her made his entrails churn.

After a time the rain let up once again. He left the stadium through one of the underground-level gates and went back into the center of the city. At this hour Kundalimon usually took his walk, down Mueri Way and into the park. Curabayn Bangkea was prepared. He waited at the mouth of a narrow alley in the shadows of the street just below Mueri House: ten minutes, fifteen, half an hour. The street was deserted. Almost everyone was at the games.

And there was the young man now, by himself.

"Kundalimon?" Curabayn Bangkea called softly.

"Who? What?"

"Over here. Nialli Apuilana sent me. With a token of love from her for you."

"I know you. You are Cura—"

"Right. Here, let me give it to you."

"She is at the games today. I thought I would go to her."

"Go to your Queen instead," Curabayn Bangkea said, and wrapped a silken strangling-cloth around Kundalimon's neck. The emissary struggled, kicking and using his elbows, but struggle was useless against Curabayn Bangkea's great strength. He drew the cloth tight. He imagined this man's hands on Nialli Apuilana's breasts, this man's lips covering her mouth, and his grip tightened. For a moment Kundalimon made harsh rough hjjk-noises, or perhaps they were merely death-rattles. His eyes bulged. His lips turned black, and his legs gave way. Curabayn Bangkea eased him to the ground and dragged him deeper into the alleyway. There he left him lying, propped up against the wall like a drunk. He wasn't breathing. Wrapping the strangling-cloth around his own wrist as though it were an ornament, Curabayn Bangkea returned to his wagon, which he had left three streets away. In half an hour more he was back at the stadium. He was surprised at how calm he felt. But it had all gone so smoothly: a very skillful job, no question of it, quick and clean. And good riddance. The city was cleaner now.

Husathirn Mueri was in one of the grand Presidium boxes near the center aisle. Curabayn Bangkea looked across to him, and nodded. It seemed to him that Husathirn Mueri smiled, but he wasn't sure of that.

He took his seat in the commoners' section, and waited to be invited to Husathirn Mueri's box.

The summons was a long time in coming. They had run the long race, and done the vaulting one, and were getting ready for the relays. But eventually a man Curabayn Bangkea recognized as a servant of Husathirn Mueri appeared. "Guard-captain?" he said.

"What is it?"

"Prince Husathirn Mueri sends me to you with his good wishes. He hopes you've been enjoying the games."

"Very much."

"The prince invites you to share a bowl of wine with him."

"It would be an honor," Curabayn Bangkea said.

After a time he realized that the man didn't seem to be leading him toward the central row of boxes where the aristos sat. Rather, he was taking him on some route around the far side, to the arched corridor that encircled the stadium.

Perhaps Husathirn Mueri had changed his mind, Curabayn Bangkea decided, about meeting with him in such a conspicuous place as his own box. Maybe he was afraid that the job had been botched, that there had been witnesses, that it wasn't such a good idea to be seen in public with him until he knew what had actually happened. Curabayn Bangkea felt his anger returning. Did they think he was such a bungler?

There was Husathirn Mueri now, coming along the corridor toward him. Stranger and stranger. Where were they supposed to share that bowl of wine? In one of the public wine-halls downstairs?

He's *ashamed* to be seen with me, Curabayn Bangkea thought, furious. That's all it is. A highborn like him doesn't ask a mere guardsman into his box. But then he shouldn't have told me he was going to. He shouldn't have told me.

Husathirn Mueri looked happy enough to see him, though. He was grinning broadly, as he might if he were going to a rendezvous with Nialli Apuilana.

"Curabayn Bangkea!" he called, from twenty paces away. "There you are! I'm so pleased we were able to find you in this madhouse!"

"Nakhaba favor you, your grace. Have you been enjoying the games?"

"The best ever, aren't they?" Husathirn Mueri was alongside him now. The servant who had led Curabayn Bangkea to him vanished like a grain of sand in a windstorm. Husathirn Mueri caught him by the arm in that intensely confidential way of his and said, under his breath, "Well?"

"Done. No one saw."

"Splendid. Splendid!"

"It couldn't have gone off better," said Curabayn Bangkea. "If you don't mind, your grace, I'd like to talk about the reward now, if I could."

"I have it here," Husathirn Mueri said. Curabayn Bangkea felt a sudden warmth at his side, and looked down at the smaller man in astonishment. The blade had entered so swiftly that Curabayn Bangkea had had no chance even to apprehend what was happening. There was blood in his mouth. His guts were ablaze. Pain was starting to spread through his entire body now. Husathirn Mueri smiled and leaned close, and there came a second stunning burst of warmth, and more pain, far more intense than before; and then Curabayn Bangkea was alone, clinging to the railing, sagging slowly to the ground.

5

By the Hand of the Transformer

To Hresh the games seemed endless. The crowd was roaring with excitement all about him, but he longed to be anywhere else, anywhere at all. Yet he knew there was no hope of leaving the stadium until the last race was run, the last weight was tossed. He would have to sit here, bored, wet, aching with the knowledge of irretrievable loss and struggling desperately to hide the pain that he felt. Nialli Apuilana sat beside him, completely caught up in what was going on down there on the field, cheering and shouting as each race was decided, just as though their conversation of the night before had never taken place. Just as though she was unable to realize that she had struck him in the heart, a blow from which he could never recover.

"Look there, father!" she said, pointing. "They're bringing out the cafalas!"

Yes, they were going to run the cafala race now, a comic event, each rider atop one of the plump short-legged beasts trying frantically to make his sluggish mount move forward against its will. It had always been one of Nialli Apuilana's favorites: so silly, so completely absurd. One of his little jokes, in fact. He was simply being playful when he had added a cafala race to the original roster of games. But the others had taken him seriously, had loved the idea, in fact; and now it was one of the high points of the day.

Hresh had never cared much for games himself, not even in his boyhood in the cocoon. Sometimes he had played at kick-wrestling and cavern-soaring with the others, but never with any enthusiasm. He had been too slight, too small, too strange for such things. Spending time with gray-furred old Thaggoran the chronicler had been more to his liking, or, once in a while, wandering by himself in the maze of ancient abandoned corridors beneath the main dwelling-chamber.

But games were important all the same. They provided amusement; they held the attention of the flighty; and, what was far more significant, they focused the spirit on divine matters—the quest for excellence, for perfection. And so he had devised this annual festival in Dawinno's honor, Dawinno being the god of death and destruction but also of mutability, of transformation, of inventiveness and wit, of a thousand channels of energy. And, having devised the games, he was stuck here whether he liked it or not, watching them to the end.

The rain came and went, now a faint misty drizzle, now a sharp slanting flurry. No one seemed to care. The stadium was covered only at its perimeter: the center sections, even the chieftain's box, lay open to the sky. Between showers, warm drying winds blew and sometimes the sun appeared, and that was comfort enough for onlookers and contestants alike. In their fascination with the games they paid no attention to the rain. Hresh, sodden and disconsolate, feeling no fascination, suspected he was the only one it bothered.

And now the cafalas were off and away waddling down the muddy track. Usually it was a Beng who won the cafala race. The Bengs, in their wanderings at the edge of hjjk country long before the Union, had found herds of wild cafalas and domesticated them for their meat and their thick wool. They had been the great cafala experts ever since.

But that was a Koshmar lad at the head of the pack, wasn't it? Yes. Yes. Jalmud, it was, one of Preyne's younger sons. Nialli Apuilana was standing, waving her arms frenetically, urging him on. "Go, Jalmud! Go! You can do it!"

The boy was sitting hunched well forward on his cafala, knees dug deep into the animal's rain-soaked bluish wool, his fingers tugging at its floppy, leathery black ears. And the dull-eyed flat-snouted cafala was responding heroically, chugging steadily forward, head bobbing, legs splaying wide. It was taking a good lead now.

"Jalmud! Jalmud!" Nialli Apuilana called. "Go! Beat those Bengs!" She was jumping about now, imitating the clumsy rhythm of the cafala, laughing as he hadn't heard her laugh in a long while. She seemed more like a young girl at her first cafala race than like a woman who would never see one again.

Hresh, watching her watching the race, felt a sharp pang of grief. He kept looking at her as if expecting her to vanish right then and there. But there was a little time yet. There were the things she had promised to tell him, first. About the Queen, about the Nest. She was one who kept her promises.

How soon would she leave? A few days, a week, a month?

She had always been an adventuresome child, ever inquisitive, ever eager to learn. Fondly Hresh saw her now as she had been when a little girl, bright-eyed and forever laughing, stumbling along beside him through the corridors of the House of Knowledge, bubbling with questions: What is this, Why is that?

No question of it: she would go. She saw it as the great adventure of her life, a grand quest, and nothing else mattered to her, nothing. Not father, not mother, not city. It was like a spell, an enchantment. It would be impossible for him to hold her back. He had seen the glow on her. She loved Kundalimon; and, Dawinno help her, she loved the Queen. The one love was natural and much to be praised. The other was beyond his understanding, but also, he knew, beyond his power to alter. Whatever had been done to her in the Nest while she was a captive there had changed her irreparably. And so she would go to the hjjks again; and, just as surely, this time she wouldn't return. She would never return. It seemed unreal to him: just a little while longer, and then he would lose her forever. But he was helpless. The only way to keep her here would be to lock her away like a common criminal.

"Jalmud!" Nialli Apuilana shrieks. She seems to be in ecstasy.

The race is over. Jalmud stands grinning at the altar of Dawinno accepting his wreath of victory. Handlers are trying to round up the wandering cafalas, which have gone straying in all directions.

A helmeted figure appears just then at the entrance to the chieftain's box, a thickset man wearing the sash of the guards of the judiciary. He inclines his head toward Taniane and says in a low voice, "Lady, I have to speak with you."

"Speak, then."

The guard glances uncertainly at Hresh, at Nialli Apuilana.

"For your ears alone, lady."

"Then whisper it."

The guard pushes his helmet back, leans forward, very close to her. "No," Taniane mutters harshly, when he has spoken only a few words. She puts both her hands to her throat for a moment. Then she begins to beat them against her thighs, angrily, in fierce agitation. Hresh, astonished, stares at her with amazement. Even the guard seems appalled at the effect the message has had on her, and he steps back, making the signs of all the gods with rapid, nervous gestures.

"What is it?" Hresh asks.

She shakes her head slowly. She is making holy signs too. "Yissou save us," she says in a strange hollow tone, repeating it several times.

"Mother?" Nialli Apuilana says.

Hresh catches Taniane by the forearm. "By the gods, Taniane, tell me what's happened!"

"Oh, Nialli, Nialli—"

"Mother, please!"

In a voice like a voice from the tomb Taniane says, "The boy who came to us from the hjjks—the emissary—"

In exasperation: "Mother, what is it? Is he all right?"

"He was found a little while ago in an alleyway down the street from Mueri House. Dead. Strangled."

"Gods!" Hresh cries.

He turns toward Nialli Apuilana, holding out his arms to comfort her. But he is too late. With a terrible cry of pain the girl turns and flees, bounding wildly over the side of the chieftain's box and rushing off into the crowd, shoving people out of her way with furious force as though they are no more than straws. In a moment she is out of sight. And an instant later a second guardsman comes chugging up, running as clumsily as a cafala, breathless, wild-eyed. He clutches the side of the chieftain's box with both hands, trying to make the world hold still beneath him. "Lady!" he blurts. "Lady, a murder in the stadium! The guard-captain, lady—the guard-captain—"

It was near midnight. The rain was over, and thick white mists rose from the ground everywhere, like phantoms of the dead issuing into the air. An impromptu meeting of the key members of the Presidium had been going on all evening—it had seemed the only thing to do—and they had discussed the murders interminably, going around and around, as if talking about them could bring back the dead. Finally Taniane had sent them all away, with nothing accomplished. Only Husathirn Mueri remained. She had asked him to stay behind.

The chieftain was at the edge of collapse. This day had been a thousand years long.

Not one murder but two. Violent death was all but unknown in the city. And on a single day, two of them, and the day of the Festival at that!

Giving Husathirn Mueri a cold, acrid look, she said, "I merely told you to stop him from preaching. Not to have him killed. What kind of beast are you, to have a man killed like that?"

"Lady, I didn't want him dead any more than you," said Husathirn Mueri hoarsely.

"Yet you sent that guard-captain of yours off to do it."

"No. I tell you no, lady." Husathirn Mueri looked as worn and ragged as she felt herself. His black fur was heavy with sweat, and the white stripes that ran through it were dulled by the day's grime. His amber eyes had the glassy gleam of extreme fatigue. He threw himself down on the stone bench facing her desk and said, "What I told Curabayn Bangkea was nothing more than you told me: that he had to shut him up, that he had to stop him from doing any more preaching. I didn't say anything about killing. If Curabayn Bangkea killed him, it was entirely his own idea."

"*If* Curabayn Bangkea killed him?"

"That can't ever be proven, can it?"

"The very strangling-cloth he used was wrapped around his wrist."

"No," Husathirn Mueri said wearily. "There was a strangling-cloth on him when he was found, I'll grant you. But many men of Curabayn Bangkea's sort carry strangling-cloths, more for ornament than anything else. That there was one around his wrist proves nothing. Nor can we be sure that it was the one that was used to kill Kundalimon. And even if it was, lady, there's always the possibility that whoever killed Kundalimon killed Curabayn Bangkea also, and then put the strangling-cloth on him to throw suspicion on him. Or let me give you yet another hypothesis: that Curabayn Bangkea had discovered the murderer, and had taken the strangling-cloth from him to offer as evidence, when he was killed. By the murderer's accomplice, perhaps."

"You have an abundance of hypotheses."

"It's the way my mind works," said Husathirn Mueri. "I can't help that."

"Indeed," Taniane said sourly.

What she longed to do was send forth her second sight and try to see just how deeply involved Husathirn Mueri actually had been in this miserable thing. It still seemed to her, knowing him as she did, that very likely he had deliberately chosen to interpret her orders as instructions to have Kundalimon removed. Kundalimon had been Husathirn Mueri's rival, after all, for Nialli Apuilana's affections. Had won those affections beyond question, actually. How convenient for Husathirn Mueri to misunderstand her words and send his creature Curabayn Bangkea off to murder him. And then to have the guard-captain murdered too, by way of silencing him.

It all fit together. And an aura of guilt seemed to hover like a dull stinking cloud of marsh-gas around Husathirn Mueri even as he sat here.

But Taniane couldn't simply go on a fact-finding expedition in his mind with her second sight. It would be a scandalous intrusion. It was beyond all propriety. She'd have to make a formal charge first, and call him to trial, for that. And if in fact he was innocent, she would have gained nothing for herself except an unalterable enemy, who happened to be one of the shrewdest and most powerful men in the city. That wasn't a risk worth taking.

Was it ever in my mind without my consciously knowing it, she wondered, to have Kundalimon done away with? And did I somehow convey that to Husathirn Mueri without fully realizing what I was asking?

No. No. No.

She hadn't ever meant the boy any harm. She wanted only to protect the children of the city against the madness of the hjjk-teachings that he was spreading. She was certain of that. To have ordered the death of her daughter's first and only lover—no, that had never been in her mind at all.

Where was Nialli now? No one had seen her since her disappearance from the stadium.

"You still suspect me?" Husathirn Mueri asked.

Taniane stared stonily at him. "I suspect everyone, except perhaps my mate and my daughter."

"What assurance can I give you, lady, that I had no part in the boy's death?"

Shrugging, she said, "Let it pass. But it was that underling of yours, that guard-captain, I think, who took it upon himself to have Kundalimon killed, or to kill him himself."

"Very likely so, I agree."

"How do we account for the killing of Curabayn Bangkea, though?"

Husathirn Mueri spread his hands wide. "I have no idea. Some rowdies at the games, maybe, catching him in a dark corner. With an old score that needed settling. He was captain of the guards, after all. He threw his weight around freely. He must have had enemies."

"But on the very same day of Kundalimon's murder—"

"A coincidence that only the gods could explain. Certainly I can't, lady. But the investigation will continue until we have the answer, if it takes a hundred years. Both deaths will be resolved. I promise you that."

"In a hundred years nothing of this will matter. What matters now is that an ambassador from the Queen of Queens has been murdered while in our city. While in the midst of treaty negotiations."

"And that troubles you, does it?"

"I don't want us getting embroiled in a war with the hjjks until we're ready for such a thing. Yissou only knows what goes on in the minds of hjjks, but if I were the Queen I'd regard killing Her ambassador as a very serious provocation indeed. An act of war, in fact. And we're very far from being ready to fight them."

"I agree," said Husathirn Mueri. "But this isn't any such provocation of that sort. Consider, lady." He ticked off the points on his fingers. "One: His embassy was finished. He had presented his message; that was all he was sent here to do. He wasn't a negotiator, just a messenger, and not even a very competent messenger. Two: He was a citizen of this very city, returning after a long absence brought about by his having been kidnapped. He wasn't the Queen's subject in any way. She had him only because Her people stole him from us. What claim could she have to him? Three: There's no sort of contact between Dawinno and the Nest, and therefore no reason to think they'll ever find out what became of him, assuming they care in the slightest. When we make our response to their treaty proposal, if we do, we're not obliged to say anything about where Kundalimon might happen to be at the moment. Or perhaps we won't reply to them at all. Four—"

"No!" Taniane snapped. "In Yissou's name, no more hypotheses! Doesn't your mind ever stop ticking, Husathirn Mueri?"

"Only when I sleep, perhaps."

"Then go to your bed, and I'll go to mine. You've convinced me. The killing of that boy isn't going to bring the hjjks down upon us. But there's a gaping wound in our commonwealth all the same, which can be healed only by finding these murderers."

"The one who killed Kundalimon, I do believe, is already dead himself."

"Then there's still at least one killer loose among us. I give you the job of finding him, Husathirn Mueri."

"I'll spare no effort, lady. You can count on that."

He bowed and left. She looked after him until he turned the corner of the hallway and was gone.

The day was over at last. Home, now. Hresh was already there, waiting for her. The news of Kundalimon's death had affected him more than she would have expected. Rarely had she seen him so distraught. And then, Nialli Apuilana—the girl had to be found, she had to be comforted—

A very long day indeed.

This is the deep tropical wilderness, where the air clings to your throat with every breath, and the ground is soft and resilient, like a moist sponge, beneath your feet. Nialli Apuilana has no idea how far she's come from the city in her flight. She has no clear idea of anything. Her mind is choked and congested by grief. No thoughts pass through it.

Where thought had been, there is only second sight now, operating in some automatic way, carrying information about her surroundings to her in dim pulsing pulsations. She is aware of the city far behind her, crouching on its hills like a huge many-tentacled monster made of stone and brick, sending out waves of cold baleful menace. She is aware of the swamps through which she is running, rich with hidden life both great and small. She is aware of the vastness of the continent that stretches before her. But nothing is clear, nothing is coherent. The only reality is the journey itself, the mad roaring need to run, and run, and run, and run.

A night and a day and a night and nearly another day have passed since she fled from Dawinno. She had ridden a xlendi part of the way, driving it furiously into the southern lakelands; but somewhere late on that first day she had paused to sip water at a stream, and the xlendi had wandered off, and she has gone on foot ever since. She scarcely ever stops, except to sleep, a few hours at a time. Whenever she does halt she collapses into a darkness that is the next thing to death, and when after a time it lifts from her she gets up and begins running once more, without goal, without direction. A fever is on her, so that she seems to be on fire everywhere, but it gives her strength. She is a molten thing, cutting a blazing path through this unknown domain. She eats fruits that she snatches from bushes as she runs. She stoops to pluck fungi with shining yellow caps from the ground, and crams them into her mouth without pausing. When thirst overcomes her she drinks any water she finds, fresh or still. Nothing matters. Flight is all.

Her body has long since slipped into that strange crystalline realm that lies beyond fatigue. She no longer feels the throbbings of her weary legs, no longer records the protests of her lungs or the pains that shoot upward through her back. She moves at a graceful lope, running swiftly in a kind of mindless serenity.

She must not allow her mind to regain awareness.

If it does, she will hear the lethal words again. *Found in an alleyway. Dead. Strangled.*

The vision of Kundalimon's slender body will come to her, twisted, rumpled, staring sightlessly toward the gray sky. His hands outstretched. His lips slightly apart.

Found in an alleyway.

Her lover. Kundalimon. Dead. Gone forever.

They would have gone north to the Queen together. Together they would have descended hand in hand into the Nest of Nests, down into that warm sweet-smelling mysterious realm beneath those distant plains. The song of Nest-bond would have engulfed their spirits. The pull of Queen-love would have dissolved all disharmonies in their souls. Dear ones would have come up to embrace them: Nest-thinkers, Egg-makers, Life-kindlers, Militaries, every caste gathering round to welcome the newcomers to their true home.

Dead. Strangled. My only one.

Nialli Apuilana had never known that love such as theirs had been could exist. And she knows that such love can never exist for her again. She wants nothing now but to join him in whatever place it is where he has gone.

She runs, seeing nothing, thinking nothing.

It is twilight again. Shadows deepen, falling across her like cloaks. Gentle warm rain falls, on and off. Thick golden mists rise from the moist earth. Thick soft woolly clouds spiral up around her and take the forms of the gods, who have no forms, and in whose existence she does not believe. They surround her, looming higher than the towering smooth-trunked vine-tangled trees, and they speak to her in voices that tumble downward to her ears in shimmering harmonics richer than any music she has ever heard.

"I am Dawinno, child. I take all things, and transform them to make them new, and bring them forth into the world again. Without me, there would be only unchanging rock."

"I am Friit. I bring healing and forgetfulness. Without me, there would be only pain."

"I am Emakkis, girl. I provide nourishment. Without me, life could not sustain itself."

"Me, child, I am Mueri. I am consolation. I am the love that abides and infuses. Without me, death would be the end of everything."

"And I am Yissou. I am the protector who shields from harm. Without me, life would be a valley of thorns and fangs."

Dead. Strangled. Found in an alleyway.

"There are no gods," Nialli Apuilana murmurs. "There is only the Queen, holding us in Her love. *She* is our comfort, and our protection, and our nourishment, and our healing, and our transformation."

In the deepening darkness, golden light encloses her. The jungle is ablaze with it. The lakes and pools and streams shimmer with it. Light pours from everything. The air, thick and torrid, swirls with the holy images of the Five Heavenly Ones. Nialli Apuilana holds her hand before her face to shield her eyes, so strong is that light. But then she lowers the hand, and lets the light come flooding upon her, and it is kind and loving. She draws new strength from it. She runs onward, deeper into that crystalline realm of tirelessness.

She hears the voices again. Dawinno. Friit. Emakkis. Mueri. Yissou. Destroyer. Healer. Provider. Consoler. Protector.

"The Queen," Nialli Apuilana murmurs. "Where is the Queen? Why does She not come to me now?"

"Ah, child, She is us, and we are She. Do you not see that?"

"You are the Queen?"

"The Queen is us."

She considers that.

Yes, she thinks. Yes, that is so.

She is able to think again, now. Her eyes are open. She can see the stars, she can see the many worlds, she can see the shining web of Queen-love binding the worlds together. And she knows that all is one, that there are no differences, no gradations, no partitions dividing one form of reality from another. She had not realized that before. But now she sees, she hears, she accepts.

"Do you see us, child? Do you hear us? Do you feel our presence? Do you know us?"

"Yes. Yes."

Shapes without form. Faces without features. Potent sonorities resonating through the descending shadows. Light, cascading from everything, coming from within. Density, strangeness, mystery. Godhood all about her. Beauty. Peace. Her mind is ablaze, but it is a cool white fire, burning away all dross. Out of the earth comes a roaring sound that fills all the sky, but it is a sweet roaring, enfolding her like a cloak. The Five Heavenly Ones are everywhere, and she is in their embrace.

"I understand," she whispers. "The Queen—the Creator—Nakhaba—the Five—all the same, all just different faces of the same thing—"

"Yes. Yes."

Night is coming on swiftly now. The heavy sky behind her is streaked with blue, with scarlet, with purple, with green. Ahead lies darkness. Lantern-trees are awakening into light. Creatures of the jungle show themselves everywhere, wings and necks and claws and scales and jaws shining on all sides of her.

She drops to her knees. She can go no farther. With the return of thought has come the reality of exhaustion. She digs her hands into the warm moist ground and clings to it.

But it seems for a moment, as she crouches there gasping and shivering in her great weariness, that she is alone once again, except for the creatures that screech and cackle and hiss and bellow all about her in the deepening night. She feels a tremor of fear. Where have the gods gone? Has she run so fast that she has left them behind?

No. She can still feel them. She need only open herself to them, and they are there.

"Here, child. I am Mueri. I will comfort you."

"I am Yissou. I will protect you."

"I am Emakkis. I will provide for you."

"I am Friit. I will heal you."

"I am Dawinno. I will transform you. I will transform you. I will transform you, child."

This was Thu-Kimnibol's fifth week in the City of Yissou. Real negotiations in the matter of the military alliance between Salaman and the City of Dawinno hadn't yet begun: only the preliminaries, and sketchy ones at that. Salaman seemed in no hurry. He side-stepped Thu-Kimnibol's attempts to get down to the harder issues. Instead the king kept him diverted with a constant round of feasts and celebrations as though he regarded him as a member of his own family; and the girl Weiawala shared his bed each night as if they were already betrothed. Very quickly he had come to accept and enjoy her eagerness, her passion. It had renewed his taste for life.

He was untroubled by the slow pace. It was giving the wound of Naarinta's death a chance to heal, this far from old and familiar associations. And there were even older associations here. In an odd way Thu-Kimnibol was pleased to be back in what was, after all, the city where he had spent the formative years of his life, from his third year to his nineteenth. Vengiboneeza, his birthplace, seemed like a dream to him, nothing more, and Dawinno, great as it was, somehow insubstantial and remote. His whole life there, his princely house and his mate and his pleasures and his friends, had faded until they rarely entered his mind any longer. Here, in the dark shadow of Salaman's bizarre titanic wall, in this dense dank claustrophobic warren of a city, he was beginning to feel somehow at home. That was surprising. He didn't understand it. He didn't even try. As for his mission, his embassy, the less hurry the better. An alliance of the sort he had in mind was best not forged in haste.

He went riding often in the hinterlands beyond the wall, usually with Esperasagiot and Dumanka and Simthala Honginda, sometimes with one or two of the king's older sons. It was the king who had suggested these excursions. "Your xlendis will want exercise," he said. "The streets of the city are too narrow and winding. The beasts won't have room in them for stretching their legs properly."

"What about the chance of running into hjjks out there?" Thu-Kimnibol asked. "I get the idea that they're crawling all over the place."

"If you stray very far to the northeast, yes. Otherwise you won't be bothered."

"Toward Vengiboneeza, you mean?"

"Right. That's where the filthy bugs are. A million of them, maybe. Ten million, for all I know. Vengiboneeza boils with them," Salaman said. "They infest it like fleas." He gave Thu-Kimnibol a cunning look. "But even if you do meet up with a few hjjks while you're out riding, what of it? You knew how to kill them once upon a time, so I recall."

"Very likely I still do," Thu-Kimnibol said quietly.

He was cautious outside the city, all the same. Usually he rode through the tame farming territories south of the city, and once or twice he and Esperasagiot went a short way into the unthreatening forests on the eastern side, but he never ventured toward the north. Not that the thought of running into hjjks troubled him much; and he cursed Salaman for that sly suggestion of cowardice. It would be good sport, slicing up a few hjjks. But he had a mission to carry out here, and getting himself killed in a brawl with the bugs would be worse than stupid: it would be irresponsible.

Then Salaman himself suggested that they go for a ride. And Thu-Kimnibol was surprised to see the king leading him toward the west, across a high plateau that gave way to a rough, ravine-crossed district where their xlendis were hard pressed to manage their footing. It was a troublesome broken region. Danger might be hiding anywhere. Salaman felt a need to test his guest's courage, perhaps. Or to demonstrate his own. Thu-Kimnibol kept his irritation out of view. "It was here," the king said, "that we destroyed the hjjks, the day of the great battle. Do you remember? You were so young."

"Old enough, cousin."

They stood a time, staring. Thu-Kimnibol was aware of the old memories, veiled as they were by time, stirring within him. First the hjjks thrown into confusion by that device of Hresh's, which sent their vermilions stampeding into those boulder-strewn gullies. And then the battle. How he had fought that day! Cutting them to pieces as they milled around in bewilderment! Six years old, was he? Something like that. But already twice the size of any child his age. With his own sword, and not a toy sword, either. The finest hour of his life: the child-warrior, the boy-swordsman, hacking and slashing with fury and zeal. The one and only time in his life, it was, that he had tasted the true joy of warfare. He longed to feel the wine of it on his lips again.

On his second ride with Salaman the king was even bolder; for this time he headed into the high wooded lands east and north of the city, precisely the region he had warned Thu-Kimnibol against, and kept on going for hours without turning back. As they proceeded on and on during the day, it began to seem to Thu-Kimnibol that Salaman might have it in mind to ride all the way to Vengiboneeza, or some such insanity. Of course that was impossible, a journey that would take weeks, and certain death at the end of it. But the hjjks were supposed to be plentiful to the northeast even this close to the city. If it was so risky to take this route, why had the king chosen it now?

They rode in silence, deep into the afternoon, along a lofty ridge that stretched as far as the eye could see. The countryside grew increasingly wild. Once a passage of bloodbirds briefly darkened the sky just overhead. On a hot sunny knoll a sinister congregation of the large pale insects called greenclaws, thick many-jointed things half the length of a man's body, moved slowly about in the warmth. Later they rode past a place where the ground was in turmoil as though a giant auger were turning beneath it, and, looking down, Thu-Kimnibol saw scarlet eyes huge as saucers looking back at him out of the soft tumbled soil, and great yellow teeth clacking together.

At last they halted in a quiet grassy open place atop a high point along the ridge. The sky was deepening in color. It had the color of strong wine now. Thu-Kimnibol stared eastward, into the gathering shadows. Vengiboneeza was somewhere out there, far beyond the range of sight. He barely remembered it, only scattered scraps and bits, the image of a tower, the cobbled pavement of a great boulevard, the high sweep of a vast plaza. That gleaming ancient city, thick with ghosts. And its million hjjks, swarming furiously in their hive. How the place must reek of them!

After a time Thu-Kimnibol thought that he could see figures, angular and alien, moving about in the shallow canyon below the ridge, very far off.

"Hjjks," he said. "Do you see them?"

They were very small at this distance, hardly more than specks, yellow banded with black.

Salaman narrowed his eyes, stared closely. "Yes, by Yissou! One, two, three, four—"

"And a fifth one, on the ground. With its belly in the air."

"Your eyes are younger than mine. But yes, I can make them out now. You see how near to Yissou they venture? Forever prowling closer and closer." He took a closer look. "The two large ones are females. Warriors, they are. Among hjjks it's the females who are stronger. Escorting the other three somewhere, I suppose. A team of spies. The one on the ground's badly hurt, by the looks of it. Or dead. Either way, they'll be feasting in a little while."

"Feasting?"

"On the dead one. They waste nothing, the hjjks. Didn't you know that? Not even their own dead."

Thu-Kimnibol laughed at the monstrous grisliness of the idea. But then, reconsidering, he felt himself shuddering. Could Salaman be serious? Yes, yes, apparently he was. Indeed, the quartet of distant hjjks seemed to be crouching over the body of the fallen one now, methodically pulling it apart, wresting its limbs from it and splitting them open to get at whatever meat they might contain. He watched in horror, unable to look away. Disgust made his skin crawl, his guts writhe. The busy claws, the avid beaks, the steady, diligent, efficient process of feeding—how loathsome, how hateful they were—

"Are they cannibals, then? Do they murder one another for their flesh?"

"Cannibals, yes. They see nothing wrong with eating their own dead. A thrifty folk, they are. But murderers, no. Killing their own kind is a sin they don't seem to practice, cousin. My guess is that this one ran into something even nastier than itself. Yissou knows there's danger all over the place in this open country, wild beasts of a hundred sorts."

"Thrifty, you say!" Thu-Kimnibol spat. "Demons is what they are! We should exterminate them to the last one!"

"Ah, you think so, cousin?"

"I do."

Salaman smiled broadly. "Well, then we think alike. I thought you'd find this ride instructive. Do you see what we face here, now? Why my wall, which I know you all find so amusing, is of the size that it is? We journey just a short way from the city, and there they are, committing their abominations right in front of our eyes, and not caring in the slightest that we're watching."

Thu-Kimnibol glared. Something throbbed in his forehead. "We should go down there and kill them as they eat. Two of us, four of them—those aren't bad odds."

"There may be a hundred more behind those trees. Do you want to be their next meal, cousin?" The king tugged at Thu-Kimnibol's arm. "Come. The sun has gone down, and we're far from the city. We should turn back, I think."

But Thu-Kimnibol was unable to take his eyes from the grim scene in the canyon below.

"A vision comes to me as I stand here," he said softly. "I see an army, thousands of us, riding out across this land. From your city and ours, and all the small settlements between. Traveling swiftly, striking quickly, slaughtering every hjjk we find. Going right on without stopping, right into the heart of the great Nest, right into the Queen's own hiding-place. A lightning strike that they won't be able to withstand, no matter how many of them there are. The Queen is their strength. Kill Her and they're helpless, and we'll be able to wipe the rest of them out at our ease. What do you say, Salaman? Isn't that a wondrous vision?"

The king nodded. He looked pleased. "We think alike, cousin. We think alike! Do you know how long I've waited for someone from Dawinno to say such things to me? I had almost given up hope."

"You never considered launching the war on your own?"

What might have been annoyance awoke in the king's eyes for a moment. "There aren't enough of us, cousin. It would be certain disaster. Your city, once it took in all those Bengs—that's where the troops I need are. But what chance is there that I'd get them? Your city's too comfortable, Thu-Kimnibol. Dawinno's not a city of warriors. Yourself excepted, of course."

"Perhaps you underestimate us, cousin."

Salaman shrugged. "The Bengs were warriors once, when they were wanderers in the plains. But even they've grown fat and easy down there in the warm southlands. They don't remember how much grief the hjjks gave them long ago. Dawinno's too far from hjjk territory for anyone down there to care about them. How often do you see hjjks roaming as close to your city as these are to ours? Once every three years? We live with their presence every day. Among you there's some little flurry of anger when a child is stolen, and then the child comes back, or is forgotten, and everything is as it was before."

Tightly Thu-Kimnibol said, "You make me think my mission's pointless, cousin. You tell me to my face that I speak for a nation of cowards."

There has been a sudden shift in mood. The two men stare at each other in a way that is very much less friendly than it was only a little while before. The rebuke hangs in the air between them for a long silent moment. Down below, the feast is still going on: harsh sounds, sounds of rending and crunching, drift upward on the cool evening air.

Salaman says, "It was weeks ago that you said you're here to propose an alliance, that Dawinno wants to join forces with us and make war against the hjjks. Exterminate them like vermin, that's what you said you'd like to do. Fine. Excellent. And now you put forth this pretty vision of our two armies joining and marching north. Splendid, cousin. But forgive me if I'm skeptical. I know what people are like in Dawinno. Alliance or no alliance, how can I be sure that your people will actually come up here and fight? What I want is a guarantee that you can deliver the army of Dawinno to me. Can you give me that guarantee, Thu-Kimnibol?"

"I think I can."

"Think-you-can isn't good enough. Take another look down there, cousin. See them gnawing and grinding their comrade's flesh. Can you make your people see what you see now? Those are hjjks, just a few hours' ride from my city. Every year there are more of them. Every year they get a little closer." Salaman laughs bitterly. "What does it matter to the people of Dawinno that the hjjks are camped on our doorstep, eh? It's the flesh of *our* sons and daughters, not theirs, that they'll be feeding on one of these days, eh, cousin? Do they realize, down south, that when the hjjks are through here, they'll go on to pounce on Dawinno? Their appetites can't be checked. They'll go south, sure as anything. If not right away, then twenty, thirty, fifty years from now. Are your people capable of looking that far ahead?"

"Some of us are. Which is why I'm here."

"Yes. This famous alliance. But when I ask you if Dawinno will really fight, you give me no answer."

Salaman's eyes are bright with fierce energy, now. They drill remorselessly into Thu-Kimnibol's. Thu-Kimnibol's head is beginning to ache. Diplomatic lies are on the tip of his tongue, but he forces them back. This is the moment for utter honesty. That too can sometimes be a useful tool.

Bluntly he says, "You must have good spies in Dawinno, cousin."

"They do a decent job. How strong is your peace faction, will you tell me?"

"Not strong enough to get anywhere."

"So you actually think your people will go to war against the hjjks when the time comes?"

"I do."

"What if you overestimate them?"

"What if you underestimate them?" Thu-Kimnibol asks. He stares down at the king from his great height atop his xlendi. "They'll fight. I give you my own guarantee on that, cousin. One way or another, I'll bring you an army." He points with a jabbing finger into the canyon. "I'll find a way of making them see what I see now. I'll wake them up and turn them into fighters. You have my pledge on that."

A disheartening look of continuing skepticism flickers across Salaman's face. But almost immediately other things seem to be mixed into it: eagerness, hope, a willingness to believe. Then the whole mixture vanishes and the king's expression once more becomes guarded, stony, gruff.

"This needs further discussion," he says. "Not here. Not now. Come. Or we'll be riding back in the dark."

Darkness was indeed upon them by the time they reached the city. Torches blazed atop the wall, and when Salaman's son Chham rode out from the eastern gate to greet them the look of anxiety on his face was unmistakable.

The king laughed it away. "I took our cousin out toward Vengiboneeza, so that he could smell the breeze that blows from that direction. But we were never in danger."

"The Protector be thanked," Chham exclaimed.

Then, turning to Thu-Kimnibol: "There's a messenger here from your city, lord prince. He says he's been riding day and night, and it must be true, for the xlendi he arrived on was so worn out it looked more dead than alive."

Thu-Kimnibol frowned. "Where is he now?"

Chham nodded toward the gate. "Waiting in your chamber, lord prince."

The messenger was a Beng, one of the guardsmen of the justiciary, a younger brother of the guard-captain Curabayn Bangkea. Thu-Kimnibol recalled having seen him on duty at the Basilica now and then. Eluthayn was his name, and he looked ragged and worn indeed, a thin shadow of himself, close to the point of breaking down from fatigue. It was all he could do to stammer out his message. Which was a startling one indeed.

Salaman came to him a little while afterward.

"You look troubled, cousin. The news must be bad."

"Suddenly there seems to be an epidemic of murder in my city."

"Murder?"

"During our holy festival, no less. Two killings. One was the captain of our city guard, the older brother of this messenger. The other was the boy the hjiks sent to us carrying the terms of the treaty they were offering."

"The hjik envoy? Who'd kill him? What for?"

"Who can say?" Thu-Kimnibol shook his head. "The boy was harmless, or so it seemed to me. The other one—well, he was a fool, but if simply being a fool is reason to be murdered, the streets would run red with blood. There's no sense to any of this." He frowned and went to the window, and stared off into the shadowy courtyard for a time. Then he turned toward Salaman. "We may have to break off our negotiations."

"You've been recalled, have you?"

"The messenger said nothing about that. But with things like this going on there—"

"Things like what? A couple of murders?" Salaman chuckled. "An epidemic, you call that?"

"You may have five killings here every day, cousin. But we aren't used to such things."

"Nor are we. But two killings hardly seems—"

"The guard-captain. The envoy. A messenger racing all this way to tell me. Why is that? Does Taniane think the hjjks will retaliate? Maybe that's it—maybe they think there might be trouble, maybe even a hjjk raid on Dawinno—"

"We killed the envoy that was sent to us, cousin, and we never heard a thing about it. You people are too excitable, that's the problem." Salaman stretched a hand toward Thu-Kimnibol. "If you haven't been officially recalled, stay right where you are, that's my advice. Taniane and her Presidium can take care of this murder business without you. We have work of our own to do here, and it's barely only begun. Stay in Yissou, cousin. That's what I think."

Thu-Kimnibol nodded. "You're right. What's been happening in Dawinno is no affair of mine. And we have work to do."

Alone in his chambers atop the House of Knowledge in the early hours of the night, Hresh tries to come to terms with it all. Two days have gone by since Nialli Apuilana's disappearance. Taniane is convinced that she is somewhere close at hand, that she's gone into seclusion until her grief has burned itself out. Squadrons of guardsmen are at work combing the city for her, and the outlying districts.

But no one has seen her. And Hresh is convinced that no one will.

She has fled to the Queen: of that he's sure. If she reaches them safely, he thought, she'll spend the rest of her life among them. A citizen of the Nest of Nests, that's what she'll be. If she thinks of her native city at all, it'll be only to curse it as the place where the man she loved was murdered. It's the hjjks that she loves now. It's the hjjks, Hresh tells himself, to whom she belongs. But why? Why?

What power do they have over her? What spell did they use to pull her toward them?

He feels baffled and impotent. These events have all but paralyzed him. Thought has become an immense effort. His soul seems to be encased in ice. The murders—when had there last been a violent death in Dawinno? And Nialli Apuilana's disappearance—he must try to think—to think—

Someone had said yesterday that a girl riding a xlendi had been seen that rainy afternoon, out by the perimeter of the city. Seen only at a distance, just at a distance. There were plenty of girls in the city, plenty of xlendis. But suppose it had been Nialli. How far could she get, alone, unarmed, not knowing the route? Was she lost and close to death somewhere out there in the empty plains? Or had bands of hjjks been waiting to receive her and lead her onward to the Nest of Nests?

You can't possibly know what it's like, father. They live in an atmosphere of dreams, of magic, of wonder. You breathe the air of the Nest, and it fills your soul, and you can never be the same again, not after you've felt Nest-bond, not after you've understood Nest-love.

She had promised to explain all that to him before she left. But there hadn't been time, and now she is gone. And he still understands nothing, nothing at all. Nest-bond? Nest-love? Dreams? Magic? Wonder?

He glances toward the huge heavy casket of the chronicles. He has spent his lifetime ransacking the hodgepodge of ancient half-cryptic documents in that casket. His predecessors had copied and recopied those tattered books, and copied them again, during the hundreds of thousands of years in the cocoon. Ever since he was a child staring over Thaggoran's shoulder, he has looked to the chronicles as an inexhaustible well of knowledge.

He opens the seals and the locks and begins to draw the volumes forth and lay them out one by one on the work-tables of polished white stone that encircle the room.

Here is the Book of the Long Winter, with its tales of the coming of the death-stars. Here is the Book of the Cocoon, which tells how Lord Fanigole and Balilirion and Lady Theel led the People to safety in the time of cold and darkness. Here is the Book of the Way, containing prophecies of the New Springtime and the glorious role the People would play when they came forth again into the world. And this is the Book of the Coming Forth, which Hresh himself had written, except for the first few pages which Thaggoran who was chronicler before him had done: it tells of the winter's end, and the return of the warmth, and the venturing of the tribe into the open plains at last.

This one is the Book of the Beasts, which describes all the animals that once had been. The Book of Hours and Days, telling of the workings of the world and the larger cosmos. This one here, with its binding hanging all in faded scraps, is the Book of the Cities, in which the names of all the capitals of the Great World are inscribed.

And these three: how sad they are! The Book of the Unhappy Dawn, the Book of the Wrongful Glow, the Book of the Cold Awakening, three pitiful tales of times when some chieftain, believing in error that the Long Winter was over, had led the People from the cocoon, only to be driven swiftly back by the icy blasts of unforgiving winds.

Concerning the hjjks, all he finds are old familiar phrases. *In the dry northlands, where the hjjks dwell in their great Nest,* or, *And in that year the hjjks did march across the land in very great number, devouring all that lay in their path,* or, *That was the season when the great Queen of the hjjk-folk despatched a horde of her people to the City of Thisthissima, and another vast horde to Tham.* Mere chronicle-phrases, no real information in them.

He keeps rummaging. These books down here at the bottom have no names. They are the most ancient of all, mere elliptical fragments, written in a kind of writing so old that Hresh can perceive only the edge of its meanings. Great World texts is what they are, poems, perhaps, or dramatic works, or holy scriptures, or quite possibly all three things at once. When he touches the tips of his fingers to them, their frail vellum pages come alive with images of that glorious civilization that the death-stars had destroyed, of that splendid era when the Six Peoples had walked the glowing streets of the grand cities; but everything is murky, mysterious, deceptive, as though seen in a dream. He puts them back. He closes the casket.

Useless. The Book of the Hjjks, that's what he needs. But he knows there's no such thing.

"Three days," said Taniane bleakly. "I want to know where she is. I want to know what kind of insanity came over her."

Fury and frustration were churning her soul fearfully on this bright, windy autumn day. She hadn't slept. Her eyes were rough and raw. She felt chills and shakes. And yet she couldn't slow down. Restlessly she prowled the stone-floored chamber at the rear of the Basilica that she had turned into the command center for the search for Nialli Apuilana, and for the investigations of the two murders as well.

Behind her, tacked helter-skelter to a wall-board, were documents by the dozens—statements of citizens who claimed to have seen Nialli Apuilana on the fateful afternoon, wild third-hand tales of supposed murder plots overheard in taverns, vague and tentative reports from the city guards on their investigations thus far. None of it was worth a thing. She knew no more than she had on the first afternoon, which was nothing at all.

"You have to try to be calm," Boldirinthe said.

"Calm! Yes." Taniane laughed bitterly. "Yes, of course. Above all else I must try to be calm. Two killings, and my daughter nowhere to be found, hiding in some cellar, maybe, or more likely dead, and you want me to be calm!"

They were all staring at her. The room was full of important people just then. Hresh was there, suddenly haggard and old, and Chomrik Hamadel, the keeper of the Beng talismans, and Husathirn Mueri, and the Beng justiciar Puit Kjai, and the acting captain of the guards.

"Why would you think she's dead?" Puit Kjai asked.

"What if it's a general conspiracy? Murder the hjjk ambassador, murder the captain of the guards, murder the chieftain's daughter, perhaps the chieftain herself, next—"

They were staring and staring. She saw by their expressions that they had begun to think she had cracked under the strain. They might be right about that.

Softly Boldirinthe said, "Nialli Apuilana hasn't been murdered, Taniane. She's alive and she'll be found. I've asked the Five Heavenly Ones, and they tell me that she is safe, that she is well, that she is—"

"The Five!" Taniane said. Almost a shriek, it was. "You've asked the Five! We should ask Nakhaba too, I suppose. Ask all the gods we know, and some that we don't. And the Queen of the hjjks—perhaps we ought to consult Her also—"

"Perhaps that wouldn't be such a bad idea," said Hresh.

Taniane glanced at him in astonishment. "This isn't any time for being facetious."

"You were being facetious. I'm serious."

"What are you talking about, Hresh?"

Diffidently he said, "It's something that's best discussed between you and me only, I think. Concerning the hjjks. And Nialli."

Her hand moved in impatient circles. "If it involves the security of the city, it ought to be brought out into the open right here and now. Unless you feel Puit Kjai is unworthy of hearing it, or Husathirn Mueri, or Boldirinthe—"

He looked at her strangely. "It involves our daughter, and where I think she has gone, and why."

"Then it's a security matter. Out with it, Hresh!"

"Since you insist." Hresh sighed. But he was silent until she prodded him with a quick imperious gesture. "They were going to run off to the Nest," he said then, bringing the words out with difficulty. "Nialli and Kundalimon. To the Nest of Nests, the great one where the Queen lives, in the far north. You know they were lovers, and twining-partners also. And they wanted no part of life in this city, neither of them. The Nest drew them like a magnet. They came to me and babbled about Nest-bond, about Queen-love, dreams and magic, how the sweet air of the Nest fills one's soul and transforms you forever—"

His words were blades. Taniane pressed her hand to her heart. He was right that this should never have been poured out in front of all these others. It was family business, scandalous, mortifying. But too late now.

"They told you this?" Taniane said leadenly.

"Yes."

"When?"

"The day before the games. They came to me to ask my blessing."

Taniane said, incredulous, "You knew they were going to leave, and you kept it to yourself?"

His expression darkened. In a thin voice he said, "As I told you before, we'd have done better discussing this in private. But you insisted, remember. I kept what Nialli had told me to myself, Taniane, because I knew you'd have tried to stop her from going."

"Which you had no objection to?"

"What was I to do? Order them thrown into prison? Even that wouldn't have accomplished anything. You know the girl. Nothing stops her. She's like a force of nature. She told me her plans out of love, so that I'd understand it when she disappeared. She knew I wouldn't take any steps to prevent her."

Taniane shook her head in disbelief. At Hresh's stupidity, at Nialli Apuilana's willfulness. And at her own idiocy in pushing her into Kundalimon's arms. No, not idiocy. It had been for the good of the city. There were things she had needed to learn, and only Nialli Apuilana could have discovered them for her. She would do it all again.

"So you think that's where she's gone? To the Nest?"

"To the Nest, yes. The Nest of Nests."

"Even though Kundalimon is dead?"

"*Because* Kundalimon is dead," Hresh said. "She sees the Nest as a place of love and wisdom. When she heard he was dead, she went running to the hjjks to take refuge."

The room was terribly silent.

Taniane trembled with rage and disbelief. "But it would take months, or years, even, to get to them. Who knows how far it is to the great Nest? How could Nialli even think of trying to do it alone?" For a moment she felt herself teetering on the brink. It was too much. Hresh's perfidy, Nialli Apuilana's madness. And now a room full of wide-eyed faces and gaping mouths, everyone too amazed to speak. Pitying her. Perhaps feeling contempt for her, even. Pretends to rule the city, can't even control her own daughter. No. No. She wasn't going to let this overwhelm her. Fiercely she said, "You're talking foolishness, Hresh. The girl may have been crazed with love, and maybe even some sort of hjjk insanity that the boy poured into her. But she wouldn't ever have been crazy enough to go off on a trip like that by herself. Not Nialli. No, Hresh. I still think she's in the city somewhere. Hiding, like a wounded animal. Until she gets over her grief."

"Dawinno grant that you're right," Hresh said.

"You don't think I am?"

"I saw her with Kundalimon the day before she vanished. I talked with her. I know how she felt about him. And about the hjjks."

Angrily Taniane said, "Then you look for her your way, and I'll look for her mine. You're the one with the powers. If you think she's heading for the hjjks, send your wonderful mind after her, and track her down, and talk her into coming home, if you can. Meanwhile I'll keep my guardsmen out searching for her." She looked toward Husathirn Mueri, who was in charge of the murder investigations, and to Chevkija Aim, the young Beng who was the acting captain of the guards. "I want reports every four hours, day and night. Understood? The girl's someplace nearby. She has to be. Find her. This has gone on long enough."

Husathirn Mueri, slick and smooth as ever, smiled as though she had asked for nothing more than an extra copy of some routine report. In his most resonant way he declared, "Lady, I'm confident we'll have her back by nightfall. Or by tomorrow at the latest. I feel sure of it. By all the gods, I'm sure of it!"

And moved his head in a slow half-circle, looking around the room at each of the others in turn, as if defying them to contradict him. With a flourish he requested permission to withdraw and get about his task.

Taniane nodded. It was time to get away from this room herself. Her shoulders quivered. She realized suddenly that she was at the end of her endurance, on the verge of tumbling down in a sobbing heap. That was new, this weakness. She battled to control herself. She couldn't let herself break down in front of these people, whose conflicting ambitions she had held in check so long by strength, by guile, and, when necessary, by sheer force of will. Force of will was what she needed now. But she felt so weak—so drained of the power that had always been hers—

There was someone beside her, then. She heard heavy wheezing breaths. She felt soft arms, warm comforting flesh.

Boldirinthe. The enormous bulk of the offering-woman enfolded her in a steadying embrace.

"Come with me," Boldirinthe said gently. "You need to rest now. Come. We'll pray together. The gods will watch over Nialli Apuilana. Come with me, Taniane."

I could pray to Dawinno, Hresh tells himself. But he doubts it would do any good. It was Dawinno, after all, who had taken Nialli Apuilana away—not Dawinno the Destroyer, but Dawinno the Transformer, the god in his higher manifestation. Dawinno seems to want her to live with the hjjks. That was why the god had allowed her to be taken the first time, so that they could fill her mind with love for them. And now he has sent her to them again. If that is what Dawinno wants—Blessed be Dawinno! Who can know his ways?—then no amount of prayer is going to bring her back.

The girl has been swept from him by the hand of the Transformer, who has uses of his own for her that go beyond mere mortal understanding.

After a time Hresh's hand reaches for the little amulet that dangles against his breastbone, the one that he took from the body of old Thaggoran when the rat-wolves killed him in the frosty plains, long ago, just a few days after the tribe had left the cocoon. It is an oval bit of what might have been polished green glass, obviously ancient, with inscriptions in its center so faint and fine that no one can make them out. Thaggoran had said it was a Great World thing. Hresh has worn it almost constantly ever since Thaggoran's death.

He touches it now, fondling its smooth worn surface. It has no real power that he had ever been able to discover. But it was a thing of Thaggoran's; and in those first days when Hresh became chronicler he had touched the amulet often, hoping desperately that Thaggoran's wisdom would descend from it to him. And perhaps it has.

"Thaggoran?" he says, looking into the dimness of the darkened room atop the House of Knowledge. "Can you hear me now, wherever you are? It's me, Hresh."

There is silence, a silence so profound that it roars. It deepens into a stillness deeper even than any silence could be: not only the absence of any sound, but the absence even of the possibility of it. And then a murmur as of a gentle wind comes drifting in. There is a lightness in the air, a barely perceptible glow.

Hresh feels a presence entering the chamber. It seems to him that he can see gaunt grizzled bent-backed old Thaggoran before him, eyes red-rimmed and rheumy with age, his fur pure white.

"You," Hresh says. "You, here, old man?"

"Yes. Of course. What is it, child?"

"Help me," Hresh says softly. "Just this one last time."

"Why, child, I thought you always insisted only on doing things by yourself!"

"Not now. Not any longer. Help me, Thaggoran."

"If that is what you need, yes. But wait a moment. Look there, boy. There, by the door."

There is that all-consuming roaring silence again, and then the even deeper stillness once more, and another gradual ghostly stirring in the darkness beyond the door; and then the sound of soft wind once more. A second figure has come in, just as grizzled, just as frail with age, or even more so: Hresh's other great mentor, it is, the wise man of the Helmet People, Noum om Beng, who in the Vengiboneeza days had ordered him to call him "father," and had taught him deep wisdom by means of oblique questions and sudden unexpected slaps in the face.

"So you're here too, father?"

A tall gaunt figure, flimsy as a water-strider: who can it be but Noum om Beng? He nods to Thaggoran, who offers him a salute as one would to an old comrade, even though in life they had never met. They whisper together, shaking their heads and smiling knowingly, as if discussing their wayward pupil Hresh and saying to each other, "What will we do with him? The boy is so promising, and yet he can be so dense!"

Hresh smiles. To these two he would always be an unruly boy, though by now he is as old and grizzled as they, and the last tinge of color will soon be gone from his own whitening fur.

"Why do you call us?" asks Noum om Beng.

"The hjjks have taken my daughter once again," he tells the two half-visible spectral figures who stand side by side in the shadows at the far side of the room. "The first time, they simply seized her and carried her off. She was able to escape from them, then. But now I fear something far worse. It's her spirit they've captured."

They are silent. But he feels their benign presence, sustaining him, nourishing him.

"Oh, Thaggoran, oh, father, how frightened I am, how sad and weary—"

"Nonsense!" Noum om Beng snaps.

"Nonsense, yes. You have ways, boy," comes Thaggoran's hoarse wispy voice. "You know that you do! The shinestones, Hresh. Now is the time at last to make use of them."

"The shinestones? But—"

"And then the Barak Dayir," comes the thin whisper of Noum om Beng. "Try that, too."

"But first the shinestones. The shinestones, first."

"Yes," Hresh says. "The shinestones."

He crosses the room. With quivering hands he draws the little talismans from their place of safekeeping. The shinestones are still mysteries to him after all these years. Thaggoran had died before he had any chance to tell Hresh how they were used.

Tools of divination is what they are, that much he knows: natural crystals, found deep in the Earth beneath the cocoon. They can be used in some way to focus one's second sight and provide glimpses of things that could not be seen by ordinary methods.

Carefully he lays them out in the five-sided pattern he remembers from a day long ago when he had spied on Thaggoran in the cocoon. It seems to him that Thaggoran stands by his elbow, guiding him.

The shinestones are shining black things, bright as mirrors, which burn with some cool inner light. This one, Hresh knew, is named Vingir, and this is Nilmir, and these are Dralmir, Hrongnir, Thungvir. He stares a long while at the stones. He touches them, one by one. He feels the force that lies within them. Then, with reverence, he opens himself to them.

Tell me tell me tell me tell me—

There comes a warmth. A tingling. Hresh brings his second sight into play, and feels the stones interacting with it somehow.

"Go on," Thaggoran says hoarsely, from the shadows.

Tell me tell me tell me—

The stones grow warmer. They throb under his hands. In fear and anguish he frames the question whose answer he is half afraid to learn.

My daughter—is she still alive?

And he conjures up the image of Nialli Apuilana with his mind.

A moment passes. The image of Nialli begins to blaze with celestial radiance. A fiery corona of white light surrounds it. Nialli Apuilana's eyes are bright and keen. She is smiling; her hand is extended lovingly toward him. Hresh feels the vitality of her, the deep surging energy of her.

She's alive, then?

The image comes toward him, glowing, arms outstretched.

Yes. Yes, it must be so.

Her presence is almost overpoweringly real. Hresh feels as though she were actually in the room with him, only an arm's length away. Surely that's proof that she lives, he thinks. Surely. Surely.

He stares in wonder and gratitude at the shinestones.

But where is she, then?

The shinestones can't tell him that. Their warmth diminishes, the tingling ceases. The light within them seems to be flickering. The image of Nialli he has conjured up is beginning to fade. He looks toward Thaggoran, toward Noum om Beng. But he can barely find the two old ghosts. They look faint, filmy, insubstantial, in the darkness across the room.

Fiercely Hresh puts his hands to Vingir and Hrongnir. He touches Dralmir, the largest shinestone, pressing down hard. He brings the tips of his fingers to bear on Thungvir and Nilmir, and begs the stones to give him an answer. But he gets nothing from them. They have told him all they mean to tell him this day.

But Nialli is alive. He's certain of that much.

"She's gone to the hjjks, hasn't she?" Hresh asks. "Why? Tell me why."

"The answer is in your hands," Thaggoran says.

"I don't understand. How—"

"The Barak Dayir, boy," says Noum om Beng. "Use the Barak Dayir!"

Hresh nods. He sweeps the shinestones into their case and takes from its pouch the other and greater talisman, the one that the tribe calls the Wonderstone, a thing older even than the Great World, which is feared by all, and which only he knows how to use.

He has come to fear it too, in these latter years. When he was a boy he thought nothing of using it to soar to the farthest realms of perception; but no longer, no longer. The Barak Dayir is too powerful now for him. Whenever he touches his sensing-organ to it now, he can feel it pulling the waning strength from him; and the visions that it gives him carry so great a freight of meaning that often they leave him dazed and stunned. In recent years he has used it only rarely.

He places the stone before him, and looks down into its mysterious depths.

"Go on," Thaggoran says.

"Yes. Yes."

Hresh raises his sensing-organ, coils it around the Wonderstone without actually touching it; and then, in a swift convulsive gesture, he seizes the talisman in the innermost coil and presses the tip of his sensing-organ to it.

There is a sharp sensation of dislocation and shock, as though he is plunging down an infinite shaft. But with it comes the familiar celestial music that he associates with the device, descending about him like a falling veil, enfolding him, sustaining him. He knows there is nothing to fear. He enters that music, as he has done so often before, and allows himself to be dissolved by it and swept aloft by it, and carried upward into a world of light and color and transcendental forms where all things are possible, where the entire cosmos is within his grasp.

Northward he soars, traversing the great breast of the planet, flying high over dark land scaled and crusted with the myriad deposits of the Earth's long history, the rubble and debris left behind by the world that had been before the world.

The City of Dawinno is below him, white and grand and lovely, nestling in its lush hills beside its sheltered bay. To the west he sees the immense ominous black shield of the sea lying with monstrous weight across half the Earth, concealing deep mysteries beyond his comprehension. He goes higher and higher yet, and onward, northward, over the zone where the city gives way to scattered outer settlements, and then to farms and forest.

As he climbs he seeks the hot bright spark that is the soul of Nialli Apuilana. But he feels no trace of her.

He is well to the north, now, looking down on tiny farming villages, bright specks of white and green against the brown of newly tilled fields, and beyond them into the land that hasn't yet been resettled in the New Springtime, where the wild beasts of the Long Winter still roam free in the forests and the parched and eroded relics of abandoned Great World cities lie shriveling like shards of bone on the dry windy uninhabited plateaus. From them, dead as they are, the formidable resonant presence of the Six Peoples whose domain all this once had been still radiates.

No Nialli. He is mystified. Had they come for her in a magic chariot, and carried her in the twinkling of an eye across the thousands of leagues to the Nest?

He continues northward.

Now the City of Yissou slides into view far to the north, huddling like a wary tortoise behind its immense wall; and then in another moment he is past it, and coming over Vengiboneeza now, its turquoise and crimson towers all aglow with swarming insect life. There is a Nest here, above the ground, sprawling like a strange gray growth over the ancient Great World structures, but no Nialli. He has reached so great an altitude that he can make out the sweeping curve of the shoreline moving sharply to his right as he advances into the north. The entire coast of the continent slants notably eastward as it goes from south to north, so that the City of Yissou can lie far to the east of Dawinno and nevertheless be near the sea, and Vengiboneeza be farther eastward still, but also have its easy access to the water.

Onward. Beyond Vengiboneeza, into territory he has never dared enter except in imagination.

This is the land of the hjjks. They had ruled it in Great World days and they had never relinquished command of it, not even in the brutal worst of the Long Winter, when rivers and mountains of ice covered everything. Somehow they endured; somehow they provided for themselves when all other creatures were forced to flee to the milder south.

Now the ice is gone, laying bare the sorry barren land. Hresh looks down on red buttes and mesas, on knobby terraced promontories rising above dismal gray-brown wastes where no grass would grow, on empty riverbeds streaked with white saline outcroppings, on a chilly desolate landscape of forbidding aridity.

And yet there is life here.

The Barak Dayir brings him incontrovertible impulses of it. Here, here, here: the unmistakable blaze of life. No more than isolated sparks far from one another in this miserable netherworld over which he hovers; but they are sparks with a terrible intensity that nothing could quench.

They are hjjk sparks, though, only hjjk sparks, no trace here of anything but hjjks.

He senses insect souls by twos and threes, or tens and twenties, or a few hundreds, little bands of hjjks and some not so little, moving across the bleak face of these northlands on errands which even the Wonderstone can't interpret for him. The scattered traveling bands move with a determination stronger than iron, less pliant than stone. Nothing, Hresh knows, would halt them, neither cold nor drought nor the wrath of the gods. They could have been planets, journeying on unswervable orbits across the sky. The strength that comes from them is terrifying.

These, Hresh thought, are the inhuman bowelless hjjks his people have always dreaded, the invulnerable and implacable insect-men of myth and fable and chronicle.

Is it to these monsters that his daughter has gone, seeking Nest-bond, seeking Queen-love? How could she have done it? What love, what mercy can she expect from them?

And yet—yet—

He tunes his perceptions, he extends and deepens the range of the Barak Dayir, and in amazement he tumbles through the net of his own preconceptions, he falls like a plummeting star into a new realm of awareness, and just as he has seen life behind the lifelessness it seems to him now that he sees souls behind the soullessness. He feels the presence of the Nest.

Many nests, actually. Widely spaced across the land, settlements largely underground, warm snug tunnels that radiate in a dozen directions from a central core, so that they remind him of nothing so much as the cocoon in which his own people had passed the seven hundred thousand years of the Long Winter. They teem with hjjks, uncountable multitudes of them, moving with the purposefulness and singlemindedness that the People regard with such horror. But it isn't a soulless purposefulness. There is a plan, a central organizing principle, an inner coherence; and each of those millions of creatures moves in accordance with its part in it. It is as Nialli Apuilana had said, that day she spoke before the Presidium: they are no mere vermin. Their civilization, strange though it might be, is rich and complex, even great.

In each Nest lies a slumbering Queen, a great somnolent creature, swaddled and guarded, about whom the entire intricate life of the settlement revolves. Hresh, sensing the Queens now, is powerfully tempted to touch the mind of one of them with his own, to sink down into that sleeping vastness, to enter its powerful spirit and attempt to comprehend it. But he doesn't dare. He doesn't dare. He holds back, uneasy, uncertain, gripped by the timidities of age and fatigue, telling himself that that is not what he came here for, not now, not yet.

His roving mind seeks his daughter. Does not find her.

Not here? Not even here?

Farther north, then, perhaps. These are only subordinate Nests, subordinate Queens. Seek elsewhere, then. He feels the lodestone pull of the huge capital that lay beyond them, the home of the Queen of Queens, to which these great quiescent creatures are mere handmaidens.

Nialli? Nialli?

On and on he goes. Still no hint of her presence. Now he feels his disembodied consciousness approaching the Nest of Nests, ablaze on the northern horizon like a second sun. A terrible irresistible warmth comes from it. From it comes the incandescent all-loving soul-embrace of the Queen of Queens, calling to him, drawing him in.

No Nialli here. I have misled myself. She didn't go to the Nest after all. I've gone in the wrong direction. Taken myself thousands of leagues away from where I should have looked.

Hresh halts his flight. The bright radiance on the horizon grows no closer. Time for him to return. He's traveled as far this day as he can. The Queen of Queens is calling, but he won't answer that summons, not now. It's a powerful temptation: to enter the Nest, to fuse his soul with Hers, to learn more of what the world within this great hjjk-hive is like. The Hresh of the old days, wild little Hresh-full-of-questions, wouldn't have hesitated. But this Hresh knows that he has responsibilities elsewhere. Let the Queen wait a little longer for him.

The warmth of the Nest burns in his flesh. The heat of Queen-love courses through his spirit. But with a powerful effort he makes himself turn, pulls away, begins the homeward journey.

Southward now he flew, past the barren lands, past radiant Vengiboneeza, past Yissou, past the dry plateaus of ruined fragmentary cities. The familiar warm greenness of his own province came into view. He could see the bay, the shore, the hills, the white towers of the city that he himself had built. He saw the parapet of the tall narrow House of Knowledge, and saw himself within the building, sitting sightless at his desk, the Barak Dayir clutched in his sensing-organ. A moment later he was united with himself once more.

"Thaggoran?" he called, looking around the room. "Noum om Beng? Are you still here?"

No, they're gone. He's alone, dazed, shaken, dumbfounded by the voyage he has just made. Somehow the night has fled while he journeyed. Golden light out of the east floods the room.

And Nialli—he has to find Nialli—

Surely she's somewhere nearby, as Taniane had argued all along. Certainly she lives; the shinestones wouldn't have deceived him about that. The life-impulses he had detected had been unmistakably hers. But where, where? In exhaustion he contemplated the Barak Dayir, wondering if he could muster the energy for another excursion.

I'll rest a little while, he told himself. Ten minutes, half an hour—

He became aware of the sounds of shouting in the street far below.

An uprising? An invasion? With an effort Hresh rose and went outside, to the parapet. People were running and calling to one another down there. What were they saying? He could make nothing out—nothing—

A gust of wind blew him a few syllables only: "Nialli! Apuilana!"

"What is it?" Hresh called. "What's happened?"

His voice would not carry. No one could hear him. Fearfully he rushed down the endless winding staircase to the ground floor, and out into the street. He stood clinging to the gate of the building, gasping for breath, his legs trembling, and looked around. No one there. Whoever had been shouting had moved along. But then others came, a band of boys on their way to school, tumbling and leaping, tossing their notebooks about. When they saw him they halted, adopting a more sober demeanor as befitted an encounter with the chronicler. Their eyes, though, were bright and jubilant.

"Is there news?" he demanded.

"Yes, sir. Yes, sir. Your daughter, sir—the lady Nialli Apuilana—"

"What of her?"

"Found, sir. In the lakelands. The hunter Sipirod found her. They're bringing her back right now!"

"And is she—"

He couldn't get the whole question out soon enough. The boys were on their way again already, scampering and cavorting.

"—all right?"

They called something back to him. Hresh was unable to make out the words. But their tone was cheerful and the sense of it was clear. All was well. Nialli lived and was returning to the city. He gave thanks to the gods.

"You must come with me, Mother Boldirinthe," the earnest young guardsman said. "The chieftain requires it. Her daughter is in great need of healing."

"Yes. Yes, of course," the offering-woman said, smiling at the guardsman's solemnity. He was a Beng, like most of the guards, blocky and thick-tongued, with a heavy manner about him. But he was very young. Much was forgivable, on that account. "Don't you think I knew I'd be summoned? Four days lying in those vile swamps—what a shape the girl must be in! Here, boy, help me up. I'm getting as big as a vermilion."

She extended her arm. But the guardsman, with unexpected diligence and courtesy, rushed around behind her chair and slipped his own arm around her to lift her to her feet. She tottered a bit. He steadied her. It was hard work for him, strong though he was. Boldirinthe chuckled at her own unwieldiness. Flesh was accumulating on her with the force of an avalanche, new layers of it every day. Soon she'd be entombed within herself, virtually unable to move. Her legs were like pillars, her belly was a rippling massive mound. That was a matter of little concern to her, though. She was grateful to the gods for having let her live long enough to undergo this transformation, and for having provided her with the sustenance out of which she had created her vastness. Many others hadn't been so fortunate.

"Over there," she said. "That satchel on the table—hand it to me—"

"I can carry it for you, mother."

"No one must carry it but me. Hand it here. There's a good boy. You have a wagon waiting?"

"In the courtyard, yes."

"Take my arm. That's it. What's your name?"

"Maju Samlor, mother."

She nodded. "Been in the guards long?"

"Almost a year."

"Terrible thing, your captain's murder. But it won't go unpunished, will it?"

"We seek the slayer day and night," said Maju Samlor. He grunted a little as she swayed and lurched, but held her steady. At a cautious pace they proceeded into the courtyard. This was twice in two days that she had left her cloister, now, for only yesterday she had attended the meeting that Taniane had called at the Basilica. That was unusual for her, in these days, to go out so often. Movement was so difficult. Her thighs rubbed together with each step, her breasts pulled her groundward like weights. But perhaps it would do her some good, she thought, to bestir herself more frequently.

The long satchel she carried was more of a burden to her than she had expected. She had loaded it that morning with the things she would need in caring for Nialli Apuilana—the talismans of Friit and Mueri, of course, but also the wands of healing, which were carved of heavy wood, and an array of herbs and potions in stone jars. Too many things, maybe. But she managed to hobble out to the wagon without dropping it.

Her hillside cloister was near the head of the steep street known as Mueri Way. Just a hundred paces or so farther uphill was Mueri House. The alleyway in which Kundalimon had been murdered lay midway between Mueri House and her cloister.

It angered Boldirinthe that blood—innocent blood—had been shed so close to her holy precinct. How could anyone, even a madman, have dared violate this place of healing by casting an aura of violent death over it? Each morning since the killing she had sent one of her junior priestesses to the site to perform a rite of purification. But she hadn't gone to it herself. Now, as Maju Samlor tugged at the reins and the xlendi moved forward into the street, she turned to look toward the fatal place.

A crowd seemed to have gathered. She saw thirty or forty people, or perhaps more, bustling about the narrow entrance to the alley. The ones going in carried string-bags bulging with fruit, and others bore bunches of flowers, or armloads of greenery of some sort—boughs pulled from trees, so it looked. The ones coming from the alley were empty-handed.

Boldirinthe turned to Maju Samlor, frowning. "What's going on there, do you think?"

"They're bringing offerings, mother."

"Offerings?"

"Nature-offerings. Branches, fruits, flowers, things like that. For the one who died, you know, the boy from the hjjks. It's been going on two or three days."

"They place offerings on the spot where he died?" That was strange. Her priestesses had said nothing about it to her. "Take me over there and let me see."

"But the chieftain's daughter—"

"She can wait another few minutes. Take me over."

The guardsman shrugged and pulled the wagon around, and drove it up the street to the mouth of the alley. At closer range, now, Boldirinthe realized that there were only a few adults in the crowd. Most were boys and girls, some of them quite young. From where she sat it was hard for her to get a good view of what was going on, nor did she want to dismount and investigate directly. But she could see that someone had set up some kind of shrine in there. At the far end where the line of offering-bearers terminated the green boughs were piled higher than a man's head, and they were draped with bits of cloth, glittering metallic ribbons, long bright-colored paper streamers.

For a long moment she sat there watching. Some of the children noticed her, and waved and called her name, and she smiled to them and returned their greetings. But she did not leave the wagon.

"Would you like a closer look?" Maju Samlor asked. "I could help you out, and—"

"Another time," Boldirinthe said. "Take me to Nialli Apuilana now."

The guardsman turned the wagon and headed it down the hill.

So now they're worshiping him, Boldirinthe thought in wonder. The one who died: they are making him a god. Or so it would appear. How strange. It's all so very strange, everything that has happened that is in any way connected to that boy.

She found it bothersome that such things should be going on. That there should be a shrine in the alleyway, that the children should be bringing offerings to Kundalimon as though he were a god, seemed improper to her.

Perhaps it's not so serious, though, she told herself.

She thought of all the unorthodoxies that she'd seen arise during her long life. Had any of them done any real harm? These were unstable times. The coming of the New Springtime had shaken the People out of the narrow ways of the cocoon by sending them out to face the unknown mysteries of the larger world; and it wasn't surprising that they would grasp at new salvations when the old ones didn't appear to be producing immediate gratification.

Some of the novelties had been short-lived. Like that odd cult of human-worship that had sprung up during the last days in Vengiboneeza, when a few of the simpler folk had met secretly to dance around a statue of a human that they found somewhere in the old city, and had made prayers and sacrifices before it. But that had died out in the time of the second migration.

On the other hand, the worship of the alien god Nakhaba had been integrated into the life of the tribe after the union with the Bengs, and that seemed to be permanent. And other creeds had come into fashion from time to time, centering around the stars, the sun, the great ocean, and even less likely things. Boldirinthe had heard it whispered around that Nialli Apuilana was a worshiper of hjjks, and kept some holy talisman of theirs in her room in the House of Nakhaba.

Well, so be it, thought Boldirinthe. She was a godly woman, devout enough to understand that there is godliness in everything. The Five Heavenly Ones weren't necessarily the only repositories of the sacred. They were simply the ones that she had sworn to serve. It wasn't that they were true and the other gods false: just that to her they were the most efficacious, the ones who partook most fully of the holy. If these children wanted to make offerings to the memory of Kundalimon, so be it. So be it. Worship is worship.

"Hurry," Boldirinthe said to the guardsman. "Can't you make that xlendi of yours go any faster? Nialli Apuilana is very weak, you know. She needs me urgently."

"But you just said—"

"If you won't use the whip, give it to me. You think I'm afraid to hit with it? Go faster, boy. Faster!"

Nialli Apuilana lay on a pallet in one of the upstairs rooms of the chieftain's residence, her eyes closed, her breathing slow and shallow. Her fur was matted and damp. Now and then she muttered something unintelligible. She seemed lost in some realm beyond consciousness, farther than sleep but just this side of death. Seeing her thus entranced, Boldirinthe was reminded of something out of her distant youth, out of the cocoon days: the strange being—Hresh said he was a human—whom the tribe had called the Dream-Dreamer, who had lain for years deep in unending sleep, only to awaken and die on the day when the People received the omens of the Going Forth. He had slept the same way, as if he were more in another world than in this one.

A somber little group surrounded Nialli Apuilana's bedside. Taniane was there, of course, looking taut and drawn, as though about to crack. Hresh, too, seemed to have aged years in a few days. And also Husathirn Mueri and Tramassilu the jewelry-maker, and Fashinatanda, Taniane's blind and doddering old mother, and the architect Tisthali and the grain-merchant Sturnak Khatilifon and his mate Sipulakinain, who was ill, a mere charred ember of herself, with death's hand practically at her shoulder. And there were still others, some of whom the offering-woman couldn't place at all.

What such a mob as this was doing in a sickroom was beyond

Boldirinthe's comprehension. No doubt they all wanted to offer help. But they were pressing too close on the poor girl, overheating the air, draining the room of vitality. With quick impatient flutterings of her hands Boldirinthe cleared them all out, all but Taniane and Sipulakinain, whose presence seemed somehow significant. She let old Fashinatanda stay also, silent in a corner, seemingly unaware of anything that was going on.

"Where was she found?" Boldirinthe asked.

"In the lakelands," said Taniane. "Lying on her face in the mud beside a little pond, according to Sipirod, with a bunch of animals grouped around her and watching her closely, some caviandis and stinchitoles, a little herd of scantrins, a couple of gabools. Sipirod said it was the most amazing thing she had ever seen, those animals gathering around her. It was almost as if they were guarding her. She must have been there two days or so. Burning with fever, said Sipirod. She must have been drinking the pond water. And of course she had no food."

"Has she been conscious at all?"

"Delirious, only. She babbles sometimes—the Queen, the Nest, all of that. And calls Kundalimon's name. They were lovers, did you know that? They were going to elope to hjjk country together, Boldirinthe!"

"Poor girl. No wonder she ran." But then the offering-woman made a grunting sound of dismissal. None of that mattered now.

"Bring that table over here, will you? Set my satchel on it. There, where I can get at it. And give me something to sit on, beside the bed. It's all I can do to keep myself on my feet, you know."

She lifted Nialli Apuilana's arm and ran her fingers along the length of it, feeling for the life-currents. They were very feeble. The girl was warm but her soul-river was flowing sluggishly, like quicksilver beginning to congeal. Boldirinthe turned her face away from Taniane, not wanting the chieftain to see the extent of her concern. Another few hours in that swamp and there'd have been a dead girl here. It was possible that they would lose her yet.

No. I won't allow it, Boldirinthe thought.

From her satchel she drew the two great wands of healing and laid them alongside Nialli Apuilana, who barely stirred. She took out her herbs and ointments, and set them in a row on the table. She placed the talisman of Friit the healer at Nialli Apuilana's head and that of Mueri the comforter at her feet.

To Sipulakinain she said, "Bring me that brazier. We'll burn the leaves of Friit in it, and see to it you breathe the smoke yourself. It'll do you some good too."

"I'm on the mend, Boldirinthe," said Sipulakinain.

The offering-woman gave the grain-merchant's mate a skeptical look. "Yissou be praised for that," she said without conviction.

Together they worked to light the aromatic herb. Taniane watched, silent, motionless. In the far corner the old woman Fashinatanda prayed in a toneless mumble, seeing nothing. Purplish smoke curled upward.

"More," Boldirinthe said. "Another five sprigs."

Sipulakinain's hands trembled. But she fed the herbs to the blaze. Boldirinthe took Nialli Apuilana's ankles and held them. She felt the congestion in the girl's lungs, the weariness in her heart. Her soul-center was chilled and enfeebled. Nialli Apuilana was strong, though. These weaknesses could be driven from her.

The smoke grew thick in the room.

Now the gods became visible.

Boldirinthe had long had the skill of seeing the Five Heavenly Ones clearly. It was not something she ever spoke of to others, for she knew that the gods, real though they were, had never appeared to anyone else in actual manifestations, only as powerful abstract presences. It was different with her. They had forms and faces, familiar ones. Mueri the Consoler was much like Torlyri to her, a tall strong handsome woman whose dark fur was marked with white. Dawinno the Destroyer had the look of Harruel, a fierce red-bearded giant. Yissou was wise and remote, sparse of fur, almost like a human. The Provider, Emakkis, was fat and jolly. Friit the Healer was very serious, and frail, a little like Hresh. They stood now by her side. She indicated the sleeping girl, and they nodded, and Friit told her what must be done, and Boldirinthe, though she felt a stab of uneasiness, made ready unhesitatingly to do it.

"You have to leave the room now," she said to Taniane.

"I—"

"There's too much strength in you. We want only the sick and the old and the fat in here now."

Taniane's mouth opened, and closed again. She gave Boldirinthe a look of astonishment and, perhaps, anger. But she went out without a word.

Boldirinthe applied the ointments of healing now, one to Nialli Apuilana's lips, another to her breasts, a third to the place between her thighs. Nialli Apuilana stirred and murmured as the heat of these herbal creams began to penetrate her skin.

"Get the old one," she said to Sipulakinain. "I want her sitting on the bed, with her hands on the girl's feet. You sit up there, and take her head against your bosom. I'm going to twine with her."

Sipulakinain nodded. Though she was weak and uncertain on her feet herself, she slipped her arm around the shoulders of the trembling old grandmother and led her to the bedside, and placed her in the position Boldirinthe had requested. She lay down then and cradled Nialli Apuilana's head.

Ponderously Boldirinthe maneuvered her cumbersome body about until her sensing-organ was within reach of Nialli Apuilana's. There was no question of her lying down beside the girl on the pallet in the usual twining position, but twining might be accomplished in other ways. She looked up and saw Mueri smiling at her, saw Friit holding his hand high in approval. Yissou himself helped to move her into position.

Now came a moment of uncertainty and unease.

Boldirinthe was too old to feel fear, but she was not beyond apprehensiveness. She had twined with Nialli Apuilana once before, years ago, on the girl's twining-day—on the very eve, as it had turned out, of her capture by the hjjks—when she had come to Boldirinthe for the traditional instruction in the art. Boldirinthe hadn't forgotten what that twining had been like.

That other time Boldirinthe had been expecting nothing more than the usual childish chaos of a first twining, the soft unformed vulnerable young soul struggling painfully to focus itself amidst the embarrassment of the new intimacy; but instead Nialli Apuilana, when the union of their two souls had been achieved, had revealed herself to be strong and fierce, as hard and as firm-edged as some machine, a thing of shining metal and driving force. That was frightening, to encounter such strength in one so young. Boldirinthe had been exhausted by their twining. She hadn't expected ever to repeat that experience. Nor was she eager to.

But the Five had commanded it. Boldirinthe touched her sensing-organ to that of the unconscious girl, and began to enter into communion with her.

The girl's soul was remote and elusive. There were moments when Boldirinthe felt she would be unable to reach it; there were moments when she felt Nialli Apuilana's spirit slipping away entirely, separating from the girl's body. But Fashinatanda and Sipulakinain served as barriers to prevent her soul's departure. They contained it. And, little by little Boldirinthe was able to surround it and take it into her capacious embrace.

Now Nialli Apuilana's sleeping self opened gladly to her.

Her soul was infinitely deeper and stranger and richer than it had been that other time, four years earlier. Nialli Apuilana had been a girl, then; now she was a woman, with all that that implied of depths of understanding. She had coupled; she had twined; she had loved.

And she had accepted the Five Heavenly Ones.

What a surprise that was! There hadn't been a shred of belief in Nialli Apuilana the other time. Not unusual, such godlessness, among the modern young ones. But Nialli Apuilana hadn't simply been indifferent to the goodness of the gods before: she had sealed herself up against it, she had rejected it outright.

Now, though, to her vast amazement, Boldirinthe felt the essence of the Five within the girl's soul. There was no doubt of their presence, new and fresh. The auras of all of them were there, Friit and Emakkis, Mueri and Dawinno, and preeminently Yissou the Protector, casting a glow of godliness through the corridors and channels of her soul. Boldirinthe had not remotely expected that. Their holy fire burned in her, and it was all, or almost all, that was keeping her alive. Perhaps they had come to her as she lay close to death in that swamp.

But the Nest was present within her also. The Queen was present within her.

Boldirinthe could feel the great massive alien power of the insect monarch, surrounding and infiltrating every aspect of the girl's spirit, interpenetrating even the auras of the Five in a manner as blasphemous as it was improbable. Hjjk-light blazed like an angry fire. Hjjk-mists swathed Nialli Apuilana's soul. Tenacious claws clung everywhere. Surely this was something that had befallen her during her captivity. The offering-woman had to struggle to keep herself from recoiling from these mysteries, or from being drawn down into them.

But she knew what to do. She was here to heal. With the help of the gods she would drive out the evil.

Unhesitatingly she set about her work. She grappled with the dark thing within the chieftain's daughter. She hacked at it, she speared it, she slashed it to its heart. It seemed to weaken. Its claws flailed and thrashed. The offering-woman pulled one claw free, and another, and another, though they sprang back nearly as quickly as she ripped them away. The thing fought back with cold malevolent fury, lashing her with lattices of force, showering her with torrents of icy flame. She stood her ground against the onslaught. She had spent all her life in preparation for this moment. Again and again the sluggish invincible monster stirred and rose and leaped, and each time Boldirinthe fought it down, and again it leaped and again it was cast down, and the offering-woman forged new weapons and went forward, battling with all her strength.

Slowly, grudgingly, the thing retreated to the depths of the girl's soul and crawled into the lair that it maintained there. Not that it had yielded; but it had given ground. There was hope now that Nialli Apuilana could fight the rest of the battle herself. Boldirinthe had done all she could.

To Friit the offering-woman said, "Take command of her now, I beg you, and give her strength."

"Yes, I will do that," the god replied.

"And you, Dawinno. Emakkis. Mueri. Yissou."

"Yes," said each of them in turn.

Boldirinthe made a passageway for them, and the gods entered her, uniting themselves with the auras of themselves that were already within her. They bolstered Nialli Apuilana where she was flagging, and restored her where she was weakened, and filled her where she had been drained.

Then, one by one, they departed.

The last of them to leave was Mueri, who paused and touched Boldirinthe's own soul, embracing it most tenderly as Torlyri might have embraced her long ago. Then Mueri too was gone.

Nialli Apuilana stirred. Her eyes opened. She blinked several times, very quickly. She frowned. She smiled.

"Sleep, girl," Boldirinthe said. "You'll be strong again when you wake."

Nialli Apuilana nodded dreamily. Turning to Sipulakinain, Boldirinthe said, "Send in Taniane. Only Taniane."

The chieftain brought a cloud of worry in with her; but it dissipated the moment she saw the change in Nialli Apuilana. At once her own vigor returned, and the light flooded back into her eyes. Boldirinthe was too tired for gratitude. "Yes, the job's done, and done well," she said. "Keep that crowd out of here, now. Let the girl rest. Afterward, warm broths, the juice of fresh fruits. She'll be up and around in a couple of days, good as new, I promise you."

"Boldirinthe—"

"Not necessary," the offering-woman said. The girl's eyes were closed again. She had slipped into a deep, healthy, healing sleep. Auras glowed around her. But Boldirinthe still could see the wounded Nest-creature crouching deep behind the outer aspect, the hidden hjjk within, glowing like an angry red sore, and she shivered a little.

She knew, though, that she had dealt it a terrible blow. The rest was up to Nialli Apuilana. And to the Five.

"Help me up," she said, wheezing a little, patting her brow. "Or get one or two of the others, if you can't do it alone."

Taniane laughed. And raised her easily from her bench, as though Boldirinthe were no bigger than a child.

Outside, in the gray stone hallway where green glowglobes flickered, Husathirn Mueri approached her and took her by the arm. He looked edgy and forlorn.

"Will she live, Boldirinthe?"

"Of course she'll live. Never any doubt about that."

She tried to move on. This day she had gone down into the deepest abyss and returned from it, a costly business, hard on the soul. She had no wish to stand here chattering with Husathirn Mueri now.

But he was holding her. Wouldn't let her go. A warm insincere grin starting to spread across his face.

"You're too modest," he said. "I know a little of the healing arts myself. That girl was dying until you came here to treat her."

"Well, she's not dying now."

"You have my deepest gratitude."

"I'm sure that I do."

She stared at him a long moment, trying to see behind his words. There were always meanings behind his meanings. Even when he sneezed it seemed somehow devious.

Finding Husathirn Mueri likable was something that Boldirinthe had never managed to do, which troubled her, for she disliked disliking anyone; and he was Torlyri's son, which made the matter worse. She had loved Torlyri as she loved her own mother. And here was Husathirn Mueri, quick and clever and handsome, and warmhearted, after a fashion, and looking a good deal like Torlyri with those brilliant white stripes running through his black fur; and Boldirinthe couldn't like him at all. It was his slyness, she thought, and his unbridled ambition. Where had those traits come from? Not from Torlyri, certainly. Nor from his father, that hard and austere Beng warrior. Well, she told herself, the gods have their mysteries. Each one of us is a special mystery of the gods.

Softly Husathirn Mueri said, "You know that I love her."

Boldirinthe shrugged. "So do we all."

"I mean it in another fashion."

"Yes. Of course you do."

His foolishness saddened her. She had no wish to see anyone hurt himself this way. Wasn't Husathirn Mueri aware how strange she was, the girl he claimed to love? He must at least suspect by now that she had taken Kundalimon as her lover. And that after refusing the best young men the city had to offer. Well, Kundalimon was dead; perhaps Husathirn Mueri no longer regarded him as important. But what would he say if he knew that he had another and greater rival, no less than the Queen of Hjjks? How he would turn away in horror! But he'd have to twine with Nialli Apuilana to find it out, and Boldirinthe doubted that he had much chance of that.

She moved on, slowly, toward the outer door.

"May I have a few more words with you?" Husathirn Mueri asked.

"If you walk with me. Standing in one place is unpleasant for me, now that I'm so huge."

"Let me carry your satchel."

"The satchel is my holy burden. What do you want to say to me, Husathirn Mueri?"

She thought it would be something more about Nialli Apuilana. But instead he said, "Are you aware, Boldirinthe, that some sort of cult is already beginning to spring up around the murdered ambassador from the hjjks?"

"I know there's a shrine of some sort in his memory, yes."

"More than just a shrine." He licked his lips nervously. "I have the guardsmen's reports. The children are praying to him. And not only the children, but it started with them. They've got some little bits of his clothing, and things from his room, hjjk things that somehow were taken after he died. Boldirinthe, they're making him into a god!"

"Are they?" she said indifferently. "Well, such things happen from time to time. As they please. It'll change nothing for me. The Five remain sufficient for my needs."

Sourly he said, "I didn't expect you to start worshiping Kundalimon. But doesn't this trouble you at all?"

"Why does it trouble you?"

"Don't you understand, Boldirinthe, they're setting up a boy who was half hjjk by spirit, or more than half, as a figure of power in the city! They want favors from him. They want guidance. And they'll confer favors in return. Do you really want to see a new religion get started here? A new priesthood, new temples, new ideas? Anything could come out of that. Anything. While Kundalimon was alive he went around preaching Nest-stuff to them, and suggesting to them that they follow him back to the Nest. And the children loved it. They ate it up. I have absolute proof of that. What if this—this cult—falls under the control of someone who can build on what Kundalimon was starting? Will we all find ourselves loving the hjjks, and begging them to love us? Will Nakhaba and the Five be swept away? You're too casual about it, Boldirinthe. This will grow only worse, and very rapidly, like fire spreading in the drylands. I can feel it. I'm not without a certain shrewdness in these matters, you know."

His face was flushed and disquieted. His amber eyes, gleaming with feverish excitement, were like polished glass beads. Something was at work in him, no doubt of that. She could not remember having seen him so agitated. It wasn't much like Husathirn Mueri to display such open emotion.

It was the last thing she needed right now, this frantic outburst. She was still shaken by the shock of what she had seen in Nialli Apuilana's soul. What she needed was to return to her cloister and rest. A quiet dinner with dear old Staip, a few bowls of wine, and bed—yes—

Let come what may, she thought. New cults, new gods, anything. I've worked hard today. I'm tired. I long for my couch.

Coolly she said, "Perhaps you're making a great deal out of very little. The children liked Kundalimon, yes. He amused them. He told them interesting stories. Now they mourn him. They bring offerings to his spirit. I saw them at it as I came here today. A harmless gesture, a memorial, nothing more. And in a few days it'll all blow over. He'll become part of history, something for Hresh to enter in his chronicles, and that'll be the end of it."

"And if you're wrong? If there's a revolution here instead? What then, Boldirinthe?" He waved his hands excitedly.

But she had had enough.

She said, "Speak to Taniane if these things bother you, Husathirn Mueri. I'm fat and old, very fat, very old, and whatever changes will come, if they do, will probably come when I'm no longer here to see them. Or if I still am, well, I've seen more changes than you can imagine in my lifetime already. I can stand to see some more. Let me go, now. May Mueri give you peace, eh? Or Nakhaba, if you prefer. All gods are one, to me."

"What? But you are sworn to the Five!"

"The Five are my gods. But all gods are godly." She made a sign of Mueri at him, and moved slowly onward past him to the door, and down the steps to the waiting wagon.

The boy's name was Tikharein Tourb. He was nine. He wore the black-and-yellow Nest-guardian talisman on his breast.

The girl was Chhia Kreun. She had the wrist-amulet.

They stood before a congregation of eleven children and three adults. Aromatic boughs were piled high in the little rough-walled basement room, so that the pungent odor of sippariu sap mingled with the sweetness of dilifar needles to make the air almost intoxicatingly strong.

"Hold hands," said Tikharein Tourb. "Everyone, touch together! Close your eyes."

Chhia Kreun, standing next to the boughs, was virtually in a trance. She began to chant, unknown words, thick and harsh. Perhaps they were hjjk words. Who could say? They were sounds that Kundalimon had taught them. What they might mean, no one knew. But they had a holy sound.

"Everyone," Tikharein Tourb cried. "Come on! Everyone, say the words! Say them! Say them! It is the prayer to the Queen!"

The negotiations, such as they were, were stalled. Since the news had come of those murders in Dawinno, Thu-Kimnibol had fallen into some sort of black pit of brooding. Salaman watched him with surprise and growing uneasiness. All day long he paced the halls of the palace like some huge beast, and at the royal feasts each night he said practically nothing.

What was bothering him, so he said, was the lateness of the autumn caravan from the City of Dawinno. It was nine days late arriving at Yissou. "Where is it?" Thu-Kimnibol kept asking. "Why isn't it here?" He seemed obsessed by its failure to arrive. But there had to be more to it than that. For a caravan to be a few days late wasn't sufficient cause for so much fretting.

"There must be bad weather somewhere down south," Salaman said, trying to soothe him. Thu-Kimnibol was too explosive, too unpredictable, when he was this troubled. "Heavy storms along the way, flooding on the highway, some such thing."

"Storms? We've had nothing but one golden day after another."

"But perhaps to the south—"

"No. The caravan's late because there's trouble in Dawinno. Once killing begins, where does it stop? There's some upheaval going on there."

So that's what's worrying him, Salaman thought. He still thinks he should have gone home the moment he got word of the murders. He feels guilty because he's up here doing nothing while Dawinno may be in an uproar. If Taniane had wanted him to come home, though, Taniane would have asked him to come home. The fact that she didn't must mean there's no problem there.

"My prayers go with you, cousin," Salaman said unctuously. "Yissou grant that all is well in your city."

But the days went by, five more, six, seven, and still no caravan. Now Salaman too was puzzled. The caravans were always punctual. In winter and spring Yissou sent caravans south, and in summer and autumn they came northward from Dawinno. They were important to the economic life of both cities. Now Salaman found himself plagued with fretful merchants and manufacturers whose warehouses were piled high with goods ready to offer. Who would they sell them to, they asked him, if the caravan didn't come? And the marketplace vendors who dealt in goods from Dawinno had the opposite problem. They needed to restock; but where was the caravan? "Soon," Salaman told them all. "It's on its way." Yissou! Where was it? He was getting as edgy as Thu-Kimnibol.

Was something really wrong down south? He did, of course, have a few spies in Dawinno. But he hadn't heard from them in weeks. The distance between the two cities was so great, the time of travel so long. We need some better way of getting news from abroad, the king told himself. Something faster, something that doesn't involve asking couriers to travel hundreds of leagues. Something using second sight, maybe. He made a note to give the matter some thought.

Thu-Kimnibol continued to pace and scowl. Salaman found himself beginning to do it too.

Gods! Where was that caravan?

Husathirn Mueri said, "I trust your daughter's recovery is proceeding well, lady."

"As well as can be hoped for," said Taniane, in a dull, toneless way.

He was astounded to see how tired she looked. Her shoulders were slumped, her hands lay limply in her lap, her fur was faded and without sheen. Once she had seemed to him more like Nialli Apuilana's older sister than her mother, but no longer.

Maybe the state of Nialli Apuilana's health had been the wrong topic to open with. He went on quickly to something else.

"As you requested, lady, I have the latest report on the search for Curabayn Bangkea's murderer. The report is that no progress has been made."

Taniane stared at him balefully. "There won't ever be any progress there, will there, Husathirn Mueri?"

"I think not, lady. It was such a casual crime, it seems—"

"*Casual?* Murder?"

Suddenly there was cold fire in her eyes.

He said, "I meant only that it must have been a sudden brawl, something that came up out of nowhere, perhaps even without reason. Of course, we'll continue the investigation in every way possible, but—"

"Forget the investigation. It isn't leading anywhere."

Her brusqueness was startling. "Just as you wish, lady."

"What I want you to get your guardsmen thinking about is this new religion we have. This cult. It seems to be traveling through the city like a pestilence."

"Chevkija Aim is leading a vigorous program of suppression, lady. In the past week alone we've uncovered three chapels, and we have—"

"No. Suppression isn't going to work."

"Lady?"

"I'm hearing disturbing news. Men like Kartafirain, Si-Belimnion, Maliton Diveri—property-holders, men who get around and know what's going on. They say that as fast as we close down one chapel, two more open. Everyone out there is talking about Kundalimon. A prophet, they call him. A holy prophet. Queen-love's spreading among the workers faster than a new drink. It's becoming obvious very quickly that the policy of suppression's going to cause more trouble than it cures. I want you to tell Chevkija Aim to call off his campaign."

"But we have to suppress it, lady! The thing is outrageous heresy. Are we simply going to allow it to spread?"

Her eyes narrowed. "Are you so godly, Husathirn Mueri?"

"I know a danger when I see it."

"So do I. But didn't you hear what I just said? Suppressing it may prove to be more risky than letting it thrive."

Perhaps so, he thought.

"I don't like this new religion any more than you do," she said. "But it could be that the best way of controlling it just now is by *not* trying to control it. We need to learn something about it before we can decide how dangerous it really is. It may be simple foolishness of the common people, or perhaps it's active subversion by the hjjks, and how can we know which it is, eh? Except by looking at it. What I want you to do is drop everything else and find out what's really taking place. Send guardsmen to snoop around in those chapels. Infiltrate them. Listen to what's being said."

Husathirn Mueri nodded. "I'll see to it personally."

"Oh, and one more thing. Check up on the people who are about to go with the caravan to Yissou, will you? Make sure none of *them* are cultists. That's the last thing we need, to have this business infect Yissou also."

"A very good point," said Husathirn Mueri.

The Dawinno caravan had arrived at last, more than two weeks over-due: eleven xlendi-drawn wagons with red-and-gold banners, clip-clopping up the Southern Highway amid clouds of tawny dust.

That night there was a grand celebration: bonfires burning in the plazas, street musicians playing until dawn, feasting and carousing galore, little sleep, much revelry. The coming of the caravan was always a signal for unfettered rejoicing in Yissou, where the prevailing mood was more often one of constraint and caution: it was as though the arrival of the merchants from the south caused the great stone wall of the city to swing apart and warm sultry winds out of the tropics to blow through the narrow winding streets. But the lateness of the caravan, the uncertainty about whether it would get there at all, made its arrival an even bigger occasion than usual.

To Salaman, in his private palace chamber, came the merchant Gar-dinak Cheysz, the most useful of his agents in Dawinno. He was a plump but somber man, with fur of a curious grayish-yellow cast, and a mouth that drooped on one side from some weakness of the facial muscles. Though born in Yissou, he had lived most of his life in Dawinno. Salaman had employed him for years.

"There's much confusion in Dawinno," Gardinak Cheysz began. "That's why we were late. Our departure was delayed by it."

"Ah. Tell me."

"You know that a boy called Kundalimon, who had been taken from Dawinno many years ago by the hjjks, returned to the city in the spring, and—"

"I know all that. I also know that he was murdered, and the captain of the city's guards was also. This is old news."

"You know these things, do you?" Gardinak Cheysz paused a moment, as if to reorder his thoughts. "Very well. Very well, sire." From a courtyard outside the palace came wild skirling sounds, some kind of discordant piping, and the sound of laughter. "Do you know also, sire, that on the day of the two murders the daughter of the chieftain Taniane went mad, and disappeared from the city?"

That was something new. "Nialli, is that her name?"

"Nialli Apuilana, yes. A difficult and unruly girl."

"What else could be expected but unruliness and difficulty, from the child of Taniane and Hresh?" Salaman smiled grimly. "I knew Hresh when he was a boy, when we were in the cocoon. A mad little child he was, forever doing forbidden things. Well, so this Nialli Apuilana went insane and vanished. And the delay in your setting out, then—a period of mourn-ing, was it?"

"Oh, she's not dead," said Gardinak Cheysz. "Though I hear it was a close thing. They found her raving and feverish in the swamps east of the city, a few days later, and the offering-woman nursed her back to health. But it was touch and go for days, they say. Taniane could deal with nothing else. Not a shred of government business transacted all the while the girl lay ill. Our permit to depart lay on her desk, and lay there, and there it lay, unsigned. And Hresh—he nearly went out of his mind himself. He locked himself up in the tower where he keeps all his old chronicles and hardly came out at all, and when he did he said nothing to anyone about anything."

Salaman shook his head. "Hresh," he muttered, with mingled respect and contempt. "There's no mind like his in all the world. But a man can be brilliant and a fool all at once, I suppose."

"There's more," said Gardinak Cheysz.

"Go on, then."

"I mentioned the dead hjjk emissary, Kundalimon. They've begun to make him into a god in Dawinno. Or at least a demigod."

"A god?" the king said, blinking several times very quickly. "What do you mean, a god?"

"Shrines. Chapels of worship, even. He's considered a prophet, a bearer of revelation, a—I can hardly tell you what. It goes beyond my understanding. There's a cult, that's all I can tell you, sire. It seems absurd to me. But it's caused tremendous commotion. Taniane, when she finally would turn her attention to something other than her daughter, sent out word that the new religion was to be suppressed."

"I'd have credited her with more sense than that."

"Exactly. They thrive under persecution. As she quickly discovered. The original order for suppression has already been rescinded, sire. The guards were trying to find the places where this Kundalimon is worshiped—there's a new captain of guards, by the way, one Chevkija Aim, a young Beng, very ambitious and ruthless—and they were attempting to eradicate them. They'd desecrate the shrines, they'd arrest the worshipers. But it was impossible. The people wouldn't stand for it. Therefore the persecutions have been called off, and the cultists' numbers are growing from day to day. It's happened so fast you wouldn't believe it. Before we could leave for Yissou we had to take an oath that we weren't believers ourselves."

"And what's this new faith all about, can you say?"

"I tell you, sire, such things are beyond me. The best I can make it out, it calls for surrender to the hjjks."

"Surrender—to—the—hjjks?" Salaman said, slowly, incredulously.

"Yes, sire. Accepting Queen-love, sire. Whatever that may mean. You may know, the boy Kundalimon came bearing a proposal of a treaty of peace with the hjjks that would have divided the continent between us and them, with the boundary—"

"Yes. I know about that."

"Well, the cult leaders are calling for immediate signing of the treaty. And more than that: for establishment of regular peaceful contact between the City of Dawinno and the land of the hjjks, with certain hjjks known as Nest-thinkers invited to live among us, as the treaty requires. So that we can come to understand their holy teachings. So that we can come to comprehend the wisdom of the Queen."

Salaman stared. "This is madness."

"So it is, my lord. And that's why the caravan was delayed, because everything's up in the air in the city. Perhaps it's a little quieter by now. By the time we finally left, the chieftain's daughter had apparently recovered—the story is going around that she's become a leader of the new cult, by the way, but perhaps that's only a story—and that gave Taniane time for government affairs again. And Hresh has reappeared too. So it may be that things are getting back to normal. But it was a hard few weeks, let me tell you, sire."

"I imagine so. Anything else?"

"Only that we've brought eleven wagons full of fine goods, and look forward to a happy visit in your city."

"Good. Good. We'll talk again tomorrow, perhaps, Gardinak Cheysz. I want to hear all this a second time, by daylight, to see if it seems any more real to me then." He grimaced and threw his hands high. "Make peace with the hjjks! Invite them to Dawinno so that they can teach their philosophy! Can you believe it?" He reached under his sash, pulled out a pouch filled with exchange-units of the City of Dawinno, and tossed it to Gardinak Cheysz. The spy caught it deftly and saluted. His drooping mouth jerked upward in what might have been an attempt at a smile, and he went from the room.

The same night, in a tavern in another part of the city. Esperasagiot, Dumanka, and a few other members of the crew of the caravan that brought Thu-Kimnibol to Yissou have gotten together with some of the newcomers. The hour is late. The wine has been going down freely. They are all old friends. The men of Thu-Kimnibol's crew had often served in the regular merchant caravans that pass between the two cities. Among those who came in today was Esperasagiot's brother, Thihaliminion, nearly as good a hand with xlendis as Esperasagiot himself. Thihaliminion had been wagon-master to the caravan that has just arrived.

There are some local folk in the party, too—a harnessmaker named Gheppilin, and Zechtior Lukin, a meat-cutter, and Lisspar Moen, a woman whose trade is the making of fine porcelain dishes. Friends of Dumanka's, they are. New friends.

Thihaliminion has been speaking for some time of the sudden rash of unusual events in the City of Dawinno: the murders, the disappearance and subsequent madness of the chieftain's daughter, the emergence of the new cult of Kundalimon. Laughing into his wine, he says, "It's like the end of the world. Everything is going strange at once." He shakes his helmeted head. "But why am I laughing? It's no laughing matter!"

"Ah, but it is," says Dumanka. "When all else has gone foul, laughter still remains. When the gods send us disaster, what else can we do but laugh? Weeping won't heal anything. Laughter at least buries our sorrows in merriment."

"You were ever a mocker, Dumanka," Thihaliminion tells the quartermaster. "You take nothing seriously."

"On the contrary, brother," Esperasagiot says. "Dumanka is one of the most serious men I know, behind that bawdy grin of his."

"Then let him be serious, if he will. What's happening in Dawinno is serious stuff, as you'll find out when you get back there. It's easy enough to laugh when you're hundreds of leagues away."

"Brother, he meant no offense! It's only his way, don't you see? He was only making sport with words."

"No," Dumanka says. "That wasn't what I was doing."

"No?" Esperasagiot says, frowning.

"I was being as serious as I know how to be, my friend. If you'll give me a moment, I'll explain myself."

"We're all wasting our breath with this talk," Thihaliminion says, in something like a growl. "We could be drinking instead of talking."

"No. Give me a moment. I think this is no waste of breath at all," Dumanka says, and the others look at him, for they have never heard the quartermaster speak so solemnly before. "I said we should laugh when the gods send us misery, rather than weep, and I think I'm right about that. Or if not to laugh, then to shrug; for what good is it to moan and grumble over the will of the gods? These people here—"

"Enough, Dumanka," Thihaliminion says, a little too sharply.

"One or two more words, I beg you. These three here, Zechtior Lukin, Lisspar Moen, Gheppilin—do you know them? No, of course not. But I do. And there's wisdom in them, let me tell you. They've plenty to teach us all on the subject of bowing to the will of the gods. Have you ever considered, good Thihaliminion, why it was that the sapphire-eyes took it so easily, when the gods threw death-stars down to destroy their world? Everyone knows the sapphire-eyes could have hurled the death-stars back, if they'd cared to, but—"

"Nakhaba! What can the sapphire-eyes possibly have to do with the lunacy that's running rampant in our city? Will you tell me that, Dumanka?"

"Pass the wine, and I'll explain. And then you may want to listen to Zechtior Lukin, and even to read a little book that he's written, eh, Thihaliminion? Because there may be comfort in it for you, if you're as troubled by the difficulties in Dawinno as you seem to be." Dumanka nods toward the meat-cutter, a short thick-bodied man with a look of great strength and force about him. "The thing that Zechtior Lukin has taught me in our conversations," he says, "is the same thing that I've practiced all my life without having a name to put to it, which is that I acknowledge the absolute greatness of the gods and the role they play in our fates. They decide everything, and we must obey cheerfully, because the only other choices we have are to obey sadly, or to obey angrily, and those simply get us to the same place, but not as merrily. So we have to accept whatever comes, be it death-stars or hjjks, be it strange new religions or bloodshed in the streets, be it anything at all. What Zechtior Lukin and his Acknowledgers believe, good friend—and these two here are Acknowledgers too, Lisspar Moen and Gheppilin, and so am I, so have I always been, though I've only just discovered it—is a creed that brings peace to the soul and calmness to the mind, and has made me a better man, Thihaliminion, no doubt of it, absolutely a better man. And when I return to Dawinno, let me tell you, I'll will be bringing Zechtior Lukin's little book with me, and spreading the truth it contains to everyone who'll listen."

"Just what we need," Thihaliminion says, staring broodingly into his wine-cup. "One more new religion."

Thu-Kimnibol knocked and entered. Salaman, half dozing over a nearly empty bottle of wine, came instantly awake.

"You wanted to see me, cousin?"

"I did. You've had a chance to catch up on the news from your city, have you?" Salaman asked. "Taniane's daughter going mad? And Taniane herself so upset over it that she couldn't be bothered to govern her city for a time?"

Thu-Kimnibol's fur flared, his eyes grew bright. Tightly he said, "Yes. So I've heard."

"And have you heard also of the new hjjk-loving religion which has sprung up down there? It was the murder of the envoy Kundalimon that got it going, I'm told. My agents tell me that they're speaking of him in Dawinno as a holy prophet, who died for love of the People."

"Your agents are very efficient, cousin."

"They're paid to be. What they inform me is that the Kundalimon-worshipers are in favor of signing the Queen's treaty. Is it true that they want to invite hjjk missionaries to Dawinno to teach them the mysteries of hjjk wisdom?"

"Cousin, why are you asking me these questions?"

Crisply Salaman said, "Because you promised me that your people would fight, when the time comes. Instead this is what they do. This foolishness. This idiocy."

"Ah," Thu-Kimnibol said. "So that's it."

"It *is* idiocy, cousin."

"But useful idiocy, I think."

The king looked up, wonderstruck. "Useful?"

Thu-Kimnibol smiled. "Of course. The peace faction's playing right into our hands. They're carrying things to the extreme that will destroy them. Can you imagine what it would be like, cousin, with Dawinno full of hjjk preachers, clicking and hissing on every streetcorner, and everyone down there walking around with talk of Nest-bond and Queen-love and such on his lips, and the hjjks marching up and down the coast in droves, free as you please, going to visit their new colony in the south?"

"A nightmare," Salaman said.

"A nightmare indeed. But one that can be put to good use, provided there are still a few in Dawinno who haven't yet lost their minds, and I think there are." Thu-Kimnibol leaned close. "What I need to do is make them see the picture I've just sketched for you. Show them how the hjjks are trying to subvert us from within. Don't you realize, I'll say, that the new religion's designed to deliver us all into the clutches of the bugs? The Queen's love is a worse thing than the Queen's hatred, I'll tell them. At least we know where we stand with hatred. And in fact Queen-love and Queen-hate are the same thing wearing different masks. Friends, I'll say, this is a deadly threat. Accepting the treaty means opening our arms to our enemies. Do you want hjjks overrunning Dawinno the way they did in Vengiboneeza? And so on and so forth, until this new cult is driven underground, or put out of business altogether."

"And then?"

"And then we begin to sing the praises of war," said Thu-Kimnibol. "The virtues of carrying the attack to our foe, making the world safe for the People. War against the hjjks! Our only salvation! A war which you and I, cousin, must plan very carefully before I leave here. And then I'll go back to Dawinno and tell them that Salaman's our loyal ally, that he's waiting for us to join him in this holy endeavor, that our two cities must stand together against the bugs. After that, we simply need to arrange to start the war. Almost any sort of small incident ought to do it. What do you think, cousin? Isn't this new religion of hjjk-worship precisely the thing we've been waiting for?"

Salaman nodded. Then he began to laugh.

The boy Tikharein Tourb touched the shining Nest-guardian talisman that hung around his neck and said, "If only it would show us the Queen, Chhia Kreun! Maybe we could see Her with it, eh? If we used the talisman and our second sight at the same time, let's say."

"She's too far away," the girl said. "Second sight won't reach that far."

"Well, we could try twining, then."

Chhia Kreun stifled a giggle. "What do you know about twining, Tikharein Tourb?"

"Enough. I'm nine, you know."

"Thirteen's the twining-age."

"You're only eleven. But you act as though you know it all."

She groomed herself elaborately, plucking and smoothing. "I know more than you, at any rate."

"About twining, maybe. But not Nest-truth. Anyway, this isn't getting us anywhere. Look, what if I were to hold the Nest-guardian in my sensing-organ, and you and I were to twine, right here in front of the altar—"

"You can't be serious."

"I am! I am!"

"It's forbidden to twine until we're old enough. Besides, we don't know how. We may think we do, but until the offering-woman shows us, we—"

"Do you want to see the Queen or don't you?" Tikharein Tourb asked scornfully.

"Of course I do."

"Then what do you care about what's forbidden, or what the offering-woman is supposed to show us? The offering-woman doesn't mean anything to us. That's the old way. Nest-truth is everything. And this thing on my chest is the repository of Nest-truth." He ran his hand over the bit of hjjk-shell as if caressing it. "Kundalimon said so himself. If I hold it, and we twine—and maybe everyone else stands by us, chanting the chants at the same time—maybe then the Queen will appear to us, or we'll appear to the Queen—"

"Do you think so, really?"

"It's worth trying, isn't it?"

"But—twining—"

"All right," he said. "I'll find someone who's old enough to teach me how to twine. And then she and I will see the Queen together, and you can do as you please."

He turned as if to go. Chhia Kreun made a little gasping sound, and reached out toward him.

"No—wait—wait, Tikharein Tourb—"

6

Difficult Weather

Thu-Kimnibol will leave for Dawinno in another day or two, or at most perhaps three, as soon as his caravan is ready to take to the road. This is the night of the farewell dinner Salaman is giving in his honor. The black wind is howling tonight. Hail rattles against the windowpanes. There was hail last night too, hard little pellets that cut and stung and burned like bits of solidified flame. Tonight it's even wilder. And there's a darkness to the east that hints at the possibility of snow to follow.

The season is changing. Darkness comes early now. The first storms of the oncoming winter are beginning to blow through the City of Yissou.

For Salaman the coming of the hard weather meant the beginning of a difficult time. It was like that every year, but every year it was a little worse. He was losing resilience as he aged. His spirit, melancholy by nature, darkened even more when the black winds returned, and more and more year by year. This was likely to be the worst ever. Overnight, with the change, the last shred of his patience had fled: he was all irascibility now. The brunt fell on those who were closest to him, and they walked warily. Everything and everyone annoyed him: even Thu-Kimnobol, his honored guest, his dear and cherished friend, who tonight had the seat of grace that he had coveted long ago, beside the king, above Chham, above Athimin.

"By the Destroyer, it cuts right through the wall, that wind!" Thu-Kimnibol said, as they were serving the roasted thandibar haunch. "I'd forgotten about the winter weather here!"

Salaman, red-eyed from too much wine, poured himself another glass. Thu-Kimnibol's comment had come like a slap in the face. The king swung around and glared at him.

"You miss your easy Dawinno climate, do you? There's no winter there at all, is there? Well, you'll be home soon enough."

Winter, true winter, was something the tribe had not had to cope with in the Vengiboneeza days. That city nestled between mountains and sea in a zone of privileged climate, where the cool season was short and mild, bringing nothing worse than steady rains for a time. And the City of Dawinno, far to the south, lay becalmed in soft year-round warmth. But King Salaman's city, though sheltered by its location within the ancient death-star crater, was exposed on its eastern side to the harsh winds that blew at year's end from the heart of the continent, where the Long Winter had not yet entirely relinquished its grip.

Yissou's winter was brief, but it could be savage. When the black winds blew, trees were stripped of their leaves and the soil became dry and barren. Crops perished and livestock turned gaunt. Sometimes, not often, there was snow. The souls of the city's men and women grew crabbed and sour in that time of wind. They lost all generosity, and anger was general: there were bitter disputes between friends and mates, even violence. Though it lasted only a matter of weeks, everyone prayed constantly for the season to end, as in generations now forgotten their ancestors had prayed for an end to the Long Winter.

"It'll grow worse," said Salaman's mate Thaloin in bleak gloomy tones. "You're lucky you're leaving, prince. It'll seem like the Long Winter come again here, in another few weeks."

"Be quiet," Salaman said brusquely to her.

"My lord, you know it's true! This is only the first of it, this wind!"

"Will you be quiet, woman?" Salaman cried. He slapped the flat of his hand against the bare wood of the table so fiercely that glasses and tableware jumped, and some wine was spilled.

To Thu-Kimnibol he said, "She exaggerates. Now that she's growing old the cold weather bothers her bones and makes her cranky. But I tell you, we have only a few weeks of trying winds here, and sometimes a little snow, and then it's spring." He laughed harshly, a heavy, forced laugh that cost him some aching of the ribs. "I enjoy the shifting of the seasons. I find it refreshing. I wouldn't want to live where the weather is unvaryingly fine. But of course I regret it if you've been caused any small discomfort since it turned colder, cousin."

"Not at all, cousin. I can abide some chilling."

"Our little winter isn't really all that harsh. Eh? Eh?" The king glanced around the table. Chham nodded, and Athimin, and then all the others, even Thaloin. They knew his moods all too well. The wind gusted wildly again. Salaman felt his temper rising another notch. He struggled to contain it.

Raising his glass, he waved it vaguely in Thu-Kimnibol's direction. "Enough of this talk. A toast, a toast! To my dear friend and beloved cousin Thu-Kimnibol!"

"Thu-Kimnibol," Chham echoed quickly.

"Thu-Kimnibol," the others chimed in.

"My dear friend," Thu-Kimnibol said, lifting his own glass. "Who'd have thought it, twenty years ago, that I'd sit here tonight, at this very table, in this very seat, by Salaman's hearth-fire, thinking, How splendid he is, what a great friend, what a staunch ally! To you, dear Salaman!"

The king studied him as he drank. He seemed sincere. He *was* sincere. They *had* become friends. The last thing I would have expected, he thought. His eyes filled with tears. Dear Thu-Kimnibol. Good old Thu-Kimnibol. How I'll miss you, when you leave here!

"Wine!" he called. "Wine for Thu-Kimnibol! And wine for the king!"

Weiawala hopped up at once to refill their glasses. As she came within range of Thu-Kimnibol, he slipped his hand along her waist, and down the side of her leg. He never missed a chance to fondle her and stroke her. From the moment soon after his arrival when she had begun to share his bedchamber, he'd scarcely looked at any other woman here. Good, Salaman thought. A royal mating will come of this, perhaps. There's reason to think Thu-Kimnibol can make himself chieftain in Dawinno after Taniane's reign is over, since there seems to be no woman there who's fit to have the job. How useful, then, to have one of my own daughters sitting on Dawinno's throne at Thu-Kimnibol's side.

He took a deep pull of his wine. He was beginning to feel a little better now. The wind seemed to be dying down.

"Dear Thu-Kimnibol," he said again, after a time.

There was a sound like the slap of a giant hand against the palace wall. The wind's brief lull was over. The gale was back with twice the fervor of before. And with its return, Salaman's little moment of good feelings was gone. Suddenly there was a pounding in his head, a constriction in his breast.

"What a terrible night it is," Thaloin whispered to Vladirilka. "It'll drive the king mad." It was only the barest thread of a whisper. But Salaman's hearing was unnaturally keen when the black winds were blowing. Her words reached him with the force of a shout.

"What's that? What? You think I'll go mad, is that what you say?" he cried, springing up. Thaloin shrank back, one arm across her face to protect herself. The room grew very still. Salaman loomed over her. "A terrible night. This terrible season. A terrible night. This terrible season. The Long Winter come again, you say. You complain all the time, woman. Can't you ever be content with what you have? I ought to turn you out into the cold so you can see what it's *really* like!" Thu-Kimnibol was staring at him. The king gripped the edge of the table to steady himself. Rage is coursing like lava through his brain. In another moment he'll be roaring. It's all he can do to keep from knocking Thaloin across the room. His own mate, whom he cherishes. Perhaps she's right. Perhaps he's mad already. This damnable wind, this accursed season.

I'm ruining the feast, he thinks. I'm shaming myself and my whole family before Thu-Kimnibol.

"You must excuse me," he says to his guest in a hoarse, ragged fragment of a voice. "This wind—I'm not well—"

He looks around the room, half glaring, half apologetic. Dares them all to speak. No one does. His three mates are terrified. Thaloin is ready to fling herself down under the table. Vladirilka looks appalled. Only Sinithista, the calmest and sturdiest of them, seems in any way composed. "You," he says, beckoning her to his side out of his group of women, and goes sweeping off with her to his bedchamber amidst the screaming of the wind.

In the depths of the night a terrible fantasy overcomes the king. Salaman imagines that he is lying not with his familiar mate Sinithista but with a female of the hjjks, whose hard scaly body is pressed close against him.

Her black-bristled fore-claws caress his cheeks. Her powerful multiple-jointed hind legs are clasped tightly about his thighs, and her mid-limbs hold him by the waist. Her huge gleaming many-faceted eyes, bulging like toadstools, stare passionately into his. She makes harsh rasping sounds of delight. Worst of all, he is pressing himself to her with equal fervor, his fingers running tenderly over the orange breathing-tubes that dangle beside her head, his lips seeking out her fierce sharp beak. And his mating-rod, stiff and immense with lust, is plunged deep into some mysterious orifice of her long rigid thorax.

He cries out in horror, a dreadful wailing bellow of pain and rage that might almost have toppled the city wall itself, and pulls himself free. In a wild bound he springs from the bed, and goes searching madly about the room for a glowberry candle.

"My lord?" Sinithista called, in a small, plaintive voice.

Salaman, standing naked and trembling convulsively beside the window, managed to find the light and uncover it. No hjjk, no. Only Sinithista, sitting up in bed and staring at him in astonishment. She was shivering. Her breasts were heaving, her sexual parts were swollen in arousal. He looked down at his mating-rod, throbbing painfully, still rigid. All a dream, then. He had been coupling with Sinithista in his drunken sleep, and had taken her for—for—

"My lord, what is it that troubles you?" Sinithista asked.

"Nothing. Nothing. An ugly dream."

"Come back to bed, then!"

"No," he told her sternly. If he lets himself sleep again this night the dream will seize him anew. Perhaps if he banishes Sinithista from the chamber—no, no, that would be worse, being alone. He does not dare to close his eyes a moment. Behind his eyelids the dreadful image of that monster would burst forth again.

"My lord." The woman was sobbing now.

He pitied her. He had abandoned her in mid-coupling, after all. He had not been with her in many weeks, not since his fascination with Vladirilka had overwhelmed him, and now he appeared to be spurning her.

But he wasn't going to return to the bed.

Salaman went to her and touched her lightly on the shoulder, and whispered, "This dream has so disturbed me that I must have some air. I'll come to you again later, when my mind is clear. Go back to sleep."

"My lord, your outcry was so frightening—"

"Yes," he said. He found a robe and threw it on, and went from the room.

There was nothing but darkness in the palace. The air was frigid. A ghastly wind was ripping down out of the east, and white swirls of snow rode on it like angry ghosts. But he couldn't stay here. The entire building seemed polluted by his monstrous nightmare. He went down and down, and out to the stables. Two grooms looked up sleepily at him as he entered, saw it was the king, and rolled over again. They were accustomed to his moods. If he wanted a xlendi in the depths of the night, well, that was nothing new to them.

He selected a mount and rode out, toward the city wall, to his private pavilion.

The storm raged above him, so strong a wind that it was a wonder it didn't blow the Moon itself out of the sky. There was more snow with it than he could remember, already enough to encrust the ground with white to a depth of a fingertip or so, and coming down more swiftly all the time. He looked back and by the blurred moonlight he saw that the xlendi's hooves were leaving a sharply pronounced track in the whiteness.

Tethering his mount below the pavilion, Salaman raced up the staircase to the top. His heart was hammering at his ribs. In the pavilion the king grasped the window-ledge and hung his head outside, heedless of the icy gusts. He needed to cleanse it of every vestige of the dream that had coursed through his sleeping wine-sotted mind.

The landscape beyond the city, fitfully illuminated by such moonlight as could break through the storm's burden of snow, was white as death. A knife-blade wind scooped up the fallen crystals, swept them onward, whirled them into sinister patterns. The king was unable to get the taste of the hjjk-woman's beak from his mouth. His mating-rod had subsided now, but it still ached with the pain of unfulfilled desire and it seemed to him that a cool fire burned along its entire shaft, the sign of some corrosive hjjk fluid that he must have come in contact with during that ghastly coupling.

Perhaps I should go out there, Salaman thought, and strip off my robe and roll naked in the snow until I'm clean—

"Father?"

He whirled. "Who's there?"

"Biterulve, father." The boy peered in uneasily from the vestibule of the pavilion. His eyes were very wide. "Father, you frighten us. When my mother said you'd arisen and gone rushing madly from your bedchamber—and then you were seen leaving the palace itself—"

"You followed me?" Salaman cried. "You spied on me?"

He lurched forward, seizing the slender boy, pulling him roughly into the pavilion, and slapped him three times with all his strength. Biterulve cried out, as much perhaps in surprise as pain, after the first blow, but was silent thereafter. The king saw his son's astounded eyes gleaming into his by the light of the Moon and the reflection of that light on the whirling flakes of snow. He released the boy and staggered back toward the window.

"Father," Biterulve said softly, went to him as though heedless of all risk, holding his arms outstretched.

A great convulsive shiver passed through the king, and Salaman gathered Biterulve in and held the boy in a hug so tight it forced a gust of breath from him. Then he let him go, and said very quietly, "I should not have struck you. But you shouldn't have followed me here. You know that no one is permitted to come upon me in the night in my pavilion."

"We were so frightened, father. My mother said you were not in your right mind."

"Perhaps I wasn't."

"Can we help you, my lord?"

"I doubt that very much. Very much indeed." Salaman reached for the young prince again, collecting him in the curve of his arm and pulling him tight against him. Hollowly he said, "I had a dream tonight, boy, such a dream as I won't disclose in any way, not to you, not to anyone, except to say that it was a dream that could peel a man's sanity from him like the skin from a fruit. That dream still afflicts me. I may never wash myself clean of it."

"Oh, father, father—"

"It's this beastly season. The black wind beats on my skull. It drives me crazier every year."

"Shall I leave you by yourself?" Biterulve asked.

"Yes. No. No, stay." Brooding, the king spun around and stared into the darkness beyond the wall again. He kept the boy at his side. "You know how much I love you, Biterulve."

"Of course I do."

"And that when I struck you just now—it was the madness in me that was striking, it wasn't I myself—"

Biterulve nodded, although he said nothing.

Salaman hugged him to him. Gradually the fury in his soul subsided.

Then, peering into the night, he said, "Am I mad again, or do you see a figure out there? Someone riding on a xlendi, coming up from the Southern Highway?"

"You're right, father! I see him too."

"But who'd come here in the middle of the night, in weather like this?"

"Whoever he is, we have to open the gate for him."

"Wait," Salaman said. He cupped his hand to his mouth and cried, in a voice like a trumpet, "Hoy! You out there! You, can you hear me?"

It was all he could do to make his voice carry above the storm.

The xlendi, stumbling in the snow, seemed near the end of its strength. The rider looked little better. He rode with his head down, clinging desperately to his saddle.

"Who are you?" Salaman called. "Identify yourself, man!"

The stranger looked up. He made a faint croaking sound, inaudible in the wind.

"What? Who?" Salaman shouted.

The man made the sound again, less vigorously even than the last time.

"Father, he's dying!" Biterulve said. "Let him in. What harm can he do?"

"A stranger—in the night, in the storm—"

"He's just one man, and half dead, and there are two of us."

"And if there are others out there, waiting for us to open the gate?"

"Father!"

Something in the boy's tone cut through Salaman's madness, and he nodded and called to the rider again, telling him to head for the gate. Then the king and his son went below to throw it open for him. But it was with the greatest difficulty that the stranger managed to guide his mount inside the wall. The beast wobbled a zigzag path through the snow. Twice the man nearly fell from the staggering xlendi, and when he was finally within he let go of the reins and simply toppled over the animal's side, landing trembling on his knees and elbows. The king signaled to Biterulve to help him up.

He was a helmeted Beng. Though swaddled in skins and pelts tied tightly about him with yellow rope, he looked nearly frozen. His eyes were glazed, and a glossy coating of ice clung to his fur, which was of an odd pale pinkish-yellow cast, very strange for a Beng.

"Nakhaba!" he cried suddenly, and a shiver ran through him so fierce that it seemed likely to hurl his head free of his shoulders. "What weather! The cold is like fire! Is this the Long Winter come again?"

"Who are you, man?" Salaman asked sternly.

"Take me—inside—"

"Who are you, first?"

"Courier. From the chieftain Taniane. Bearing a message to the lord Thu-Kimnibol." The stranger swayed and nearly fell. Then he pulled himself erect with some immense effort and said, in a deeper, stronger voice, "I am Tembi Somdech, guardsman of the City of Dawinno. In Nakhaba's name, take me to the lord Thu-Kimnibol at once."

And he fell face forward into the snow.

Salaman, scowling, gathered him up into his arms as easily as if the man were made of feathers. He gestured to Biterulve to collect all three xlendis, his own and his father's and the stranger's, and tie their reins together so that they could be led. On foot they proceeded inward to the core of the city. There was a guardhouse a few hundred paces away.

As they approached it, Salaman saw something so strange that he began to wonder whether he had never left his bed this night, but still lay dreaming by Sinithista's side. There was a plaza yet another few hundred paces deeper still into the city, and Salaman, standing outside the guardhouse with the unconscious stranger in his arms, was able to see down the street into it. Within the plaza some twenty or thirty capering figures were dancing round and round by torchlight. They were men and women both, and a few children, all naked, or nearly so, wearing no more than sashes and scarves, and moving in wild jubilant prancing steps, flinging their arms about, violently throwing their heads back, kicking their knees high.

As Salaman watched, astounded, they completed the circuit of the plaza and disappeared down the Street of Sweetsellers at its farther end.

"Biterulve?" he said, wonderingly. "Did you see them too, those people in the Plaza of the Sun?"

"The dancers? Yes."

"Has the whole city gone mad tonight, or is it only me?"

"They are Acknowledgers, I think."

"Acknowledgers? What are they?"

"A sort of people—people who—" Biterulve faltered. He made a sign of confusion, turning his palms outward. "I'm not sure, father. You'd have to ask Athimin. He knows something about them. Father, we have to get this man indoors, or he'll die."

"Yes. Yes." Salaman stared toward the plaza. It was empty now. If I go down there, he wondered, will I see their footprints in the snow, or are Biterulve's words part of my dream also?

Acknowledgers, he thought. Acknowledgers. What is it that they acknowledge? Or whom?

He carried the man inside the guardhouse.

Three blurry-eyed guardsmen, all too obviously caught sleeping, came lurching out. When they saw it was the king, they coughed and cringed in horror, and made obeisance; but he had no time to give attention to such creatures now. "Get a bed for this man, and some warm broth, and put dry clothing on him," he ordered. To Biterulve he said more quietly, "Check the saddlebags of his xlendi. I want to see that message before Thu-Kimnibol does."

He waited, staring at his fingertips, until the boy returned.

Biterulve came in, some minutes later, with a packet in his hand. "This is it, I think."

"Read it to me. My eyes are weak tonight."

"It's sealed, father."

"Break the seal. Do it carefully."

"Is this wise, father?"

"Give it to me!" Salaman snapped, seizing the packet from him. Indeed it bore the red seal of Taniane, with the chieftain's imprint in it. A secret message, for Thu-Kimnibol. Well, there were ways of dealing with seals. He shouted to the guardsmen to bring him a knife and a torch, and heated the seal until it was soft, and pried it up. The packet, when unfastened, opened into a broad vellum sheet.

"Read it to me now," the king said.

Biterulve put his fingers to the sheet and the words sprang to life on it. At first he seemed puzzled, not having been trained in the Beng-influenced writing now in favor in the City of Dawinno; but it took him only a moment to adjust his mind to it. "It's very short. *Come home at once, regardless of whatever you're doing,* is what Taniane says. And she says, *Things here are very bad. We need you.*"

"That's all?"

"Nothing else, father."

Salaman took the sheet from him, folded it again, carefully resealed it. "Put it in the saddlebags where you found it," he told the boy.

One of the guardsmen appeared. "He refuses the broth, sire. He's too weak for it. He seems starved and frozen. He's dying, is what I think."

"Force the broth into him," the king said. "I won't have him die on my hands. Well, man, don't just stand there!"

"No use," the second guardsman said. "He's gone, sire."

"Gone? Are you sure?"

"He sat up, and cried out something in Beng, and his whole body shook in a way that was fearful to watch. Then he fell down on the bed and didn't move again."

These southerners, Salaman thought. A few weeks of riding through the cold and they fall down dead.

But for the guardsmen's benefit he made a few quick holy signs, and intoned a Yissou-have-mercy, and told them to summon a healer just in case there was still some life in the man after all. But also make arrangements for his burial, he ordered. To Biterulve he said, "Take that xlendi to the palace stables and bring the saddlebags to my private chamber, and put them under lock and key. Then go to the hostelry and wake up Thu-Kimnibol. Let him know what's happened. Tell him he can collect his message when he comes to the palace in the morning."

"And you, father?"

"To the pavilion for a little while, I think. I need to clear my mind."

He went outside. Glancing down the street to the left, he stared into the Plaza of the Sun, to see if the Acknowledgers had come back to it to dance again. No, the plaza was deserted. He touched his hand to his throbbing forehead, bent, scooped up a few fingers' worth of snow, and rubbed it against his brow. That was a little better.

It was almost dawn. The wind howled unabated. But the snow was ceasing, now. It mantled·the ground to a surprising depth. He couldn't recall a snowfall this heavy in thirty years. Was that why those people had come out? To dance in it, to rejoice over the strangeness of it?

Acknowledgers, he thought. Acknowledgers.

I have to speak with Athimin about them in the morning.

He ascended the wall and stood for a long while at the window of his pavilion, staring out into the bleakness of the southern plains, until his mind was utterly void of thought and his aching body had yielded up some of the tautness of its tense muscles. Eventually a pink light began to appear in the east. This whole night has been a dream, Salaman told himself. Feeling strangely unweary, as though he had passed into some state beyond even the possibility of fatigue—or as though, perhaps, he had died without noticing it, somewhere during the night—he went slowly down the stairs and rode back through the awakening city to the palace.

Athimin was the first to come to him that morning as he sat enthroned, waiting in eerie tranquility, in the Hall of State. There was something odd about the prince's movements as he approached the throne, something hesitant, that Salaman didn't like. Ordinarily Athimin carried himself in a burly, decisive way, as befitted the next-to-oldest of the king's eight sons. But now he seemed not so much to stride as to skulk toward the throne, giving his father wary glances as though peeping at him over the top of an arm that was flung defensively across his face.

"The gods grant you a good morning, father," he said, sounding oddly tentative. "They tell me you didn't sleep well. The lady Sinithista—"

"You've talked to her already, have you?"

"Chham and I breakfasted with her, and she seemed troubled. She told us you'd had a profound dark dream, and had gone rushing out in the night like one who's possessed—"

"The lady Sinithista," Salaman said, "should keep her royal mouth shut, or I'll shut it for her. But I didn't ask you here to discuss the nature of my dreams." He gave the prince a sharp look. "What are Acknowledgers, Athimin?"

"Acknowledgers, sir?"

"Acknowledgers, yes. You've heard the term before, have you?"

"Why, yes, father. But it surprises me that you have."

"It was in the night just past, also, one of my many adventures this night. I was outside the guardhouse near the Plaza of the Sun, and I looked down the street and saw lunatics dancing naked in the snow. Biterulve was with me, and I said, 'What are those?' and he said, 'They are Acknowledgers, father.' And he could say nothing more about them than that. You'd be able to give me better information, he told me."

Athimin shifted his weight uneasily from one foot to the other. Salaman had never seen him like this before, so uncertain, so restive. The king began to smell the smell of treachery.

"Acknowledgers, sir—these dancers you saw—these people you rightly call madmen—"

"Lunatics is the word I used. Those who are driven mad by the Moon. Though there was precious little moonlight visible through the driving snow while they were dancing. Who are these people, Athimin?"

"Unfortunate strange folk is what they are, whose minds have been turned by drivel and nonsense. They are just such folk as would dance when the black wind blows, or frolic naked in the snow. Or do many another strange thing. Nothing fazes them. They hold the conviction that death isn't important, that you should never at any time care about risk, but just do whatever seems right to you, without fear, without hindrance."

Salaman leaned forward, gripping the armrests of the Throne of Harruel.

"So this is some new philosophy, then, you say?"

"More like a religion, sir. Or so we think. There's a system of belief that they teach one another—they have a book, a scripture—and they hold secret meetings, which we have yet to infiltrate. We've only begun to understand them, you see. The sapphire-eyes folk seem to be what they most admire, because they stayed calm when the Long Winter was coming on, and were indifferent to death. The Acknowledgers say that this is the great thing taught by Dawinno the Destroyer, that we need to show indifference to dying, that death is simply an aspect of change and is therefore holy."

"Indifference to dying," said Salaman, musing. "Acceptance of death as an aspect of change."

"That's why they call themselves Acknowledgers," Athimin said. "The thing that they acknowledge is that death can't be avoided, that it is in fact the design of the gods. And so they do whatever comes into their heads to do, father, regardless of risk or discomfort."

Salaman clenched his fists. He felt fury rising in him again after these hours of early morning calmness.

So the City of Dawinno wasn't the only place plagued by an absurd new creed? Gods! It sickened him to hear that such madness was loose virtually under his very nose. This could lead to anarchy, this cult of martyrdom. People who fear nothing will do anything. And worship of death wasn't what his city needed. What was needed here was life, nothing but life, new flowering, new growth, new strength!

He rose angrily to his feet.

"Insanity!" he cried. "How many such lunatics do we have in this city?"

"We've counted a hundred ninety of them, father. There may be more."

"You seem to know a great deal about these Acknowledgers."

"I've been investigating them all this month past, sir."

"You have? And said not a word to me?"

"Our findings were only preliminary. We needed to know more before—"

"More?" Salaman bellowed. "Madness is spreading like a pestilence in the city, and you needed to know more before you could tell me even that such a thing exists here? I was to be kept in the dark about it all? Why? And for how long? How long?"

"Father, the black winds were blowing, and we felt—"

"Ah. Ah, I understand now." He stepped forward and brought his arm up in the same instant, and struck Athimin ferociously across the cheek. The prince's head rocked back. Sturdy as he was, he nearly lost his balance at the force of the blow. For an instant there was fiery rage in the younger man's eyes; then he recovered, and took a step away from the throne, breathing heavily and rubbing the place where he had been struck. He stared at his father with a look of utter disbelief on his face.

"So this is how it begins," said Salaman very calmly, after some moments. "The old man is considered so unstable, so easily deranged, that during the troublesome season he has to be kept from learning of significant developments that have occurred in the city, so that he won't become so upset by them that he'll take unpredictable action. That's the start of it, shielding the old man from difficult knowledge at a time of the year when he's known to behave rashly. The next step is to shield him even from the mildly disturbing things, so that he'll never feel any distress at all, for who knows? He might be dangerous when he's troubled in any way, even the slightest. And a little while after that, the princes gather and conclude among themselves that he's become so capricious and volatile that he can't be trusted even in the times of calm weather, and so he's gently removed from the throne, with the softest of apologies, and sent to live under guard in some smaller palace, while his eldest son takes his place on the Throne of Harruel, and—"

"Father!" Athimin cried in a strangled voice. "None of this is true! By all the gods, I swear that no such thoughts have entered the minds of any of—"

"Keep quiet!" Salaman thundered, raising his hand as though to strike him again. He gestured furiously to the throne-room guards. "You—you— convey Lord Athimin to the North Prison immediately, and have him kept in custody there until I send further word concerning his disposal."

"Father!"

"You'll have plenty of time to reflect on your errors while you're sitting in your cell," the king said. "And I'll have writing materials sent to you, so you can prepare a full report on these deranged Acknowledgers of yours, telling me everything that you were too cowardly or too perfidious to tell me until I pulled some of it from you this morning. For there's more: I'm certain there's more. And you'll tell me all of it. Do you understand me?" He made a sweeping gesture. "Take him out of here."

Athimin threw him a stunned, bewildered look. But he said not a word, nor did he resist in any way while the guards, looking no less astonished than he, led him from the great hall.

Salaman reseated himself. He leaned back against the smooth obsidian. He drew deep, steady breaths. For all his shouting and fury, he saw that he was beginning now to glide easily back into that curious godlike calmness that had come over him in his pavilion at dawn.

But his hand was tingling from the blow he had given Athimin.

I have struck two of my sons this same night, he thought.

He couldn't remember having hit any of them ever before, and now he'd struck two in a matter of hours, and sent Athimin to prison besides. Well, the black winds were blowing. And Biterulve had broken a rule by coming to him in the pavilion. Maybe he thought that because he'd been allowed there once, he could come at any time. Athimin, too—what audacity, keeping the news of the Acknowledgers to himself! Downright dereliction of duty, it was. Which had to be punished, even if it was one of the royal princes who was guilty of it. *Especially* if it was one of the royal princes.

And yet, to strike the gentle Biterulve—and the steady and capable Athimin, who might well be king here one day if anything evil befell his brother Chham—

No matter. They'd have to forgive him. He was their father; he was their king. And the black winds were blowing.

Salaman sat back and idly stroked the armrests of the throne. His mind was tranquil, and yet it was whirling at a pace almost beyond his comprehension. Thoughts, ideas, plans, swirled through it like raging gales, one after another. He made unexpected connections. He saw new possibilities. Is it martyrdom that these Acknowledgers long for? Good. Good. We'll have a use for some martyrs around here soon. If martyrdom is what they love, well, then, martyrdom is what they will have. And everyone will be the better off for it, they and we both.

He would have to have a talk with the leader of these Acknowledgers.

There were sounds in the hall outside. "The Prince Thu-Kimnibol," called a herald.

The lofty figure of Harruel's son stood in the doorway.

"Almost ready to leave us, are you?" Salaman asked.

"Another few hours and we'll be ready to set out," said Thu-Kimnibol. "If the storm doesn't start up again." He came farther into the room. "I hear from your son that a messenger from Dawinno arrived during the night."

"A Beng, yes, a guardsman. He was caught in the storm, poor man. Died practically in my arms. He was carrying a letter for you. Over there, on that table."

"With your permission, cousin—" Thu-Kimnibol said.

He snatched it up, stared at its face intently for a moment, ripped it open without pausing to inspect the seal. He read it slowly through, perhaps several times, running his fingers carefully over the vellum. Reading did not appear to be an easy thing for Thu-Kimnibol. He looked up finally and said, "From the chieftain. A good thing I'm about ready to leave here, cousin. I'm ordered to go back to Dawinno right away. There's trouble there, Taniane says."

"Trouble? Does she say what kind of trouble?"

Thu-Kimnibol shrugged. "All she says is that things are very bad." He began to pace. "Cousin, this worries me. First the murders, and then the autumn caravan comes bearing word of upheavals and confusions and a new religion, and now this. Come home at once, she says! Things are very bad! Yissou, how I wish I were there now! If only I could fly, cousin!" He paused, steadying himself. In an altogether different tone he said, "Cousin, can you tell me anything about this?"

"About what, cousin?"

"These troubles in Dawinno. I wonder if perhaps you've had some report from sources of your own, something that could let me know what to expect."

"Nothing."

"Those efficient, highly paid agents of yours—"

"Have told me nothing, cousin. Nothing whatever." There was a sticky little moment of silence between them. "Do you think I'd conceal news of your own city from you, Thu-Kimnibol? You and I are allies, and even friends, or have you forgotten?"

A little shamefacedly Thu-Kimnibol said, after a moment, "Forgive me, cousin. I simply wondered—"

"You know as much as I do about what's going on down there. But listen, listen, cousin: it may not be as bad as Taniane thinks. She's had a hard season. She's getting old, she's weary, she has a difficult daughter. You may find things a little shaky there, but I promise you you won't find chaos, you won't find the place in flames, you won't find hjjks preaching the love of the Queen in the Presidium building. Taniane's simply decided that she needs your steadying hand close by her in these troubled times. And that's what you'll provide. You'll help her do whatever's needed to restore order, and all will be well. After all, you're coming home with an alliance, and after the alliance comes a war. I tell you this, cousin, nothing brings a troubled land back to its senses faster than the prospect of war!"

Thu-Kimnibol smiled. "Perhaps so. What you say makes sense."

"Of course it does." Salaman made an elaborate gesture of farewell. "On your way, then. You've done all you can here. Now your city needs you. A war is coming, and you'll be the man of the hour when the fighting begins."

"But *will* it begin? We talked of the need for some incident, Salaman, some provocation, something to get the whole thing going, something I can use to persuade my people to send troops north to join forces with you—"

"Leave that to me," Salaman said.

It had also been a season of difficult weather to the south, in the City of Dawinno: no black winds there, nor hail or snow, but the rains came daily for week after week, until hillsides crumbled into muddy streams and floodwaters ran in the streets. It was the worst winter since the founding of the city. The sky was a leaden gray, the air was cool and heavy, the sun seemed to have vanished forever.

The simpler folk began to ask each other if a new death-star had struck the Earth and the Long Winter had returned. But simple folk had been asking themselves such things ever since the departure from the cocoon, whenever the weather was not to their liking. The wiser ones knew that the world had no new Long Winters to fear in their lifetimes, that such catastrophes came to the Earth only once in millions of years and that the one that had lately afflicted the planet was over and done with. Even those wiser ones, though, chafed at the dreary days and nights of endless rainfall and suffered when the swirling waters poured through the lower floors of their splendid homes.

Nialli Apuilana rarely left her room high up in the House of Nakhaba. With the help of Boldirinthe's potions and aromatic herbs and prayers, she had driven out the fevers and pestilences that had entered her as she lay exhausted in the swamp, and regained her strength. But doubts and confusions assailed her, and there were no potions for those. She spent most of her time alone. Taniane came to see her once, a strained and unsatisfactory visit for both of them. Not long afterward Hresh paid a call, and took her hands in his, and held them and smiled, and stared into her eyes as though he could ease her of all that troubled her with a glance.

Other than Hresh and Taniane, she saw no one. A note came from Husathirn Mueri, asking if she'd care to dine with him. She let it pass unanswered.

"You're a smart one," the young Beng priest who had the room just down the hall from her said one day, meeting her as she came out to get her tray of food. "Staying holed up in there all the time. If I could, I'd do the same thing. This filthy rain goes on and on."

"Does it?" Nialli Apuilana asked, without interest.

"Like a scourge. Like a curse. Nakhaba's curse, it is."

"Is it?" she said.

"Whole city washing away. Better off staying indoors, is what I say. Oh, you're a smart one!"

Nialli Apuilana nodded and smiled faintly, and took her tray, and retreated into her room. Afterward she made a point of looking out before going into the hall to make certain that no one was there.

Sometimes, after that, she went to the window and watched the rain. Most often she sat crosslegged in the center of the room, absentmindedly grooming herself hour after hour while letting her thoughts drift without direction.

Now and again she would take the hjjk star down from the wall, the amulet of plaited grass that she had carried back with her from the Nest years ago. Would hold it, would stare into the open place at its center, would let her mind drift. Sometimes she could see the pink glow of Nest-light coming from it, and dim figures moving about: Militaries, Egg-makers, Kindlers, Nest-thinkers. Once she thought she even had a glimpse of the Queen-chamber itself, of the great unmoving mysterious bulk within it.

But the visions were vague ones. Most of the time the star showed her nothing at all.

She had no clear idea of where to go next, or what to do, or even who she was. She felt lost between worlds, mysteriously suspended, helpless.

Kundalimon's death had been the death of love for her, the death of the world. No one had understood her as he had; and she had never felt such an understanding of anyone else. It hadn't been just the twining, and certainly not the coupling, that had bound them together. It was the sense of shared experience, of knowledge held in common. It was Nest-bond. They had touched the Queen; the Queen had touched them; the Queen then had stood as a bridge between their souls, making it possible for them to open themselves to one another.

It had only been a beginning, though. And then Kundalimon had been taken away. And everything had seemed to end.

What didn't end was the rain. It fell on the city and on the bay, on the hills and on the lakes. In the farming district of Tangok Seip, on the eastern side of the Emakkis Valley where the inner range of coastal mountains began to rise, it fell with such force that it peeled the soil from the slopes in torrential mud-slides such as had never been seen since the founding of the city. Whole hillsides sheared away and flowed down into the bottomlands.

A Stadrain farmer named Quisinimoir Flendra, taking advantage of a lull in the latest storm to chase after a prize vimbor bull that had broken free from its compound, was crossing the rain-soaked breast of a hill when the earth gave way practically at his feet. He dropped down and dug his fingers into the sodden earth, sure that he'd be swept over the edge into this newly formed abyss and buried alive. There was a terrible sickening sound, a kind of sucking roar, a liquid thunder.

Quisinimoir Flendra held tight and prayed to every god whose name he could remember: his own first, the All-Merciful, and then Nakhaba the Interceder, and then Yissou, Dawinno, Emakkis. He was struggling to remember the names of the other two Koshmar gods when he realized that the hill had stopped collapsing.

He looked down. The earth had broken away in a crescent just in front of him, revealing a sheer face of brown earth laced with exposed roots.

Other things were showing too. A great tiled arch, for one; a row of thick columns, their bases hidden somewhere deep in the earth; a scattering of shards and fragments of ruined structures strewn over the newly exposed face of the shattered hillside like so much trash. And also there was the mouth of a stone-vaulted tunnel, leading into the hill. Quisinimoir Flendra, hanging head-down, was able to make out the beginnings of a cave. He peered in astonishment and awe into its mysterious depths.

Then the rain started up again. The hill might collapse a little further, and take him down with it. Hastily he scrambled down the back face of the hill and headed for his house.

He said nothing about what he had seen to anyone.

But it remained with him, even entering his dreams. He imagined that the Great World people still lived inside that hill: that slow solemn massive sapphire-eyes folk were moving about in there with reptilian grace, speaking to one another in mystic poetry, and with them were pale fragile long-limbed humans, and the little flowery vegetals, and the dome-headed mechanicals, and all the other amazing beings of that splendid era, living on and on in a kind of cocoon much like the cocoon that Quisinimoir Flendra's own tribe had inhabited all during the Long Winter.

Why not? We had a cocoon. Why not them?

He wondered if he dared to investigate the place again, and decided that he didn't. But then it struck him that there might be treasure in that cave, and that if he didn't go in there to look for it someone else sooner or later would.

When there had been three straight days without rain he went back to the broken hillside, carrying a rope, a pick, and some clusters of glow-berries. He let himself down very carefully over the edge of the cave-in and wriggled into the tunnel. Paused, listened, heard nothing, warily went deeper.

He was in a stone-vaulted room. Another one lay beyond. A rockfall blocked access beyond that. There was no sign of any life. The silence had a weight of thousands of years. Quisinimoir Flendra, prowling cautiously, saw nothing useful at first, only the usual bits and fragments that these ancient sites contained. But toward the back of the inner room he found a box of green metal, half buried in the detritus on the floor of the cave, that came apart like wet paper when he poked it.

There were machines inside: of what kind, he had not the slightest idea. There were eleven of them, little metal globes, each one larger than his fist, with little studs and projections on their surfaces. He picked one up and touched one of the studs. A beam of green light burst from an opening in the thing and with a little whooshing sound it cut a round hole the size of his chest in the wall of the cave just opposite him, so deep that he couldn't see how far it went. Hastily he let the globe drop.

He heard pebbles falling in the new opening. The hillside creaked and groaned. It was the sound of rock masses shifting about somewhere far within.

All-Merciful save me! It's all going to fall in on me!

But then everything was still again, except for the faint dry trickle of falling sand in the hole he had so inadvertently carved. Quisinimoir Flendra, scarcely daring to breathe, tiptoed to the mouth of the tunnel, pulled himself up quickly and frantically to the safety of the hilltop, and ran all the way back to his house.

He had heard about such machines. They were things of the Great World. You were supposed to report such finds to the House of Knowledge in the city. Well, so be it. The scholars of the House of Knowledge were welcome to anything they could find in that cave. He didn't even want a reward. Let them have it all, he thought. Just so long as I don't have to go near any of those things again—so long as they don't ask me to go back in there myself to show them where everything is—

Suddenly, with a shudder, Nialli Apuilana imagines that her room is full of hjjks. She isn't even holding the plaited star when they come. They simply burst into being all around her, congealing out of the air itself.

These aren't the gentle wise creatures of her feverish recollections. No, she sees them now as others of her kind have always seen them: huge frightening glossy-shelled bristle-limbed things with ferocious beaks and great glittering eyes, milling in hordes about her, clicking and clattering in a terrifying way. And behind them she glimpses the immense mass of the Queen in Her resting-place—motionless, gigantic, grotesque. Calling to her, offering her the joys of Nest-bond, offering her the comforts of Queen-love.

Queen-love?

Nest-bond?

What did those things mean? They were empty noises. They were food that carried no nourishment.

Nialli Apuilana trembles and draws back, pressing herself into the farthest corner of the room. She shuts her eyes, but even so she is unable to blot out the sight of the nightmare creatures that crowd up against her, clicking, clicking, clicking.

Get away from me!

Horrid hideous insects. How she loathes them! And yet she knows there was a time once when she had wanted to be one of them. For a time she had actually thought she was. Or had all that been a dream, just a phantom of the night just past—her sojourn in the Nest, her talks with Nest-thinker, her taste of Nest-truth? Had she really lived gladly among the hjjks, and come to love them and their Queen? Was such a thing possible, to love the hjjks?

Kundalimon. Had she dreamed him too?

Queen-love! Nest-bond! Come to us, Nialli! Come! Come! Come!

Strange. Alien. Horrible.

"Get away from me!" she cries. "All of you, get away!"

They stare reproachfully. Those immense eyes, glittering, cold. *You are one of us. You belong to the Nest.*

"No! I never was!"

You love the Queen. The Queen loves you.

Was it true? No. No. She couldn't possibly have believed it, ever. They had put a spell on her while she was in the Nest, that was all. But now she's free. They'll never have her again.

She kneels and huddles into herself. Trembling, sobbing, she touches her arms, her breasts, her sensing-organ. Is this hjjk? she asks herself, feeling the thick lustrous fur, the warm flesh beneath.

No. No. No. No.

She presses her forehead to the floor.

"Yissou!" she calls. "Yissou, protect me!" She prays to Mueri to give her ease. She prays to Friit to heal her, to rid her of this spell.

She tries to banish that terrible sound of clicking from her mind.

The gods are with her now, the Five Heavenly Ones. She feels their presence like a shield about her. Once she had told anyone who would listen that they were nothing but silly myths. But since her return from the lakelands they have been with her. They are with her now. They will prevail. The hjjks who have come crowding into her room grow misty and insubstantial. Tears flow down her cheeks as she gives thanks, gives praise, offers blessings.

Then after a time she begins to grow calm.

As mysteriously as it has come, the convulsion that has overtaken her spirit is gone from her, and she is herself once again. The loathing, the disgust, vanishes. I am free, she thinks. But not quite. She can't see the hjjks any more, but she still feels their pull. She loves them as she did before. Into her mind once more comes an awareness of the sublime harmony of the Nest, of the industriousness of its inhabitants, of the great throbbing waves of Queen-love that sweep constantly through it. Queen-love throbs also in her heart. Nest-truth remains with her yet.

She doesn't understand. How can she sway from one pole to the other like this? How can it be possible to have the Five within her, and the Queen also? Is she of the city or of the Nest, of the People or of the hjjks?

Both, perhaps. Or neither.

Who am I? she wonders. What am I?

Another time Kundalimon came to her.

He appeared toward evening. She hadn't taken the trouble to light the lamps in her little room and the early darkness of the rain-swept city was beginning to settle upon everything. She saw him standing near the wall opposite the door, where the woven-grass star that the hjjks had given her long ago was hanging.

"You?" she whispered.

He made no reply. He merely stood before her, smiling.

There was something shimmering and golden about him. But within that luminous aura he looked just as he had in the final few weeks of his life, slender almost to the point of frailty, yet sturdy enough in his wiry way, with warm radiant eyes. At first Nialli Apuilana was afraid to look too closely at him, fearing that she would see the signs of violence on his body. But then she found the courage to do it, and saw that he was unharmed.

"You aren't wearing your amulets," she said.

He smiled and said nothing.

Perhaps he's given them to someone, she thought. To one of the children with whom he used to speak in the streets. Or he has returned them to the Nest, now that his embassy is over.

"Come closer," she said to him. "Let me touch you."

He shook his head, smiling all the while. Waves of love continued to stream from him. All right. No need to touch him. She felt a great calmness; she felt total assurance. There was much in the world that she did not understand, and perhaps never would understand. But that didn't matter. What mattered only was to be calm, and loving, and open, and accepting of whatever might befall.

"Are you with the Queen?" she asked.

He said nothing.

"Do you love me?"

A smile. Only a smile.

"You know that I love you."

He smiled. He was like a great bower of light.

He stayed with her for hours. Finally she realized that he was beginning to fade and vanish, but it happened so slowly that it was impossible to tell, moment by moment, that he was leaving her. But at last he was altogether gone.

"Will you come back?" she asked, and heard no answer.

He came again, though, always at nightfall, sometimes standing beside her cot, sometimes by the star of grass. He never spoke. But always he smiled; always he filled the room with warmth, and that same profound sense of ease and calmness.

Thu-Kimnibol was almost ready to set out for home now. He looked down at Salaman's daughter Weiawala and felt the waves of fear and sadness and loss coming from her. Her chestnut-hued fur had lost all sheen. Her sensing-organ rose at a tense angle. She seemed forlorn and desperately frightened. And she looked terribly small, smaller than she had ever seemed to him before; but from his great height all women looked small, and most men.

"So you're going now, are you?" she asked, her eyes not quite meeting his.

"Yes. Esperasagiot has the xlendis groomed, Dumanka's got the wagons provisioned."

"This is goodbye, then."

"For now."

"For now, yes." She sounded bitter. "Your city is calling you. Your queen."

"Our chieftain, you mean."

"Whatever she's called. She says come, and you hop to it. And you're a prince, they say!"

"Weiawala, I've been here for months. My city needs me. I've had a direct command from Taniane to return. Prince or not, how can I refuse to obey her?"

"I need you too."

"I know," Thu-Kimnibol said.

He studied her, feeling perplexed. It would be no great task to sweep her up in his arms and go to Salaman with her and say, "Cousin, I want your daughter as my mate. Let me take her to Dawinno with me, and in a few months we'll return and hold the formal ceremony in your palace." Certainly that was what Salaman had had in mind from the first moment, when he had offered this girl to him "to warm your bed tonight," as the king in his cheerfully crude way had put it.

It was not as a concubine but as a potential mate that Salaman had given Weiawala to him. Thu-Kimnibol had no doubt of that. The king wanted nothing more than to atone for the old breach between them by linking his family in marriage to the most powerful man in Dawinno. And the prospect had obvious merit for Thu-Kimnibol, too. A king's son himself, mated to the daughter of that king's successor—he'd have a strong claim to the throne of Yissou, if that throne became vacant and for some reason no son of Salaman was in a position to take it.

But two obstacles lay in the way.

One was simply that it was too soon after Naarinta's death for him to be taking a new mate. He was of the highborn class; there were proprieties to observe; there were the feelings of Naarinta's family to consider. Of course he'd mate again, but not now, not so swiftly.

But beyond that was a deeper chasm. He felt no love for Weiawala, at least not the kind of love that led to mating. They had been inseparable, yes, since his arrival. They had coupled again and again, eagerly, passionately. But never once had they twined. Thu-Kimnibol hadn't felt the desire for such intimacy, and she had shown no sign of interest in it either. That was significant, he thought. Without twining a marriage is hollow.

And, after all, she was hardly more than a child—no older, he suspected, than his niece Nialli Apuilana. How could he mate with a child? He was past forty. An old man, some might say. No. Weiawala had been a fine companion for him these months in Yissou, but now it was over. He had to leave her behind, and put her from his mind, however she wept and begged.

None of this seemed remotely honorable to Thu-Kimnibol. But he wasn't going to take Weiawala home with him to Dawinno, all the same.

As he stood there uncomfortably searching for the words that would pacify her, or at least to allow him to make a graceful escape, the king's son Biterulve of the pale fur came up to them, that handsome, quick-witted boy. He put out his hand and took Thu-Kimnibol's in a firm and confident way.

"A safe journey to you, cousin. May the gods watch over you."

"My thanks to you, Biterulve. We'll meet again before long, that I know."

"I look forward to it, cousin." Biterulve glanced quickly from Thu-Kimnibol to Weiawala, and back to Thu-Kimnibol again. For an instant the unasked question hung in the air between them; then it was gone. Biterulve appeared to be sizing things up: the distance between them, the look in her eyes.

It was another awkward moment. Biterulve was Weiawala's full brother: their mother was Sinithista. He was the king's favorite, that was very obvious. Of all the young princes he seemed the cleverest, and the gentlest by far, with little of the haughtiness that marked Chham and Athimin or the boisterousness of the other sons. Here was his sister being abandoned before his eyes, though. Gentle as he was, he might find that hard to swallow. Was he going to force the issue and create an embarrassment for everyone?

Apparently not. With sublime tact Biterulve turned to Weiawala and said, "Well, sister, if you and Thu-Kimnibol have made your farewells, come with me now to our mother. She'll be glad to have us breakfast with her."

Weiawala stared at him dully.

"And then afterward," Biterulve said, "we'll all go to the top of the wall, and watch as our cousin from Dawinno sets out on his journey. So come. Come." He slipped his arm around the girl's shoulders. He was hardly any taller than she was, and scarcely more sturdy. But in a smooth and persuasive fashion he drew her away. Weiawala turned back once, giving Thu-Kimnibol a panicky look over her shoulder; and then she was gone from the room. Thu-Kimnibol felt a surge of gratitude. How wise the boy was!

Salaman, though: would he be so understanding, would he be helpful?

Well, he'd repair matters with him later, somehow. It shouldn't be hard to make the king see that the time hadn't been ripe for him to take a mate from the royal family of the City of Yissou. Making Weiawala understand that would probably be more difficult. But she was young. She'd forget. She'd fall in love with someone else.

And if ever I become king of this place, he thought, I'll give a high position to this princely Biterulve, and keep him by my side. And if I'm never granted a son, he'll be king after me in Yissou. We'll alternate the dynasties, a son of Salaman's following the son of Harruel.

He laughed at his own foolishness. He was looking a great many steps ahead. Too many, perhaps.

Esperasagiot had the wagons waiting in the courtyard outside. The wagonmaster was studying the gray heavy sky with displeasure. Anger made his bright golden fur stand out full and thick. He gave Thu-Kimnibol a scowling glance. "If my say ruled, I'd say it was no weather for journeying."

"It could be better, yes. But today's the day we leave this place."

Esperasagiot spat. "They say these winter storms are likely to last only another week or two."

"Or three, or four. How can anyone know? The chieftain has summoned me, Esperasagiot. Do you love this bleak city so much that you want to wait here for spring?"

"I love my xlendis, prince."

"Won't they be able to withstand the cold?"

"Their kind withstood worse in the Long Winter. But it'll do them no good to be out there. As I've told you: these are city-bred animals. They're accustomed to warmth."

"We'll keep them warm, then. Ask King Salaman's grooms for extra blankets. And we'll take care not to push them too hard. We'll go at a steady pace, the kind you like. If this miserable season is almost over, well, we'll only have to cope with the cold for a matter of days. But by the time it lifts, we'll be far along on the road to Dawinno."

Esperasagiot smiled frostily. "As you wish, prince."

He went off toward the stables. Thu-Kimnibol caught sight of Dumanka at the far side of the courtyard, inventorying the provisions that were to be loaded on the wagons. The quartermaster waved cheerfully without interrupting his work.

It was midday when all the preparations at last were done and they rode out through the southern gate. The sun was bright and the wind was barely blowing. But the landscape beyond the wall was a forbidding one. Leafless trees rose like dead things everywhere, and a dusting of frost clung to the north-facing slopes. Toward late afternoon the east wind intensified, sweeping across the dry plateau like a scimitar. The only sign of life came from the lantern-trees that lay just south of the city, for even in this hard season they hadn't been abandoned by the tiny birds responsible for their glow. As the early night came on they began to send forth a blinking, feeble light, but that was nothing to inspire any great degree of cheer.

Thu-Kimnibol looked back. Tiny figures watched them from the top of the wall. Salaman? Biterulve? Weiawala? He waved at them. A few of the figures, not all, waved back.

The wagons moved onward. The City of Yissou vanished behind them. Slowly, warily, the ambassadors from the City of Dawinno wended their way south across the forlorn wintry land.

7
Rumblings of War

Aweek after Thu-Kimnibol's departure, Salaman had the commander of the Acknowledgers brought to the palace. Zechtior Lukin, his name was. Athimin, newly released from prison and more than a little chastened, went with half a dozen guards into the run-down eastern quarter of the city to get him, anticipating a fight. But Athimin was surprised to find that Zechtior Lukin had no more qualms about going to speak with the king than he did about dancing naked in the streets when the black winds were blowing. He behaved as though he'd been expecting Salaman to summon him all along—as though he'd been wondering why the summons had taken so long to come.

There were some surprises for Salaman, too, in his meeting with the Acknowledger leader.

He had imagined that the head of the sect would be some wild-eyed fanatic, excitable and irascible, who would foam at the mouth, would shout and rant and babble incomprehensible slogans. He was right about one part of that, at least: Zechtior Lukin was a fanatic, beyond any doubt. Everything about him, the iron set of his jaw and the cold, bleak stony look of his eyes and his hard, thick-muscled frame, covered with gray, grizzled fur, spoke of extraordinary singlemindedness of purpose and dedication to his unlikely cause. And very likely he was irascible, too.

But a shouter? A ranter? A babbler of slogans? No. This man was cool and tough, with an air of icy reserve that Salaman immediately recognized as much like his own. He could surely have been a king, this one, if things gone a little differently in the early years of the city. Instead he had become a butcher, a meat-cutter, who spent his days not in a stone palace but in a slaughterhouse, chopping joints and loins and flanks while blood ran in rivers around him. And in the evenings he and his followers met in a drafty gymnasium in the eastern quarter, and drilled one another in the strange tenets of their creed.

He stood calmly before the king, square-shouldered, unintimidated.

"How long is it since you people first started this?" Salaman asked.

"Years."

"Three years? Five?"

"Almost since the founding of the city."

"No," Salaman said. "That's impossible, that you could have been in existence that long a time without my even hearing about you."

Zechtior Lukin shrugged. "There were very few of us, and we kept to ourselves. We studied our texts and held our meetings and practiced our disciplines, and we didn't go out looking for recruits. It was our private thing. My father Lakkamai was the first of us, and then—"

"Lakkamai?" Another surprise. In the cocoon and in Vengiboneeza Lakkamai had been a silent man, who kept to himself and seemed to have no depths to his soul. He had been the lover of the offering-woman Torlyri in Vengiboneeza, but when the Breaking Apart had happened Lakkamai had abandoned Torlyri without a qualm, to go off with Harruel as one of the founders of the tiny settlement that would become the City of Yissou. He had died long ago. Salaman couldn't remember his ever having taken a mate, let alone siring a son.

"You knew him," Zechtior Lukin said.

"Many years back, yes."

"Lakkamai taught us that what happened to the Great World was by design of the gods. He said that everything that happens is part of their plan, whether it seems good or ill to us, and that when the Great World people chose to die, it was because they understood the will of the gods and knew that it was their time to go from the world. So they lifted no hand to avert the death-stars, and allowed them to strike the world, and the great cold descended on them. He learned these things, he said, while speaking with Hresh, the chronicler of the Koshmar people."

"Yes," said Salaman. "You talk with Hresh, your mind becomes filled with all sorts of fancies and strangenesses."

"These are truths," said Zechtior Lukin.

Salaman let the blunt contradiction pass. There was no point in arguing with the man. "So there were originally only a few of you. A couple of families only, is that it? But now my son says that there are a hundred ninety of you."

"Three hundred seventy-six," Zechtior Lukin said.

"I see." One more black mark for Athimin. "So now you've decided to go out looking for new recruits after all, is that it? Why?"

"In dreams I saw the hjjk Queen hovering in the air over the city. I felt the tremendous presence of Her like a great weight above us. This was last year. And I saw that the day of reckoning is coming. The hjjks, as everyone knows, were exempted from the destruction of the Great World. The Five Heavenly Ones had some other purpose in mind for them, and brought them safely through the time of cold and snow so that they could perform that purpose in the New Springtime."

"And you know what that purpose is, of course."

"They are meant to destroy the People and their cities," said Zechtior Lukin calmly. "They are the scourge of the gods."

So he's crazy after all, Salaman thought. What a pity that is.

But with calmness that matched the Acknowledger's he said, "And how would that serve the purposes of the Five? They brought us safely through the Long Winter to be the inheritors of the world—so say all our chronicles. Why did the gods bother to preserve us, if all they had in mind was to let the hjjks destroy us now? It would have been simpler just to leave us out in the cold and let the Long Winter finish us off hundreds of thousands of years back."

"You don't understand. We were tested, and we have failed the test. As you say, we were spared from the cold so that we might inherit the world. But we have taken the wrong turn. We build cities; we live in ever more comfortable houses; we grow soft and lazy. It's worse in Dawinno than it is here, but everywhere the People fall away from the intent of the Five. What was our aim, after all, in building these cities? Only to duplicate the ease and comfort of the Great World, so it would appear. But such a duplication is wrong. If the gods wanted the world to be as it was when the sapphire-eyes lived, they would merely have left the Great World as it was. Instead they destroyed it. As they will destroy us. I tell you, king, the hjjks will be the instruments of our correction. They will fall upon us; they will shatter our cities; they will force us out into the wild lands, where we will finally accept the disciplines that the gods intended for us to learn. Those few of us who survive the onslaught will make another attempt at building a world. This is Dawinno's will: he who transforms."

"And if you all die of freezing, dancing in the plazas at night, is that going to create this wonderful new world for you?"

"We do not freeze. We will not die."

"I see. You're invulnerable."

"We are very strong. You saw us, that night, at our festivals. You haven't seen us at our training. Our spiritual exercises, our physical drills. We are warriors. We have developed immense endurance. We can march for days without sleep or food. We are unafraid of cold or privation. We have given up our individual selves, to form a new unity."

All this was astonishing to Salaman. The philosophies of Lakkamai's son were gibberish and lunacy; but all the same the king felt a great kinship of temperament with this man, and much affection for him. His strength, his ferocity, were evident. Secretly he had built an entire little kingdom within the kingdom. He had the true force of royalty about him. They could almost have been brothers. And yet he was crazy. It seemed an immense pity.

He said, "You must let me see you at your training."

"This very night, if you wish, King Salaman."

"Done. Perform your most difficult exercises for me. And then, my friend, you and your friends will need to start packing. You'll be leaving here."

Zechtior Lukin seemed unsurprised by that, and even indifferent, as he appeared to be toward everything that came his way.

"Where would you have us go?" he asked calmly.

"Northward. Obviously you're unhappy here in Yissou, living amidst our contemptible softness. And I tell you truly that I have no great eagerness to have you spread your creed of inevitable destruction in the city that I love. So it's in your interest and mine also for you to leave, wouldn't you say? You wouldn't want to go south, of course. Life's too easy there. Besides, as our city expands into the lands to the south and Dawinno grows northward, we're bound to trespass on your privacy. So go north, Zechtior Lukin. Cold doesn't bother you, you say. Hunger is unimportant to you. And there's plenty of land to the north where you can found a settlement that lives according to your principles and precepts. It could well be the capital of the great and pure and proper world that we of the cities have failed to create."

"You mean, we should go into the hjjk lands?"

"I mean that, yes. Beyond Vengiboneeza, even. Deep into the cold dry northlands. Choose the territory to please yourselves. It may be that the hjjks will leave you unmolested. From what you say, your ways are very much like theirs, anyway—warriors, unafraid of discomfort, free of individual ambition. They may welcome you because you're so much like them. Or they'll simply ignore you. Why should a few hundred settlers matter to them, when they have half a continent? Yes: go to the hjjks. What do you say, Zechtior Lukin?"

There was a silence. Zechtior Lukin's face was expressionless: no look of anger, no defiance, not even dismay. *Something* was going on in his mind, but he looked as untroubled as if the king had asked him some question about the price of meat.

"How much time will you allow us to prepare ourselves for the journey?" he asked, after a little while.

Nialli Apuilana has had all the solitude she can bear. She has been in hibernation all the winter long, like some animal that goes through a metamorphosis every year, and lies hidden away, wrapped in its own web, until the time arrives to come forth. Now the time is here. On a day in late winter when the rain is falling on Dawinno in torrents that are stupendous even for that season of merciless downpours, Nialli Apuilana leaves her room in the House of Nakhaba early in the afternoon. Now and then she has gone out late at night, but this is the first time since her recovery that she's been out in daytime. There's no one around to see her. The storm is so furious that the streets are deserted. Not even the guards are out. A light gleams behind every window: everyone's indoors. But she laughs at the fury of the storm. "It's really much too much," she says out loud, looking upward, addressing herself to Dawinno. It is Dawinno who moves the great wheel of the seasons, now sending sun and now storms. "You're overdoing it a little, don't you think?" All she's wearing is a sash. Her fur is drenched before she has taken five steps. It clings to her like a tight cloak, and water streams down her thighs.

She crosses the city to the House of Knowledge and climbs the winding stairs to the uppermost floor. She hadn't doubted for an instant that Hresh would be there; and indeed he is, writing away in one of his huge old books.

"Nialli!" he cries. "Have you lost your wits, going out in weather like this? Here—let me dry you off—"

He swaddles her in a cloth, as if she's a child. Passively she lets him enfold her and rub her dry, though it leaves her fur ruffled and wild.

When he's done she says, "We should start to tell each other things, father. The time for doing that is long overdue."

"Things? What kind of things?"

"About—the Nest—" she says hesitantly. "About—the Queen—"

He looks incredulous. "You actually want to talk about the hjjks?"

"About the hjjks, yes. The things you've learned, and what I have. They may not be the same things. You've always said you need to understand the hjjks better. You aren't the only one. I do too, father. I do too."

Chevkija Aim indicated an arching doorway of weatherbeaten smoke-gray wood at the end of a blind alleyway just off Fishmonger Street, flanked on either side by grubby-looking commercial buildings with facades of soiled red brick. Husathirn Mueri had never been in this part of the city before. It was some sort of industrial district, more than a little disreputable. "It's all the way down there," the guard-captain said. "A basement room. You go in and turn left, and down the stairs."

"And is it safe for me just to walk right in?" Husathirn Mueri asked. "They won't recognize me and panic?"

"You'll be all right, sir. There's not much light in there. You can just barely make out shapes, let alone faces. Nobody'll know who you are." The lithe young Beng grinned and nudged Husathirn Mueri's arm with surprising familiarity. "Go on in, sir! Go on! I tell you, you'll be all right."

Indeed the room, long and narrow and rich with the salty reek of dried fish, was very dark. The only sources of light were two faint glowberry clusters mounted on the wall at the far end. A boy and a girl stood there, beside a table containing fruits and aromatic boughs that was probably the altar.

Husathirn Mueri, squinting, saw only darkness. Then his eyes adapted to it and saw a congregation of perhaps fifty people seated close together on rows of rough black barrels. They were muttering and chanting and occasionally stamping their feet in response to the words of the children at the altar. Here and there a towering Beng helmet rose above the crowd, but most of them were unhelmeted. The voices he heard were deep, thick, the voices of ordinary people, working-folk. Husathirn Mueri felt a new level of uneasiness. He had never gone among working-folk much. And to spy on them now, in their own sanctuary—

"Sit!" Chevkija Aim whispered, half shoving him down on one of the barrels in the last row. "Sit and listen! The boy is Tikharein Tourb. He's the priest. The priestess is Chhia Kreun."

"Priest? Priestess?"

"Listen to them, sir!"

He stared in disbelief. It seemed to Husathirn Mueri that he had arrived at the threshold of some other world.

The boy-priest made thick strange sounds, horrid chittering clicking noises that seemed much like hjjk-talk. The worshipers before him replied with the same bizarre noises. Husathirn Mueri shivered and put his hands over his face.

Then suddenly the boy called out, in a high clear voice, "The Queen is our comfort and our joy. Such is the teaching of the prophet Kundalimon, blessed be he."

"The Queen is our comfort and our joy," replied the congregation, sing-song.

"She is the light and the way."

"She is the light and the way."

"She is the essence and the substance."

"She is the essence and the substance."

"She is the beginning and the end."

"She is the beginning and the end."

Husathirn Mueri trembled. At the sound of that sweet innocent voice he felt a touch of terror. The light and the way? The essence and the substance? What madness was this? Was he dreaming it?

He felt a choking, gagging sensation and covered his mouth with his hand. The basement room was windowless, and the air was close and hot.

The musky salt tang of the barrels of dried fish, the gamy odor of sweaty fur, the rich pungent aroma of the sippariu and dilifar boughs on the altar—it was all starting to sicken him. He began to grow dizzy. He knotted his hands together and pressed his elbows hard into his ribs.

They were all crying out in hjjk-sounds again, the boy and the girl and the congregation.

At any moment, Husathirn Mueri imagined, the floor might open beneath him and he would find himself looking down into some vast pit where swarms of glittering hjjks moved in such multitudes that the earth seemed to be boiling with them.

"Easy, sir, easy," Chevkija Aim murmured beside him.

He watched the boy and the girl moving about now, taking fruits and boughs from the altar and showing them to the congregation, and replacing them again, while the worshipers stamped their feet and made the droning, clicking sounds. What did it all mean? Where had it come from, so suddenly?

The boy was wearing a shining yellow-and-black amulet on his chest, much like the one dead Kundalimon had worn. The same one, perhaps. The girl had a wrist-talisman that was also of hjjk-shell. Even in the dimness these objects gleamed with a preternatural brightness. Husathirn Mueri remembered how the shells of the hjjks had gleamed as they moved on their mysterious rounds through the streets of Vengiboneeza when he was a child.

"Kundalimon guides us from on high. He tells us that the Queen is our comfort and our joy," the boy called again.

And again the congregation responded, "The Queen is our comfort and joy."

But this time a burly man three rows in front of Husathirn Mueri rose and shouted, "The Queen is the one true god!"

The congregation began to repeat that too. "The Queen is the one true—"

"*No!*" the boy cried. "The Queen is not a god!"

"Then what is She? What is She?" For a moment the rhythm of the service was broken. People were rising everywhere, calling out, waving their arms. "Tell us what She is!"

The boy-priest leaped atop the altar. Instantly he had their attention again.

"The Queen," he said, in that same eerie high sing-song, "is of god-essence, by virtue of Her descent from the people of the Great World, who lived in the sight of the gods. But She is not a god Herself." The boy seemed to be parroting some text he had learned by rote. "She is the architect of the gateway through which the true gods one day will return. Such is the word of Kundalimon."

"The humans, you mean?" the burly man asked. "Are the humans the true gods?"

"The humans are—they are—" The boy on the altar faltered. His eyes seemed to turn glassy. He had no prepared text for this. He looked down toward the girl, and she reached out with her sensing-organ, coiling it about his ankle in an astonishingly intimate way. Husathirn Mueri caught his breath, amazed. The gesture seemed to steady the boy; he regained his poise and cried, "The revelation of the humans is yet to come! We must continue to await the revelation of the humans! Until then the Queen is our guide." He made hjjk-clicks. "She is our comfort and our joy!"

"She is our comfort and our joy!"

They were all clicking in response, now. The sound of it was horrifying. The boy had them under control once more. That was horrifying too.

"Kundalimon!" they cried. "Martyred Kundalimon, lead us to the truth!"

The boy-priest held his arms high. Even at this distance Husathirn Mueri could see how his eyes blazed with conviction.

"She is the light and the way."

"She is the light and the way."

"She is the essence and the substance."

"She is the essence and—"

"Look," Husathirn Mueri whispered. "The girl's got her sensing-organ on his, now."

"They're going to twine, sir. Everybody here is going to twine."

"Surely not. All in one place together?"

"It is what they do," said Chevkija Aim casually. "They all twine and let the Queen enter their souls, so I do hear. It is their custom."

Numb with disbelief, Husathirn Mueri said, "This is the greatest vileness that ever has been."

"I have officers outside. We can clear all these hjjk-lovers out of here in five minutes, if you give the word, and smash the place up."

"No."

"But you've seen what they—"

"No, I said. The persecutions mustn't be resumed. That's the chieftain's express order, and you know it."

"I understand, sir, but—"

"Then no one is to be arrested. We'll leave this chapel absolutely undisturbed, at least for now. And keep it under careful observation. How else will we understand what kind of threat we face, if we don't look the enemy right in the face? Do you follow me?"

The guard-captain nodded. His lips were tightly clamped.

Husathirn Mueri looked up. In front of him the dark shapes of the congregation were rising, moving about, joining into groups. The hjjk-clicking sound could no longer be heard, and in its place came an intense deep humming. No one took any notice of the two men whispering in back. The air in the narrow long room seemed to grow superheated. It might burst into flames at any moment.

Quietly Chevkija Aim said, "We should leave, now."

Husathirn Mueri made no response.

It seemed to him that he had become rooted in place. At the far end of the room the boy and the girl were unashamedly twining before the altar, and, two by two, the members of the congregation were beginning to enter into the communion. Husathirn Mueri had never heard of such a thing. He had never dreamed of it. He watched it now in terrible fascination.

Chevkija Aim whispered, "If we stay, they'll want us to do it too, sir."

"Yes. Yes. We have to go."

"Are you all right, sir?"

"We—have to—go—"

"Give us your hand, sir. There. That's it. Come on, now. Up. Up."

"Yes," Husathirn Mueri said. His feet felt dead beneath him. He leaned heavily on Chevkija Aim and tottered and stumbled toward the door.

She is the light and the way. She is the essence and the substance. She is the beginning and the end.

The cool fresh air outside struck him like a fist.

Hresh said, "What I believed about them, once upon a time, is what everybody's always believed. That they're a malevolent alien folk. Our sworn enemies, strange and menacing. But lately I've been beginning to change my mind about that."

"So have I," said Nialli Apuilana.

"How so?"

She shrugged. "It'll be easier for me if you speak first, father."

"But you said you'd come here to tell *me* things."

"And I will. But it has to be an exchange: what you know for what I know. And I want you to go first. Please. Please."

Hresh stared at her. She was as baffling as ever.

After a moment he said, "All right. I suppose it began for me that time you addressed the Presidium: when you said the hjjks have to be regarded as something other than monsters, that in fact they're intelligent creatures with a deep and rich civilization. You called them human, even. In the special sense of that word that I sometimes have used. It was the first hint you'd given of what you experienced while you were in the Nest. And I realized that what you said must certainly have been true at one time, for they were a part of the Great World, and in the visions of the Great World that I once was able to have I saw them, living among the sapphire-eyes and the humans and the others in peace and harmony. How could they have been demons and monsters, and still a part of the Great World?"

"Exactly so," Nialli Apuilana said.

Hresh looked up at her. There was something even stranger than usual about her today. She was like a coiled whip.

He went on:

"Of course what they were in the Great World and what they may have become by now, hundreds of thousands of years after the Great World, aren't necessarily the same. Maybe they *have* changed. But who can say? We have people like Thu-Kimnibol who've been convinced from the start that the hjjks are evil. Now, though, we have some among us who take the opposite position entirely. This new religion, I mean. I hear that in the chapels the hjjks are spoken of as the instruments of our salvation: benevolent holy creatures, no less. And Kundalimon is looked upon as some sort of prophet." Hresh gave her a searching glance. "You know about the chapels? Do you go to them?"

"No," Nialli Apuilana said. "Never. But if they're teaching that the hjjks are benevolent, they're wrong. The hjjks have no benevolence. Not as we know the meaning of the word. But neither are they evil. They're simply—themselves."

"Are they monsters, then, or holy creatures?"

"Both. And neither."

Hresh considered that a moment.

"I thought you worshiped them," he said. "That you wanted nothing more than to go to them, to live among them for the rest of your life. They live in an atmosphere of dreams and magic and wonder, you said. You breathe the air of the Nest, you told me, and it fills your soul."

"That was before."

"And now?"

Wanly she shook her head. "I don't know what I want. Or what I believe, not any more. Oh, father, father, I can hardly tell you what confusion I feel! Go to the Nest, says a voice within me, and live in eternal Queen-love. Stay in Dawinno, says another voice. The hjjks aren't what you've taken them to be, says that voice. One is the voice of the Queen, and the other—the other—" She looked at him with eyes bright with pain. "The other is the voice of the Five. And their voice is the one I want to obey."

Hresh peered at her, not believing it. This was the last thing he would have expected to hear from her.

"The Five? You accept the authority of the Five? Since when? That's something new, Nialli."

"Not their authority, no, not really."

"What then?"

"Their truth. Their wisdom. It came to me as I lay in the swamp. They entered me. I felt it, father. I thought I was dying, and they came to me. You know that I had no belief before that. But I do now."

"I see," Hresh said vaguely. But he didn't see at all. The more she told him, the less he seemed to understand. Even as he had begun to feel the pull of the Nest—which was partly her doing—she appeared to be turning away from it. "So there's no likelihood that you'll try to return to the Nest, now that you have your strength back?"

"None, father. Not any more."

"Speak only the truth to me, girl."

"It is the truth. You know that I would have gone with Kundalimon. But now everything is changed. I've begun to doubt everything I once believed, and to believe everything I once doubted. The world's become a mystery to me. I need to stay right here and sort things out before I do anything."

"Can I believe you, I wonder?"

"I swear it! I swear by any god there is. I swear it by the Queen, father."

She reached her hand toward his. He took it and held it as though it were a precious object.

Then he said, "What a puzzle you are, Nialli! Almost as great a puzzle as the hjjks themselves!" He smiled tenderly. "You'll always be a puzzle to me, I suppose. But at least I think I'm beginning to understand the hjjks."

"Are you, father?"

"Look at this," he said. "A newly discovered text, very ancient."

Carefully he drew a vellum scroll from the larger of his two caskets of chronicles, and undid its fastening. He laid it on the table before her.

Nialli Apuilana leaned forward to peer at it. "Where was it found?"

"In my collection of chronicles. It was there all along, actually. But it was in Beng, a very ancient form of Beng almost impossible to understand. So I didn't pay much attention to it. Puit Kjai suggested finally that I ought to look at it, when I told him I was doing research in hjjk history. He was the keeper of the Beng chronicles, you know, before they were turned over to me. He helped me learn how to read it."

She put her hands to the manuscript. "May I?"

"It won't do you any good. But go ahead."

He watched her as she bent over the text. The writing was unintelligible to her, of course. These ancient Beng hieroglyphics were nothing like the characters in use nowadays, and wouldn't tune themselves easily to a modern mind. But Nialli Apuilana seemed determined to master them. How very much like me she is in some ways, Hresh thought. And how different in so many others.

She murmured under her breath, pressed her fingertips harder, struggled to bring sense out of the page. When it seemed to him that she had wrestled with it long enough he reached for the manuscript to decipher it for her, but she shook him away and continued to work at it.

He looked at her and his heart overflowed with warmth. He had so many times given her up for lost; and yet here she was, quietly sitting with him in his study, as she had so often done when she was a child.

Her strength and determination as she toiled over the ancient manuscript delighted him. Seeing her like this, he could see Taniane reborn in her, and it took him back to the days when he was young, when he and Taniane had roamed Vengiboneeza together in search of the secrets of the Great World.

But Nialli was something more than a mere duplicate of her mother. He could see the Hresh in her too. She was volatile and impulsive, a spooky willful child, as he had been. Before her capture by the hjjks she had been outgoing and exuberant, but also—as he had been—lonely, alienated, inquisitive, odd. How he loved her! How deeply he felt for her!

She looked up from the scroll. "It's like the language they speak in dreams. Nothing will hold still long enough for me to find its meaning."

"So I felt also. But not any longer."

She gave him the manuscript. He put his fingers to it and the strange archaic phrases rose to his mind.

"It's a document of the very early years of the Long Winter," he said. "When all the tribes of the People were newly cocooned. There were some warriors of the Bengs who wouldn't believe that they had to spend all their lives in hiding, and one of them made a Going Forth to see if the outer world could be reclaimed. You must realize that this was thousands of years before our own three premature departures from the cocoon, what we call the Cold Awakening, the Wrongful Glow, and the Unhappy Dawn. Most of the text is missing, but what we have is this—

"And then I stood in the land of ice and a terrible death of the heart came upon me, for I knew that I would not live.

"Then did I turn, and seek again the place of my people. But the mouth of the cave I could not find. And the hjjken-folk came upon me and seized me where I stood, laying their hands upon me and carrying me away, but I was free of fear, for I was a dead man already, and who can die the death more than once? There were twenty of them and very frightsome of aspect, and they did lay their hands on me and take me to the warm dark place where they lived, which was like unto the cocoon, but greatly larger, in the ground extending farther than I could see, with many avenues and side-passages going in every way.

"And there was in this place the Great Hjjken, a monster of huge

244 / ROBERT SILVERBERG

and most formidable size, the sight of which made the blood run backward in my vessels. But she touched the soul of my soul with the second sight of her, and she said unto me, *Behold, I give you peace and love,* and I was not afraid. For the touch of her soul on my soul was like being taken into the arms of a great Mother, and I did marvel greatly that so huge and frightsome a beast could be so comforting. And also she said, *You are come to me too soon, for my time is not yet. But when the world wakens into warmth will I embrace you all.*

"Which was all she said, and never did I speak with her again. But I did stay among the hjjken twenty days and twenty nights, the count of which I did keep most carefully, and lesser hjjken did ask of me with the voices of their inner minds a great many questions concerning my People and how we live and what we believe, and also they did tell me something of what it is that they believe, though that is all hazy in my mind, and was even as they told it me. And I did eat of their food, which is a dreadful mash that they do chew and spit forth for their companions to eat after them, and which gave me sore revulsion at first, though later hunger overcame me and I did eat of it and find it less hateful than might be thought. Then when they ceased to question me did they say to me, *We will take you to your nation now,* and let me forth into the bitter cold and deadly snows, and did conduct me thenceforward—"

Hresh laid the scroll down.

"That's where it ends?" Nialli Apuilana asked.

"It breaks off there. But what there is of it is clear enough."

"And what does it tell you, father?"

"It explains, I think, the taking of captives by the hjjks. They've been doing it for thousands of years. Evidently it's so they can study us. But they care for the captives and eventually they let them go, some of them, at least, as they did with that poor foolish Beng warrior who they found wandering around on the icefields."

"So this is what has led you to cease thinking of them as monsters."

"I never believed they were monsters," said Hresh. "Enemies, yes, ruthless and dangerous enemies. Remember, I was there when they attacked Yissou. But perhaps they aren't even that. After all this time we don't really know *what* they are. We've never even begun to understand them. We hate them simply because they're unknown."

"And they probably always will be."

"I thought you said you understood them."

"I understand very little, father. I may have thought I did, but I was wrong. Who understands why the Five send us storms, or heat or cold, or famines? They must have their reasons, but how can we presume to say what they are? So it is with the Queen. She's like a force of the universe. It's impossible to understand Her. I know a little of what the Nest is like, its shape and smell and how life is lived there. But that's mere knowledge. Knowledge isn't understanding. I've started to see that no one who is of the People can even begin to understand the Queen. Except—just possibly—someone one who has been in the Nest."

"But you have been in the Nest."

"Just a minor one. The truths I learned there were minor truths. The Queen of Queens who dwells in the far north is the only source of the real revelations. I thought they were going to take me to Her when I was older; but instead they let me go and brought me back here to Dawinno."

Hresh blinked in bewilderment. "They *let you go?* You told us that you escaped!"

"No, father. I didn't escape."

"Didn't—escape—"

"Of course not. They released me, as they did that Beng in that chronicle of yours. Why would I have wanted to leave a place where I was completely happy for the first time in my life?"

The words struck him like blows. But Nialli Apuilana went serenely on.

"I had to leave. I never would have gone of my own will. Whether the Nest is a place of good or evil, one thing is true of it: while you're in it you feel utterly secure. You know that you live in a place where uncertainty and pain are unknown. I surrendered myself completely to it, and gladly, as who wouldn't? But they came for me one morning and said I had stayed with them as long as was necessary, and led me outside, and took me on vermilion-back to the edge of the city, and turned me loose."

"You told us you had escaped from them," Hresh said numbly.

"No. You and mother decided I had escaped from them, I suppose because you weren't able to imagine that anyone could possibly prefer to remain in the Nest instead of coming home to Dawinno. And I didn't contradict you. I didn't say anything at all. You assumed I had escaped from the clutches of the evil bug-monsters, as any sensible person would have wanted to do, and I let you think so, because I knew you needed to believe that, and I was afraid you'd say I had lost my mind if I told you anything approaching the truth. How could I tell you the truth? If everyone in the city thinks the hjjks are dreadful marauding demons, and always has thought so, and I stand up and say that they aren't, that I found love and truth among them, will I be believed? Or will I simply be met with pity and scorn?"

"Yes. Yes, I see that," said Hresh. His shock and dismay were slowly beginning to lift. She waited in silence. At last he said, very softly, "I understand, Nialli. You *had* to lie to us. I see that now. I see a great many things now." He put the ancient Beng scroll away, closed the casket of the chronicles, let his hands rest on the lid. "If I had known then what I know now, it might have been different."

"What do you mean?"

"About the hjjks. About the Nest."

"I don't understand what you're saying."

"I have an idea of what the Nest is like, now. The great living machine that it is. The perfection of its pattern, the way it all rotates around the tremendous directing intelligence that is the Queen, who is Herself the embodiment of the guiding force of the universe—"

It was Nialli Apuilana's turn to look amazed. "You sound almost like someone who's been to the Nest!"

"I have," Hresh said. "That's the other thing I had to tell you."

Her eyes went bright with shock and incredulity. *"What?* To the Nest? You?" She recoiled and stood up, bracing herself with both her hands against the edge of the table, staring at him open-mouthed. "Father, what are you telling me? Is this some kind of joke? These aren't joking matters."

Taking her hand in his again, he said, "I've seen the small Nests, like the one where you were taken. And then I approached the great one, and the great Queen within it. But I turned back before I reached it."

"When? How?"

He smiled gently. "Not in the actual flesh, Nialli. I wasn't really there. It was with the Barak Dayir, only."

"Then you *were* there, you were!" she exclaimed, clutching his arm in her excitement. "The Barak Dayir shows you true visions, father. You told me so yourself. You've seen into the Nest! And so you must know Nest-truth. You understand!"

"Do I? I think I'm very far from understanding anything."

"That isn't so."

He shook his head. "Perhaps I understand a little. But only a little, I think. Only the beginning of the beginning. What I had was simply a fleeting vision, Nialli. It lasted just a moment."

"Even a moment would be enough. I tell you, father, there's no way you can touch the Nest without experiencing Nest-truth. And therefore knowing Nest-bond, Egg-plan, all of it."

He searched his mind. "I don't know what those words mean. Not really."

"They're the things you spoke of a moment ago. When you talked of the Nest as a great living machine, and spoke of the perfection of its pattern."

"Tell me. Tell me."

Her expression changed. She seemed to disappear deep within herself. "Nest-bond," she said, in an odd high-pitched way, as though reciting a lesson, "is the awareness of the relationship of each thing in the universe to everything else. We are all parts of the Nest, even those of us who have never experienced it, even those of us who look upon the hjjks as dread monsters. For everything is united in a single great pattern, which is the endless unstoppable force of life. The hjjks are the vehicle through which this force is manifested in our times; and the Queen is its guiding spirit on our world. That is Nest-truth. And Egg-plan is the energy that She expresses as She brings forth the unceasing torrent of renewal. Queen-light is the glow of Her warmth; Queen-love is the sign of Her great care for us all."

Hresh stared, thunderstruck by the girl's strange burst of eloquence. The words had come pouring out of her almost uncontrollably, almost as if someone or something else were speaking through her. Her face was aglow, her eyes were shining with absolute and unshakable conviction. She suddenly seemed swept up into some rapture of visionary zeal. She was aflame with it.

Then the flame flickered and went out, and she was only Nialli Apuilana again, the troubled, uneasy Nialli Apuilana of a moment before.

She sat stunned and depleted before him.

She is such a mystery, he thought.

And these other mysteries, those of the Nest—they were great and complex, and he knew that merely hearing of them like this could never give him a true grasp of them. He wished now that he had lingered longer when he had made his Barak Dayir voyage into the country of the hjjks. He began to see that he must before much longer make that voyage again, and experience the Nest far more deeply than he had allowed himself to do that other time. He must learn what Nialli Apuilana had learned, and he must learn it at first hand. Even if the learning of it cost him his life.

He felt very weary. And she looked exhausted. Hresh realized that they had carried this meeting as far as it could go this day.

But Nialli Apuilana apparently wasn't quite ready to end it.

"Well?" she asked. "What do you say? Do you understand Nest-bond now? Egg-plan? Queen-love?"

"You look so tired, Nialli." He touched her cheek. "You ought to get some rest."

"I will. But first tell me that you understood what I was saying, father. And I didn't really need to say it, isn't that true? You already knew all that, didn't you? You must have seen it when you looked into the Nest with your Wonderstone."

"Some of it, yes. The sense of pattern, of universal order. I saw that. But I looked so quickly, and then I fled. Nest-bond—Queen-light—no, those terms are just words to me. They have no real substance in my mind."

"I think you understand more than you suspect."

"Only the beginning of the beginning of understanding."

"That's a beginning, at least."

"Yes. Yes. At least I know what the hjjks are not."

"Not demons, you mean? Not monsters?"

"Not enemies."

"Not enemies, no," Nialli Apuilana said. "Adversaries, maybe. But not enemies."

"A very subtle shade of difference."

"Yet a real one, father."

Thu-Kimnibol was home at last. The journey south had been swift, though not nearly swift enough for him, and uneventful. Now he walked the grand, lonely halls of his great villa in Dawinno, rediscovering it, reacquainting himself with his own home, his own possessions, after his long absence. It seemed to him that he had been away ten thousand years. He was alone as he went from one echoing room to another, pausing here and there to examine the objects in the display cases.

There were phantoms and spectres everywhere. These were Naarinta's things, really: she was the one who had collected most of the ancient treasures that filled these rooms, the bits of Great World sculpture and architectural fragments and strange twisted metallic things whose purpose would probably never be known. As he looked at them his sensing-organ began to tingle and he felt the immense antiquity of these battered artifacts come crowding in about him, alive and vital, jigging and throbbing with strange energy, making the villa itself seem a dead place, though it had been built only a dozen years before.

It was still early in the day, just hours after his return from Yissou. But he had lost no time setting in motion his preparations for war. He was due to see Taniane in the afternoon; but first, messengers had gone out to Si-Belimnion, to Kartafirain, to Maliton Diveri, to Lespar Thone: men of power, men he could trust. He waited impatiently for their arrival. It was not good, being here by himself. He hadn't expected that, how painful it would be to come back to an empty house.

"Your grace?" His majordomo, Gyv Hawoodin, an old Mortiril who had been with him for years. "Your grace, Kartafirain and Si-Belimnion are here."

"Send them up. And then set out some wine for us."

Solemnly Thu-Kimnibol embraced his friends. Solemnity seemed the appropriate mood of the day: Si-Belimnion wore a dark mantle that emanated a bleak funereal glow, and even the ebullient Kartafirain was somber and subdued. Thu-Kimnibol offered them wine and they drained their cups as though it were water.

"You won't believe what has happened here while you were away," Kartafirain began. "The common folk sing hymns to the Queen of the hjjks. They gather in cellars and children lead them in nonsensical catechisms."

"This is the heritage of the envoy Kundalimon," muttered Si-Belimnion, peering moodily into his cup. "Husathirn Mueri warned us that he was corrupting the young, and indeed he was. A pity he wasn't killed even sooner."

"It was Curabayn Bangkea that did it?" Thu-Kimnibol asked.

Kartafirain replied, with a shrug, "The guard-captain, yes. So everyone says, at any rate. Someone killed him too, the same day."

"I heard about that up north. And who was it that killed him, do you suppose?"

"Very likely whoever it was that hired him to kill Kundalimon," said Si-Belimnion. "To silence him, no doubt. No one knows who it might have been. I've heard twenty different guesses, all of them absurd. In any case the investigation's just about forgotten, now. The new religion's the only thing that anyone thinks about."

Thu-Kimnibol stared. "But isn't Taniane attempting to stamp it out? That's what I heard."

"Easier to stamp out wildfire in the dry season," said Kartafirain. "It was spreading faster than the guards could close the chapels. Eventually Taniane decided that trying to eradicate it was too risky. There might have been an uprising. The common folk profess to see great blessings in the teachings of the Queen. She is their comfort and their joy, the prayer goes. She is the light and the way. They think everything will be love and peace here, once the kindly hjjks are among us."

"Unbelievable," Thu-Kimnibol murmured. "Utterly unbelievable."

"There was love and peace aplenty in the days when our parents lived in the cocoon!" cried Maliton Diveri, who had just entered the room. "Perhaps that's what they really want. To give up all this city life, and go back into the cocoon, and spend their days sleeping, or kick-wrestling, or munching on velvetberries. Pah! What this city has become disgusts me, Thu-Kimnibol. And it'll disgust you too."

"The war will put an end to all this foolishness," Thu-Kimnibol said brusquely.

"The war?"

"I've spent these months speaking with Salaman. I sense that he believes the hjjks are restless and angry, that our failure to accept their treaty has offended them, that they're going to launch war against us all. The first move will be to attack Yissou, within the year. If the Presidium ratifies, we'll be pledged by treaty to go to his aid in that case."

Maliton Diveri chuckled. "Salaman's been having nightmares of a hjjk invasion for thirty years. Isn't that why he's hidden Yissou behind that preposterous wall? But the invasion never comes. What makes him think it'll happen now? And why do you believe he's right?"

"I have good reason to think he is," Thu-Kimnibol said.

"And then?" Si-Belimnion asked. "Is this city of sudden hjjk-lovers that we have here going to lift so much as a finger to save far-off Yissou?"

"We have to help them to see the importance of honoring our new alliance," said Thu-Kimnibol quietly. "If there's an attack and Salaman beats the hjjks without our help, he'll lay claim to Vengiboneeza and everything north of it. Can we allow him to grab all that? On the other hand, if Yissou falls to the hjjks, it won't be long before we see armies of the bug-folk marching through our own lands. Which is even less acceptable. We'll make the citizens here understand that. They'll have to realize that a hjjk invasion of Yissou is an act of war against all the People of every city. Surely not everybody in this city has become a worshiper of the Queen. We'll find enough who are loyal. The rest, if they like, can stay behind and pray to their new goddess. While we're marching north to destroy the Nest."

"To destroy the Nest?" Lespar Thone asked. He was the most cautious of these princes, a man of great property and slow, wary ways. "Will that be so easy, do you think? The hjjks are ten to our one, or perhaps a hundred to one. They'll fight like the demons they are to keep us from getting anywhere near the Nest. How are we going to overcome such numbers?"

"I remind you that I've faced those numbers before," said Thu-Kimnibol. "We routed the hjjks long ago at the battle of Yissou, and we'll rout them again now."

"At the battle of Yissou the People had the aid of some Great World weapon, wasn't that so?" Lespar Thone observed.

Thu-Kimnibol gave him a sour look. "You sound like Puit Kjai. Or Staip. We won that battle by our own valor."

"Yet Hresh had some ancient thing that was of great help, so I understand," Lespar Thone insisted. "Sometimes valor alone isn't enough, Thu-Kimnibol. And against such an immense horde of hjjks, desperately determined to defend their Queen—"

"What are you trying to say?"

"The same thing Husathirn Mueri did, when we discussed all this at the Presidium. Before we can attack the hjjks with impunity we need to have some new weapons."

"Perhaps the ones found a little while ago in the countryside will fill that need," said Kartafirain.

Every head turned toward him.

"Tell me more," said Thu-Kimnibol.

"The story's been circulating by way of the House of Knowledge. I think there's something to it. It seems that during the storms there was a great mudslide in the Emakkis Valley, and some farmer who was trying to catch some of his beasts that had escaped stumbled on the mouth of a tunnel leading into a hill. In which he found certain ancient artifacts that have since been brought to the House of Knowledge. A member of Hresh's staff believes that they're Great World devices of war, or, at any rate, of destruction. I have this from someone who works there, a Koshmar, Plor Killivash by name. His sister's in my service."

Thu-Kimnibol smiled triumphantly at Lespar Thole. "There you are! If there's any substance to this, we have exactly what we need."

Si-Belimnion said, "Hresh is known to be cool to the idea of a war with the hjjks. He may not cooperate."

"Cool or not, the war will come. He'll help us."

"And if he chooses not to?"

"He's my brother, Si-Belimnion. He won't hold vital information back from me."

"All the same," Si-Belimnion said, "you might consider approaching one of Hresh's subordinates instead of Hresh himself. This Plor Killivash, for example. I hardly need to tell you, of all people, how unpredictable Hresh can be."

"A good point. We'll work around him. Kartafirain? Will you have another talk with your friend at the House of Knowledge?"

"I'll see what I can manage."

"See that you do. These weapons are just what we need. If weapons is what they really are." Thu-Kimnibol filled the wine-cups once again, and drank deep. "It troubles me," he said after a while, "that Taniane hasn't been willing to take action against this new cult of hjjk-worship. Don't tell me that she's come to love the Queen these days as much as her daughter does!"

Kartafirain laughed. "Hardly. She loathes them as much as you do."

"Then why are these chapels allowed to flourish?"

"It's as Kartafirain said," Si-Belimnion replied. "She was afraid there'd be an uprising if she continued the suppression."

"Taniane never lacked for courage in the old days."

"You'll find that she's much changed," said Si-Belimnion. "She looks old. She's hardly ever seen at the Presidium, and doesn't say much when she's there."

"Is she ill?" Thu-Kimnibol asked, thinking of Naarinta.

"Weary, only. Weary and sad. She's been chieftain longer than most of us have been alive, my friend. It's taken a terrible toll on her. And now she sees the city falling apart in her hands."

"Things can't be that bad!"

Si-Belimnion gave him a melancholy smile. "A bizarre new kind of belief sweeps through the populace. Her own daughter is lost in incomprehensible fantasies. Threats are made against her in the streets by people calling for her abdication—hotheaded members of my own tribe, mostly, I'm ashamed to say. The rain goes on and on as has never been seen here before. She thinks the gods have turned against us and that her own end can't be far off."

Thu-Kimnibol looked toward Kartafirain. "Is this true?"

"She's greatly transformed, I think. And not for the better."

"Incredible. Incredible. There was never anyone with as much vitality as that woman. But I'll speak with her. I'll show her how the war will redeem us. She'll feel young again once we go marching off to smash the hjjks!"

"She may oppose you on the war," Maliton Diveri said.

"You think so?"

"Husathirn Mueri is very close with her now. And you know, Thu-Kimnibol, he'll always take any position that stands against your own beliefs. If you're for war, he'll be against it. He's still in favor of watching and waiting, taking no action, gathering our strength. And he's certain to speak in the Presidium against your alliance with Salaman."

Thu-Kimnibol spat. "Husathirn Mueri! That slippery ghost! How can Taniane possibly trust him?"

"Who said she trusts him? She's smarter than that. But she listens to him. And I guarantee it, he'll advise against any kind of military action that you support. May well be able to sway her, too."

"We'll see about that," said Thu-Kimnibol.

Despite everything they had told him he was still unprepared for the transformation Taniane had undergone since summer. She seemed a hundred years old. It was hard to believe that this dull-eyed lusterless woman was the fiery chieftain who had ruled this city so vigorously for so many decades. The fierce masks of the former chieftains, hanging on the wall behind her, made a mockery of her fatigue. Thu-Kimnibol felt almost apologetic for his own vigor and strength.

"At last," she said. "I thought you'd never return."

"There was a great deal to discuss with Salaman. It had to be done carefully. And he went out of his way to make me feel welcome."

"A strange man, Salaman. I'd have expected him still to hate you."

"So would I. But all that's ancient history now. He was very loving."

"Salaman? Loving?" Taniane managed a faint smile. "Well, it may be. Even the hjjks are loving, so I'm told." She leaned back in her chair. In a voice that seemed to come from some deep crypt she said, "There's been madness here, Thu-Kimnibol. Things are almost beyond my control. I'm in need of all the help you can give."

"I've never heard you so despondent, sister."

"You know of the new religion? This Kundalimon-worship?"

"Hjjk-worship, you mean."

"Yes. In truth, that's what it is."

"News of it came north with the autumn caravan."

"Those who believe it—and there are hundreds of them, Thu-

Kimnibol, perhaps thousands!—are pushing me to accept the treaty with the Queen. I get petitions every day. They march outside the Presidium. They cry out at me in the streets. I tell you, that boy spread some kind of poison in the minds of the children during just the few weeks he was among us. By the gods, Thu-Kimnibol, I tell you I wish he'd been killed sooner!"

Uneasily Thu-Kimnibol said, "Surely you didn't have anything to do with his death, Taniane!"

For a moment there was a flash of the old fire in her eyes. "No. No, not at all. Am I a murderer? I had no idea the boy could do such harm. And he was Nialli's lover. What do you think, that I'd have wanted him removed because of that? No, brother, I had nothing to do with it. I wish I knew who did."

"Her lover?" Thu-Kimnibol said, shaken.

"You didn't know? They were coupling-partners, and twining-partners also. I thought everyone knew that by now."

"I've been away many months, sister."

"You seem to know of everything else that's gone on here."

"Her lover," Thu-Kimnibol said again, still struggling with the idea. "I never thought of that. But how obvious it seems now! Small wonder she went out of her mind when he was killed, then." He shook his head. It was strange to think of his brother's daughter having taken a lover of any sort, after the way she'd always kept herself aloof. But to have chosen that dreamy hjjk-reared lad—how much like her that was, he thought. And then for him to be killed. How sad. "The gods have been unkind to that girl," he said. "One shouldn't have to have so much turmoil so young. I suppose she's involved with the new religion, now?"

"Not so far as I've heard. By all rights she should be, yes. But I'm told that she stays in her room at the House of Nakhaba and hardly ever goes out. I don't see her very often, you understand." Taniane laughed bitterly. "You see how it is? My one child is as foreign to me as a hjjk. My mate hides himself as usual in the House of Knowledge, and busies himself with important matters ten million years old. My people cry out to me to sign a treaty that means the end of us. There have been calls for my abdication, do you know that, Thu-Kimnibol? *'You stay much too long,'* they tell me, practically to my face. *'It's time you stepped aside.'* By the gods, Thu-Kimnibol, I wish I could! I wish I could!"

"Taniane—my poor Taniane—" he began, in his gentlest tone.

Her eyes flared wildly. "Don't you dare talk to me like that! I don't want your pity! Or anyone's! Pity isn't what I need." In a softer tone she said, "What I need is help. Do you see how isolated I am? How helpless? And do you see what troubles are upon us? What can you offer me beside pity, Thu-Kimnibol?"

"I can offer you a war," he said.

"A war?"

"We're in alliance now with the City of Yissou, if the Presidium will ratify it. It binds us to go to Salaman's aid if his city is attacked by hjjks; and I tell you, no doubt of it, Yissou and the hjjks will be at war very soon. So, then, will we. And then it'll be treason in this city to speak favorably of hjjks, for they'll officially be our enemies. And so there'll be an end to any talk of our accepting the Queen's treaty, and an end also to this poisonous religion that has sprung up in our midst, and to all the rest of your troubles, sister. What do you say to that? Now, what do you say?"

"Tell me more," said Taniane, and it seemed to Thu-Kimnibol that years had dropped from her in a single moment.

"All of us finally together again," Boldirinthe cried. "You were gone so long, Simthala Honginda! How good it is to have you here with us at last!"

It was a joyous day for the old offering-woman, the day of her eldest son's return from the north. Even the interminable rain had relented for once. For the first time in months her whole family was gathered about her in the warm pleasant hilltop lodgings she shared with Staip: her three sons and their mates, and her daughter and hers, and the whole horde of her grandchildren. Boldirinthe sat enfolded complacently in her own massiveness, contained by her vast body as though by a mound of blankets, and they came to her one by one to be embraced. Afterward they lifted her and led her to the dining-table, and brought the food and the wine. There were grilled scantrins, first, the fleshy-legged little creatures of the bay, not quite fish and not quite lizard but something midway between, and then heaping bowls of steamed kivvinfruit, and finally a roasted haunch of vimbor in shells of pastry, with plenty of good strong black Emakkis wine to wash it down. When they had eaten they sang and told old tales, and Staip, as he always did, reminisced about the People's privations during the journeys from the cocoon to Vengiboneeza and from Vengiboneeza to the southland, and one of her grandsons recited a poem he had composed, and a granddaughter played a tinkling little tune on the serilingion, and the wine flowed freely and there was much laughter. But Boldirinthe noticed that in the midst of all this joy her son Simthala Honginda, in whose honor the gathering was being held, sat silently, smiling infrequently, seemingly forcing himself by supreme effort to pay even slight attention to what was taking place about him.

To her son's mate Catiriil, sitting beside her, she said quietly, "He says so little. What troubles him, do you think?"

"Perhaps he's finding it strange to be home again, after so long a journey."

Boldirinthe frowned. "Strange? To be home? How can that be, girl?

He's with his kin again, his mate, his son, his daughter—he is here in his own splendid Dawinno, and not in Salaman's miserable dank Yissou. But where is his spirit? Where is his spark? This isn't the Simthala Honginda I remember."

"Nor I," whispered Catiriil. "He seems still to be in some distant land."

"Has he been like this all day?"

"From the first, when the caravan arrived at dawn. Oh, we embraced warmly enough, he told me how much he had missed me, he brought out gifts for me and for the children, he told us of the disagreeable place he had been and remarked on the beauty of Dawinno, even in the rain. It was all just words, though. There was no feeling in them." Then, with a smile, Catiriil said, "It must be only that Thu-Kimnibol kept him up there in the north so long that the chill of Salaman's city entered his soul. But give me a day or two to warm him up, Mother Boldirinthe. That's all it'll take!"

"Go to him now," Boldirinthe said. "Sit with him. Serve him with wine, and see to it that his cup is never empty. Eh, girl? You know what I mean."

Catiriil nodded and crossed the room to take the seat beside her mate. Boldirinthe watched approvingly. Catiriil was so gentle, so good, such a graceful person in every way, a splendid mate for her sharp-edged son. And beautiful, too, as her mother Torlyri had been, that same rich black fur startlingly banded with white spirals, the same dark warm eyes. Torlyri had been very tall, and Catiriil was small and delicate, but sometimes, seeing her son's mate from the corner of her eye, Boldirinthe imagined she was seeing Torlyri returned from the dead, and it gave her a start. And also Catiriil had Torlyri's mild and loving nature. How odd, Boldirinthe thought, that Catiriil was so pleasing in so many ways, and her brother Husathirn Mueri so difficult to like.

Catiriil was doing her best to cheer Simthala Honginda up. She had gathered a little group around him—his brother Nikilain, and Nikilain's mate Pultha, who was an absolute well of laughter and high spirits, and Timofon, his close friend and hunting companion, the mate of Simthala Honginda's sister Leesnai. They were joking with him, teasing him a little, centering all their attention and love on him. If a group like that couldn't lift Simthala Honginda from his bleakness, Boldirinthe thought, then no one could. But it seemed to be working.

Abruptly Simthala Honginda's voice rose clearly over the sounds of singing and merriment.

"Shall I tell you a story?" he said, in an oddly strained tone. "You have all told stories: now I'll tell you one, or several." He gulped the last of his wine and said without waiting for a response, "At one time in the hills east of Vengiboneeza there lived a bird with one body and two heads. You never saw it, did you, father? I didn't think so. But this is a tale. It seems that one of the heads once noticed the other head eating some sweet fruit with great enjoyment, and became envious, and it said to itself, 'I will eat poison fruit, then.' And so it did; and the whole bird died."

The room was completely quiet. There were some awkward attempts at laughter when Simthala Honginda was done speaking, but they died away as quickly as they were born.

"You liked that story, eh?" he cried. "Another one, then? Wait. Wait, let me have some wine."

Catiriil said, "Perhaps you're tired, love. We could—"

"No," said Simthala Honginda, refilling and draining his cup almost at once. "Another story. The story of the serpent whose head and tail quarreled with each other as to which should be the front. The tail said, 'You're always in the lead. That isn't fair. Let me lead once in a while.' And the head replied, 'How can I change places with you? The gods have decreed that I am the head.' But the quarrel went on and on, until the tail, in anger, wrapped itself around a tree, and the serpent could not proceed. Finally the head relented, and allowed the tail to go first, whereupon the serpent fell into a pit of flame and perished. Which is to say that there is a natural order to things, and when that order is disturbed, everything will go to ruin."

The silence this time was even more tense.

Staip, half rising from his seat, looked toward his son and said, "I think perhaps you should put your wine-cup away now, boy. What do you say?"

"I say that I haven't had nearly enough, father! But you don't like my stories, I take it. I thought you would, but it seems that I'm wrong. Well, then. No more stories. Only straightforward speech will it be, then. Direct and plain. Do you want to hear about my journey to the north? Do you want to know what our embassy achieved in Salaman's kingdom?"

Softly Catiriil said, "You're upsetting your mother, you know. You don't want to do that, do you? Look how pale she's become. Perhaps we should go out for a little fresh air, love. The rain has stopped, and—"

"No," Simthala Honginda said fiercely. "No, she should hear this too. She's still the offering-woman, isn't she? She's a high official of the tribe, is she not? Well, then. She must hear it." His hand trembled as he reached for yet another cup of wine. "What I have to tell you is that there will be war soon," he cried. "With the hjjks, it'll be. Salaman and Thu-Kimnibol have arranged it between them, some provocation, some pretext that'll touch it off, and we'll be plunged into the full fury of it, like it or not. This I know from what I heard, and what I overheard, and what I found by prowling about. There will be war! Thu-Kimnibol and Salaman will have it no other way! And we'll all blindly follow them over the edge of the cliff!" He took a deep draught of the wine. More moderately he said, "They're mad, those two. And their madness will infect all the world. Or perhaps it's the world's madness that has infected them. Perhaps we've already gone so far down the wrong road that this is the inevitable outcome, that Thu-Kimnibol and Salaman are the appropriate leaders for our time."

Boldirinthe stared, horror-stricken. She felt her heart beating furiously in the depths of her immense body.

Catiriil rose now and took the cup from Simthala Honginda, and whispered in his ear, trying desperately to calm him down. He responded angrily at first, but something she said appeared to reach him, and he nodded and shrugged, and spoke more gently to her, and after a moment she slipped her arm through his and led him quietly from the room.

Quietly Boldirinthe said to Staip, "Can what he said be true? Will there be war, do you think?"

"I'm no confidant of Thu-Kimnibol's," said Staip impassively. "I know no more than you do of any of this."

"There must be no war," she said. "Who will speak for peace in the Presidium? Husathirn Mueri will, I know. And Puit Kjai. And Hresh, perhaps. And certainly I will, if they give me a chance. And you? Will you speak?"

"If Thu-Kimnibol wants war, there will be war," said Staip, sounding as though he spoke from the other side of the grave. "What of it? Will you have to go to battle? Will I? No, no, no, this is no affair of ours. The gods determine everything. This is no affair of ours, Boldirinthe. If there is to be war, I say, let it come."

"War?" Husathirn Mueri said. He looked at his sister in astonishment. "A secret understanding with Salaman? A trumped-up provocation?"

"So Simthala Honginda insisted," said Catiriil. "So he said, in front of Staip, in front of Boldirinthe, in front of the whole family. It was bubbling inside him all day, and finally it came out. He'd been drinking heavily, you understand."

"Would he say the same things to me, if I went to see him?"

"He's never been really close to you, you know."

Husathirn Mueri laughed. "How kind you are! What you mean, but aren't willing to say, is that he dislikes me intensely. Eh, Catiriil?"

She shrugged almost imperceptibly. "I'm aware that you and he have never been friendly. What he said at dinner is something he really had no right to reveal. It's almost treasonous, isn't it, blurting out state secrets like that? He may not want to take you into his confidence."

"No right to reveal that we're being tricked into fighting a war that'll ruin us, simply to gratify Thu-Kimnibol's lust for battle? You call that treasonous? It's Thu-Kimnibol who's committed the treason, Catiriil."

"Yes. So I think also. That's why I've brought this to you."

"But you doubt that I can get Simthala Honginda to give me the details of it himself."

"I doubt it very much, brother."

"All right. All right. This is valuable enough for now, simply knowing what Thu-Kimnibol and Salaman have cooked up together. I'll take it from there."

"And may the gods be with us, whatever may come," Catiriil said.

"The gods," Husathirn Mueri said softly to himself, with a little chuckle, when his sister was gone. "Yes. May the gods be with us, indeed."

To me they are nothing at all, they are only names. Those were Nialli Apuilana's words, that astounding time when she had raved in such frenzy before the Presidium. *Our own inventions, to comfort us in our difficult times.* Husathirn Mueri had never forgotten that moment, nor those words.

Nothing but names. His own view exactly. In truth he knew himself to be a worse case even than Nialli Apuilana, for he had no beliefs at all, other than that life was nonsense, a cruel joke, a series of random events, that there was no reason for our being here other than that we are here. She at least had swallowed the hjjk myth that a cosmic plan governs the world and that everything is part of a preordained pattern. He had never seen evidence of that. And so he had no moral center, and knew it; he was capable of taking any position that seemed useful to the moment, favoring war one day and opposing it the next, as circumstances required. All that mattered was attaining power and comfort in his own lifetime, for that one lifetime was all there was, and everything was a joke in any case.

Husathirn Mueri had tried once to expound on these things to Nialli Apuilana, hoping to prove to her that they shared a set of common beliefs. But she had looked at him in shock and dismay, and had said to him in the coldest voice he had ever heard, "You don't understand me at all, Husathirn Mueri. You don't understand a thing about me at all."

So be it. Perhaps he didn't.

But he did understand the implications of the astonishing tale Catiriil had brought to him this day. He was surprised to see how little surprise he felt. Of *course* Thu-Kimnibol had gone north to stir up a war with the hjjks; of *course* the bellicose Salaman would gladly conspire with him to bring it about. And doubtless Taniane would lend what was left of her waning energies and all of her still considerable power to the task of mobilizing the Presidium's approval.

But possibly there was still a way to head them off. Just possibly, he thought. Or, if a war couldn't be avoided, at least to expose the perfidious role Thu-Kimnibol had played in bringing it about. The city could only suffer, if it went to war against the insect-folk. The losses would be terrible, the disruption of the fabric of life perhaps irreparable. And in the aftermath, those who had fomented the war would be brought down by it, and those who had tried in vain to prevent it would rise to greatness.

Husathirn Mueri smiled.

I'll see what I can do, he thought.

And may the gods be with me indeed.

They had marched for weeks, going northward all the time. Behind them the world was gliding happily onward once again into spring, but in these forlorn lands on the far side of Vengiboneeza an iron winter still seemed to prevail. To Zechtior Lukin that made no difference. The chill of winter and the hot blasts of summer were all the same to him. He scarcely noticed the change of seasons, except that the hours of darkness lasted longer at one time of the year than at another.

Now they were in a gray land. The ground was gray, the sky was gray, the wind itself was gray with a burden of dark sand when it came roaring out of the east. The only color came from the vegetation, which seemed to be striking back against the grayness with sullen fury. The tough sparse saw-edged grass was an angry carmine; the big rigid dome-shaped fungi were a deathly yellow and exploded into clouds of brilliant green spores when they were trampled; the trees, tall and narrow, had gleaming blue leaves shaped like spines, and constantly dropped a rain of viscous pink sap that burned like acid.

Low chalky hills like stubby teeth formed chains in the distance. The open country between them was flat and dry and unpromising, no lakes, no streams, only an occasional brackish spring oozing out of some salt-crusted crack in the ground.

"Which way now?" Lisspar Moen asked. She was the daily march-herald, who transmitted Zechtior Lukin's orders to the others.

He nodded toward the hills and indicated a continued north-northeasterly route.

"Hjjk country?" she said.

"Our country," Zechtior Lukin told her.

Striding along behind him in the gray plain were the Acknowledgers of Yissou, three hundred forty of them now.

Of his original three hundred seventy-six followers, a dozen or so had been too old and feeble to undertake the risks of beginning a new life in the wilderness, and another few had, when the moment of departure was at hand, simply recanted their faith and refused to go. Zechtior Lukin had anticipated something of that sort. He made no attempt to coerce them.

Coercion had no part in his philosophy. He acknowledged the supremacy of the gods in all things. If the gods decreed that some of his followers would choose not to follow him, he was prepared to accept that. Zechtior Lukin, expecting nothing of the world but what the world daily presented to him, had never known a moment's disappointment.

There had been some losses on the march, too. He accepted those calmly too. The gods would always have their way.

A raiding party of hjjks had captured five of his people as the marchers were passing the vicinity of Vengiboneeza. Knowing that the ancient sapphire-eyes capital was held now by the insect-folk, Zechtior Lukin had chosen a route cutting well to the east of it. But not far enough, it seemed. At twilight, in a mountain pass shrouded in close-hanging mist, came a sudden attack, shrieks and scuffles, great confusion, and, after a moment, the realization that whatever had happened was over. A few abandoned knapsacks lay on the ground, and one hand-cart was overturned. There was no hope of giving chase: the high country surrounding them was dark and pathless. Zechtior Lukin was grateful that the hjjks had taken as few as they had.

Natural perils took others. This was an untamed land. A scattering of loose boughs turned out to conceal the mouth of a pit, and scarlet claws and yellow fangs were waiting at its bottom. A few days later a huge low-slung beast clad in thick brown scales hard as stone burst madly out of nowhere, swinging its small dull-eyed head from side to side like a club, killing those it struck. Then there was a comic hopping creature with merry golden eyes and absurd tiny forearms; but from its tail there sprang a spike that squirted poison. And at midday once came a swarm of winged insects, as dazzling as colored jewels, that filled the air with a milky spray. Those that breathed it fell ill, and some did not recover.

"These things are to be expected," Zechtior Lukin said.

"We acknowledge the will of the gods," his people replied.

The survivors went on undaunted. Zechtior Lukin waited for the Five Heavenly Ones to tell him that they had come to the place where they should build their city.

On the far side of the chalky hills the grayness lifted. The land here was pale brown streaked with red, a sign perhaps of fertility, and there was a river running from east to west that was split into three forks. Along the riverbanks the vegetation had shining green foliage and some of the shrubs bore fat purplish fruits with wrinkled skins. They proved to be edible.

"Here we will stay," Zechtior Lukin said. "I feel the presence of the Five here."

He chose a little ridge between the two southernmost forks that seemed likely to be above the river's floodplain, and they set up the tents that they would live in until they had constructed the first buildings. Three women who were gifted with unusually powerful second sight went some distance apart to send word to Yissou of their location; for Zechtior Lukin had promised the king that he would do that. Salaman had shown him a method, combining twining and second sight, that would allow contact to be maintained over great distances. Zechtior Lukin was skeptical. But promises were to him like sacred oaths, and he sent the women off to transmit the message.

He said, "I call this place Salpa Kala," which meant the Place of the Heavenly Ones.

On the morning of the fourth day after the Acknowledgers had settled at Salpa Kala three hjjks appeared without warning, as though they had risen from the earth, and went unhesitatingly to Zechtior Lukin as he was supervising the raising of a tent. He was aware that they were behind him even before he turned: he could feel a hard icy pressure against his consciousness that was the bleak, remote, arid coldness of their austere souls.

Calmly one of them—he could not tell which; it spoke in the silent buzzing droning voice of the mind—said, "This place is forbidden to you. You will leave here tonight and return to your own land."

"This place is Salpa Kala, and the Five Heavenly Ones have given it to us to be our home," Zechtior Lukin replied evenly.

By second sight he sent forth the vision he once had had, of the immensity of the Queen of the insect-folk hovering in the air above Yissou, as though to say that he knew of her greatness, and accepted it as he accepted all things; but what he attempted to transmit also was that he had been told by the gods, the same high gods who guide the destinies of the hjjks, that he must come to this place and establish a settlement here.

But if what he had sent forth had reached the hjjks, or had impressed them in any way, they gave no sign of it.

"You will leave here tonight," said the rasping hjjk-voice again.

"We will not yield the gift of the gods," said Zechtior Lukin.

The hjjks said nothing further. Zechtior Lukin studied them calmly, staring at their long shining bodies, their many-faceted eyes, their segmented orange breathing-tubes, their jutting beaks, their six slender bristly limbs. The shortest of the three was a head taller than he was, but he doubted that it weighed any more than a child, so parched and fleshless did its body seem. In the clear morning air their hard yellow-and-black carapaces reflected the sunlight with an unpleasant glare. He felt no fear of them.

After a time he shrugged and turned his back to them, and went back to the job of directing the raising of the tent.

"What will we do?" Gheppilin the harnessmaker asked, when the hjjks had gone stalking off.

"Why, we'll hold our ground," he said. "It's ours by gift of the gods, is it not?"

He gave orders to his Acknowledgers to break out weapons: swords, spears, knives, clubs. At sundown they gathered in a tight circle beside their clustered baggage and waited for the hjjks to return.

The three who had come before—Zechtior Lukin assumed, at least, that they were the same ones—stepped out of the shadows.

"You are still here," the droning hjjk-voice said.

"This place is ours."

"It is no place for flesh-folk. Go back or die."

"The gods have brought us here," said Zechtior Lukin. "The gods' will be done."

There was a shrill cry from the far side of the encampment. Zechtior Lukin looked about quickly; but the one quick glance was enough. A horde of dark angular figures had emerged from the thickets by the river, hjjks by the hundreds, perhaps by the thousands. It seemed as if every pebble along the bank had been transformed in that moment into a hjjk. Already his people were in chaos.

Zechtior Lukin lifted his spear. "Fight!" he bellowed. "Fight! Cowardice is ungodly!"

He thrust the weapon into the bright shining eye of the hjjk nearest him, pulled it free, used the edge of its blade to slash the breathing-tube of the second one.

"Fight!"

"We'll all be killed!" Lisspar Moen called to him.

"We owe the gods a death, and tonight they'll have it, yes," Zechtior Lukin said, and struck down the third of the hjjks just as it raised its clacking beak above him. "But we'll fight all the same. We'll fight to the end."

The insect-folk swarmed everywhere in the encampment. Their spears flashed. Their harsh screeching cries drowned out the voices of the Acknowledgers.

Lisspar Moen's right, Zechtior Lukin told himself. We're all going to die now.

So it seemed he had misunderstood the will of the gods. Evidently they hadn't meant him to be the one who built the new world after all. That seemed clear. Very well: this too was the will of the gods, even as the descent of the death-stars upon the Great World had been their will, seven hundred thousand years before.

He wondered for a moment whether it was right even to attempt to resist. If the gods had ordained his death and the death of all his people this night, as surely they had, should he not put down his spear and wait peacefully for his end with folded arms, just as the sapphire-eyes had done when the Long Winter swept over them?

Maybe so. Looking quickly around, he saw some of his people trying to hide or flee, but others standing calmly, offering themselves with an Acknowledger's true resignation to the spears of the hjjks.

Yes. Yes, he thought. That is the proper way.

But he realized that he himself couldn't do it. Here at the last, with destruction at hand, he felt impelled to resist, futile though it was, and contrary to all that he had believed and taught. He didn't have it in him, after all, to submit so obligingly to slaughter. In the final hour of his life Zechtior Lukin found himself staring at an aspect of his soul that he had not expected ever to find.

False Acknowledger! Hypocrite!

At least he was capable of acknowledging that much. He pondered the matter for an instant and thrust it from his mind. After all, he was what the gods had created, for good or ill.

Λ wide ring of hjjks surrounded him. Their shining eyes were like huge glittering dark moons. With a snarl, he set himself in a square battle-stance as they moved in on him.

He struck and struck and struck again, until he was able to strike no more.

8

The Sword of Dawinno

Husathirn Mueri said, "A moment, if I may, Hresh."

The chronicler, who had been about to enter the House of Knowledge, halted on the steps and gave Torlyri's son an inquiring look. Husathirn Mueri took the steps two at a time and was at Hresh's side an instant later. He said in a low voice, "Do you know what's going on in this city, Hresh?"

"In general or in particular?"

A quick smile. "You don't know, then. Your brother's out at the stadium this very minute, putting the army through its drills."

Hresh blinked. It was only three days since the Presidium had voted to ratify the new alliance with the City of Yissou. Taniane and Thu-Kimnibol had spoken strongly in favor and only a few cautious ones like Puit Kjai had objected that the agreement would sooner or later drag Dawinno into war. More likely later than sooner, Hresh had thought then. But things seemed to be moving more quickly than he had expected.

"We have no army," he said. "Only a city guard."

"We have an army now. Thu-Kimnibol and his friends have put it together overnight. The Sword of Dawinno, it's called. Your brother insists that we're going to be at war with the hjjks any minute, and we have to get ready for it." Husathirn Mueri made a hoarse sound that Hresh realized, after a moment, was laughter. "Imagine it! Half the city's sitting in the Kundalimon chapels right now singing the praises of the insect Queen, and the other half's out by the stadium getting ready to go and kill Her!"

"If there is war," Hresh said slowly, "then of course we must be prepared to fight. But why does Thu-Kimnibol think—"

"The alliance with Salaman requires us to go to war, if Yissou is attacked."

"I know what it requires. But the hjjks haven't made any hostile moves."

"Not yet."

"Is there any reason to believe they will?"

Husathirn Mueri looked thoughtfully into the distance. "I have reason to think so."

"Salaman's been telling us for years that the hjjks mean to invade him. I gather that wall of his has gotten higher and higher until it looms over his city in the most incredible way. But meanwhile no invasion has ever come. All the supposed hjjk threats against him have been strictly in his mind. Why should things be any different now?"

"I think they are," Husathirn Mueri said.

"Because Salaman has rejected the Queen's offer of a peace treaty and we've ignored it?"

"That's part of it. But my guess is that it's only a small part. I think that there are those among us who are actively engineering a war by provoking the hjjks to take action against us."

"What are you saying, Husathirn Mueri?"

"I could say it again, if you wish."

"You're making a very grave accusation. Do you have any proof?"

Husathirn Mueri stared again into the distance. "I do."

"The Presidium should have it, then."

"It involves a person or persons very close to yourself, Hresh. *Very* close."

Hresh scowled. "All this ponderous hinting at conspiracies is annoying, Husathirn Mueri. Speak out frankly or let me be."

Husathirn Mueri looked dismayed. He said in his most ingratiating way, "Perhaps I've been too forward. Perhaps I'm leaping to conclusions too swiftly. I hesitate to implicate those who may be innocent, at least at this point. But let me put it another way, shall I? There are certain great forces in the universe that are pushing us to war, is what I believe. It's inevitable. Sometimes a thing simply is inevitable, the way the coming of the death-stars was inevitable. Do you understand me, Hresh?"

This was maddening, this pious philosophizing out of an unbeliever like Husathirn Mueri. But Hresh saw that he wasn't going to get anything explicit or even coherent out of him. He was determined to be evasive and elliptical, and no amount of questioning could break through his defenses.

It was always a temptation, when you were talking with Husathirn Mueri, to want to probe him with your second sight, to see what meanings lay concealed behind his words. Hresh resisted it. Surely Husathirn Mueri would be prepared for such a thrust, and would have a counterthrust ready.

With some irritation Hresh said, "Well, may the gods spare us, but if the hjjks do strike against Yissou, then we're bound to go to Salaman's defense. That's done and agreed. As for your talk of conspiracies, I regard that as mere talk until I have reason to think otherwise. But in any event, why be so troubled by Thu-Kimnibol's army? If a war's coming, should we go into it unprepared?"

"You miss the point, though you utter it with your own lips. Don't you see? It's *Thu-Kimnibol's* army. If war's this close, and I think Thu-Kimnibol's correct that it is, then the responsibility for organizing an army belongs to the Presidium. There has to be an official mobilization. It can't simply be a private patriotic venture of one powerful prince. Can't you see that, Hresh? Or are you so blinded by your love for your half-brother that you've forgotten that he's his father's son? Do you want another Harruel here? Think about that, Hresh."

Hresh felt a stab of shock.

In an instant the years dropped away from him, and he was a boy again, and it was the Day of the Breaking Apart. Here stood the folk of Koshmar's tribe, and there, opposite them, were those who had opted to depart from Vengiboneeza with Harruel. Hresh's mother Minbain, Harruel's mate, was among them; but Hresh had just chosen not to go. "There are important things for me still to do here," Hresh had said.

And Harruel swelled with wrath, and his powerful arm swung in sudden fury.

"Miserable boy! Flea-ridden little cheat!"

The blow was only a glancing one. But it was enough to knock Hresh off his feet and send him flying through the air. He landed in a heap, stunned and trembling. And stayed there until Torlyri went to him and lifted him and held him in her warm embrace.

"Think about it," said Torlyri's son now. "Is it your brother Thu-Kimnibol who's drilling that army on the stadium grounds now? Or is it King Harruel?" Husathirn Mueri gave him a close, searching look. Then he turned and was gone almost at once.

As Hresh entered the vestibule of the House of Knowledge, haunted by all that Husathirn Mueri had told him and deep in thoughts of the anguished past and the foreboding future, Chupitain Stuld stepped out of one of the inner offices and said, "Shall I bring the artifacts from Tangok Seip up to your study now, sir?"

"The artifacts from Tangok Seip?"

"The ones the farmer found in the cave, after the mudslide. You said you'd look at them today."

"Ah. Yes. Yes. Those tools, you mean."

He tried to shake off the fog that had engulfed him. His mind was scattered from one end of the world to the other.

That cache of Great World artifacts, yes. Chupitain Stuld had been after him persistently for the past few days to examine those things. She was probably right, he supposed. It was weeks since their discovery and he hadn't even bothered to look at them. Other preoccupations had distracted him completely. But Plor Killivash had said the find was important. The least he could do, he told himself, was take a look.

Chupitain Stuld was waiting for an answer.

"Bring them upstairs, yes," he said. "In half an hour, will you? I have a few things to do first."

He made his way up the spiral ramp and into his private chamber.

Somehow he is outside the building, on the parapet. Then, without even troubling to take the Barak Dayir from its pouch, he feels himself rising, floating off into the upper air, soaring above the city, climbing effortlessly higher and higher, beyond the clustering clouds, into the sky above the sky. Everything up here is black, streaked with scarlet. Streams of cool air rush past him like rivers. Tiny pellets of ice strike his fur. There are crystals of ice on his fingertips. He dances on nothingness.

Looking down, he can see everything, as if through a clear window in the darkness. The entire city lies open to his gaze.

He sees the stadium grounds, and the troops of the Sword of Dawinno marching in formation, while at their head the impressive figure of Thu-Kimnibol struts and prances, gesturing emphatically and barking commands.

He sees Nialli Apuilana walking in a park, moving like one lost in a dream. Mysteries shroud her soul. A bright crimson line of conflict runs through it as though it is splitting apart.

Behind her, a considerable distance behind, lurks Husathirn Mueri. He is a mystery too: obvious enough on the surface, hungry for power and pathetically obsessed with Nialli Apuilana. But what lies beneath? Hresh senses only a void. Can it be, such emptiness in the son of Torlyri and Trei Husathirn? There must be more within him than that. What, though? Where?

Hresh's gaze moves on.

Here is his garden of captive animals, now. The furry enigmatic blue stinchitoles, the gentle thekmurs, the stanimanders. The twittering sisichils frisk as though they know he's watching them. The stumbains—the diswils—the catagraks—all the multitudinous horde of wondrous creatures that Dawinno the Transformer has tumbled forth upon the face of the thawing Earth, and which Hresh's hunters have brought together for him here.

The caviandis. There they are beside their stream, the two slender gentle creatures. How lovely the sleekness of their purple fur, the brightness of their thick yellow manes. They look up and see him in the sky far above, and they smile.

He feels the warmth of their spirits radiating toward him. She-Kanzi, He-Lokim: his friends, his friends. His caviandi friends.

Their wordless greeting comes floating up to him, and his wordless reply descends. They speak again, and he replies; and then he asks, and they answer. Without words, without concepts, even. A simple, silent communion of being, an ongoing exchange of spirit that could not possibly be expressed other than as itself.

———
———
———
———

He knows by now they have no use for words as he understands words, just as "He-Lokim" and "She-Kanzi" are not names as he understands names. They live outside the need of such things, just as they and all their kind live outside the need for the building of cities, or the fabrication of objects, or any other such "civilized" thing. The otherness of them is the central fact of their nature: their strangeness, their non-Peopleness.

Their souls flood into his, and he into theirs, and suddenly there comes to him a vision within the vision he is having. He sees a second Great World upon the Earth, different from the first but no less glorious, a world not of six races but of dozens, of hundreds, of People and caviandis and stinchitoles and thekmurs, of sisichils and stanimanders and catagraks, of all the creatures that lived—united, locked in perpetual understanding sharing in everything, a world deeper and richer in its fullness than even the old Great World had been, a world that embraced everything that lived upon the Earth—

A sudden discordant voice within him asks:

Even the hjjks?

And he answers at once, without pausing to think:

Yes. Even the hjjks. Of course, the hjjks.

But then, considering it, he asks himself if the hjjks would in fact join any such new confederation of races. They had, after all, been part of the earlier one. And the Transformer has had all the hundreds of centuries since the time of the Great World to alter and elevate them. It might be that they have moved so far beyond the other races of the Earth now that they are incapable of joining them as equals in anything.

Was that so? Hresh wonders. Have they become gods? Is *She* a god, the great Queen of the hjjks?

In that instant, but only for an instant, his dreaming mind flashes northward into the bleakness of the cold lands, where the horizon is lit by a brilliant incandescent glow. And he beholds there the vast secret Queen, lying motionless in Her hidden chamber while She directs the destinies of all the millions of insect-folk, and, for all Hresh can tell, of the rest of the world as well. He feels the force and power of that immense mind, and of that great living machine, the Nest over which She rules. He observes the meshing of the parts, the weaving of gleaming pistons, the spinning of the web of life.

Then it is gone and he hovers again in the indeterminate void; but the tolling echo of that immensity lingers in him.

A god? Ruling over a race of gods?

No, he thinks. Not gods.

The Five Heavenly Ones, *they* are gods: Dawinno, Emakkis, Mueri, Friit, Yissou—the Transformer and Destroyer, the Provider, the Comforter, the Healer, the Protector.

And Nakhaba of the Bengs: *he* is a god. The Interceder, he who stands between the People and the humans, and speaks with them on our behalf. So old Noum om Beng had taught him, when he was a boy in Vengiboneeza.

And therefore it must be so, Hresh tells himself, that the humans also are gods, for we know that they are higher even than Nakhaba, and older than the Great World.

Perhaps they are the ones who brought the other five races of the Great World into being, the hjjks and the sea-lords, the mechanicals and vegetals, the sapphire-eyes. Could it be? That they had grown weary of living alone on the Earth, the humans, and had created the others to join with them in a new great civilization, which would flourish for many years, and then perish as all civilizations perished?

Where are they, then, if they are gods?

Dead, like the sapphire-eyes and the vegetals and the mechanicals and the sea-lords?

No, Hresh thinks. For how can gods die? They have simply withdrawn from the world. Perhaps their own Creator has summoned them elsewhere, and they are building a new Earth for Him far away.

Or else they are still with us, nearby but invisible, biding their time, keeping themselves aloof while they await the working-out of their great plan, whatever that may be. And the hjjks, awesome though they are, are simply an aspect of that plan, not the designers and custodians of it.

Perhaps. Perhaps.

And if there is to be a new Great World, the hjjks must be part of it. We must turn to them as fellow humans, as Nialli Apuilana once had said. But now instead we are about to go to war with them. What sense does that make? What sense, what sense, what sense?

He can't say. Nor can he sustain himself aloft any longer. His soul comes spiraling downward through the darkness, crashing toward the ground. As he falls from the skies Hresh looks toward the city that rises to meet him, and catches one final glimpse of his brother Thu-Kimnibol, proudly parading before his troops on the stadium grounds. Then he passes through some zone of incomprehensible strangeness; and when he is conscious again, he finds himself at his own desk, dazed, stunned.

His mind is in a whirl. Things are as they always have been for him. Too many questions, not enough answers.

The voice of Chupitain Stuld cut through his confusion. "Sir? Sir, I've brought the Tangok Seip artifacts. Sir? Sir, are you all right?"

"I—it—that is—"

She came rushing into the room and hovered before him, eyes wide with anxiety. Hresh scrambled to pull himself together. Fragments of dream circled and spun in the bedlam of his soul.

"Sir?"

He summoned all the serenity he could muster.

"A moment of reverie, is all—deep in thought—"

"You looked so strange, sir!"

"Nothing's wrong. A moment of reverie, Chupitain Stuld. The wandering mind, very far away."

"I could come back another time, if you—"

"No. No. Stay." He pointed to the box she was holding. "You have them in there? Let me see. Inexcusable, that I've let them wait this long. Plor Killivash's already studied them, you say?"

For some reason that produced a flurry of turmoil in her. He wondered why.

She began to lay the objects out on his desk.

There were seven of them, more or less spherical, each one small enough to be held with one hand. By their elegance of design and richness of texture Hresh knew them at once to be Great World work, each of them fashioned of the imperishable colored metals characteristic of the extraordinary craftsmen of that vanished era. The vaults of Vengiboneeza had yielded hundreds of devices like these. Some of them no one had ever learned how to operate; a few had produced one single startling effect and then had never functioned again; still others he had managed to master and use effectively for years.

Things like these were unearthed only rarely, now. This new cache was a remarkable find. It was a measure of the turmoil in his own soul that he'd left them to his assistants for so long, without bothering to examine them himself.

He looked at the seven objects but didn't touch any of them. He knew the dangers of picking such things up without knowing which of the various protrusions on them would activate them.

"Does anybody have any idea what they do?"

"This one—it dissolves matter. If I touched this knob on the side, a beam of light would come out and dissolve everything between here and the wall. This one casts a cloak of darkness over things, a kind of veil that's impossible to see through, so you could walk through the city and no one would notice you. And this one, it cuts like a knife, and its beam is so powerful we couldn't measure the depths of the hole it cut." Chupitain Stuld gave him a wary look, as if unsure that he was paying attention. She picked up another of the things. "Now, this one, sir—"

"Wait a moment," said Hresh. "I see only seven instruments here."

She looked troubled again. "Seven. That's right, sir."

"Where are the others?"

"The—others?"

"I seem to recall being told that there were eleven of these things, the day they were brought in. A couple of months ago, it was—during the rainy time, I remember—eleven Great World artifacts, that's what you said, I'm sure of it, or perhaps it was Io Sangrais who told me—"

"I was the one, sir," said Chupitain Stuld in a very small voice.

"Where are the other four?"

Distress had turned to fright in her, now. She moved quickly back and forth in front of the desk, moistening her lips, frantically grooming herself.

Hresh gave her just a minute jab of second sight. And felt the roiling fear within her, the shame, the contrition.

"Where are they, girl?" he asked gently. "Tell me the truth."

"Out—on—loan—" she whispered.

"On loan? To whom?"

She stared at the floor.

"To Prince Thu-Kimnibol, sir."

"My brother? Since when is he interested in ancient artifacts? What in the name of Nakhaba does he want with them, I wonder? How would he even have known they were here?" Hresh shook his head. "We don't loan things, Chupitain Stuld. Especially new acquisitions that haven't been properly studied. Even to someone like Prince Thu-Kimnibol. You know that."

"Yes, sir."

"Did you authorize this loan?"

"It was Plor Killivash, sir." A pause. "But I knew about it."

"And didn't tell me."

"I thought it was all right. Considering that Prince Thu-Kimnibol is your brother, and—"

Hresh waved her into silence. "He has them now?"

"I think so, sir."

"Why did he want them, do you know?"

She was trembling. She tried to speak, but no words would come.

Through Hresh's mind ran Chupitain Stuld's description of the arti-facts that remained, the ones that Thu-Kimnibol hadn't bothered to take. *This one dissolves matter . . . This one casts a cloak of darkness . . . This one cuts like a knife, and its beam goes so deep we couldn't measure it . . .*

Gods! These were the devices that Thu-Kimnibol had chosen to leave behind. What sort of destruction were the other ones capable of working?

At this moment, he knew, Thu-Kimnibol was out drilling his army on the stadium grounds, getting ready for his war against the hjjks. It had taken him only a few days to assemble his troops.

And now he had his weapons, too.

Taniane said, "It's not Thu-Kimnibol's army, Hresh. It's *our* army. The army of the City of Dawinno."

"But Husathirn Mueri—"

"The gods confound Husathirn Mueri! He's going to oppose us every step of the way, that's obvious. But war is coming, beyond any question. And therefore I authorized Thu-Kimnibol to begin organizing an armed force."

"Wait a minute," Hresh said. He looked at Taniane as though she were some stranger, and not his mate of forty years. "*You* authorized him? Not the Presidium?"

"I'm the chieftain, Hresh. We're facing a crisis. It's no time for long-winded debate."

"I see." He stared at her, scarcely believing what he heard. "And this war? Why are you so sure it's on the way? You and Thu-Kimnibol and Husathirn Mueri too, for that matter. Is it all agreed? Has some kind of secret resolution to start a war been passed?"

Taniane was slow to reply. Hresh, waiting, sensed the same evasiveness coming from her that had emanated earlier from Husathirn Mueri, and even from Chupitain Stuld. They were all trying to hide things from him. A web of deception had been woven here while he slept, and they were desperately eager to keep him from penetrating it now.

She said finally, "Thu-Kimnibol obtained proof, while he was in Yissou, that the hjjks intend to launch an attack against King Salaman in the very near future."

"Proof? What sort of proof?"

The evasiveness deepened. "He said something about having gone riding out into hjjk territory with Salaman, and coming upon a party of hjjks, and forcing them to surrender secret military plans. Or something like that."

"Which they were conveniently carrying in little baskets around their necks. Personally signed by the Queen, with the royal hjjk seal stamped on them."

"Please, Hresh."

"You believe this? That the invasion of Yissou that Salaman's been fretting about since the beginning of time is actually going to happen the day after tomorrow?"

"I do, yes."

"What proof is there?"

"Thu-Kimnibol knows what it is."

"Ah. I see. All right, let's say the hjjks finally are going to invade. How timely for Salaman that this is going to happen right after he and my brother have concluded a treaty of mutual defense between Dawinno and Yissou, eh?"

"You sound so angry, Hresh! I've never heard you this way."

"And I've never heard you this way, either. Dancing around my questions, talking about proof but not producing any, letting Thu-Kimnibol set up an army right here in the city without taking the trouble even to discuss it in the Presidium—"

Now she was staring at him as if *he* were a stranger. Her eyes were hooded, her expression was cold.

He couldn't bear it, this wall of suspicion that had arisen between them suddenly, rearing as high as Salaman's lunatic rampart. The urge came to him to ask her to twine with him, to join him in the communion that admits of no suspicion, of no mistrust. Then all would be made known between them; then once again they would be Hresh and Taniane, Taniane and Hresh, and not the strangers they had become to each other.

But he knew that she'd refuse. She'd plead weariness, or an urgent meeting an hour from now, or some other such thing. For if she twined with him she would have no secrets from him; and Hresh saw that she was full of secrets that she was determined not to share with him. He felt a great sadness. He could always find out everything he wanted to know by taking recourse to the Barak Dayir, he knew. The powers of the Wonderstone would carry him anywhere, even into the guarded recesses of Taniane's mind. But the idea was repugnant to him. Spy on my own mate? he thought. No. No, I'll let the city be destroyed and everyone in it, before I do that.

After a long silence Taniane said, "I've taken such actions as I deem necessary for the security of the city, Hresh. If you disagree, you have the right to state your objections in the Presidium. All right?" Her stony glare was awful to behold. "Is there anything else you want to tell me?"

"Do you know, Taniane, that Thu-Kimnibol has gone behind my back to remove newly discovered Great World artifacts from the House of Knowledge for use as weapons?"

"If there's a war, Hresh, weapons will be necessary. And there's going to be a war."

"But to take them from the House of Knowledge, without even telling—"

"I authorized Thu-Kimnibol to see to it that the army was properly equipped."

"You authorized him to steal Great World things from the House of Knowledge?"

She eyed him steadily and unflinchingly. "I seem to remember that you used Great World weapons against the hjjks at the battle of Yissou."

"But that was different! That was—"

"Different, Hresh?" Taniane laughed. "Was it? How?"

For Salaman it was a bad day atop the wall. Everything was unclear. A hash of harsh chattering nonsense clogged the channels of his mind. Vague cloudy images drifted to him now and then. A lofty tower which might signify Thu-Kimnibol. A flash of luminescent flame which perhaps stood for Hresh. A tough weatherbeaten tree, whipping about in a storm, which he thought might represent Taniane. And some other image, that of someone or something serpentine and slippery, impossible for Salaman to interpret at all. Things were happening in Dawinno today. But what? What? Nothing that he was picking up made sense. He tuned his second sight as keenly as he could. But either his perceptions were weak today or the transmissions from his spies were muddled beyond his ability to decode them.

He was in his pavilion, sweeping his sensing-organ from side to side in broad arcs. Casting his mind outward along it into the great empty spaces that surrounded Yissou, he trawled southward for news. On the far side of the wall, the whole city's width away, stood his son Biterulve, seeking word from the north.

The new communications network was finally in place. It had taken all the winter to build it: finding the volunteers, training them, sending them out to establish the outposts that would masquerade as farms. But now he had his agents strung like beads along a line stretching southward nearly to the City of Dawinno, and north toward hjjk territory as far as seemed safe to intrude.

From all sides came the buzz and crackle of second-sight visions flooding toward him, relayed station by station along the line. The king concentrated the full force of his powerful mind on them. He came here every day at dawn now, to listen, to wait.

It wasn't easy to achieve, this mind-transmission. The messages were always blurred and difficult to interpret, and often ambiguous. But what other way was there, short of having couriers ride constantly back and forth? At best the news they brought would be weeks late. That was unthinkable, now. Events were moving too quickly. If he had a Wonderstone as Hresh did, perhaps he could let his spirit rove hither and yon as he wished, peering into anything and everything. But there was only one Wonderstone, and Hresh had it.

Nothing was working for him today, though. The messages that were coming in were worthless. Murk and mist, darkness and fog, no clarity at all. A waste of time and energy.

Well, so be it. Salaman let his weary sensing-organ go limp. A better day tomorrow, perhaps. He moved toward the stairs.

Then, like an agitated voice calling to him out of the sky, the presence of his son came to him.

—Father! Father!

—Biterulve?

—Father, can you hear me? It's Biterulve!

—I hear you, yes.

—Father?

—Tell me, boy. Tell me!

There was silence then. Salaman felt fury rising. Plainly the boy had something important to tell him; but just as plainly, Biterulve's messages and his own replies weren't in coordination.

Salaman swung around and inclined his sensing-organ toward the direction Biterulve's output was coming from. It was maddening: so inexact, so imprecise, mere approximations of meaning, images and sensations rather than words, which must be deciphered, which must be interpreted. But certainly there was news from the north. Salaman had no doubt of that. He could feel the boy's unmistakable excitement.

—Biterulve?

—Father! Father!

—I hear you. Tell me what it is.

He sensed the boy struggling. Biterulve had great sensitivity, but it was of an odd kind, more keen over long distances than close at hand. Salaman hammered his fists against the brick walkway of the wall. He raised his sensing-organ until it could go no higher, and stroked the air with his outspread arms as though that way he could pull the message more clearly from his son.

Then came an image unquestionable in its clarity.

Bloodied bodies lying on a plain between two streams. Hundreds of them. Zechtior Lukin's people.

Gaunt shadowy figures stalking among them, stooping now and then as though taking trophies.

Hjjks.

—They're dead, father. The Acknowledgers. Every one of them. Can you hear me?

—I hear you, boy.

—Father? Father? It came through so clearly, through the northern relay posts. They've all been killed, in the hjjk country, in a place where rivers fork. All the Acknowledgers, completely wiped out.

Salaman nodded, as though Biterulve were standing right beside him. With a fierce burst of mental strength he hurled toward the boy a message so vehement that he was certain it would get through, to say that he had received and comprehended the news; and after a moment came confirmation from Biterulve, and the boy's relief that he had managed to make himself understood.

At last, Salaman thought.

Now the wheels begin to turn.

The Acknowledgers had found the martyrdom they wanted. Time now to send the second force, the army of vengeance, which would probably meet martyrdom too, though far less calmly. And then to make ready for the all-out war that was sure to follow.

The king swung about again toward the south. For a moment he stood resting, breathing easily, gathering force. There could be no ambiguities or mysteries this time. The message had to travel along the relay chain with no distortion whatever, and get through to Thu-Kimnibol in distant Dawinno untainted by error.

He summoned the images. The bodies by the riverbank. The dark angular shapes moving among them. The new army, setting out from Yissou, bravely marching into the territory of the enemy to avenge the murder of Zechtior Lukin and his people. The violent collision of forces that was sure to come. The hjjks, aroused, issuing threats.

And then the gates of Dawinno opening, and an immense force of warriors emerging, with Thu-Kimnibol at their head.

Salaman smiled. He raised his sensing-organ and held it rigid. Power throbbed in it from the base of his spine and traveled to the tip. He closed his eyes and let the word burst forth from him. It soared southward from station to station in a bright blaze of energy, like a thunderbolt leaping across the vast spaces between the two cities.

—I invoke the terms of our alliance. We are at war.

Something is wrong. Nialli Apuilana, alone in her room in the House of Nakhaba, feels a sudden tremor, a heaving and a wrenching, as if the world has been pulled free of its base and is plummeting wildly through the heavens. She goes to the window. Everything seems quiet in the streets. But her second sight shows her the sun, suddenly huge, hanging just above her in the air with rivers of blood dripping down from it. In the blackness of the sky the icy green tails of comets whirl and spin.

She trembles and looks away and covers her eyes with her arms. After a time she prays, first to the Five, and then to the spirit of Kundalimon.

And then, without knowing why, she thinks to reach out to the Queen as well.

Taking the hjjk star from its place on the wall, Nialli Apuilana holds it before her face, gripping it lightly by its sides. She peers into the open place at its center, narrowing the focus of her vision down until that small open place is the only thing she can see.

It is dark in there. Perhaps some sort of image lurks in the deepest part of the darkness, but she isn't at all sure it is there, and, if it is, it is blurred and faded and unclear, a mere ghost of a ghost. Once the star had been able to show her the Nest, or so she had thought. But now—

Nothing. Only dark hazy shadows that elude her gaze, try as she might to penetrate them. Of the Nest there is no trace.

Where has it gone? she wonders.

Was it ever there at all?

—*Do you want to see?* a voice within her asks.

—*Yes.*

—*What you see may change you.*

—*I've been changed so many times already. What harm can one more do?*

—*Very well. See, then, what is there to be seen.*

It seems to her then that the shadows are lifting, that the darkness at the core of the star is brightening, that once more she can look through the place at the center of the star into the familiar subterranean corridors that had for a time been her home. Figures are moving about. She grips the star more tightly, stares more intently.

Figures, yes—

She sees them all too clearly now.

Monstrous. Weird. Distorted. Heads like hatchets, arms like swords. Huge cold burning eyes like mirrors of black glass that throw back a thousand malevolent refractory images at once. Glistening beaks that snap and clack and thrust themselves like daggers at her through the opening in the star. Nialli Apuilana hears the harsh hissing sound of their mocking laughter. The star itself, that simple thing of plaited grass, is covered with sharp black bristles now. Its center is a dark hairy mouth, gleaming, gaping, a wet and slippery hole that makes soft insinuating sucking noises at her.

Something is pulling at her, trying to draw her down into the heart of the little plaited star.

The temptation to yield is powerful. Return to the Nest, yes, allow the bond to be rebuilt, sit at the feet of Nest-thinker, absorb his wisdom. Be taken before the Queen to experience Her touch. Wasn't that what she wanted? Wasn't it what she has always wanted? And Kundalimon. The greatest temptation of all. They'd give Kundalimon back to her. *Come to us and Kundalimon will be yours again.* Was it so? How tempting it sounds.

How easy it would be to surrender. How good to return to the nest . . . how comforting . . . how safe.

No. No. How can it be, any of it?

Nialli Apuilana resists with all the strength of her soul.

Still she is drawn inward. But then gradually, as she continues to struggle, the force of the pull recedes. Shuddering, she throws the star aside and watches it skitter into a far corner of the room, where it comes to rest against the wall, tipped up on end. But even from there it calls to her. *Come to us. Come. Come.*

The nightmare images refuse to leave her. The beaks and claws, the bristling mouth, the myriad cold gleaming eyes. They blaze in her mind no matter how she tries to drive them from her. She thought she had fought and won this battle already, weeks ago. But no, no, the Queen's grip is not yet fully broken.

She fights for breath. Her heart races. Her skin breaks out in cold fiery pricklings.

Her head swims with mysteries.

The walls of her little room seem to be closing in on her. Streams of blood flow across the floor. Severed limbs arise and dance wildly about her. A baleful green light comes pulsing up from the star that lies beside the wall. Thin bristly arms reach out through its center, groping for her. Harsh whispering voices, distant but seductive, call to her.

"No," she says. "I'm not yours any more."

She edges backward, keeping her eyes on the star as she moves slowly toward the door, fumbling behind herself to open it, then slipping hurriedly out into the hallway. She slams the door and holds it shut, leaning against it, drawing air deep into her lungs, waiting for the dizziness to go from her, for the pounding in her chest to subside.

Free. Free.

What next, though?

There is only one person in the city she can turn to.

I'll go to my father, she thinks.

"They want to destroy the Queen, if they can," Husathirn Mueri said. "You have my word on it."

He was in the chapel of Kundalimon in the alleyway just off Fishmonger Street. It wasn't one of the regular days of communion. Only Tikharein Tourb and Chhia Kreun were with him now: the boy-priest, the girl-priestess.

Somewhat to his own surprise, Husathirn Mueri had become a regular communicant of the new creed. What had begun as spying had become— was it faith? Or spying still? He was unsure. The chapel, that dingy place reeking of dried fish where sweaty lower-class folk came four times a week to cry forth their love of the Queen, had become his special refuge in the storm that was sweeping Dawinno. To Chevkija Aim he maintained that he was still conducting an investigation. Inwardly he wasn't so clear that that was what he was doing.

The boy said, "But are they capable of such a thing? Is anyone? It seems hard to believe."

"That the Queen can be destroyed?"

"That they would be so evil as to attempt it."

"They'll kill her," said Husathirn Mueri, "as they killed Kundalimon. There are no limits to their hatred of Nest-truth."

"Then it was Thu-Kimnibol who killed Kundalimon?" the girl said, amazed.

Husathirn Mueri turned to her. "Surely you knew that. It was done at his orders by the guard-captain, Curabayn Bangkea. Who then was murdered also, to keep him silent."

"You know this to be true?" asked Tikharein Tourb.

"It's true, all right. By all the gods, it's true!" said Husathirn Mueri.

Tikharein Tourb stared at him a long while, as if weighing and judging him. The boy's narrowed green eyes were cold as the ice that lies at the heart of the world. Only once before had Husathirn Mueri seen eyes like those: the bleak pale ones of the emissary Kundalimon. And even Kundalimon's gaze at its most remorseless had held some hint of compassion. These eyes were wholly icy, wholly terrifying.

The fierce roaring silence went on and on. Tikharein Tourb and the girl stood silent, statue-still. After a time Husathirn Mueri saw the boy's sensing-organ quiver and grow rigid and steal toward the side, until its tip was touching the tip of Chhia Kreun's. They might almost have been entering into communion right before him. Perhaps they were.

Then the boy said, "Swear to me by your love of the Queen that it was Thu-Kimnibol who had Kundalimon murdered."

"I swear it," said Husathirn Mueri unhesitatingly.

"And that the purpose of this war that Thu-Kimnibol has stirred up is to bring about the destruction of the Nest and the death of Her who is our comfort and our joy."

"That's its purpose. I swear it."

Again Tikharein Tourb stared. What a frightening child he is, Husathirn Mueri thought. And the girl also.

"Then he will die," said the boy finally.

Hresh was in his garden of animals, sitting with small brightly colored beasts all about him. The two purple-and-yellow ones, the caviandis, were by his side, and he was gently stroking them. He glanced up as Nialli Apuilana came rushing in.

"Father—" she cried at once. "Father, I've had something strange happen—something so very strange—"

He looked at her in a bland incurious way, as though she had not said anything at all. His eyes were remote and his expression was milder even than usual. There was a great sadness about him that she had never seen before: he seemed bowed down under it, a beaten man, very old and frail.

That frightened her. Her own chaotic fears and confusions receded into the background. She had come here in terror and in need; but his need, she saw, was even greater than hers.

"Is something wrong, father?"

Hresh made a little shrugging gesture and slowly moved his head from side to side like some wounded beast. He seemed terribly far away. After a time he said, "It's certain now. There's going to be war."

"How do you know?"

"I felt the signal just now, coming from the north. Perhaps you felt it too. There'll be no holding it back. Everything is in place and the word has been given to begin."

She stared at him blankly. "I'm not sure what you mean, father."

"You don't know about the alliance Thu-Kimnibol brought back with him from Yissou?"

She shook her head.

"We've agreed to help defend Salaman if he's ever attacked by the hjjks. Which is about to happen—an attack provoked by Salaman himself, I suspect. Perhaps with some help from my brother. Once Yissou is invaded, our army will go north, and there'll be all-out war."

"Which is precisely what those two have always wanted."

Hresh nodded. Tonelessly he said, "Much blood will flow, ours and theirs. Great sins will be committed. Hjjk armies will march through our cities putting them to the torch, or we'll destroy the Nest, or perhaps both will happen. It makes no difference what happens in the end. Whether we win or lose, everything we've achieved will be destroyed."

He looked forlorn and bereft. Nialli Apuilana wanted to hold him, to comfort him.

She said softly, "You mustn't worry yourself like this, father. Salaman is dreaming. The hjjks won't attack Yissou and there isn't going to be any all-out war."

"They invaded Yissou once," Hresh said.

"That was different. Yissou was right on the path of a hjjk swarming-drive."

"A what?"

"A swarming-drive. The Nest, great as it is, can hold only so many. A time arrives when the population has to divide. And then they come bursting out, thousands of them, millions sometimes, carrying a young Queen with them. And they march. For a thousand leagues if they have to, or sometimes more, until they reach the place where they mean to go. The gods only know how they decide where that place is. But they let nothing stop them until they're there. And then they build a new Nest."

Hresh looked up, his eyes alive for an instant with sudden interest in the old Hresh manner.

"And is this what was happening when they attacked Harruel's settlement?"

"Yes. They probably didn't have any specific intention of harming the settlement. But when they swarm they go marching blindly straight ahead, and nothing will turn them. Nothing."

"Well, and if they swarm in the same direction again?"

"It won't happen. They never swarm twice in the same direction. I know how eager Thu-Kimnibol is to have a war, and Salaman too. But they'll be disappointed."

"Let's pray that they are."

"Unless a war with the hjjks is something that the Five intend for us to have," Nialli Apuilana said. "In which case, may Dawinno help us all. I tell you, though, father, that there'll be no war."

He stared at her, smiling in that strange new sad way of his. The caviandis turned also to look at her. There was a curious bright glow of—what? Sadness also? Compassion?—in their big gleaming violet eyes.

Hresh said, in a voice so soft she could barely hear him, "Despite all you say, I feel the war rushing toward us like a great storm, Nialli. Who can stop a storm?"

"I've lived in the Nest, father. I know the hjjks won't ever arbitrarily launch a war against us. That isn't their way."

"And if we begin the war? We have an army now, do you know that?"

She caught her breath. "Since when?"

"It's brand-new. Thu-Kimnibol organized it. They're at the stadium right now, marching and drilling. Once armies exist, wars are easy to bring about."

"Does Taniane know about this?"

"Yes. And approves of it." Hresh smiled ruefully. "They have Great World weapons, taken from the House of Knowledge without my awareness or consent. Taniane finds that acceptable also."

"She wants war?"

"She expects it, at least. Is resigned to it. Will give her wholehearted support to it."

Nialli Apuilana stared at Hresh, horrified.

She could see the People's armies streaming northward into the land of the hjjks, and hordes of hjjk Militaries coming forth to meet them.

A terrible clash, frightful carnage. Thu-Kimnibol unleashing his pur-loined Great World weapons and working great devastation. Whole legions of Militaries blown into vapor at the touch of a button. The hjjk forces, vast though they were, driven back, ever back, the invaders advancing triumphantly into the dark northern territories. Swarm after swarm of Militaries sent to meet them, called in from every Nest of the north, each in turn destroyed by the inexorable drive of the attackers.

The Nest in danger! The Queen!

Yes, the Nest of Nests besieged. Everything in confusion there, Nest-plenty lost, Nest-truth denied, Egg-plan set awry, the wise Nest-thinkers scurrying to take cover in the dust, Egg-makers and Life-kindlers trying to flee and hacked down as they ran, and at last, the most terrible assault of all, even the Queen of Queens Herself rooted out of Her deep chamber and put to death—

Unthinkable. For the second time that day the world swayed and reeled about Nialli Apuilana.

This war must not be, she thought.

She wanted to cry out, to rage and scream her defiance of the war-makers, to send warning to the Nest of the treachery of her people, send it by dreams or second sight or Barak Dayir or any other means she could find. And more. To throw herself in the path of the forces of Thu-Kimnibol and Salaman as they set forth into the sacred territories of the Queen, and by her own will and strength hold them back from this unlawful strife. She would prevent it if it cost her her own life.

She clenched her fists fiercely. She would do anything to defend the Queen and the Nest. She would—

She would—

She would do—

What?

Nothing.

Nothing.

It was all gone. She felt only a void where, a moment before, there had been white-hot wrath.

In one bewildering instant all her fury, all her indignation, had died away, leaving her in a strange suspended state, empty, baffled. Why should she care what happened to the Nest? Why was she so eager to sacrifice her life for the sake of the Queen?

And then, stunned, she realized that all those fierce and desperate thoughts that had come welling up so spontaneously out of her soul had had no substance behind them.

They were shams. Mere automatic responses, empty of true feeling. The last flicker of the old loyalty to the Queen that once had burned within her. But *these* were her people, here. *This* was her city.

Across her mind now, like a red line of fire, came the recollection of the horrors she had seen this morning when she had stared into the star of grass, the things that had sent her fleeing in chaos to her father for solace. The claws, the clicking beaks, the mocking alien eyes. She heard the hissing laughter, the whispers of seduction. And she knew now what that terrible vision had been telling her.

Once more she summoned the image of the disruption of the Nest by the triumphant armies of the People, the ruination of Nest-plenty, the savaging of Nest-truth, the thwarting of Egg-plan, the terrible destruction even of the Queen of Queens. She confronted it all, even that, bringing it to vivid life in her thoughts.

And to her astonishment, none of it mattered to her at all. She was unable to find that fiery indignation which the same images had kindled in her just a moment before. She was free. Today she had finished the task of breaking the spell at last.

What is it to me, if the Nest is destroyed? If the Five have willed our path and the path of the hjjks to collide, why, then it must happen, and so be it. So be it. And if the collision comes, my loyalty must be with my own.

Everything was clear to her now.

The thing she must mourn, if the war did come, was not the fate of the insect-folk whose advocate she had been so long, but rather the loss of the young men and women of the People—her People—who would perish in the campaign, dead long before their time, a tragic pointless waste. There was the real horror: the thought of their blood staining the bleak wastelands of the north for leagues in every direction.

"Nialli?"

Hresh's voice, cutting through her thoughts like a voice from another world.

She made no response. Her mind churned with unaskable questions and inconceivable answers.

Who are these hjjks whom I have claimed to love?

Why, they are the creatures who stole me from my mother and father, and took me to a strange place, and transformed me into that which I was never meant to be.

Why did I want to defend them against my own kind?

Because they magicked my soul, and won me to their cause.

And Kundalimon, whom you loved? What about him?

I still love him. But they had done to him what they did to me, so that they could use him; and they would have used me through him, if he had lived.

"Nialli? Nialli?" Hresh again, calling her from the far side of the sky.

As though in trance she said, "Yes, father?"

"What's happening to you, Nialli?"

She opened her eyes. "An awakening," she said. "From a very long dream."

The caviandis were close by her sides, warm and soft, nuzzling her. Gently she stroked them.

Hresh said, "Are you sure there's nothing wrong?"

"Yes. Yes. I'm fine." She smiled. "Don't be sad, father. The gods are still watching over us. They're still guiding us." Taking his hand in hers, she said, "I think I'll go now, if that's all right with you. I want to talk to Thu-Kimnibol."

The warriors of the Sword of Dawinno were everywhere on the stadium field, running, jumping hurdles, dueling with blunt wooden swords. Thu-Kimnibol knew he had little time left to toughen them up. Any day now, the army that Salaman had sent into hjjk territory to avenge the death of his Acknowledgers would be set upon by the defenders of the Nest. Then the period of feinting would be at an end and the war would begin in earnest. Long before news came south of the destruction of Salaman's expeditionary force, Thu-Kimnibol knew, his own army would have to begin marching north to rendezvous with the king at Yissou.

"Jump higher, you sleepy bastards!" That was Maju Samlor. Most of Thu-Kimnibol's drillmasters were city guardsmen. "You run like pregnant women!" came another guardsman's voice from the far side of the stadium. "Put some wind into it!" And in another corner a huge Beng decked out in an immense seven-horned helmet laughed so loudly he could be heard clear across the field, and sent three men whirling with one great sweep of his quarterstaff.

Thu-Kimnibol rose and applauded. The warriors needed encouragement. It was just as Esperasagiot had said of his xlendis, long ago when they were first setting out for Yissou: they were city-bred, with no experience of the long haul. Even the strongest of them needed to be hardened for the battle ahead.

There was irony in that. Thu-Kimnibol remembered his father telling him that in the long sleepy days of the cocoon the warriors had had machines to work out on, to keep their muscles from rusting. All day long they grunted and toiled over devices with names like the Wheel of Dawinno, the Loom of Emakkis, the Five Gods: and yet the thousands of years of cocoon life went by and there was never an enemy to face, sealed away in the mountainside as they were. Now the People lived out in the open, where enemies abounded everywhere. But even so city life was too comfortable. It had led them to grow soft.

"Jump!" Maju Samlor called again. "Higher! Stretch those legs! Keep your sensing-organ out of the way, you idiot!"

Thu-Kimnibol laughed. Then he looked up and saw Chevkija Aim approaching him down the rows of seats. The guard-captain saluted and said, "Dumanka's here, lordship. And Esperasagiot and his brother."

"Good. Bring them to me."

The three men emerged from the passageway under the stands, Dumanka first, then the two Bengs. They offered gestures of respect. Esperasagiot said, "You know my brother, prince? A good man with a xlendi, he is. His name's Thihaliminion."

Thu-Kimnibol looked him over. Thihaliminion was a hair taller than Esperasagiot, with pure Beng fur of the brightest gold. He seemed two or three years younger than his brother. "High praise, if Esperasagiot thinks you know how to handle xlendis. This is the first time I've ever heard him admit that he isn't the only man in the world who understands those beasts."

"Prince!" Esperasagiot cried.

Thihaliminion inclined his head. "What I know, I know from him. He has been my teacher in xlendis. Just as Dumanka here has been my teacher in obedience to the gods."

"Acknowledgers, are you? All three?"

"All three, prince," Dumanka said. The quartermaster slapped his hands together gleefully. "And what peace and joy it is, the faith we hold! I'll show you our little book, sir. Which I got in Yissou, from a certain meat-cutter, Zechtior Lukin by name. When you read it you'll attain understanding of the great truth of the world, which is that all is as it is meant to be, that there's no use railing against fortune, because it's the gods who send us our fortune, and what point is there—"

"Enough, good friend," said Thu-Kimnibol, holding up a hand. "Convert me another time. We have an army to train just now. For which you'll be very useful."

"Whatever your lordship asks," said Dumanka.

"I heard something of your Zechtior Lukin when we were in Yissou," Thu-Kimnibol said. "Or of his teachings, at any rate. It was Salaman the king who told me. Death isn't anything to lament or regret, that's the idea. For it's part of the divine plan of the gods. And so we have to accept it unquestioningly, no matter what form it comes to us in. Do I have it right?"

"In a nutshell, you do," said Esperasagiot.

"Good. Good. How many are there in Dawinno now who follow these Acknowledger teachings now, would you say?"

"Some two hundred, prince, and more of us all the time." The wagonmaster glanced over his shoulder. "I see some of our people on this field right now."

"And you three are the chief teachers?"

"I was the one that learned the creed in Yissou," Dumanka said, "and taught it to Esperasagiot and Thihaliminion. They've been spreading it fast as they can."

"Spread it even faster. I'll be counting on you. I want all my men to be Acknowledgers by the time we march north. I want soldiers about me who have no fear of dying."

He dismissed them.

The dull clangor of the wooden training-swords resounded like merry music on the drill-field. A bright vision sprang into Thu-Kimnibol's mind: the Nest ablaze, hjjks strewn dying on the ground by the thousands, their beaks clacking impotently, the Queen writhing in Her death-throes—

"Sir?" Chevkija Aim again. "Nialli Apuilana's here to see you."

"Nialli? Why in the name of all the gods would she—" He grinned. "Ah. Yes. To lecture me about the evils of the war, I suppose. Tell her to come some other time, Chevkija Aim. Next week. Next year."

"Very good, lordship."

But Nialli Apuilana had come up right behind him. Chevkija Aim's golden fur flared in irritation.

"The Lord Prince Thu-Kimnibol is busy now with—"

"He'll see me."

"He instructs me to tell you—"

"And *I* instruct you to tell him that his kinswoman the chieftain's daughter has urgent business with him."

"Lady, it's impossible for you to—"

This squabble could go on all day. "It's all right, Chevkija Aim," Thu-Kimnibol said. "I'll speak with her."

"Thank you, kinsman," Nialli Apuilana said, not particularly graciously.

It was so long since Thu-Kimnibol had seen her—not since his departure for Yissou—that she seemed almost a stranger to him. He was astonished by how much she had changed: not so much in the way she looked as in the aura, the vibration, that surrounded her. She seemed stronger, deeper, purged of the last of her girlishness. She radiated strength and passion, and a new maturity. Her soul burned with an unmistakable luminous glow. And there was a formidable regality about her now. It enfolded her like a glittering mantle. It gave her a fiery beauty. He had never seen that in her before. It amazed him now. He felt as though he were seeing her for the first time.

They confronted each other in silence for a long moment.

He said finally, "Well, Nialli? If you're here to do battle with me, let's get on with it. These are busy days for me."

"You think I'm your enemy?"

"I know you are."

"Why is that?"

He laughed. "How could you be anything other? We have troops here, preparing for war. The enemy we'll march against is the Nest. Surely you know that. And you're the one who stood up in the Presidium and told us all how wonderful and wise and noble the hjjks are."

"That was a long time ago, kinsman."

"You said that making war on them was unthinkable, because they're such great civilized beings."

"Yes. I said that. And in some ways it's true."

"In *some* ways?"

"Some, yes. Not all. I put it all too simply that day at the Presidium. I was very young then."

"Ah. Ah, yes, of course."

"Don't smile at me in that patronizing way, Thu-Kimnibol. You make me feel like a child."

"I don't mean to do that. You hardly seem like a child to me, believe me. But I don't have to be as wise as Hresh to realize that you've come here today—at the urging, I suspect, of Puit Kjai and Simthala Honginda and other such peace-loving types—to denounce me and the war that I'm about to launch against your beloved hjjks. All right. Denounce me, then. And then let me get on with what I have to do."

Her eyes sparkled defiantly. "You don't understand me at all, do you, Thu-Kimnibol? I've come to you today to offer my support and help."

"Your *what?*"

"I want to join you. I want to go north with you."

"To spy on us for the Queen?"

She shot him a blazing look, and he could see her choking back some hot angry retort. Then she said, in a frosty tone, "You don't know a thing about the beings you're going out there to fight. I've experienced them at the closest possible range. I can guide you. I can explain things to you as you approach the Nest. I can help you ward off dangers you can't even begin to imagine."

"You give me very little credit if you think I'm such a fool, Nialli."

"And you give me very little, if you think I'd act as traitor to my own blood."

"Do I have any reason to think you'd be anything else?"

Her gaze was icy. Her nostrils flared and her fur rose, and he saw her biting down on her lower lip.

Then, to his complete amazement, she extended her sensing-organ toward him.

In a deadly calm voice she said, "If you doubt my loyalty, Thu-Kimnibol, I invite you to twine with me here and now. And then you can decide for yourself whether I'm a traitor or not."

This was strange country out here, five days' journey to the north of Dawinno and then some days more inland. Hresh had never seen it before, and he doubted that many others had, either. There were no farming settlements on this side of the interior hills, and the main road from Dawinno to Yissou passed well to the west.

It was broken land, cut by canyons and gullies. Dry cool winds blew from the center of the continent. Earthquakes had shattered this region many times, and the passage of ancient glaciers had ground it to ruin again and again, so that the bones of the world lay exposed here, great dark stripes cutting through the soft reddish rock of the hillsides.

A single xlendi drew his wagon. It might have been wiser to take two; but he knew so little about handling xlendis that he had decided not to risk the difficulties he'd encounter if the pair turned out to be ill-matched. He let the xlendi amble at its own pace, resting when it felt like it.

He had taken just a little with him in the way of provisions, enough to see him through the first few days. After that he would depend on the countryside for whatever he needed.

Nor had he brought anything from the House of Knowledge, any of his books or charts or ancient artifacts. Those things no longer mattered. He wanted to leave everything behind: everything. This was to be the final adventure of his life, this pilgrimage. Best not to be impeded by baggage out of the past.

With one exception: the Barak Dayir, in its little velvet pouch, tied about his waist beneath his sash. At the very last, he hadn't been willing to abandon that.

Day after day he rode calmly onward, allowing his path to choose itself. Constantly he scanned the horizon, hoping to catch sight of roving parties of hjjks.

Where are you, children of the Queen? Here is Hresh-full-of-questions, come to talk with you!

But he saw no hjjks.

He was, he supposed, somewhere close by the lesser Nest where Nialli Apuilana had been taken by her captors years ago. But if there were hjjks hereabouts, they were keeping themselves out of sight; or else they were so sparse in these parts that he hadn't passed near their encampment.

No matter. Eventually he'd find hjjks, or they would find him, in good and proper time. Meanwhile he was content to wander on, this way and that, across the broken land.

This cool windy region seemed fertile, in its way. There were great trees with thick black trunks and wide-spreading crowns of yellow leaves, each spaced far from the next as if it would tolerate no competition, choking off any of its own kind that tried to sprout within its zone of dominance. Sprawling shrubs with white woolly leaves clung to the ground like a dense coating of fur. Other plants, basket-shaped ones with tightly interwoven branches, rolled and tumbled freely as though they were beasts of the field.

But if there were plants that looked like animals here, so also did Hresh see animals that might well have been plants. A whole grove of snaky green creatures stood on their tails in holes in the ground. They might well have been rooted where they stood. He watched them rising up suddenly to snap some hapless bird or insect from the air and coiling back down again, and never once saw one come all the way out of its den. Then there were others that were no more than huge mouths with vestigial bodies, propped immobile against rocks and uttering booming seductive cries that brought their prey to them as if in trance. He remembered having encountered some such creatures when he was a boy, on the journey from the cocoon to Vengiboneeza. They had almost lured him then; but now he was invulnerable to their sinister music.

Hresh had told no one that he was leaving Dawinno. He had gone around to speak one last time with those he cared for most, Thu-Kimnibol, Boldirinthe, Staip, Chupitain Stuld, and, of course, Nialli Apuilana and Taniane. But he had told none of them, not even Taniane, that what he was actually doing was saying farewell.

That had been hard, hiding the truth that way. Especially from Taniane. He had suffered for it. But Hresh knew that they'd try to stop him from going, if they were aware of what he had in mind. So he had simply slipped out of the city in the mists of dawn. Now, with Dawinno far behind him, he felt no regrets at all. A long phase of his life had ended, a new phase was beginning.

If he regretted anything, it was that he had built the city so well. It seemed to him now that he had led the People down the wrong path, that it had been a mistake to build the City of Dawinno in the image of magnificent Vengiboneeza, to try to recreate the Great World here in the New Springtime. The gods had cleansed the Great World from the Earth because it had run its course. The Great World had developed as far as it could. It had reached a stand-still point. If the death-stars had not come to shatter it, its perfection would have given way imperceptibly to decay. For a civilization, unlike a machine, is a living thing, which must either grow or decay, and there is no third alternative.

He had wanted the People to attain the grandeur of the Great World, which had been hundreds of thousands of years in the making, in one sudden leap. But they hadn't been ready for that. They were, after all, only a single generation away from the cocoon. Under the pressures of that leap they had passed from that primitive simplicity into their own corruption and decay, with scarcely a pause for ripening into real humanity.

This evil war, for example—

A crime against the gods, against the laws of the city, against the essence of civilization itself. But he knew that nothing he could do would stop it.

And so he understood that he had failed. In the time that remained to him he would do what he could to atone for that. But he refused to mourn the errors that he had made, or those that others were about to make; for he had done his best. That was the one great consolation. He had always done his best.

"I remember the day you were born," Thu-Kimnibol said in wonderment. "Hresh and I stayed up all night together, the night before, and—"

"Don't," she said.

"Don't what?"

"Don't talk about what you remember. Don't talk about when I was young."

He laughed. "But am I just supposed to pretend, Nialli, that I'm not—"

"Yes. Pretend, if that's what you have to do. Just don't remind me that you were already grown up when I was born. All right? All right, Thu-Kimnibol?"

"But—Nialli—"

Then he laughed.

"Come here," she said.

She pulled him close. He enveloped her in his arms. He was all over her, hands, lips, sensing-organ, touching, stroking, nibbling, murmuring her name. He was like a great river, sweeping over her, carrying her away. And she was letting herself be carried away. She had never expected anything like this. Nor had he, she guessed.

She wondered if she'd ever get used to the immensity of him. He was so huge, so powerful, so very different from Kundalimon. How strange that was, to be swallowed up in him this way. But also very pleasing. I think I can get used to it, given a little time. Yes, she thought, as she felt him trembling against her, and began to tremble herself. Yes, I definitely can get used to it.

The shape of the land was beginning to change. For the past few days he had had a ridge of low hills to his left and another to his right, with what seemed like an endless plain stretching between them. But now the two ridges were converging to form a narrow enclosed valley with no exit at its far end. Hresh halted beside a stream bordered with thick gray rushes to consider what he should do. It seemed pointless to proceed into that apparent cul-de-sac. Best to fall back, perhaps, and look for some way across the hills to the east.

"No," came a voice that was not a voice, speaking words that were not words. "You will do better to go forward."

"In truth, yes. It is the only way." A second voice, addressing him in the silent speech of the mind.

Startled, Hresh looked around. After these days of unbroken solitude the voices had the impact of sudden thunder.

At first he saw nothing. But then he detected a flash of purple in the depths of the streamside rushes. The slender tapering snout of a caviandi, and then another, rose into view. Coming now from their hiding places, the lithe little fish-hunting creatures walked toward him unafraid, holding up their hands with delicate fingers outspread.

"I am She-Thikil," said one.

"I am He-Kanto," the other declared.

"Hresh is my name."

"Yes. We know that." She-Thikil made a soft small sound of friendship and put her hand into his. Her fingers were thin and hard, quick fish-catching fingers. He-Kanto took his other hand. And from them both came the invitation to communion of the sort that he had had in his own garden with the other pair, his captives, He-Lokim, She-Kanzi.

"Yes," Hresh said.

Their souls came rushing toward his, and a surge of warmth and friendship leaped from them to him.

So kindness to one caviandi was kindness to all. When he had opened himself in communion to the two caviandis in his garden he had unknowingly enrolled himself in league with the entire caviandi race. These two had followed his wagon for days, secretly prodding the xlendi along the right path, the one that led to the Nest. Steering him away from places where perils lay hidden, guiding him toward grazing-grounds where beast and master could find fresh water and provender. His journey, Hresh realized, had been far less random than he had thought.

And now he knew he must not turn aside. The true path was ahead of him, into the narrowing valley.

Gravely he thanked the caviandis for their help. He had one last glimpse of their great dark shining eyes, gleaming at him from the tops of the rushes. Then the sleek little creatures sank down into that dense thicket of reeds and disappeared.

He returned to the wagon. He nudged the xlendi forward with a quick touch of second sight.

As the canyon narrowed, the stream that ran down its center grew swifter, grew wild and fierce, until by twilight it was sweeping along beside Hresh with a steady pounding roar. Looking ahead, he saw that the canyon was indeed open at the far end, but the opening was a mere slit through which the stream must be hurtling with cataract force.

Had the caviandis betrayed him? It seemed impossible. But how could he pass through that crack of an opening with his wagon?

He went onward, all the same.

Clearly now Hresh heard the thousand echoing and answering voices of the cataract. Overhead a great blue star had appeared in the sharp cool air and its reflection glittered in the stream. The path was so narrow now that there barely was room for the wagon beside the turbulent water. Here the ground trended slightly upward, which must mean that the bed of the stream cut ever deeper as it approached the opening ahead.

"Here he is at last," said a dry voice that was like a whitening bone, a silent voice, a mind-voice. "The inquisitive one. The child of questions."

Hresh looked up. Outlined against the deepening darkness of the sky was the angular figure of a hjjk, standing motionless and erect, holding in one of its many hands the shaft of a spear longer even than itself.

"Child?" Hresh said, and laughed. "A child, am I? No, friend. No. I'm an old man. A very weary old man. Touch my mind more carefully, if you doubt me, and you'll see."

"The child denies that he is a child," said a second hjjk, appearing on the opposite side of the cliff that loomed above him. "But the child is a child all the same. Whatever he may think."

"As you wish. I am a child."

And indeed he was: for suddenly time fell inward on itself, and he was little wiry Hresh-full-of-questions again, scrambling hither and yon around the cocoon, plaguing everyone with his need to know, driving Koshmar and Torlyri to distraction, vexing his mother Minbain, irritating his playmates. All the weariness of the latter days dropped away from him. He was alive with his old furious energy and fearlessness, Hresh the chatterer, Hresh the seeker, Hresh the smallest and most eager for knowledge of all the tribe, who had hovered again and again by the hatch of the cocoon, dreaming of darting through one day into the unknown wonderful world that lay outside.

The hjjks began to descend the cliff, picking their way toward him over the jagged rock. He waited serenely for them, admiring the agility with which they moved and the way the light of the great blue star, which he realized now was only the Moon, glinted on their rigid, shining yellow-and-black shells. Five, six, seven of them came scrambling down. Not since his childhood had he seen a hjjk. He had thought them fearsome and ugly then; but now he saw the strange beauty of their lean, tapered forms.

The xlendi stood quite still, as if lost in xlendi dreams. One of the hjjks touched it lightly along its long jaw with a bristly forearm, and it turned at once and began to go forward. There was a dark cavern here, a mere crevice that Hresh had not noticed, which led through the heart of the cliff. Starlight was visible ahead. Hresh could hear the distant roar of the cataract as the xlendi plodded onward.

After a time they emerged onto a ledge on the cliff's outer face. To

Hresh's right the stream, a milky torrent now, erupted through the crack in the rock and went plunging outward into space to land in a foaming basin far below. To his left a winding path led down the side of the cliff into a broad open prairie in which, in the darkness, nothing of consequence could be seen.

"The Queen has been expecting you," a dry silent hjjk-voice said, as the wagon began its descent into that dark realm beyond.

9

To the Nest of Nests

All week long the messages had been coming to Salaman with rising urgency and intensity from the relay stations to the north and to the south.

Thu-Kimnibol was advancing at the head of a vast army from Dawinno. He was close to Yissou now, no more than a few days' march away, perhaps less. Every relay agent along the road had underscored the awe he felt at the size of that oncoming force. Had Thu-Kimnibol brought everyone of fighting age in Dawinno with him? It almost seemed that way.

On the northern front the army of the king, four hundred strong, had pressed deeper and deeper day by day into the hjjk lands, following the route the little colony of Acknowledgers had taken.

We have found them, came the report finally. *All dead.*

And then:

We've been attacked by hjjks ourselves.

And then:

There are too many of them for us.

And then silence.

"Twice now the insect-folk have attacked our people without provocation," Salaman told the people of Yissou, speaking from his pavilion atop the wall to a great horde of citizens in the plaza below. "They have slaughtered the innocent settlers whom Zechtior Lukin led into unoccupied territory. And now they have massacred the army we sent forth to rescue Zechtior Lukin's people. There can be only one policy now."

"War! War!" came the cry from a thousand throats.

"War, yes," Salaman replied. "All-out war, by all the People against this implacable enemy. The hjjks have threatened the existence of this city since its earliest days: but now, with the help of our allies from Dawinno, we will bring the fire to their own domain, we will cut them to mincemeat, we will drag forth their loathsome Queen into the light of day and put an end at last to Her unspeakable life!"

"War! War!" came the cry again.

And later that afternoon, when Salaman had returned to the palace and had taken his seat upon the Throne of Harruel, his son Biterulve came to him and said, "Father, I want to go with the army when it sets out into the hjjk country. I ask your permission for this, as I must. But I beg you not to withhold it."

Salaman felt a hand tightening about his heart. He had never expected anything like this.

"You?" he said, staring amazed at the pale slender boy. "What do you know of warfare, Biterulve?"

"I feared you'd say that. But you know I've been riding with my brothers in the lands outside the wall for a long time now. I've learned some skills of fighting from them as well. You mustn't keep me from this war, father."

"But the danger—"

"Would you make a woman of me, father? Worse than a woman, for I know that there'll be women in our fighting brigades. Am I to stay home, then, with the old ones and children?"

"You're no warrior, Biterulve."

"I am."

The boy's quiet insistence carried a force Salaman had never heard from him before. He saw the anger in Biterulve's eyes, the injured pride. And the king realized that his gentle scholarly son had put him in an impossible situation. Refuse permission and he robbed Biterulve forever of his princeliness. He'd never forgive him for that. Let him go, and he might well fall victim to some thrusting hjjk spear, which Salaman himself could scarcely bear to contemplate.

Impossible. Impossible.

He felt his anger rising. How dare the boy ask him to make a decision like this? But he held himself in check.

Biterulve waited, expectant, unafraid.

He gives me no choice, Salaman thought bitterly.

At length he said, sighing, "I never thought you'd have any appetite for fighting, boy. But I see I've misjudged you." He looked away, and made a brusque gesture of dismissal. "All right. Go. Go, boy. Get yourself ready to march, if that's what you need to do."

Biterulve grinned and clapped his hands, and ran from the room.

"Get me Athimin," the king said to one of his stewards.

When the prince arrived, Salaman said to him dourly, "Biterulve has just told me he plans to go with us to the war."

Athimin's eyes brightened in surprise. "Surely you'll forbid him, father!"

"No. No, I've given permission. He said I'd be making a woman of him, if I forced him to stay home. Well, so be it. But you're going to be his protector and guardian, do you understand? If a finger of his is harmed, I'll have three of yours. Do you understand me, Athimin? I love all my sons as I love my own self, but I love Biterulve in a way that goes beyond all else. Stay at his side on the battlefield. Constantly."

"I will, father."

"And see to it that he comes home from the war in one piece. If he doesn't, you'd be wise to stay up there yourself in the hjjk wastelands rather than face me again."

Athimin stared.

"Nothing will harm him, father," the prince said hoarsely. "I promise you that."

He went out without another word, nearly colliding as he did with a breathless messenger who had come scampering in.

"What is it?" Salaman barked.

"The army of Dawinno," the runner said. "They've reached the lantern-tree groves. They'll be in the city in a couple of hours."

"Look yonder," Thu-Kimnibol said. "The Great Wall of Yissou."

Under a sky of purple and gold a massive band of the deepest black stretched along the horizon for an impossible distance, curving away finally at the sides to disappear in the obscurities beyond. It might have been a dark strip of low-lying cloud; but no, for its bulk and solidity were so oppressive that it was hard to understand how the ground could hold firm beneath its impossible weight.

"Can it be real?" Nialli Apuilana asked finally. "Or just some illusion, some trick that Salaman makes our minds play upon ourselves?"

Thu-Kimnibol laughed. "If it's a trick, it's one that Salaman has played on himself. The wall's real enough, Nialli. For twice as many years as you've been alive, or something close to that, he's poured all the resources of his city into constructing that thing. While we've built bridges and towers and roads and parks, Salaman's built a wall. A wall of walls, one to stand throughout the ages. When this place is as old as Vengiboneeza, and twice as dead, that wall will still be there."

"Is he crazy, do you think?"

"Very likely. But shrewd and strong, for all his craziness. It's a mistake ever to underestimate him. There's no one in this world as strong and determined as Salaman. Or as mad."

"A crazy ally. That makes me uneasy."

"Better a crazy ally than a crazy enemy," Thu-Kimnibol said.

He turned and signaled to those in the wagons just behind him. They had halted when he had. Now they began to move forward again, up the sloping tableland toward the high ground where that incredible wall lay athwart the sky. Nialli Apuilana could see small figures atop the wall, warriors whose spears stood out like black bristles against the darkening air. For a moment she imagined that they were hjjks, somehow in possession of the city. The strangeness of this place inspired fantasy. She found herself thinking also that the wall, colossal as it was, was merely poised and lightly balanced on its great base, that it would take only a breeze to send it falling forward upon her, that already it had begun slowly to topple in her direction as the wagon rolled onward. Nialli Apuilana smiled. This is foolishness, she thought. But anything seemed possible in the City of Yissou. That black wall was like a thing of dreams, and not cheerful dreams.

Thu-Kimnibol said, "It was only a wooden palisade when I was a boy here. Not even a very sturdy one, at that. When the hjjks came, they'd have swarmed over it in a moment, if we hadn't found a way of turning them back. Gods! How we fought, that day!"

He fell into silence. He seemed to lose himself in it.

Nialli Apuilana leaned against his comforting bulk and tried to imagine how it had been, that day when the hjjks came to Yissou. She saw the boy Samnibolon, who would call himself Thu-Kimnibol afterward, at the battle of Yissou: already tall and strong, never tiring, holding his weapons like a man, striking at the hordes of hjjks in the bloody dusk as the shadows lengthened. Yes, she could see him easily, a boy of heroic size, as now he was a man of heroic size. Fighting unrelentingly against the invaders who threatened his father's young city. And something in her quivered with excitement at the thought of him hot with battle.

The warlike boy Samnibolon, who had become this warlike man Thu-Kimnibol: they were the utter opposite of the gentle Kundalimon, that shy and strange bearer of the Queen's love and the Queen's peace. Nialli Apuilana had loved Kundalimon beyond any doubt. In some way she still did. And yet—and yet—when she looked at this fierce Thu-Kimnibol she found herself swept by irresistible love and desire. It had come over her for the first time at the drill-field, to her astonishment and joy. It had come over her a hundred times since. Here beneath the terrible walls of Salaman's city it seemed stronger than ever. She had known him since she was a child; and yet she realized now she had not actually known him at all, not until these past few weeks had brought them so strangely together.

All his life, she thought, he has waited for a chance to fight again;

and now he will. And suddenly she realized that what she loved him for was that strength, that oneness of character, that had defined him since his earliest boyhood, when this city's wall had been nothing more than a palisade of wood.

Her love for Kundalimon glowed imperishably within her: she was certain of that. And yet this other man, Kundalimon's opposite in all things, now filled her soul so thoroughly that there seemed no room for anyone else.

Hresh had never touched such perfection before. He had not ever imagined it was possible. Truly the Nest functioned as smoothly as any machine.

He knew this was only a minor hjjk outpost, certainly not the great Nest of Nests; and yet it was so huge and complex that even after many days within it he had no clear idea of its plan. Its tunnels, warm and sweet-smelling and dimly lit by some pink glow that emanated from the walls, radiated in bewildering patterns, running this way and that, crossing and recrossing. Yet all those who traversed these corridors moved swiftly and unhesitatingly in obvious clear knowledge of the route.

The hjjks had fabricated their huge subterranean city in the simplest way, digging the tunnels with their bare claws—Hresh had watched them at work, for they never ceased expanding the Nest—and lining the walls with a pulp made of soft wood, which they chewed themselves and spat out into great soggy mounds that could be scooped up and pressed into place. Wooden beams served to prop the tunnel roof at regular intervals. He had expected something more complex from them. This was not very different except in size from the sort of nests the ants and termites of the forest built for themselves.

And, like those small insects of the forest floor, they had evolved an elaborate system of castes and professions. The biggest ones—females, they were, though apparently not fertile—were the Militaries. They were ordinarily the only ones who ventured into the world beyond the Nest. It was Militaries who had brought Hresh here.

A parallel caste of sterile males, the Workers, had charge of constructing and expanding the Nest, and of maintaining the intricate systems of ventilation and heating that kept it livable. They were thick-bodied and short, with little of the eerie grace that the slender Militaries displayed.

Then there were the reproductive cadres, the Egg-makers and Life-kindlers: smaller, stockier even than the Workers, with short limbs and blunt, rounded heads. When they were mature, they were taken before the Queen, who brought them to full fertility by penetrating them in some way and flooding them with a substance She herself secreted: this was known as Queen-touch. Life-kindlers and Egg-makers mated, then, and brought forth eggs that hatched into small pale larvae. A caste known as Nourishment-givers reared and nurtured these in outlying caverns. It was they who determined which caste the new hjjks would belong to, in accordance with the orders of the Queen, and shaped them for it by the manner of food they provided. The number of each caste's members never changed: as the life of each hjjk Military or Worker or Egg-maker or Life-kindler neared its appointed end, its replacement was already being reared in the caverns of the Nourishment-givers.

Hresh learned all these things from the members of a different caste yet, one with which he felt a great personal kinship of spirit: the Nest-thinkers, the philosophers and teachers of the insect-folk.

Whether these were male or female, he couldn't tell. They were as tall as Militaries, which argued that they were female, but they had the blocky frame of Workers, barely narrowing at all at the places where one segment of their bodies gave way to the next, as though they might be male. In any event they were unconcerned with sexual matters. They sat all day in dark sealed chambers, to which the young came for instruction. Hresh went to them too, and listened solemnly as they explained the workings of the Nest to him. He was never sure if he ever spoke twice with the same Nest-thinker. They seemed indistinguishable. After a while he fell into the habit of regarding them all as one, a single individual—Nest-thinker.

Nest-thinker it was who opened the mysteries of the Nest to him, Nest-thinker who showed him how every aspect of the life of the Nest was coordinated perfectly with every other aspect, Nest-thinker who instructed him in Nest-truth, who taught him the intricacies of Egg-plan and Queen-love, who offered him the comfort of Nest-bond.

It was Nest-thinker, ultimately, who brought him before the Queen.

That was the deepest mystery of all: the city's giant immobile monarch, hidden in a chamber sunken far beneath the other levels, guarded by the elite caste of Queen-attendants—warriors of immense size and indomitable valor who encircled Her place of repose in an impenetrable legion.

"The Queen can never die," Nest-thinker told Hresh. "She was born when the world was young and will live to its final age." Was he supposed to take that literally? Surely the Queen's life-span was great. Perhaps She lived so long that to the others She seemed immortal. But immortal?

Hresh had no idea how long he had been in the Nest before they took him to the Queen. Time had little meaning here: his days often passed in a dreamy haze of contemplation. He had slipped into a strange peaceful otherness. The storms of the outer world, the turmoil and bustle of the City of Dawinno, seemed to him now like phantasms out of some other life. But ultimately a day arrived when Nest-thinker said to him, "You are for the Queen today. Follow me."

Together they descended a narrow, spiraling ramp, its earthen floor worn to a high polish by the passage of generations of feet. Hresh wondered if any of those feet had been feet like his. He doubted it. Very likely only the hard bristly claws of hjjks had traveled this way before today.

Down and down and downward still they went. The shaft was like an auger boring its way backward through the depths of time. Crisp unknown odors floated up toward him. A pulsing black glow was the only illumination.

The deeper they went, the faster they moved. The long-legged Nest-thinker set an unrelenting pace. Hresh came close to growing dizzy as the shaft wound on and on. But some unknown force steadied his soul: perhaps from Nest-thinker, perhaps from the Queen Herself.

Then at last they reached the holy of holies.

It was a long oval chamber with a high, rounded ceiling. Instead of roof-beams there was a vaulting of hexagonal plates overhead, fitted one against the other in a way that looked invulnerable even to the mightiest tremor of the Earth. At one end of the chamber—the end where Nest-thinker and Hresh had entered—was a platform where the Queen-attendants stood packed close together, their weapons pointing outward. The Queen filled all the rest of the room, end to end, wall to wall.

She was a colossal tubular vessel of flesh, soft and pink, not remotely hjjk-like in any way, without eyes, without beak, without limbs, without features of any sort. But he felt himself to be in the presence of an extraordinary being, of such power and force that it was all he could do to keep himself from falling to his knees before Her.

And yet this was only a minor Queen, Hresh knew. This was just a subordinate of the great Queen of Queens.

The only sound in the chamber was that of his own breathing. He pressed his hands to his sides, digging them deep into his fur to stop them from trembling. Queen-attendants came up close against him, surrounding him on all sides, their hard shells and bristly limbs pressing tight. Their blades lightly pricked his flesh. If he made so much as the slightest unexpected move those blades would plunge deep.

A voice that was like the tolling of an awesome bell spoke in his mind. "You have the contact focus with you?"

He understood somehow that the Queen meant the Barak Dayir, "Yes."

"Use it."

He drew the Wonderstone from its pouch. It felt fiery in his hand. A profound chill of fear coursed through him, but it was met at once by a neutralizing warmth that seemed to come from the Queen.

He took a deep breath and entered into union with the stone.

At once there is a sound like a crack of thunder, or perhaps the world splitting apart on its hinges. His mind goes soaring across a vast abyss. As if he has dissolved, as if he is traveling on the wind. Impossible for him to comprehend where he is or what is happening; he has a sense only of an immensity containing an immensity, and, somewhere deep within it, a heart of fire burning with the power of ten thousand suns.

He is no longer aware of Nest-thinker's presence, of the Queen-attendants, even of his own body. There is only that immensity surrounding him.

"What are you?" he asks.

"You know Me as the Queen of Queens."

He understands. He is within the Queen, and not the minor one of the Nest he knows. All Nests are linked; all Queens are aspects of the one Queen. And that greatest of hjjks who lies in the realm of mysteries in the north has a Wonderstone too: holds it embedded within Her vast flesh, indeed, and it is that Wonderstone now that speaks to his. The union of the Wonderstones joins him to the Queen of Queens. He is engulfed in that gigantic mass of alien flesh.

Hresh remembers now his mentor Noum om Beng saying, so very long ago, "We had what you call a Barak Dayir also. But our Wonderstone was taken by the hjjks." Yes, and swallowed by their Queen; and this was it, the other contact focus, the Wonderstone that the Bengs had had and lost, the twin to the ancient magical thing he holds clutched in his sensing-organ.

"Now you will see," says the Queen.

The heavens split wide. The years roll away, back and back and back, and the Barak Dayir traces a narrow flaming line across the centuries into the distant past. The Queen wishes to show him the vastness of Her race's heritage.

He sees the world buried in the ice of the Long Winter: he sees tongues of frost creeping down into lands that had never known cold, and green tenderness blackening under the onslaught. Creatures to which he could not give names searching desperately for refuge, and folk of his own kind fleeing pitifully hither and yon. The tall pale tailless creatures whom he knew as humans move among them, saying, *Come, come, here is the cocoon, you will be saved.*

And also he sees legions of hjjks, leaning unperturbed on their spears as the black wind whips swirling snowflakes past them.

Onward, then, back, back, into the time before the cold, into the glory of the Great World, even. Huge slow-bodied quick-witted crocodilian sapphire-eyes folk on the porticoes of their marble villas; sea-lords in their carriages, vegetals, mechanicals, all the strange and wondrous beings of that glorious era. Humans, again. And hjjks, always hjjks, myriads of them, perfectly organized, clear-minded and cold-eyed, living ever in accordance with the vast millennia-spanning scheme that was Egg-plan, moving among the other races, often spending years at a time in the Great World cities before returning to the Nest from which they came.

Will She take him backward even to the time before the Great World? No. No, the voyage has reached its end. Hresh feels himself drawn forward again with dizzying speed, the images leaping past, everything in rapid motion, comet-tails in the sky, death-stars crashing down, the air turning black, the first snowstorms, the withered leaves, the world entombed in ice, the stoic patience of the doomed sapphire-eyes, the panicky flight of the desperate beasts, and the hjjks again, always the hjjks, moving calmly outward to take possession of the frozen world even as the other races abandoned it.

There was a great stillness in the royal chamber.

They were in the Nest again. A sense of the age-old grandeur and perfection of the hjjk world resonated like the swelling sounds of an immense symphony in Hresh's soul.

The Queen said, "Now you see us as we are. Why, then, do you make yourselves our enemies?"

"I am not Your enemy."

"Your people refuse to live in peace with us. Your people even now prepare to attack us."

"What they do is wrong," Hresh said. "I ask Your forgiveness for it. I ask You to tell me if there is any way for Your people and mine to live peacefully together."

There was silence again, a very long one.

"I offered a treaty," the Queen said.

"Is that the only way? To pen us up in the parts of the world that we already hold, and prevent us from going forth to explore the rest?"

"What value is it, this exploring? One piece of land is much like another. There are not so many of you that you need the entire world."

"But to give up all hope of reaching outward into the unknown places—"

"Reaching outward! Reaching outward!" That huge pealing voice rang with royal contempt. "That is all you want, you little furry ones! Why not be content with what you have?"

"Is Egg-plan not a constant reaching-out?" Hresh asked boldly.

The Queen responded with a kind of enormous chuckle, as though answering a child so impudent that he was charming. "Egg-plan is the realization and fulfillment of that which has existed since before the beginning of time. It is not the creation of anything new, but only the final actualization of what has always been. Do you understand?"

"Yes," said Hresh. "Yes, I think I do."

"Your kind, boiling out of its hiding places when the time of cold ended, spreading like a disease over the land, multiplying your numbers unchecked, covering the Earth with cities of stone, fouling the land, darkening the air, staining the rivers as you turn them to your own use, pushing yourselves onward into places where you were never meant to be—you are the foe of Nest-truth. You are the enemy of Egg-plan. You are a wild force upon the orderly world. You are a plague, and must be contained. To eradicate you is impossible; but you must be contained. Do you understand Me, child of questions? Do you understand?"

"Yes. I understand, now."

His sensing-organ tightened on the Barak Dayir. His entire body shivered with the force of the revelations sweeping through it.

He understood, beyond any doubt. And he knew that what he had come to see was more than the Queen had realized She was telling him.

The hjjks of the New Springtime were mere shadows of those who had lived during the time of the Great World. Those ancient hjjks had been venturers, voyagers, a race of bold merchants and explorers. They had journeyed the length and breadth of this and perhaps many other worlds as well in pursuit of their aims, lacing a bright red line of accomplishment through the rich fabric of the Great World.

But the Great World was long gone.

What were these hjjks who had survived? Still a great race, yes. But a fallen one, which had lost all of its technical skills and all of its outward thrust. They had become a profoundly conservative people, clinging to the fragments of their ancient glory and permitting nothing new to emerge.

What was it they most wanted, after all? Nothing more than to dig holes in the ground and live in the dark, performing eternal repetitive cycles of birth and reproduction and death, and once in a while sending their overflow population forth to dig a new hole somewhere else and start the cycle going there. They believed that the world could only be sustained by proper maintenance of the unvarying patterns of life. And they would do anything to assure the continued stability of those patterns.

This is great folly, Hresh thought.

The hjjks fear change because they've lived through so great a fall, and they dread some further descent. But change comes anyway. It was precisely because the Great World had done so well at insulating itself from change, Hresh told himself, that the gods had sent the death-stars upon them. The Great World had attained a kind of perfection, and perfection is something the gods cannot abide.

What the hjjks who had survived the catastrophe of the Long Winter still refused to comprehend was that Dawinno would inevitably have his way with them, whether they liked it or not. The Transformer always did. No living thing was exempt from change, no matter how deep in the earth it tried to hide, no matter how desperately it clung to its rituals of life. One had to respect the hjjks for what they had made out of the shards and splinters of their former existence. It was rigid, and therefore doomed, but in its own way it was awesomely perfect.

Building a different kind of static society wasn't the answer. And for the first time in a long while Hresh saw hope for his own erratic, turbulent, unpredictable folk. Perhaps the world will be ours after all, he thought. Simply because we are so uncertain in our ways.

He had no idea how much time had passed. An hour, a day, perhaps a year. He knew that he had been lost in the strangest of dreams. There was absolute silence in the royal chamber. The Queen-attendants stood still as statues beside him.

Once more Hresh heard the tolling of the Queen's great voice in his mind:

"Is there anything else you wish to know, child of questions?"

"Nothing. Nothing. I thank You for sharing Your wisdom with me, great Queen."

With quick fierce strokes of his spearpoint Salaman sketched a map in the dark, moist earth.

"This is the City of Yissou"—a tight circle, unbroken and unbreak-able—"and this is where we are now, three days' march to the northeast. Here is where the land begins to rise, the long wooded ridge that leads to Vengiboneeza. You remember, Thu-Kimnibol, we rode out that way together once."

Thu-Kimnibol, peering intently at the sketch, grunted his assent.

"This," said Salaman, drawing a triangle to the right of what he had already inscribed in the ground, "is Vengiboneeza, utterly infested with hjjks. Here"—he poked the ground viciously, some distance beyond the triangle—"is a lesser Nest, where the hjjks dwell who slaughtered our Acknowledgers. Here, here, and here"—three more angry jabs—"are other small Nests. Then there's a great open nothingness, unless we're greatly mistaken. And here"—he strode five paces upward, and gouged a ragged crater there—"is the thing we seek, the Nest of Nests itself."

He turned and looked up at Thu-Kimnibol, who seemed immense to him this morning, mountainous, twice his true size. And his true size had been more than big enough.

Last night Salaman's spy Gardinak Cheysz had come to him to confirm what the king already suspected: that the friendship between Thu-Kimnibol and his kinswoman was more than a friendship, that in fact they were coupling-partners now. Perhaps twining-partners as well. Was that something recent? Apparently so, Gardinak Cheysz thought. At least the two of them had never been linked in gossip in the past.

An end to all hope of mating him with Weiawala, then. A pity, that.

It would have been useful linking him to the royal house of Yissou. Now Thu-Kimnibol's unexpected romance with the daughter of Taniane made it all the more likely that he'd emerge as the master of the City of Dawinno when Taniane was gone. A king there, instead of a chieftain? Salaman wondered what that would mean for himself and for his city. Perhaps it was for the best. But very possibly not.

Thu-Kimnibol said, "And what plan do you propose, now?"

Salaman tapped the ground with his spear. "Vengiboneeza is the immediate problem. Yissou only knows how many hjjks are swarming in there, but it has to be a million or more. We need to neutralize them all before we can proceed northward, or otherwise there'll be a tremendous hjjk fortress at our backs, cutting us off, as we make our way toward the great Nest."

"Agreed."

"Do you know much about the layout of Vengiboneeza?"

"The place is unknown to me," Thu-Kimnibol said.

"Mountains here, to the north and east. A bay here. The city between them, protected by walls. Thick jungle down here. We came through that jungle, on the migration from the cocoon, before you were born. It's a hard city to attack, but it can be done. What I suggest is a two-pronged assault, using those Great World weapons of yours. You come in from the waterfront side, with the Loop and the Line of Fire, and create a distraction. Meanwhile I descend out of the hills with the Earth-Eater and the Bubble Tube and blow the city to bits. If we strike swiftly and well, they'll never know what hit them. Eh?"

He sensed trouble even before Thu-Kimnibol spoke.

"A good plan," said the bigger man slowly. "But the Great World weapons have to stay in my possession."

"What?"

"I can't share them with you. They're mine only on loan, and I'm responsible for their safety. They can't be offered to anyone else. Not even you, my friend."

Salaman felt a burst of hot fury like molten rock flooding his veins. Bands of fire were tightening around his forehead. He wanted to bring his spear up in a single heedless gesture and bury it in Thu-Kimnibol's gut; and it took all the strength within him to restrain himself.

Trembling with the effort to seem calm, he said, "This comes as a great surprise, cousin."

"Does it? Why, then, I'm sorry, cousin."

"We are allies. I thought there would be a sharing of the weapons."

"I understand. But I'm obliged to protect them."

"Surely you know I'd treat them with care."

"Beyond any doubt you would," said Thu-Kimnibol smoothly. "But if they were taken from you somehow—if the hjjks of Vengiboneeza managed to ambush you, let's say, and the weapons were lost—the shame, the blame, all that would fall upon me for having let them out of my hands. No, cousin, it's impossible. You create the seaside distraction, we'll destroy Vengiboneeza from above. And then we will go on together, in all brotherhood, to the Nest."

Salaman moistened his lips. He forced himself to stay calm.

"As you wish, cousin," he said finally. "We approach the city by the water. You descend through the hills, with your weapons. Here: I give you my hand on it."

Thu-Kimnibol grinned broadly. "So be it, then, cousin!"

Salaman stood for a time, watching as the hulking figure of the prince dwindled in the distance. The king shivered with rage. From the back, Thu-Kimnibol looked just like his father Harruel. And, Salaman thought, he was just as obstinate as Harruel had been. Just as vainglorious, just as dangerous.

Biterulve approached and said, "Trouble, father?"

"Trouble? What trouble, boy?"

"I can see it in the air around you."

Salaman shrugged. "We're not to have any of the Great World weapons, that's all. Thu-Kimnibol must keep them for himself."

"None for us? Not even one?"

"He says he doesn't dare let them out of his hands." Salaman spat. "Gods, I could have killed him where he stood! He wants all the glory of killing the enemy and winning the war—while sending us naked into the field against the hjjks."

"Father, the weapons are his," said Biterulve softly. "If we'd been the ones who found them, would we have offered to share them with him?"

"Of course we would! Are we animals, boy?"

Biterulve made no reply. But the king knew from the look in the boy's gentle eyes that he was skeptical of what Salaman had said; and Salaman very much doubted that he believed it either.

Father and son regarded each other steadily for a moment.

Then Salaman, softening, put his arm over Biterulve's thin shoulders and said, "It makes no difference. Let him keep his toys to himself. We'll manage well enough by ourselves. But I tell you this, boy, and I vow it before all the gods as well: that it'll be the army of Yissou, and not that of Dawinno, that'll be first into the Nest, if it costs me everything I have. And I'll kill the Queen myself. Before Thu-Kimnibol so much as sets eyes on Her."

And, the king added silently, I'll see to it that I square things with my cousin Thu-Kimnibol when the war is over. But for the time being we are allies and friends.

* * *

It was Husathirn Mueri's turn once more this day for judiciary throne-duty in the Basilica. With Thu-Kimnibol gone from the city again, he shared the task day by day with Puit Kjai. Not that there was much in the way of litigation for any of them to handle, with the city virtually deserted except for the very young and the very old.

Still, he sat obligingly under the great cupola, ready to dispense justice if anyone required it of him. In the idle hours his mind roved to the north, where even at this moment the war that he despised was being fought. What was happening up there? Had the hjjks overwhelmed Thu-Kimnibol yet? It gave Husathirn Mueri some pleasure to imagine that scene, the hordes of shrieking clacking bug-folk streaming down from the northern hills in implacable torrents, hurling themselves upon the invaders, cutting them to pieces, Thu-Kimnibol going down beneath the onslaught of their spears and perishing just as his father before him had—

"Throne-grace?"

Chevkija Aim had entered the Basilica while Husathirn Mueri sat dreaming. The guard-captain had chosen a helmet today of black iron plates, with two shining golden claws rising to a great height from its sides.

"Are there petitioners?" Husathirn Mueri asked.

"None so far, throne-grace. But a bit of news. Old Boldirinthe's taken to her bed, and they say it'll be for the last time. The chieftain has gone to her. Your sister Catiriil's there also. She's the one who sent me to tell you."

"Should I go also? Yes, yes, I suppose I should: but not until my hours are done in the Basilica. Whether there are litigants or not, my duty is here." Husathirn Mueri smiled. "Poor old Boldirinthe. Well, her hour was long overdue, in truth. What do you say, Chevkija Aim? Will it take ten strong men to carry her to her grave, do you think? Fifteen?"

The guard-captain seemed not to be amused.

"She's the offering-woman of the Koshmar folk, sir. It's a high office, they tell me. And she was a kind woman. I'd carry her myself, if I were asked."

Husathirn Mueri looked away. "My mother was offering-woman before her, did you know that? Torlyri. It was in the old days, in Vengiboneeza. Who'll be offering-woman now, I wonder? Will there even be a new one? Does anyone still know the rituals and the talismans?"

"These are strange days, sir."

"Strange indeed."

They fell silent.

"How quiet the city is," Husathirn Mueri said. "Everyone gone to fight the war except you and me. Or so it seems."

"Our duties prevented us, sir," said Chevkija Aim tactfully. "Even in wartime, there has to be a justiciary, there have to be guardsmen in the city."

"You know I oppose the war, Chevkija Aim."

"Then it's best that your duties here kept you from having to go. You wouldn't have been able to fight well, feeling as you do."

"And would you have gone, if you could?"

"I attend the chapels now, sir. You know that. I share your hatred of the war. I yearn only for the coming of Queen-peace to bring love to our troubled world."

Husathirn Mueri's eyes widened. "Do you? Yes, you do: I forgot. You follow Kundalimon's teachings now too. Everyone does, I suppose, who's still here. The warriors have gone to war and the peace-lovers stay behind. As it should be. Where will it all end, do you think?"

"In Queen-peace, sir. In Queen-love for all."

"I surely hope so."

But do I? Husathirn Mueri wondered. His surrender to the new faith, if surrender was what it really was, still mystified him. He went regularly to the chapel; he chanted in rote, repeating the scriptures that Tikharein Tourb and Chhia Kreun recited; and it seemed to him that he felt something close to a religious exaltation as he did. That was an experience entirely new to him. But he had never been sure of his own sincerity. It was only one of the many strangenesses of these days, that he should find himself kneeling to chant the praises of the Queen of Queens, that he should be praying to the monstrous hjjks to deliver the world from its anguish.

He looked toward the hall, as if hopeful that some gaggle of angry merchants would burst in, waving a clutch of legal papers and crying curses at each other. But the Basilica was quiet.

"An empty city," he said, as much to himself as to the guard-captain. "The young men gone. The old dying off. Taniane wanders about like her own ghost. The Presidium never meets. Hresh is gone, who knows where? Hunting for mysteries in the swamps, I suppose. Or flying off on his Wonderstone to the Nest to have a chat with the Queen. That would be like him, something like that. The House of Knowledge empty except for the one girl who hasn't gone off to the war. Even Nialli Apuilana's gone to the war." Husathirn Mueri felt a pang of sadness at that thought. He had watched her ride away, the day the troops departed, standing proudly beside Thu-Kimnibol, waving excitedly. The girl was mad, no doubt of that. First telling everyone what wondrous godlike beings the hjjks were, and involving herself in that affair with the envoy Kundalimon after rejecting every logical mate the city had to offer, and then joining the army and going off to fight against the Queen: it made no sense. Nothing that Nialli Apuilana had done had ever made sense.

Just as well, Husathirn Mueri thought, that she and I never became lovers. She might have pulled me down into her madness with her.

But it still made him ache to think of her, mad or not.

Chevkija Aim said, "I think we could close the Basilica, sir. No one came yesterday when Puit Kjai was here, and I think no one will come today. And you'd be able to pay your respects to Boldirinthe before it's too late."

"Boldirinthe," Husathirn Mueri said. "Yes. I ought go to her." He rose from the justiciary throne. "Very well. The court is adjourned, Chevkija Aim."

Ascending the spiral path from the Queen-chamber should have been more taxing than the descent; but to his surprise Hresh found himself oddly vigorous, almost buoyant, and he strode briskly along behind Nest-thinker, easily keeping pace step for step as they rose from that deep well of mysteries toward the by now familiar domain of the upper Nest.

Strange exaltation lingered in him after his meeting with the Queen of Queens.

A formidable creature, yes. That pallid gigantic thing, that quivering continent of monstrously ancient flesh. Hundreds of years old, was She? Thousands? He couldn't begin to guess. That She had survived from the time of the Great World he doubted, though it was possible. Anything was possible here. He saw now more deeply than ever before how alien the hjjks were, how little like his own kind in nearly every respect.

And yet they were "human," he thought, human in that peculiar special sense that he had long ago conceived: they maintained a sense of past and future, they understood life as a process, an unfolding, they were capable of the conscious transmission of historical tradition from generation to generation. The little flitting garaboons gibbering in the forest added nothing to nothing, and ended with nothing. That was true of all the beasts below the human level, the gorynths wallowing in their oozy swamps, the angry chattering samarangs, the jewel-eyed khut-flies, and the rest. They might as well be stones. To be human, Hresh thought, is to be aware of time and seasons, to gather and store knowledge and to transmit it, above all to build and to maintain. In that sense the People were human; even the caviandis were human; and in that sense the hjjks were human too. *Human* didn't simply mean one who belonged to that mysterious ancient race of pale tailless creatures. It was something broader, something far more universal. And it included the hjjks.

To Nest-thinker he said, "That was one of the most extraordinary experiences of my life. I thank the gods I could live long enough to reach this day."

The hjjk made no reply.

"Will I be summoned to Her again, do you think?" Hresh asked.

"You will be if you are," said Nest-thinker. "That is when you will know."

There seemed to be a surliness to Nest-thinker's tone. Hresh wondered if the hjjk envied the depth of the communion he had achieved with the Queen. But there was danger in attributing People emotions to things that hjjks might say.

They were near the upper level now. Hresh recognized certain artifacts set in niches in the wall, a smooth white stone that looked almost like a huge egg, and a plaited star like the one Nialli had had, but much larger, and a small red jewel that burned with a brilliant inner flame. He had noticed them when he began his descent. Holy hjjk talismans, perhaps. Or perhaps mere decorations.

Since coming to the Nest Hresh had lived in an austere cubicle in an outlying corridor, structure—a kind of isolation ward, perhaps, for strangers from outside. It was a round chamber with a low flat ceiling and a thin scatter of dried reeds on its hard-packed earthen floor to serve him as a bed; but it was comfortable enough for his undemanding needs. He looked forward to it now. A time to rest, a time to think about what he'd just undergone. Perhaps later they'd bring him a meal of some sort, the dried fruit and bits of sun-parched meat that seemed to be the only fare in this place and to which he had adapted without difficulty.

Now they had reached the head of the spiral ramp, the place where they re-entered the upper level. Nest-thinker turned here, not to the left where Hresh's cubicle was, but in the other direction entirely. Hresh lingered behind, wondering if his sense of direction had misled him again, as it had so many times during his stay here. This time he was sure, though. His chamber lay to the left. Nest-thinker, by now a dozen paces away, swung about and looked back, and gestured brusquely to him.

"You will follow."

"I'd like to go to my sleeping-place. I think it's that way."

"You will follow," said Nest-thinker again.

In the Nest disobedience was simply not an option: if he persisted in going to his chamber, Hresh knew, Nest-thinker wouldn't be angered so much as mystified, but in any case Hresh would end up going where Nest-thinker wanted him to go. He followed. The path ramped gently upward. After a time he saw what seemed surely to be the glow of daylight ahead. They were approaching one of the surface mouths of the Nest. Five or six Militaries were waiting there. Nest-thinker delivered Hresh to them and turned away without a word.

To the Militaries Hresh said, "I'd be grateful if you'd take me to my sleeping-place, now. This isn't where I wanted Nest-thinker to bring me."

The hjjks stared blandly at him as if he hadn't said a thing.

"Come," one said, pointing toward the daylight.

His wagon was waiting out there, and his xlendi, looking rested and well fed. The implication was clear enough. He had seen the Queen, and the Queen had seen him, and so the Queen's needs had been served. Which was all that mattered here. His time in the Nest was over; now he was to be expelled.

A quiver of shock and dismay ran through him. He didn't want to leave. He had been living easily and happily here according to the rhythm of the Nest, strange as it was. It had become his home. He had supposed that he would end his days in the warmth and the silence and the sweetness of this place, dwelling here until at last the Destroyer came to take him to his final rest, which very likely would be soon. The outside world held nothing more for him. He wanted only to be allowed to penetrate ever more deeply into the way of the hjjks in whatever time might remain to him.

"Please," Hresh said. "I want to stay."

He could just as well have been speaking to creatures of stone. They leaned on their spears and stared at him, motionless, impassive. They hardly even seemed alive, but for the rippling of the orange breathing-tubes that dangled from the sides of their heads as air passed through the tubes' segmented coils.

The xlendi made a soft whickering sound. It had had its orders; it was impatient to set forth.

"Don't you understand?" Hresh told the hjjks. "I don't want to leave."

Silence.

"I ask for sanctuary among you."

Silence, icy, impenetrable.

"In the name of the Queen, I beg you—"

That, at least, brought a response. The two hjjks nearest him drew themselves up tall, and a brightness that might have been anger passed swiftly across the many facets of their huge eyes. They brought their spears up and held them out horizontally, as though they meant to push Hresh forward with them.

A silent voice said, "It is the Queen's wish that you continue your pilgrimage now. In the name of the Queen, then, go. *Go.*"

He understood that there was no hope of further appeal. They stared at him inexorably. The horizontal spears formed an impenetrable gate, cutting him off from the Nest.

"Yes," he said sadly. "Very well."

He clambered into the wagon. Immediately the xlendi set out almost at a canter across the barren gray plain. He was startled by that. The beast had been so unhurried during the journey up here from Dawinno. But Hresh suspected that the xlendi was being guided, and even propelled, by some force within the Nest, and he thought that he knew what that force was. He sat passively, letting the wagon run; and when the xlendi halted for water and forage, he sipped a little water himself and ate a little of the dried meat that the hjjks had put into his wagon, and waited for the ride to resume. And so it went, day after day, a long quiet time, almost like a dreamless sleep, first through a zone of strange flat-topped sand-colored pyramidal hills, and then into a region of eerie erosion where the fiery crimson rocks had been cut into fantastic arches and colonnades, and after that through a landscape of rough sedge and occasional stubby trees and scattered herds of some dark-striped grazing animal Hresh had never seen before, which did not even look up as his wagon went by.

Until at midday one day, while he was crossing what might not long ago have been a lake-bed, but was at this season a place of dry and cracked expanses of mud covered by a light scattering of sandy dust, he saw a figure on a vermilion just ahead, someone of the People, an unexpected sight indeed in this unknown place.

The xlendi halted and waited as the huge red creature came shambling up. The man riding it gasped.

"Gods! Can it really be you, sir? Or am I dreaming this? It must be a dream. It must."

Hresh smiled. Tried to speak. He hadn't used his voice in so long that it was harsh and ragged, a mere rasping croak. But he managed to say, "I know you, I think."

The rider vaulted down from the vermilion and ran toward him. Peering over the wagon's side, he stared at Hresh, shaking his head in wonder.

"Plor Killivash, sir. From the House of Knowledge! You don't recognize me? I was one of your assistants, don't you remember? Plor Killivash?"

"Is this Dawinno, then?"

"Dawinno? Sir, no! We're way up in hjjk territory. I'm with the army, your brother Thu-Kimnibol's army! We've been fighting for weeks. We've fought at Vengiboneeza, we've fought at a couple of the small Nests—" Plor Killivash's eyes grew wider and wider. "Sir, how did you get here? You couldn't possibly have come all this way alone, could you? And why are you here? You shouldn't be at the battlefront, you know. Sir, can you hear me? Are you all right, sir? Sir?"

Thu-Kimnibol was in his tent. The army was camped on the edge of the prairie that they called the Plains of Minbain. He had given names to all the features of this unfamiliar land: the Mountains of Harruel, Lake Taniane, the Torlyri River, Boldirinthe Valley, Koshmar Pass. For all he knew, Salaman was bestowing names of his own on the same places as he advanced through them. Thu-Kimnibol didn't care about that. To him the great jagged mountains they had gone past three weeks before were his father's mountains, and this lovely serene tableland was his mother's plain, and let Salaman call them what he would.

To Nialli Apuilana he said, "There it is again. I can feel the king approaching. Marching at the head of his troops, coming this way."

"Yes. So do I. Or something dark and fierce, at any rate."

"Salaman. No question of it."

She put her hand to his thick forearm, where just a few days before he had taken a light wound from a hjjk spear. "You speak his name as though he's the enemy, not the hjjks. Are you afraid of him, love?"

Thu-Kimnibol laughed. "Afraid of Salaman? I don't often think in terms of who it is that I fear. But only a fool wouldn't fear Salaman, Nialli. He's become some kind of monster. I told you once that I thought he was mad. But he's gone beyond madness now. Or so I think."

"A monster," Nialli Apuilana repeated. "But in war all warriors have to be monsters. Isn't that so?"

"Not like that. I watched him when our two armies were last together. He was fighting as if he wanted not just to kill every hjjk he saw, but to roast it and eat it also. There was fire in his eyes. Long ago I saw my father Harruel fight, and he was a troubled man, with great hot angry forces churning within him; but at his fiercest he seemed calm and gentle when I compare him with Salaman as he looked that day." Thu-Kimnibol's sensing-organ quivered. "I felt him again just now. Closer and closer. Well, perhaps it's best that the armies join again. I never meant for us to advance separately into the country of the hjjks."

"Will you have some wine?" Nialli Apuilana asked.

"Yes. Yes, that would be good."

Twilight was coming on. Most likely Salaman and his army would show up by midday tomorrow, if the emanations were this strong. The reunion of the two forces, after weeks of separation, was likely to be tense. And the gods only knew what a wild man the king had become by now. This entire campaign seemed to have been a voyage into ever deeper madness for him.

The trouble had started, Thu-Kimnibol thought, while they were planning the Vengiboneeza campaign: Salaman's burst of anger after being told he wasn't going to be given any of the Great World weapons had been the beginning. There had been a coldness between them ever since. They both obeyed the fiction that Salaman was commander-in-chief and Thu-Kimnibol the field general, but there hadn't been much cordiality or real cooperation between them as the fighting itself got under way.

Still, everything had gone well so far. Better even than they might have expected, in fact.

The battle of Vengiboneeza had been an overwhelming triumph. The hjjks had constructed a Nest above ground there, a weird ramshackle array of flimsy gray tubes that ran in a hundred directions, spanning the old city from the waterfront to the eastern foothills. Salaman came upon the city from the western side, setting up a great uproar of flame and explosions along the seawall, while Thu-Kimnibol's forces had descended carefully along the slopes of the great golden-brown mountain wall to the north and east. The hjjks were taken by surprise, rushing down to the water to see what the matter was while Thu-Kimnibol got ready to attack from above.

Then it was the moment to bring the Great World weapons into play. Thu-Kimnibol had used the one he called the Loop to set up an impenetrable barrier along the foothills to keep the hjjks from assailing his position. Then with the Line of Fire he raked the city with flames until the red tongues rose above the highest rooftop and the pulpy walls of the Vengiboneeza Nest blackened and shriveled. With the Bubble Tube he had caused such turbulence in the air that the city's age-old towers, those marvelous spires of scarlet and blue, of glittering purple, of brilliant gold, of midnight black, crumbled like brittle sticks. Now he called into service the most potent of his weapons, the Earth-Eater, to gobble huge craters in the fabric of the dying metropolis below him. The boulevards and avenues themselves slipped downward into chaos, whole districts collapsing and sinking from sight, and a great pall of dust and smoke rose to choke the sky as if the death-stars had come again.

The Long Winter itself hadn't been able to destroy Vengiboneeza. But Thu-Kimnibol had done it in a single afternoon, with four small devices that an ignorant farmer had found in a muddy hillside.

They had stayed all night to watch the city burn. All its immense population must have burned with it, for Thu-Kimnibol's troops saw not a single hjjk try to escape on the foothills side, and Salaman's warriors along the seawall cut down every one of those that attempted to get away by water. The armies rejoined on the far side of Vengiboneeza and set out side by side into the true hjjk heartland. Which was where Salaman's army had split off after the destruction of one of the smaller Nests behind Vengiboneeza. The king, made wild by the love of slaughter, had insisted on pursuing and killing a few hundred hjjks that had managed to get away. Thu-Kimnibol found little joy in the thought of seeing him again. Too bad Salaman hadn't decided to take a separate route all the rest of the way.

Pulling Nialli Apuilana close against him, he drew his breath deep, filling his lungs with the fragrance of her. At least tonight they'd be at their ease together. If Salaman turned up tomorrow, as seemed more and more likely, he'd deal with that problem when it presented itself.

"It still surprises me," he said softly, "when I awaken and see that it's you beside me. Even after all this time, I look at you, and I tell myself in wonder, That's Nialli there! How strange!"

"You still expect to find Naarinta, do you?" she said playfully.

"Gods! How merciless you can be! You know what I mean, Nialli. I'll always cherish Naarinta's memory, yes. But she's long gone. What I'm trying to tell you is that it continues to amaze me that I should have found such love with you, *you,* my half-brother's own child, that strange wild girl whom no one in Dawinno was able to tame—"

"And have you tamed me now, Thu-Kimnibol?"

"Hardly. But I no longer see you as anyone's child. Or strange. Or wild."

"Ah, and how do you see me, then?" she asked, smiling.

"Why, as the most—"

"Sir? Lord prince?" came a deep familiar voice from outside the tent.

Thu-Kimnibol muttered a curse. "Is that you, Dumanka? By all the gods, this had better be important, that you come interrupting me in my tent when—"

"Sir, it is! It is!"

"I'll have him flayed if it isn't," he said to Nialli Apuilana under his breath. "I promise you that."

"Go to him. Dumanka's not one to bother you over nothing."

"Yes. I suppose." Thu-Kimnibol put down his wine and made his way to the tent entrance, a little creakily, for his muscles were still sore from the last battle. He peered out.

Dumanka looked as astonished as if he'd just seen the sun moving backward through the sky. Thu-Kimnibol had never seen him in such a state.

"Lord prince—"

"Gods, man! What is it?"

"Hresh, sir. Hresh the chronicler?"

"Yes, I know who Hresh is. What of him? Is there a message from him?"

Dumanka shook his head. Hoarsely he blurted, "Sir, he's here."

"Here?"

"Plor Killivash just brought him in. Found him, sir, wandering around in a xlendi-wagon out in the patrol area. We've got him in the medic tent. He seems to be all right, just a little woolly in the head. He's been asking for you, and I thought—"

Thu-Kimnibol, stunned, waved him into silence. He turned to Nialli Apuilana. "Did you hear that?"

"No. Trouble?"

"You might call it that. Your father's here, Nialli. My lunatic brother. Dumanka says he just came wandering in out of the open country. Mueri and Yissou and Dawinno, what's *he* doing here? On the front line of the war, no less. Just what we need. Gods! Gods!"

Quietly Hresh said, "Come with me to the Queen, brother. Let me show you what She is like."

It was an hour after his arrival. He had been bombarded with surprises: Thu-Kimnibol and Nialli Apuilana sharing a tent like mates, Vengiboneeza destroyed, the hjjks being pushed back on every front. But, spent and drained as he was by his journey, startled and dismayed as he was by these developments, he kept his mind and strength focused on his purpose.

"To the Queen?" Thu-Kimnibol said. He seemed bewildered. Then he flashed a brief flickering smile, a look of patronizing indulgence. "You and I. The Queen of Queens, you mean?"

"Yes."

"To speak with Her. Not to kill Her, only to have a chat with Her."

"Yes," said Hresh.

"And how will we get there? In your little wagon?"

"I have this," Hresh said, and brought forth in his hand the little pouch that contained the Barak Dayir.

A grunt of amazement. "You've taken the Wonderstone with you?"

"The Barak Dayir is mine, brother. As were the weapons with which you destroyed Vengiboneeza."

Thu-Kimnibol made no attempt to parry that. "Let me understand you. You're proposing that we visit the Nest, but not in our actual bodies, just by using the Wonderstone to send our souls there?"

"That's right."

"And why, brother, do you want me to put myself in my enemy's power?"

"So you can begin to understand your enemy's nature: not just Her greatness, which I think you underestimate, but also Her vulnerability, which I don't think you see at all."

"Her greatness. Her vulnerability." Thu-Kimnibol frowned. "Of Her greatness I've already heard far too much. But Her vulnerability? What are you talking about?"

"Come with me, if you want to know."

Hresh's serenity was an unassailable armor. Thu-Kimnibol shot a glance at Nialli Apuilana as though begging for help.

Hresh saw now the healing wounds here and there beneath his brother's thick brick-hued fur, at least half a dozen of them. He wondered what prodigies of heroism Thu-Kimnibol had managed in battle, how many scores of hjjks he had already sent to their deaths.

Nialli Apuilana said, "What risk is there in this, father?"

"Only the risk that we'll fall under Her spell, which as you know is potent. But I think we can defeat it. I know we can. I've been able to escape from Her grasp once already."

"Are you saying that you've already made the voyage to the Nest yourself?" Thu-Kimnibol asked.

"To a minor Nest, yes. I was there for weeks. And went from there to the great one with the help of the Barak Dayir. The Queen of Queens has a Wonderstone also, one that once belonged to the Bengs. It's inside Her body. I spoke with Her, Wonderstone to Wonderstone. After which, the hjjks of the Nest where I was living sent me on my way. And guided my xlendi, I think, until I could be found by one of your men."

"Then all this is a trap," said Thu-Kimnibol.

"All of it is part of Dawinno's plan," Hresh replied.

Thu-Kimnibol fell silent. Hresh watched him patiently. He felt that he had infinite patience, now. He had never known such tranquility of spirit before. Nothing could shift him from his path.

He had noticed immediately the signs all over the tent that his brother and Nialli Apuilana were living together in intimacy. That had jolted him, but only for a fraction of an instant. Thu-Kimnibol and Nialli Apuilana each had greatness in them. That they should finally have come together in this troubled time seemed appropriate. Yes, even inevitable. Let them be.

Learning of Vengiboneeza's destruction had been a shock too, of a different sort. Vengiboneeza had been a place of wonder and majesty since time's early days. For it to be gone, that treasury of ancient miracles where he had spent his youth, ruined more completely now by this war than it had ever been by the Long Winter, was painful news.

But then he had put his regret aside. Nothing was eternal except Eternity itself. To mourn the loss of Vengiboneeza was to deny Dawinno. The gods provide, the gods take away. The flux of change is the only constant. The Transformer sweeps everything away in its time, and replaces it with something else. There had been cities greater than Vengiboneeza upon this Earth, Hresh knew, of which not a scrap remained, not even their names.

Thu-Kimnibol was staring at him. After a long while he said, "I think you need to rest, brother."

Hresh laughed. "Are you telling me that I'm senile, or simply out of my mind?"

"That you're exhausted from Yissou knows what kind of an ordeal. And that the last thing either of us needs to do right now is fly off into the clutches of the Queen."

"I've been in Her clutches already, and here I am to tell the tale. I can get free of Her again. Before this war goes any further, brother, there are things you need to know."

"Tell me about them, then."

"You have to see them for yourself."

Thu-Kimnibol stared. Another silence. An impasse.

Hresh said, "Do you trust me, brother?"

"You know I do."

"Do you think I'd lead you into harm?"

"You might. Without meaning to. Hresh-full-of-questions, you are. You poke your nose everywhere. You've always been fearless, brother. Too fearless, maybe."

"And you? Thu-Kimnibol the coward, is that who you are?"

Thu-Kimnibol grinned. "You think you can goad me into this lunacy by playing on my pride, do you, Hresh? Give me credit for a little intelligence, brother."

"I do. More than a little. I ask you again: come with me to the Queen. If you hope to rule the world, Thu-Kimnibol, and I know that you do, you need to understand the nature of the one being who stands in your way. Come with me, brother."

Hresh held out his hand. His voice was steady. His gaze was unwavering.

Thu-Kimnibol shifted his weight uneasily. He stood deep in thought, scowling, plucking at the ruff of fur along his cheeks. His face was dark with doubt. But then his expression changed. He seemed to be weakening—Thu-Kimnibol, weakening!—under Hresh's unremitting pressure. Tightly he said to Nialli Apuilana, "What do you think? Should I do this thing?"

"I think you should." Unhesitatingly.

Thu-Kimnibol nodded. A cloud seemed to have lifted from him. To Hresh he said, "How is it done?"

"We'll twine; and then the Barak Dayir will carry us to the Nest of Nests."

"Twine? You and I? Hresh, we've never done a thing like that!"

"No, brother. Not ever."

Thu-Kimnibol smiled. "How strange that seems, twining with my own brother. But if that's what we have to do, that's what we'll do. Eh, Hresh? So be it." To Nialli Apuilana he said, "If for some reason I don't come back—"

"Don't even say that, Thu-Kimnibol!"

"Hresh offers me no guarantees. These possibilities have to be considered. If I don't come back, love—if my soul doesn't return to my body after a certain while, two full days, let's say—take yourself to Salaman and tell him what has happened. Is that clear? Give our army over into his sole command. Let him have the four Great World weapons."

"Salaman? But he's a madman!"

"A great warrior, all the same. The only one, after myself, who can lead us in this campaign. Will you do that?"

"If I must," said Nialli Apuilana in a low voice.

"Good." Thu-Kimnibol drew in a deep breath and extended his sensing-organ to Hresh. "Well, brother, I'm ready if you are. Let's go to visit the Queen."

* * *

There is darkness everywhere, a great sea of dense blackness so complete that it excludes even the possibility of light. And then, suddenly, a fierce glow like that of an exploding sun blossoms on the horizon. The blackness shatters into an infinity of fiery points of piercing brightness and Thu-Kimnibol feels those myriad blazing fragments rushing past him on hot streams of wind.

Within the fiery mystery that lies ahead, he is able now to make out texture and form. He sees something that seems to him to be an immense shining machine, a thing of whirling rods and ceaseless churning pistons, moving flawlessly with never a moment's slackening of energy or failure of pattern. From it comes a pure beam of dazzling light that rises with scimitar force to cut across the sky.

The Nest, Thu-Kimnibol thinks. The Nest of Nests.

And a voice like the sound of worlds colliding says, speaking out of the core of that unthinkable tireless mechanism, "Why do you return to Me so soon?"

The Queen, that must be.

The Queen of Queens.

He feels no fear, only awe and something that he thinks might be humility. The presence of Hresh beside him gives him whatever degree of assurance he's unable to find within himself. He has never been this close to his brother in all his life: it's difficult now for him to determine where his own soul leaves off and that of Hresh begins.

They are descending, or falling, or plummeting. Whether it is by command of that great creature in the brightness before them, or Hresh is still in control of their journey, Thu-Kimnibol has no way of telling. But as they come nearer the Nest he sees it more clearly, and understands that it is no machine at all, but rather a thing of chewed pulp and soil, and what he has taken for a shining machine, rods flailing and pistons pumping in perfect coordination, is simply his perception of the stupendous oneness of the hjjk empire itself, in which not even the smallest of the newly hatched has free volition, but where everything is tightly woven in a predestined pattern with no room for imperfection.

And at the heart of that pattern lies such a creature as he has never imagined: a world in itself, that huge motionless thing. With the aid of the Wonderstone that his brother holds in the curl of his sensing-organ, somewhere thousands of leagues behind them where they have left their unconscious bodies, Thu-Kimnibol can perceive the vastness of the container of flesh that houses the mind of the Queen, the slow journey of the life-fluids through that gigantic ancient body, the ponderous workings of its incomprehensible organs.

It has waited through half of time for his coming here, so he feels.

And he has passed all his life in a dream, waiting only for this moment of confrontation.

"There are two of you," the Queen declares, in that same overwhelming tone. "Who is your other self?"

Hresh does not respond. Thu-Kimnibol sends a probe in his brother's direction, to prod him to make some reply. But Hresh seems silent, dazed, as if the effort of the journey itself has exhausted the last of his powers.

All is in his own hands, then. He says, "I am Thu-Kimnibol, son of Harruel and Minbain, brother on the mother's side to Hresh the chronicler, whom you already know."

"Ah. You have an Egg-maker in common but you come from different Life-kindlers." There is a long pause. "And you are the one who would destroy us. Why is that, that you feel such hatred for us?"

"The gods guide my hand," Thu-Kimnibol says simply.

"The gods?"

"They who shape our lives and control our destinies. They tell me that I must lead my people forward against those who stand in the way of our achieving what we must."

There comes a sound of great pealing laughter now, rising and spreading outward like the floodwaters of some mighty river, so that Thu-Kimnibol has to fight with all his strength to keep from being engulfed in that tremendous outpouring of mockery.

The words he has just spoken echo and re-echo in his ears, amplified and distorted by the tide of the Queen's laughter so that they become pathetic comic shards of foolishness—*destinies . . . lead . . . achieving . . . must . . .* His staunch declaration of purpose seems only like empty nonsense to him now. Angrily he strives to reclaim some shred of his lost dignity.

"Do You mock the gods, then?" he cries.

Again that great flood of laughter. "The gods, you say? The gods?"

"The gods, indeed. Who have brought me here today, and who will strengthen my hand until the last of Your kind has been sent from the world."

Thu-Kimnibol is aware now of Hresh, distant and vague, fluttering against him like a bird against a sealed window, as if trying to warn him against the course he has chosen. But he ignores his brother's agitation.

"Tell me this, Queen: do You so much as believe in the gods? Or is Your arrogance so great that You deny them?"

"Your gods?" she says. "Yes. No."

"What does that mean?"

"Your gods are symbols of the great forces: comfort, protection, nourishment, healing, death."

"You know that much?"

"Of course."

"And You have no belief in those gods?"

"We believe in comfort, protection, nourishment, healing, death. But they are not gods."

"You worship no one and nothing, then?"

"Not as you understand worship," the Queen replies.

"Not even Your creator?"

"The humans created us," she says, in a strange offhanded way. "But does that make them worthy of our worship? We think not." Once more the Queen's laughter engulfs him. "Let us not discuss the gods. Let us discuss the injuries you do us. How can you carry on such war against us, when you have no true understanding of what we are? Your other self has already seen our Nest. Now it is your turn. Prepare yourself to behold us."

But there is no time to prepare himself, nor does he know how, or for what. Before the Queen's voice has died away the Nest in its totality sweeps like a rushing torrent into his soul.

He sees it all: the great shining machine, the flawless world within the world, Militaries and Workers, Egg-makers and Life-kindlers, Nest-thinkers and Nourishment-givers and Queen-attendants and all the rest, every one woven together in an inextricable way in the service of the Queen, which is to say in the service of the totality. He understands how the creation of Nest-plenty and Nest-strength fosters the furtherance of Egg-plan, by which Queen-love will ultimately be extended to all the cosmos. He sees the smaller Nests here and there and across the face of the planet, each of them tied to all the rest, and to the great central Nest, by the powerful force of Nest-truth that radiates from the immensity that is the Queen of Queens.

How puny his own armies seem, against the colossal confident single force that is the hjjks! How ragged and confused, how crippled by division and vainglory! There's no hope of prevailing in this struggle, Thu-Kimnibol sees. Egg-plan is in direct conflict with the ambitions of the People, and Egg-plan must triumph through sheer will and force of numbers. He might win a battle now and then, he might deal one band of hjjks or another a grievous blow, but always the underlying force of hjjk unity will remain, always the power of the Nest will bring forth horde after horde, until in the end the upstarts out of the cocoon must inevitably be defeated.

Must—inevitably—

—be—

—defeated—

Or perhaps have been already. Despair presses against him with crushing weight. All strength seems to be leaving his limbs, and he sees that that strength was only an illusion, that he had thought of himself as a giant but had always in reality been nothing more than a flea: a bold flea and foolish flea who has dared to challenge an immortal monarch.

He is floating downward toward the colossus that is the Queen like a cinder drifting on the air. In another moment he will land on the great surface of Her and be swallowed up. When he looks toward Hresh for help his brother seems more distant even than before, a mere speck far away, already caught beyond hope of escape in the Queen's compelling force, already sinking irretrievably within the layers of Her flesh.

He is next. They both are doomed.

The Queen is like some great cosmic force, a deadly elemental thing that holds the power of ending his life with a single contemptuous flicker of Her will.

Does She mean to kill him, Thu-Kimnibol wonders, or merely to swallow him up? He considers the vastness of Her and the probable power of the Wonderstone hidden somewhere within the incalculable volumes of Her flesh; and he decides that probably She doesn't intend to kill him, but that if She tries it he'll send such a flare of defiant fury into Her, by way of Hresh with whom he lies entwined and the Wonderstone which Hresh possesses, that She will sizzle in unthinkable pain.

More likely, though, he decides, She means to absorb and neutralize, to transform him from Her foe into Her slave. That he will not allow either. Her strength is immense. And yet—and yet—

He thinks suddenly that he can see Her limits. How She could be brought to a standstill, if not defeated altogether.

The perfection of the hjjk empire hums and whirrs and gleams about him, and the power of the Queen holds him fast, and nonetheless in the midst of all that oppressive force Thu-Kimnibol knows what Hresh meant when he said that he must try to comprehend the vulnerability of the hjjks.

Their very perfection is their weak spot. The greatness of the self-contained civilization that they have built and sustained for so many hundreds of thousands of years contains the seed of its own destruction. Hresh has seen that already; and now Hresh, wherever he may be, is helping him to see it. The hjjks are a supreme achievement of the gods, Thu-Kimnibol thinks; but they will not allow themselves to understand that the essence of the gods' way is unceasing change. Time has brought change to everything else that ever lived; and it will come also to the hjjks, or they will perish.

They are too rigid. They can be broken. If they won't bend to the law of the gods, Thu-Kimnibol tells himself, then ultimately they'll suffer the fate of all that can't or won't bend. In time they will be struck by a force too strong for them to withstand; and they will shatter in an instant. Yes.

"Come, brother," he calls. "We've stayed here long enough. I've learned what you wanted me to learn."

"Thu-Kimnibol?" Hresh says dimly. "Is that you? Where are you, brother?"

"Here. Here. Take my hand."

"I am for the Queen now, brother."

"No. No, never. She can't hold you. Come: here."

Vast peals of laughter resound all about him. She thinks that She has them both. But Thu-Kimnibol is undismayed. His initial awe of the Queen had placed him at Her advantage; but that awe is gone now, overcome by anger and contempt, and there is no other way that She could hold him.

He understands that next to Her he is nothing more than a flea. But fleas can go about their business unseen by greater creatures. That's the great advantage fleas have, Thu-Kimnibol thinks. The Queen can't hold us if She can't find us. And She's so confident of Her own omnipotence that She isn't even trying very hard.

He begins to slip away from Her, taking Hresh with him.

Ascending from Her lair is like climbing a mountain that reaches halfway to the roof of the sky. But any journey, no matter how great, is done a single step at a time. Thu-Kimnibol draws himself upward, and upward again, holding Hresh in his arms. The Queen does not appear to be restraining him. Perhaps She thinks he'll fall back to Her of his own accord.

Upward. Upward. Streams of light come from behind him, but they grow indistinct as he continues. Now the blackness lies before him, deep and intense.

"Brother?" Thu-Kimnibol says. "Brother, we're free. We're safe now."

He blinked and opened his eyes. Nialli Apuilana, standing above him, made a soft little cry of joy.

"At last you're back!"

Thu-Kimnibol nodded. He looked over at Hresh. His eyes had opened slit-wide, but he seemed stunned and dazed. Reaching across, Thu-Kimnibol touched his brother's arm. Hresh seemed very cool; his arm twitched faintly as Thu-Kimnibol's fingers grazed it.

"Will he be all right?" Nialli Apuilana asked.

"He's very tired. So am I. How long were we gone, Nialli?"

"Just short of a day and a half." She was staring at him as though he had undergone some great metamorphosis. "I was beginning to think that you—that—"

"A day and a half," he said, in a musing tone. "It felt like years. What's been happening here?"

"Nothing. Not even Salaman. He marched around our camp without even stopping, and is heading on north without us."

"A madman, he is. Well, let him go."

"And you?" Nialli Apuilana was still staring. "What was it like? Did you see the Nest? Did you make contact with the Queen?"

He closed his eyes for a moment. "I never understood the half of it. How awesome She is—how mighty the Nest is—how intricate their life is—"

"I tried to tell you all, that day at the Presidium. But no one would listen, not even you."

"Especially not me, Nialli." He smiled. "They're a frightening enemy. They seem so much wiser than we are. So much more powerful. Superior beings in every way. I get the feeling that I almost want to bow down before them."

"Yes."

"At least before their Queen," he said. A note of discouragement came into his voice. The triumph of his escape seemed far behind him now. "She's almost like some sort of god. That ancient immense creature, reaching out everywhere, running everything. To resist Her seems, well, blasphemous."

"Yes," Nialli Apuilana said. "I know what you mean."

He shook his head wearily. "We *have* to resist, though. There's no way we can arrive at any kind of accommodation with them. If we don't keep on fighting them, they'll crush us. They'll swallow us up. But if we go on with the war, if we should win it, won't we be going against the will of the gods? The gods brought them through the Long Winter, after all. The gods may have intended them to inherit the world." He looked at her in perplexity. "I'm speaking in contradictions. Does any of this make sense?"

"The gods brought us through the Long Winter also, Thu-Kimnibol. Maybe they realize that the hjjks were a mistake, that they were an experiment that failed. And so we've been brought on to finish them off and take their place."

He looked at her, startled. "Do you think so? Could it be possible?"

"You call them superior beings. But you saw for yourself how limited they really are, how inflexible, how narrow. Didn't you? Didn't you? That was what Hresh wanted you to see: that they don't really want to create anything, that they aren't even capable of it. All they want to do is keep on multiplying and building new Nests. But there's no purpose to it beyond that. They aren't trying to learn. They aren't trying to grow." She laughed. "Can you imagine? I stood up in the Presidium and said we ought to think of them as humans. But they aren't. I was wrong and you were all right, even Husathirn Mueri. *Bugs* is what they are. Horrible oversized *bugs*. Everything I believed about them is something that they put into my head themselves."

"Don't underrate them, Nialli," Thu-Kimnibol said. "You may be going too far in the other direction now." Hresh made a soft sighing sound. He turned and looked at him. But Hresh seemed asleep, breathing gently and calmly. Thu-Kimnibol turned back to Nialli Apuilana. "There's one more thing, something the Queen told me that seemed even stranger than all the rest. Were you ever taught, when you lived among them, that the hjjks believe they were created by the humans?"

Now it was her turn to look startled. "No. No, never!"

"Can it be true, do you think?"

"Why not? The humans were almost like gods. The humans may have *been* the gods."

"Then if the hjjks are their chosen people—"

"No," she said. "The hjjks were *a* chosen people. Chosen to survive, to endure the Long Winter, to take over the world afterward. But they didn't work out, somehow. So the gods created us. Or the humans did, one or the other. As replacements for them." Her eyes were bright with a fervor he had rarely seen in them before. "Someday the humans are going to come back to Earth," she said. "I'm certain of it. They'll want to see what's been happening here since they left. And they won't want to find the whole place one gigantic Nest, Thu-Kimnibol. They put us in those cocoons for a purpose, and they'll want to know whether that purpose has been fulfilled. So we have to keep on fighting, don't you see? We have to hold our own against the Queen. Call them gods, call them humans, whatever they are, they're the ones who made us. And they expect that of us."

"This is the kind of country the bug-folk love," Salaman muttered. "Dead country, with all its bones showing." The king brought his xlendi to a halt and looked around at his three sons. Athimin and Biterulve were riding alongside him, and Chham just a short way behind.

"You think there's a Nest out there, father?" Chham asked.

"I'm sure of it. I feel its weight pressing on my soul. Here, I feel it. And here. And here." He touched his breast, and his sensing-organ, and his loins.

The territory ahead had a bleached, arid look. The soil was pale and sandy and the fierce blue sky glared with whipcrack intensity. The only sign of life was a malign-looking woody low dome of a plant that looked almost like a weatherbeaten skull, from which two thick strap-like gray leaves, tattered and shredded by the wind, extended across the desert floor to an enormous length. These plants grew far apart, each presiding over its little domain like a sullen immobile emperor. Otherwise there was nothing.

Athimin said, "Shall I give the order to make camp, father?"

Salaman nodded. He stared into the distance. A sour chilly breeze struck his face, a wind of trouble. "And send scouts forward. Protected by patrols just behind them. There are hjjks out there, plenty of them. I can smell them."

Strange uneasiness was growing in him. He had no idea why.

Until this moment Salaman had been confident that his army, and his army alone, would be able to march all the way to the great Nest and destroy it. Certainly they had met no real opposition thus far. The hjjks had numbers on their side, and they were strong and tireless warriors. But they didn't seem to have any real idea of how to fight. It had been that way forty years ago too, Salaman remembered, when they had tried to lay siege to the newly founded City of Yissou.

What they did was come swooping down in great terrifying hordes, shrieking and waving their spears and swords. Most of them wielded two weapons at once, some of them even more than that. It was a sight that could make the blood run backward in your veins, if you let yourself be awed by their frenzy and by the frightful look of them.

But if you stood your ground, side by side in a sturdy wedge of warriors, and met them hack for hack, chop for chop, you could beat them down. The thing was not to carry the battle to them, but let them come to you. For all their wild dancing about, they were inefficient fighters, too many of them too close together. What you had to do was get your strongest and most fearless men into a phalanx up front, and slash away at any hjjk that came too near. Try to cut its breathing-tubes: that was where they were most vulnerable, the loose dangling orange breathing-tubes that hung from their heads to the sides of their chests. Snip one of those and within moments the hjjk was down, paralyzed by lack of air.

And so Salaman's army had marched on and on and on, beyond the smoldering rubble-heap that was Vengiboneeza, into the ever more parched country to the north, eradicating the hjjks as they went. There had been four great battles so far, and each one had ended in a rout. His soul tingled with the memory of those victories—the hjjks hunted down to the last one, the severed claw-tipped limbs scattered about everywhere, the dry weightless bodies piled in stacks. Every army the Queen had sent against him had met the same fate.

Now, though, the invaders were approaching the first of the lesser Nests that rimmed the frontier of the true hjjk domain.

It was Salaman's plan to wipe out those Nests and their Queens one by one as he passed northward, so that no enemies would remain behind him when he moved into the far side of the great emptiness to begin his assault on the central Nest. He had no clear notion yet how he was going to destroy them. Pour some sort of liquid fire into their openings, perhaps. It would all have been much easier if he'd had one or two of Thu-Kimnibol's fancy weapons. But he was sure that he would find a way that would work, when the time came. He hadn't had a moment's worry on that score.

Now, though—this foul wind blowing, this sudden sense of distress, of impending disaster—

"Father!" Biterulve cried.

Out of nowhere a wall of water appeared before them, rising out of the desert like a gigantic ocean wave springing from the ground to blot out half the sky. The xlendis whinnied and reared wildly. Salaman swore and flung up his arm before his face in astonishment. Behind him he heard the panicky yelling of his men.

He needed only a moment to collect himself.

"A trick!" he bellowed. "An illusion! How can there be water in the desert?"

Indeed that titanic wave hung above them but did not descend. He saw the curling edge of white foam, the green impenetrable depths behind, the huge curve of inconceivable falling mass; but the mass did not fall.

"A trick!" Salaman roared. "The hjjks are attacking us! Form the wedge! Form the wedge!"

Chham, wild-eyed, rode up close behind him. Salaman shoved him fiercely back in the direction of the main body of the army. "Get them in formation!" he ordered. He saw Athimin already heading back, signaling, gesticulating, trying to keep the troops from scattering.

They seemed to realize that the sudden ocean wasn't real. But now the ground itself was wavering like a blanket being shaken to free it from crumbs. Salaman, appalled, saw the Earth rippling all about him. He grew dizzy and sprang down from his xlendi. An actual earthquake? Or another illusion? He couldn't tell.

The wall of water had become a wall of fire, enclosing them on three sides. The air sizzled and crackled and blazed. He felt heat pressing inward on him. Blue-tipped flames streamed upward from the quivering earth.

And now bright bolts of shimmering light were dancing in the sky like spears running amok. Salaman, whirling to avoid their blinding light, saw dragons advancing from the north, breathing fire. Ravenous mouth-creatures. Birds with fangs like knives.

"Illusions!" he cried. "They're sending Wonderstone dreams against us!"

Others saw that too. The army was rallying, trying desperately to get into fighting formation.

But then in the swirling madness he caught sight of an angular yellow-and-black figure just in front of him, clutching a short sword in one bristly claw and a spear in another. A force of hjjks had come upon them under cover of these hallucinations and was beginning an attack.

Lashing out with his blade, the king slashed a breathing-tube, and turned and saw a second hjjk coming at him from the left. He caught it in its exposed knee-joint and sent it to the ground. On his other side Chham was thrusting away now at two other insect-warriors. One was down, the other staggering. Salaman grinned. Let them send dragons! Let them send earthquakes and oceans! When it came to hand-to-hand fighting, his troops would still slaughter them without mercy.

The illusions were continuing. Geysers of blood, fountains of coruscating light, whole mountains tumbling out of the air, sudden abysses opening a hand's-breadth away—there seemed no limit to their ingenuity. But so long as you ignore it all, Salaman thought, and simply keep your mind on the task of chopping down every hjjk that comes within reach of your weapon—

There! There! Strike, cut, kill!

The joy of battle was on him now as perhaps never before. He fought his way across the field, paying no heed to writhing serpents that floated before his face, to jeering luminous ghosts issuing from sulphurous crevices opening on every side, to disembodied eyes swirling about his head, to stampeding vermilions, to tumbling boulders. His warriors, rallied by Chham and Athimin, had formed themselves into three fighting wedges arranged in a circular pattern and were defending themselves well.

But what was this? *Biterulve* in the outermost arc of one of the wedges? That was against his explicit order. The boy was never to be exposed in that way. Athimin knew that. Let him fight in the secondary line, yes, but never in the prime row of warriors. Salaman looked around in fury. Where was Athimin? He was supposed to look after his brother at all times.

There he was, yes. Five or six men down the row from Biterulve, hacking away vigorously.

Salaman called to him and pointed. "Do you see him? Get over there! Get over to him, you fool!"

Athimin gasped and nodded. Biterulve seemed heedless of his own safety. He was striking at the hjjks in front of him with a ferocity that the king hadn't imagined he possessed. Athimin was turning now, fighting his way across the confusion, going to the boy's defense. Salaman came rushing forward also, intending to slay the hjjk closest to Biterulve and shove the boy deeper into the phalanx of warriors.

Too late.

Salaman was still twenty paces away, struggling through a zone of phantom monsters and murky black cloud, when he saw as though by a quick flash of lightning a hjjk that seemed twice the height of Thu-Kimnibol rise up before Biterulve and drive his spear through the boy's body from front to back.

The king let loose a terrible roar of rage. It seemed to him as though a hot bar of iron had been thrust through his forehead. In an instant he reached the spot where Biterulve lay and sent the hjjk's head flying across the field with one swift stroke. An instant later Athimin was blurting useless apologies and explanations into his ear, and unhesitatingly Salaman, turning on him the full force of the fury that possessed him, cut him down too with the stroke of his backswing, slashing him across his chest, deep through fur and flesh and bone.

"Father—?" Athimin murmured thickly, and fell at his feet.

Salaman stared. Biterulve lay to his left, Athimin at his right. His mind was unable to absorb the sight. His soul throbbed with unanswerable torment.

What have I done? What have I done?

Everywhere about him the battle raged; and the king stood silent and still, purged in one stunning instant of all madness and bloodlust. To his ears came the sounds of sobbing wounded warriors and the moans of the dying and the savage cries of those who still lived and fought, and it was all incomprehensible to him, that he should be here in this place at this time, with two of his sons dead on the ground before him, and phantoms and monsters dancing all about, and huge-eyed shrieking insect-creatures waving swords in his face. Why? For what?

Madness. Waste.

He stood frozen, bewildered, lost in pain.

Then he felt a searing flash of pain of a different sort as a hjjk weapon went lancing through the fleshy part of his arm. It was astonishing, the agony. Sudden hot tears stung his eyes. He blinked in confusion. A heavy mist shrouded his soul. For a moment, under the shock of his wound, the years rolled away and he thought that he was the ambitious young warrior again, nearly as clever as Hresh, whose scheme it was to build a great city and a dynasty and an empire. But if that was so, why was he in this old stiff body, why did he hurt like this, why was he bleeding? Ah. The hjjks! Yes, the hjjks were attacking their little settlement. Already Harruel had fallen. Everything looked hopeless. But there was no choice but to keep on fighting—to keep on fighting—

The mist parted and his mind cleared. Biterulve and Athimin lay before him on the ground and he was about to die himself. And there came to him with complete clarity an awareness of the futility of his life, the years spent in building a wall, in hating a distant and alien enemy who might better have simply been ignored.

He turned and saw the gleaming yellow-and-black creature studying him gravely, as though it had never seen a man of the People before. It was preparing to strike again.

"Go ahead," Salaman said. "What does it matter?"

"Father! Get back!"

Chham, that was. Salaman laughed. He pointed to his two fallen sons. "Do you see?" he said. "Biterulve was fighting in the front line. And then Athimin—Athimin—"

He felt himself being pushed aside. A sword cleaved the air in front of him. The hjjk fell back. Chham's face was close up against his own, now.

The same face as his: it was like looking into a mirror that reflected back through time.

"Father, you've been wounded."

"Biterulve—Athimin—"

"Here—let me help you—"

"Biterulve—"

Thu-Kimnibol said, "What? Salaman here? And his army?"

"What's left of them," said Esperasagiot. "It's a fearful sight, sir. You'd best ride out to meet them. They hardly seem to have the strength to come the rest of the way to us."

"Can this be some sort of trick?" Nialli Apuilana asked. "Does he hate us so much that he means to draw us out of our camp and attack us?"

Esperasagiot laughed. "No, lady, there's no hatred left in him. If you saw them, you'd know. They're a beaten bunch. It's a wonder any of them made it here alive."

"How far are they?" Thu-Kimnibol asked.

"Half an hour's ride."

"Get my xlendi ready. You, Dumanka, Kartafirain to accompany me, and ten warriors."

"Shall I go also?" Nialli Apuilana asked.

Thu-Kimnibol glanced at her. "You ought to stay with your father. They tell me he's very weak this morning. One of us should be with him if the end comes."

"Yes," she said softly, and turned away.

What remained of the army of the City of Yissou had made camp, more or less, beside a small stream in the open country a little way north of Thu-Kimnibol's encampment. Esperasagiot had not exaggerated: it was a fearful sight. Only a few hundred warriors, of the great horde that had set forth from Yissou, were there, and every one of them seemed to bear wounds. They were sprawled here and there like a scattering of cast-off garments on the ground, with three ragged tents behind them. As Thu-Kimnibol approached, a grim-faced man whom he recognized as Salaman's son Chham came limping out to greet him.

"A sad and sorry reunion this is, Prince Thu-Kimnibol. It shames me to come before you like this."

Thu-Kimnibol sought for words and did not find any. After a moment he reached down and embraced the other in silence, doing it gingerly, for fear of opening some wound.

"Can we do anything for you?" he asked.

"Healers. Medicines. Food. What we need most of all is rest. We've been in retreat for—I couldn't tell you how long. A week, two weeks? We kept no count."

"I'm saddened to see how badly things have gone for you."

Chham managed a momentary flare of vigor. "They went well enough at first. We beat them again and again. We killed them without mercy. My father fought like a god. Nothing could stand before his attack. But then—" He looked away. "Then the bug-folk used tricks against us. Wonderstone illusions, magical fantasies, things out of dreams. You'll see: they'll come at you the same way, when you next encounter them."

"So there was a battle of dreams. And a great defeat."

"Yes. A very great defeat."

"And your father the king?"

Chham jerked his hand over his shoulder, toward the largest of the tents. "He lives. But not so as you'd know him. My brother Athimin was killed, and Biterulve also."

"Ah. Biterulve too!"

"And my father was gravely wounded. But also he's changed within, very much changed. You'll see. We escaped by mere luck. A sudden windstorm came up. The air was full of sand. No way for the hjjks to see where we were. We crept away unnoticed. And here we are, Prince Thu-Kimnibol. Here we are."

"Where is the king?"

"Come: I'll take you to him."

The withered, feeble man who lay on the pallet within the tent was not much like the Salaman that Thu-Kimnibol had known. His white fur was matted and dull. In places it had fallen out completely. His eyes too were dull, those wide-set gray eyes that had pierced once like augers. Bandages swathed his upper body, which seemed shrunken and frail. He didn't appear to notice as Thu-Kimnibol entered. A thin old woman whom Thu-Kimnibol recognized as the chief offering-woman of the City of Yissou sat beside him, and holy talismans were piled up all around him.

"Is he awake?" Thu-Kimnibol whispered.

"He's like this all the time." Chham stepped forward. "Father, Prince Thu-Kimnibol has come."

"Thu-Kimnibol?" A faint papery whisper. "Who?"

"Harruel's son," Thu-Kimnibol said quietly.

"Ah. Harruel's boy. Samnibolon, that's his name. Does he call himself something else now? Where is he? Tell him to come nearer."

Thu-Kimnibol looked down at him. He could hardly bear to meet that burned-out gaze.

Salaman smiled. In the same faint voice he said, "And how is your father, boy? The good king, the great warrior Harruel?"

"My father is long dead, cousin," said Thu-Kimnibol gently.

"Ah. Ah, so he is." A flicker of brightness came into Salaman's eyes for a moment, and he tried to sit up. "They beat us, did Chham tell you?

I left two sons on the field, and thousands of others. They cut us to bits. No more than we deserved, that's the truth. What a foolishness it was, making war on them, marching like idiots into their own land! It was madness and nothing but madness. I see that now. And perhaps you do too, Samnibolon. Eh? Eh?"

"I've been called Thu-Kimnibol these many years."

"Ah. Of course. Thu-Kimnibol." Salaman managed a kind of smile. "Will you continue the war, Thu-Kimnibol?"

"Until victory is ours, yes."

"There'll never be any victory. The hjjks will drive you back the way they did me. They'll drown you in dreams." Slowly, with obvious effort, Salaman shook his head. "The war was a mistake. We should have taken their treaty and drawn a line across the world. I see that now, but now's too late. Too late for Biterulve, too late for Athimin, too late for me." He laughed hollowly. "But do as you wish. For me the war's over. All I want now is the forgiveness of the gods."

"Forgiveness? For what?" Thu-Kimnibol said, his voice rising suddenly above a sickroom murmur for the first time.

Chham tugged at Thu-Kimnibol's arm, as though to tell him that the king did not have the strength for such discussions. But Salaman said, his voice louder now too, "For what? For leading my warriors off to be cut to pieces in this filthy land. And for sending my Acknowledgers to their doom, and the army that followed them also, all for the sake of stirring up a war that should never have been fought. The gods didn't mean us to strike at the hjjks. The hjjks are the gods' creatures as much as we are. I have no doubt of that now. So I have sinned; and for that I will undertake a purification, and by the grace of Mueri and Friit I will have it before I die. I should ask the forgiveness of the Queen as well, I suppose. But how would I do that?" Salaman reached up and caught Thu-Kimnibol by the wrist with surprising strength. "Will you give me an escort home, Thu-Kimnibol? A few dozen of your troops, to help us retrace our steps across all this miserable wasteland that we've crossed at such cost. To bring me back to my city, so that I can go before the gods in the shrine that I built for them long ago, and pray them give me peace. That's all I ask of you."

"If you wish it, yes. Of course."

"And will you pray for me, also, as you go onward toward the Nest? Pray for the repose of my spirit, Thu-Kimnibol. And I'll do the same for yours."

He closed his eyes. Chham gestured, beckoning Thu-Kimnibol from the tent.

Outside Chham said, "He's beside himself with guilt for my brothers' deaths. His soul is flooded with remorse, for that, for everything in his life that he sees now as a sin. I never knew a man could be so changed in a single moment."

"He'll have his escort home, you can be sure of that."

Chham smiled sadly. "He'll never see Yissou again. Two, three days—that's all he has, so the healer tells me. We'll put him to rest in hjjk country. As for those of us that remain—" He shrugged. "We're willing to put ourselves under your command for the rest of the war. If you'll have us, broken as we are. Or if you won't, we'll limp back to our city and wait to hear how you've fared."

"Join us, of course," Thu-Kimnibol said. "Join us and fight alongside us, if you have the strength to go on. Why would we refuse you? We are meant to be allies always, your city and mine."

Darkness was coming quickly on. Nialli Apuilana knelt beside her father. Thu-Kimnibol stood well back from them, in the shadows where the glowglobes couldn't reach.

"Take this amulet from around my throat," Hresh whispered. "Put it on."

Nialli Apuilana's hands tightened into fists. She knew what must be in Hresh's mind. He had worn that amulet all his life: she had never seen him without it. To give it to her now—

She glanced toward Thu-Kimnibol. He nodded. Do it, he said silently. Do it.

Unfastening the cord that held the amulet, she drew it gently free. It was a little thing, just a bit of smooth green glass, or so it seemed, with signs inscribed on it that were much too small for her to decipher. It seemed very old and worn. She felt an odd chill coming from it; but when she tied it around her neck she was aware of a faint tingling, and a distant warmth.

She stared at it, resting between her breasts.

"What does it do, father?"

"Very little, I think. But it was Thaggoran's, who was chronicler before me. A piece of the Great World, is what he told me. It's the chronicler's badge of office, I suppose. Sometimes it summons Thaggoran for me, when I need him. You have to wear it now."

"But I—"

"You are chronicler now," Hresh said.

"What? Father, I have no training! And the chronicler has never been a woman."

Hresh managed the bare outlines of a smile. "All that's changing now. Everything is. Chupitain Stuld will work with you. And Io Sangrais and Plor Killivash, if they live through the war. The chronicles must stay in our family." He reached for her hand and clutched it tightly. His fingers seemed tiny, she thought. He was becoming a child again. He opened his eyes for a moment and said, "I never expected to have a daughter, you know. To have any child at all."

"And to think, father, how much grief I've caused you!"

"Never. Only joy, child. You must believe that." His hand grew even tighter on hers. "I've always loved you, Nialli. And I always will. You'll send my love to Taniane, won't you? My partner all these years. My mate. How sad she'll be. But she mustn't be. I'll be sitting beside Dawinno, asking him so many things." He paused. "Is my brother here?"

"Yes."

"I thought he was. Send him to me."

But Thu-Kimnibol was already on his way to Hresh's side. He knelt and reached out his hand, and Hresh touched it, very lightly, fingertips to fingertips. "Brother," he murmured. "I'll carry your love to Minbain for you. And now you must go out. What follows must be just for Nialli and me. She can tell you afterward, if she likes."

Thu-Kimnibol nodded. Lightly, lovingly, he let his hand rest a moment on Hresh's forehead, as though he hoped the wisdom would pass into him at a touch. Then he rose, and left the tent without looking back.

Hresh said, "At my side, under my sash, you'll find a little velvet pouch."

"Father—"

"Take it. Open it."

She let the small piece of polished stone tumble into her palm and stared at it in wonder. She had never handled it before. No one, so far as she knew, was permitted to touch it but Hresh. She had hardly ever been allowed even to see it. In some ways it was like the amulet he had just given her, for it was very smooth, and along its edges a pattern of lines had been carved into it, lines so fine that she couldn't clearly make out the pattern. It gave off a barely perceptible warmth. But the amulet had little mass or weight, and seemed only a flimsy thing. The Wonderstone, though scarcely any larger, felt as weighty as a world to Nialli Apuilana. It made her uneasy to hold it. The power that it contained was frightening.

Hresh said, "Do you know what that is?"

"The Barak Dayir, father."

"Yes. The Barak Dayir. But what the Barak Dayir is, not even I can say. The old Beng prophet told me that it is an amplifier, which means that which makes something greater than it is. As I told you once, it was the humans who once ruled the Earth that made it, before the Great World ever was. And gave it to us, to protect us when they would no longer be here. That's all I know of it. You must keep it, now. And master the art of using it."

"But how will I—"

"Twine with me, Nialli."

Her eyes widened. "Twine—with—you, father?"

"You must. No harm can come of it, and much good. And when we are joined, take the Barak Dayir and place it by the tip of your sensing-organ, and seize it and grasp it tightly. You'll hear a music, then. And I'll help you after that. Will you do that, Nialli?"

"Of course I will."

"Come closer, then."

She cradled him in her arms. He weighs almost nothing now, she thought. All that remains of him now is the husk, and the mind that burns within it.

"Your sensing-organ, close to mine—"

"Yes. Yes."

It was a communion Nialli Apuilana had never expected to have. But the moment her sensing-organ touched his, all fear and uncertainty went from her; and it was with almost unimaginable joy that she felt the rich torrent of his spirit come flooding into hers. It was a joy so great that it dizzied her and for a moment it swept her away; but then she remembered the Wonderstone, and carefully she curled the tip of her sensing-organ around it and gripped it with all her strength. The world turned to mist. A column of music rose beneath her. A great overwhelming chord of love buoyed her upward, carrying her soul toward the sky.

But Hresh was beside her, smiling at her tenderly, serenely, holding her, steadying her, guiding her. Together they soared across the vault of the heavens. A great golden glow was streaming from the west, a brilliant outpouring of dazzling radiance, darkening now into a stunning crimson, and then into rich deep scarlet, and then to silky purple. The darkness was beginning to reach out for him. But as they journeyed toward that waiting realm, he offered her a final sharing, the gift of his light, his love, his wisdom. He told her in a single unbroken flow all that she must know, until he could tell her no more.

So now it begins, Hresh thinks. The last journey of all. The world is growing dark around him.

Nialli, he thinks. Minbain. Taniane.

The vortex comes whirling up to claim him. He stares into it.

Is that where I'm going? What will it be like? Will I feel anything? Will I be able to taste and smell? If only I could see a little more clearly—

Ah. That's better, now. But how strange it looks in there. Is that you, Torlyri? Thaggoran? How strange it all is!

Mother. Nialli. Taniane.

Oh, look, Taniane! Look!

When she emerged from the tent she found Thu-Kimnibol with Chham. The two men broke off their conversation as she approached, and looked at her strangely, as though she had been transformed into some unworldly creature of a kind they had never before beheld.

"How is it with your father?" Thu-Kimnibol asked.

"He's with Dawinno now." She was dry-eyed and oddly calm.

"Ah." A shiver passed through Thu-Kimnibol's massive frame, and he made the Five Heavenly Signs, slowly and deliberately, twice through, and Dawinno's sign a third time afterward. "There was no one like him ever," he said after a while, in a splintered voice. "We had the same mother, but I tell you I never truly felt myself his brother, because he was what he was. His mind was almost like a god's. How will it be for us without him, I wonder?"

Nialli Apuilana held out her hand to show him the Barak Dayir in it in its pouch.

"I have the Wonderstone," she said. "And I have much of Hresh within me now too. You heard him say that I'm to be the chronicler? I am to be Hresh for us now, if I can. I'll say the words for him tonight, and we'll put what remains of him to rest. But he is already with Dawinno."

"He was always with Dawinno, lady," said Chham suddenly. "Or so it was reported of him, that he walked with the gods from the day of his birth. Surely it was so. I wouldn't doubt it, though I never knew him myself. What a day of great losses this has been!"

Thu-Kimnibol said, "King Salaman has died this day also. Prince Chham—King Chham, is it now?—has just come from him."

"Then we mourn together," Nialli Apuilana said. "When I say the words for my father, I'll say them also for yours."

"If you will, lady. It would please me greatly."

"We will lay them here side by side, in this forlorn place," said Thu-Kimnibol. "Which will be forlorn no more, because Salaman and Hresh were buried here. They were the two wisest men in all the world."

Taniane, resting her left hand on the Mask of Koshmar and her right on that of Lirridon, fought back the numbness that had been growing in her soul all afternoon, a strange disagreeable coldness behind her breastbone; and with such strength as she could muster she compelled herself to follow what Puit Kjai was trying to tell her.

"An insurrection, you say? Against me?"

"Against us all, lady. An uprising that's meant to sweep away all those who hold power in the City of Dawinno."

She gave him a weary, skeptical look. "Does anyone hold power any more in the City of Dawinno, Puit Kjai?"

"Lady! Lady, what are you saying?"

Taniane glanced away. The eerie force of Puit Kjai's intense scarlet eyes was more than she wanted to meet this day. She had lived with this weariness of soul for what seemed like years, but today it seemed to have deepened almost to paralysis.

She stroked the masks. Once they had hung on the wall behind her;

but some time back, not long after the departure of Nialli Apuilana to the war and the disappearance of Hresh, she had taken them down and put them on the desk beside her, where she could see them easily and touch them when she wished. They gave her comfort and, she thought, strength. In the time of the cocoon, Boldirinthe once had told her, there had been a certain black stone mounted in the wall of the central chamber that had been sacred to the memory of the tribe's former chieftains. Koshmar used to touch that stone and pray to her predecessors when she was facing difficulties. That black stone had remained behind in the cocoon when the tribe made its Coming Forth. Taniane wished she had it now. But at least she had the masks.

To Puit Kjai she said, after a little while, "All right, go on. Who are the ringleaders of this insurrection?"

"That I cannot say."

"But you're certain that one is being planned."

Puit Kjai shrugged. "The word comes out of the chapels, from the common people. It reaches me from the daughter of the nephew of an old groom in my son's stables, who worships in the chapel of Tikharein Tourb."

"The daughter of the nephew of a groom—"

"A tenuous chain, yes. What I'm told is that they mean to kill Thu-Kimnibol when he returns from the wars, unless the hjjks do it first, and that they will put you to death also, and me, and most of the rest of the Presidium, except those who they'll keep alive to go before the city as rulers in their name. And then they'll make peace with the hjjks and beg their forgiveness."

"You say this as though you never wanted peace with the hjjks yourself, Puit Kjai."

"Not this way. Not by a violent purging of the highborn. And this is no fantasy, lady, this talk of a conspiracy. They may already, I suspect, have done away with Hresh."

"No," Taniane said at once. "Hresh still lives."

"Does he? Where is he, then?"

"Far from here, I think. But I know that he lives. There's a bond between us, Puit Kjai, that transcends all distance. I feel him close beside me no matter how far away he may be. No harm has come to Hresh. Of that I'm certain."

"Nakhaba grant that it be so," Puit Kjai said.

They faced each other in silence for a time. The powerful old Beng leader stood so tall that his helmeted head neared the ceiling. He was gaunt and thin, but there was a majesty about his very gauntness. Dimly Taniane remembered Puit Kjai's father, the ancient wise one of the Helmet People, Noum om Beng, to whom Hresh had gone for wisdom. Puit Kjai was coming to look like him now: that same frail but stern bearing, his great height compensating for the slenderness of his frame. His helmet today was a black one, with gnarled golden antlers rising from it.

At length Taniane said, "I'll look into these rumors. If you hear anything more, come to me immediately."

"You have my word on it, lady."

He offered her a blessing of Nakhaba, and went out.

She sat quietly, her hands resting on the masks.

No doubt there was truth to the story he had brought to her. The Kundalimon creed ran wild in the city these days: why shouldn't its leaders attempt to force an end to the war? There was no one to oppose them here. Thu-Kimnibol and the rest of his faction were off at the battlefront, Hresh had disappeared, the younger men of the city seemed all to have entered the chapels. She herself no longer even pretended to exercise authority. It seemed to her that the world had passed her by, that events had gone on far beyond her understanding. Truly it was time for her to step aside, she thought. Just as the rock-throwers had told her even before the war. But in favor of whom? Give the city over to the Kundalimon priests? She wished Thu-Kimnibol would return. But he was off killing hjjks, or perhaps being killed by them himself. And Nialli Apuilana was with him.

Taniane shook her head. She was tired of living in this chaos. She was eager for rest.

And this other thing, this strange numbness that had entered her breast today—what was that? As though she were being hollowed out from within. Some illness, was it? She remembered how in Vengiboneeza Koshmar had begun suddenly to seem easily tired, had admitted to Hresh that there was a burning in her chest, pain, fever; and soon afterward she was dead. Now her own hour might be coming around, Taniane thought. She wondered if she should go to Boldirinthe for a healing; and then she remembered that Boldirinthe was dead. One by one they were all dying. Koshmar, Torlyri, Boldirinthe—

All she felt was a numbness, though, not a burning, not a pain. She couldn't understand it. She turned her gaze inward, searching for the cause of it.

But just in that moment it went from her, all at once: that numbness, that deepening ache that had plagued her since daybreak. She felt it go, a sudden startling cessation of discomfort, like the snapping of a tight bond. Then in its place was something even more troublesome: an absence, a bleak emptiness, sharp and painful, a terrible black void. She understood immediately what it was, and a chill ran through her that set her fur on end. Helplessly she began to weep. Wave after wave of grief swept over her. For the first time in more than forty years she could not feel the presence of Hresh within her. He was gone. Gone forever.

* * *

Under a glittering pockmarked moon the battlefield had the icy serene look of an immense glacier, even where the ground was cratered and upturned by the most recent round of fighting. Thu-Kimnibol's warriors crept about warily on the broken earth, collecting the bodies of those who had fallen that day. Nialli Apuilana looked past them to the horizon, where she could see the bonfires of the hjjk camp. There was a respite now; but in the morning it would all begin again.

Thu-Kimnibol laughed harshly. "A war of nightmares," he said. "We hurl flame and turbulence at them. They throw illusions at us. We return counterillusions of our own. Enemies who can't see one another, blindly stumbling around."

She could feel his fatigue. He had fought ferociously this day, rallying his troops in every part of the field as phantom after phantom came toward them, even as Salaman had warned. Repeatedly he had led his forces through some field of spurting fire, or some onrushing horde of sinister monsters, through flood and avalanche, through a rain of blood, through a hail of daggers. His goal was to maneuver himself into a position where he could work real damage against the hjjks with his Great World weapons; but they understood that now, and danced about him, hiding themselves behind illusions and nibbling at his forces from ambush. She had done what she could, wielding the Wonderstone to cut through the screen of hjjk hallucinations and to confuse them with projected phantoms of her own. But it had been a difficult day, an inconclusive day. And tomorrow promised more of the same.

"Were our losses very bad today?" Nialli Apuilana asked.

"Not as bad as it seemed at first. A dozen killed, perhaps fifty wounded. Some of those who died were Chham's people, of the few that remain. The City of Yissou will be a broken place for years. A whole generation has been destroyed."

"And the City of Dawinno?"

"We haven't suffered the way Yissou has. They lost virtually an entire army in a single day."

"Whereas we're losing ours a few at a time. But in the end it'll be the same, won't it, Thu-Kimnibol?"

He gave her an enigmatic look. "Shall we surrender, then?"

"What do you say?"

"I say that if we fight, they'll whittle us away to nothing no matter how much injury we inflict on them, and if we don't fight, we'll lose our souls. I say that time is against us, and that I find myself lost in confusions and mysteries as never before in my life." He looked away from her, and stared into his open hands as though he hoped to read oracles in them. When he spoke again, it was clear he had not found them. "It seems to me, Nialli, that I lead this campaign in two directions at once. I go rushing forward eager to blast the hjjks before me as we blasted Vengiboneeza, and go riding onward to destroy the Nest and everything it contains. And yet at the same time a part of me is pulling back, urging retreat, praying for an end to the war before I harm the Queen. Can you understand what it's like to be torn in such a way?"

"I felt it myself, once. The spell of the Nest is very powerful."

"Is that why Hresh took me there, do you think? To hand me over to the Queen?"

Nialli Apuilana shook her head. "He only wanted you to see every side of the conflict. To undertand that the hjjks are dangerous but not evil, that there's greatness in them, but of a kind very far from anything we can comprehend. But when you touch the Nest it makes itself a part of you, and you a part of it. I know. It was like that for me, far more deeply, even, than I think it is for you. Remember, I was of the Nest myself."

"Yes. I know."

"And freed myself. But not completely. I'll never free myself completely. The Queen will always be within me."

Thu-Kimnibol's eyes flashed. "And is She within me also?" he cried, with anguish in his voice.

"I think that She is."

"Then how can I fight this war, if my enemy is part of me, and I'm part of Her?"

She hesitated a moment. "There's no way that you can."

"I despise the hjjks. I mean to destroy them!"

"Yes, you do. But you'll never allow yourself to do it."

"Then I'm lost, Nialli! All of us are!"

She looked off into the shadows. "This is the great test that the gods have sent us, do you see? There's no easy resolution. My father thought that we and the hjjks could enter into some sort of unity, that we could live harmoniously with them, side by side, as the sapphire-eyes and the rest lived with them in the Great World. But he was wrong, wise as he was. As I freed myself from the Queen's spell he was starting to fall under it; and he was swallowed up in it. This isn't the Great World, though. Assimilation of two such alien races is impossible. It's the natural desire of the hjjks to achieve absorption, domination. The best we can hope for is to hold them at bay, as perhaps they were held at bay by the other races in the time of the Great World."

"Why not destroy them altogether?"

"Because it's probably beyond us to do any such thing. And because if somehow we did, it would be at a terrible cost to our own souls."

He shook his head. "Is the best we can hope for a mere stand-off, then? A line drawn across the world, hjjks here, People there?"

"Yes."

"As the Queen originally proposed. Why did we resist it, then? We could simply have accepted Her treaty, and spared ourselves all this outlay of lives and toil."

"Not so," said Nialli Apuilana. "You forget an important thing. She proposed not just a division of territory, but also to send Nest-thinkers to live among us and spread Her truths and Her plan. In time they would bring us to embrace Queen-love; and that would deliver us forever into Her power. She'd control us all, as She controlled Kundalimon, as She controlled me. She'd regulate our rate of population increase, so there'd never be so many of us that we interfered with Her designs. She would designate the acceptable locations of any new cities we might build, to keep most of the world free for Her people. That was what the treaty would have done. What we must have is the boundary line, but not the infiltration of Nest-thinkers into our lives. There has already been too much of that."

"Then the war must go on until She is beaten. And then we have to eradicate every trace of Queen-worship in our city." He turned away from her and began to pace the tent. "Gods! Will there ever be an end to all this?"

Nialli Apuilana smiled. "We can make an end to it for tonight, at least."

"What do you mean?"

She moved closer to him in the darkness. "This night we can allow ourselves a little time out of war, just for each other." Her sensing-organ rose and moved tentatively against his. He shivered and seemed almost to draw back from her, as though unable to free himself from the doubts and turmoil that had engulfed him; but she stayed close by him, easing him gently out of his disquiet and apprehension. After a moment she could feel the tension begin to leave him. He came close to her, rising like a mountain above her, and encircled her with his arms. She took his hands and placed them over her breasts. They stood that way for a time, allowing the communion to build; and then they sank down slowly together, entwined in body and soul, and lay in each other's arms through the rest of the night.

It's the hour before dawn, now. Thu-Kimnibol is still deep in dreams. His massive chest rises and falls evenly, his sword-arm is flung casually across his face. Nialli Apuilana kisses him lightly and slips away from his side, going to the opposite end of the tent they share.

There she kneels and whispers the name of Yissou the Protector, and makes his sign, and then says the name of Dawinno the Destroyer, who is also Dawinno the Transformer, and makes his sign as well. She feels their presence entering her and gives thanks for it.

She touches then the amulet that nestles in the thick fur between her breasts, and calls upon her father; and after a while she sees him, shining in the darkness before her, the familiar smile on his familiar sharp-chinned face. There's someone else behind him, a much older man, white-furred and sunken-chested. Nialli Apuilana doesn't know him, but his presence seems benign. And deeper in the darkness is still another venerable stranger, a withered old Beng so thin and tall that he seems nothing more than an elongated straw that any breeze might blow away.

Now she draws the Barak Dayir from its pouch and touches it briefly to her forehead in a sign of respect, and grips it firmly with her sensing-organ.

The music rises within her. It carries her toward the heights of the world.

She climbs easily, confidently, fearing nothing: for isn't Yissou with her, and Dawinno, and her father also? Only when she's aloft, and the world is no more than a speck beneath her, does she feel the first tremor of concern. It would be so easy to go on and on from here, forever upward into that sphere of the unknown that surrounds the world, outward and outward and outward among the comets and the moons and the stars: and never to return. All she has to do is cut the mooring that blinds her to the Earth. But that's not what she's about to do.

What she seeks is the Queen: the Queen of Queens, indeed, in Her lair at the Nest of Nests, in the cold bleak northlands.

She focuses her mind and propels it forward. At first she feels a moment of uncertainty, a curious doubleness of destination. The Queen seems to be in two places at once, one of them distant and one very close at hand. Nialli Apuilana doesn't know what to make of that. But then she understands. The memory arises in her of that terrible time after Kundalimon's death and her own flight into the wilderness, when she had hidden herself in her room and struggled with all that possessed her spirit. The Queen had been within her then; and the Queen has remained within her to this day. That dark presence had never relinquished its place at the heart of her soul.

But that Queen within her is only the shadow of the true one. It's the Queen Herself, and not the shadow, with whom she has to deal today.

"Do you know me?" she calls. "I am Nialli Apuilana, daughter of Hresh."

And out of the depths of the Nest of Nests comes an answer from the great motionless pallid thing that lies hidden there.

"I know you. What do you want with Me?"

"To negotiate with you."

Derisive laughter rings down upon her like a hail of fire. "Only equals can negotiate, little one." And from the Queen comes a storm of power that makes the air shiver and bend upon itself, so that Nialli Apuilana can see the roots of the world showing through the fabric of the atmosphere.

But she will not let herself be swayed.

"You have a Wonderstone," Nialli Apuilana says. "I have a Wonderstone. We are equals, therefore."

"Are we?"

"Can You harm me?"

"Can you harm Me?" the Queen says.

Bolts of blue flame arch upward from the Nest. They dance and swirl about Nialli Apuilana in frenzied weaving motions, looking for a vulnerable place. She brushes them away as though they're gnats.

The Queen sends a storm of boulders. The Queen sends a wall of fire. The Queen sends a cloud of searing mist.

"You waste Your time. Do You think I'm a child, who can be frightened this way? What the Wonderstone sends, the Wonderstone can turn aside. We can spend all day threatening each other like this, and nothing will be achieved."

"What is it that you hope to achieve?"

"Let me show You a vision," says Nialli Apuilana.

From the Queen, after a moment, comes grudging assent.

From Nialli Apuilana to the Queen goes an image of the terrain that surrounds the Nest of Nests, as she knows it must be, though she had never seen it with her own eyes: hard sparse plains, broad endless grayness under an unforgiving sky. She draws it from the soul of Kundalimon that is still within her. Kundalimon had lived in the Nest of Nests. She shows the Queen the dry puckered soil, the pitiless saw-edged grass, the small vicious creatures that scrabble fiercely for their livelihoods in that remote and dreadful land.

And then she shows Her the dark mouths of the Nest gaping here and there in the plain, and the barely perceptible rise of the Nest itself, a faint humped swelling beneath the surface of the land, myriad corridors running off in every direction.

"Do You recognize this place?" Nialli Apuilana asks.

"Go on."

Now Nialli Apuilana shows the Queen the armies of the People advancing from east and west and south: not merely the force that Thu-Kimnibol had brought with him from Dawinno, but the warriors of all the Seven Cities of the continent, from Yissou and Thisthissima and Gharb, from Ghajnsielem, from Cignoi, from Bornigrayal, every tribe of every land, all of them united here in one cataclysmic outpouring of joined strength. And there, rising above that multitude like the tallest tree of the forest, is Thu-Kimnibol of Dawinno; and in his hand is one of the weapons of the Great World. The chieftain of Gharb has a similar weapon, and that of Cignoi, and all the others; and they hold them trained on the Nest of Nests.

Hjjks come streaming now from the Nest, the finest of the Queen's Militaries; and as they rush toward the invaders Thu-Kimnibol and the other chieftains raise their weapons high, and bright light flares and a clap like the sound of the world's final thunder sounds, and the plains are swept by fire and the Militaries fall, crisped like twigs in a firestorm. And the armies of the Seven Cities move onward toward the Nest.

They surround it now. They peer down into each of its many mouths. They raise their weapons high once again and touch the studs that bring them to life.

And force leaps from those gleaming ancient devices, an invincible force that rips the earth apart and lifts the roof from the Nest, stripping it bare, revealing the corridors and passages and channels so painstakingly constructed over so many hundreds of thousands of years. In that terrible glare all the Egg-layers and the Life-kindlers stand revealed, and the Nest-thinkers, and the uncountable hordes of workers; and they perish in the first blasts. Then the deadly power descends into deeper, more tender places, where the Nourishment-givers are holding the newborn to their mouths to give them food; and they die also, Nourishment-givers and newborn both, in the next wave of the onslaught.

And then, deeper yet, to the deepest cavern of all—

To the place where the Queen Herself lies hidden, but hidden no longer, for a flick of force has stripped the roof of Her chamber away and Her pale immense body is exposed and defenseless, while desperate Queen-attendants cluster close about Her and frantically brandish their weapons in vain. Thu-Kimnibol looms above Her, grasping a small sphere of shining metal from which a sudden amber light comes forth. And the Queen quivers and convulses and pulls away from that hot probing pressure. But where can She go, in that close chamber? Remorselessly the amber light plays up and down the length of Her. Huge bubbles and blisters begin to appear on the charred and blackening surface of Her. Black smoke rises from Her as She sizzles and crisps under that merciless amber beam. Until—

Until—

"This could never occur," comes the cold voice of the Queen.

"Are You so certain? Vengiboneeza lies in ashes. The dead bodies of the insect-folk litter the plains already for hundreds of leagues. And we have only begun."

"You are small-souled creatures. You would turn away in terror long before you reached us."

"Are You absolutely certain of that?" asks Nialli Apuilana. "Could small-souled creatures have built our cities? Could small-souled creatures have fought You as we've fought You thus far? I tell You: we have only begun."

There is a silence.

The Queen says at length, "I know you. You are of the Nest, girl. You were one of us, and then I sent you from the Nest, back to your own kind: but I meant to have you serve Me there, not to oppose Me. Why these threats? How can you utter such things? Queen-love is still within you."

"Is it?"

"I know that it is. You are mine, child. You are of the Nest, and you can never do harm to it."

Nialli Apuilana doesn't reply. By way of answer she looks within herself, to that secret place in her soul where the Queen had placed a part of Herself long ago. And seizes it, and draws it out as though it were no more than a shallow splinter in her flesh, and hurls it from her. Down it tumbles through the many layers of the sky. And as it nears the surface of the world it bursts into flames and is consumed.

"Do You still think I am of the Nest?" Nialli Apuilana asks.

There's another great silence.

Once again now Nialli Apuilana shows the Queen the vision of the final war: the Nest ripped open, its inhabitants consumed by flames, the royal chamber despoiled, the vast charred body, split apart and ruined, dead in the smoking depths.

"You know nothing of what it is to die," says Nialli Apuilana. "You know nothing of pain. You know nothing of loss. You know nothing of defeat. But You'll learn. You'll perish in flame and agony; and the worst agony of all will be the knowledge that there is no way You can take revenge upon those who did this to You."

The Queen doesn't respond.

"It will happen," Nialli Apuilana says. "We are a determined people. The gods have shaped us to be what we are."

Silence.

"Well?" Nialli Apuilana says. "Is that Your answer? Is this what You'd have us do? Because I tell You that we will do it, if You won't give us what we ask."

Silence. Silence.

The Queen says at length, "What is it, then, that you want?"

"An end to the war. A truce between our peoples. A line drawn between Your lands and ours, never to be violated."

"These are your only terms?"

"Our only terms, yes," says Nialli Apuilana.

"And the alternative?"

"War to the death. With no quarter given."

"You deceive yourself if you think there can ever be peace between us," says the Queen.

"But there can be an absence of war."

There is one last silence. It seems to stretch on forever.

"Yes," replies the Queen finally. "There can be an absence of war. So be it. I grant you what you ask. There will be an absence of war."

It was done. Nialli Apuilana bade the Queen farewell, and in a single moment withdrew from the high realm, sweeping swiftly downward toward the breast of the land, where dawn now had begun to glow. She relinquished her grasp on the Barak Dayir and sat up. She was back in the tent that she shared with Thu-Kimnibol.

He was just beginning to stir. He looked over at her and smiled.

"How strange. I slept like a child, lost to the world. And I dreamed the war was over. That a truce had been agreed on between ourselves and the Queen."

"It was no dream," said Nialli Apuilana.

10

The Queen of Springtime

The day was bright and fair, with a cool pleasant wind blowing out of the west, a sea-breeze, always a good omen. Taniane arose early, and went to the Temple of the Five to express her gratitude for the safe return of the army and to ask the gods' blessings for the time to come; and then, for she was the chieftain of all the people, she went also to the Temple of Nakhaba and made her obeisance to the god of the Bengs. Afterward she called for her wagon of state, with four fine white xlendis to draw it, and made ready to ride out to the Emakkis Gate at the northern end of the city, where a great reviewing stand had been erected so that the chieftain and the Presidium could properly greet the troops as they arrived. She had the Mask of Koshmar with her, the shining black one that she sometimes wore on high occasions of state. This day seemed worthy of Koshmar's mask.

Runners had been carrying word of the return for four days, now, stumbling breathless into the city with reports of the army's southward progress. "They're in Tik-haleret now!" came the cry, and almost at once, "They've reached Banarak," and then, "No! They're approaching Ghomino!" Thu-Kimnibol, the messengers said, rode proudly at the head of the column, with Nialli Apuilana beside him, and all the troops stretching on and on behind them as far as anyone could see.

Thu-Kimnibol had sent messengers of his own ahead as well, announcing the truce that had brought the war to its end. From the messengers, too, came the first official word of the death of Hresh. Which only confirmed what Taniane already knew, for she had not felt the presence of Hresh in the world since that day of strange numbness when Puit Kjai had come to her with his tales of insurrection; but it was hard news all the same. King Salaman also was dead, they said, dead of grief and weariness, after a great loss at the hands of the hjjks.

Taniane wondered what Hresh had been doing up there in hjjk country at the battlefront. That was the last place where she would have expected him to go. But evidently Hresh had remained Hresh to the very end, a law unto himself. Perhaps she would get the explanation of his mysterious final journey from Nialli Apuilana later.

Old Staip, trembling and unsteady, stood to Taniane's left as she took her position on the reviewing stand. Simthala Honginda and Catiriil were beside him. Puit Kjai was at her right, and Chomrik Hamadel next to him, both of them grandly helmeted. Before them, occupying the outer rim of the stand's lower level, was an array of city guardsmen led by Chevkija Aim.

One by one the other members of the Presidium mounted the stand. Taniane greeted them as they appeared. A crowd was gathering below.

Puit Kjai leaned his head toward hers and said quietly, "Be on your guard, lady. I think your enemies may well choose this day to make trouble."

"Have you any proof of that?"

"Whisperings, only."

Taniane shrugged. "Whisperings!"

"Such whisperings very often carry truth, lady."

She pointed into the distance, where she thought she saw a far-off cloud of gray dust rising over the highway. "In a little while Thu-Kimnibol will be here," she said. "And my daughter, and an army of their loyal followers. No one's going to dare to make trouble with a force like that heading this way."

"Be on your guard all the same."

"I'm always on my guard," Taniane said, running her fingers uneasily over the smooth shining surface of Koshmar's mask. She glanced around. "Husathirn Mueri isn't here. He's the only one. Why is that?"

"I think he's likely to get very little joy from Thu-Kimnibol's triumphant return."

"He's a prince of the Presidium, all the same. His place is here among us." She turned and beckoned to Catiriil. "Your brother!" she called sharply. "Where is he?"

"He said he'd be going to his chapel first. But he'll be here in time. I'm sure that he will."

"He'd better be," Taniane said.

Husathirn Mueri had risen early that day also. It had been a long night for him, fitful rest at best, and he was glad enough to leave his bed at dawn. His dreams, when he'd been able to sleep at all, had been oppressive ones: chanting hjjk warriors filing round and round him in the darkness and the Queen's crushing bulk, monstrous and bloated and pale, hovering over him like a titanic weight slowly falling from the sky.

The early service was already under way at the chapel when he arrived. Tikharein Tourb was presiding, with Chhia Kreun beside him at the altar. Husathirn Mueri slipped into the seat at the rear that he usually occupied. Chevkija Aim, deep in his devotions, gave him a perfunctory nod. The others nearby took no notice. By now it was no extraordinary thing to have a prince of the city present in a chapel.

"This is the day of revelation," the boy-priest was saying. "This is the day when the seals are broken and the book is opened, and the secrets are brought forth, and the depths give up their mystery. This is the day of the Queen; and She is our comfort and our joy."

"She is our comfort and our joy," the congregation replied automatically, and Husathirn Mueri said it with them.

"She is the light and the way," cried Tikharein Tourb, making hjjk-clicks as he spoke, and the congregation, clicking in response, echoed his words.

"She is the essence and the substance."

"She is the essence and the substance."

"She is the beginning and the end."

"She is the beginning and the end."

Chhia Kreun brought green boughs forward, and Tikharein Tourb held them aloft.

"This is the day, dear friends, when the will of the Queen is made known. This is the day when Her love will be made manifest upon us all. This is the day when the dragon devours the dark stars, and brightness is reborn. And She will be among us; and She is our comfort and our joy."

"She is our comfort and our joy."

"She is the light and the way—"

Husathirn Mueri responded with the others, dutifully repeating the phrases when he heard the cues; but the words were no more than empty formulas for him today. Perhaps they had never been more than that. This supposed religious conversion of his: he'd never fully understood it himself. Somehow he'd tricked himself into thinking he felt a glimmer of something greater than himself, something he could lose himself in. That must have been it. In any event his mind and soul were elsewhere now. He could think of nothing but Thu-Kimnibol, riding in glory through the farmlands north of the city, coming back from the war with some sort of victory to proclaim.

Victory? What had he done? Beaten the hjjks? Slain the Queen? None of that seemed remotely possible. Yet the word had preceded him: the war was over, peace had been achieved. By the heroic efforts of Thu-Kimnibol and Nialli Apuilana, and so forth and so forth—

That galled Husathirn Mueri more than anything: that by some strange trick of fate the unattainable Nialli Apuilana had been taken in mating by her own father's half-brother, the man Husathirn Mueri most loathed in all of Dawinno. He choked on the thought of that mating. Her sleek silken body against his huge coarse bulk. His hands on her thighs, her breasts. Their sensing-organs touching in the most intimate of—

No. Stop it.

He ordered himself not to think about them. All he was achieving was self-torture and despair. He fought to regain his inner equilibrium. But however he struggled to calm himself, no calmness would come. His mind was aswirl. Bad enough to have given herself to the hjjk ambassador, but then to go from Kundalimon to Thu-Kimnibol—! It was unthinkable. It was monstrous. That great lumbering vimbor. And her own kinsman, too.

Husathirn Mueri closed his eyes and tried to let thoughts of the Queen, the all-loving benevolent Queen, drive these tormenting visions of Nialli and Thu-Kimnibol from his mind. But there was no way he could pay attention to what the boy-priest was saying. Only empty noise, that was what it seemed like now. Hollow mumblings, weird magical nonsense.

Perhaps I never believed any of this, he thought. Love the Queen? What kind of madness is that, anyway?

What if I've been coming here only out of some sort of feeling of guilt? An expiation, perhaps, for what I did to Kundalimon?

The thought startled him. Could it be? He began to tremble.

Then Chevkija Aim leaned over and murmured, "Tikharein Tourb wants you to stay after the service."

Husathirn Mueri blinked and looked up. "What for?"

The guard-captain offered only a shrug. "He didn't say. But we aren't supposed to take part in the twining when the service ends. We're just supposed to wait."

"She is the essence and the substance," Tikharein Tourb called out.

"*She is the essence and the substance,*" the congregation replied. Husathirn Mueri forced himself to bellow forth the response with them.

He felt a little calmer now. Chevkija Aim, breaking in on him like that, had managed to pull him back from his feverish brooding. But he fidgeted as the string of litanies went on and on. He was due at the welcoming ceremony in a little while: the whole Presidium had to be there to hail the returning heroes. Much as he loathed the idea, he didn't dare to stay away, or it would seem he was too embittered to attend, and that would create trouble for him. But if Tikharein Tourb didn't hurry it up—

At last, though, the service was over, ending with the usual mass twinings. The faithful, when the intensity of their communions had lifted from them, filed silently out of the hall.

Husathirn Mueri and Chevkija Aim rose and went to the altar, where Tikharein Tourb waited for them.

The boy's eyes seemed more fiery even than usual today. His fur bristled with tension.

"It is just as I said in the service," he told Husathirn Mueri. "This is the day of the breaking of the seals. This is the day of the Queen. And you two are to be Her instruments."

Husathirn Mueri frowned. "I don't understand."

"The prince Thu-Kimnibol has brought shame upon the Queen. His life is already forfeit for the slaying of the holy Kundalimon; but now also he has intruded on the sanctity of the Nest of Nests and attempted to impose his will on Hers. For these and many other misdeeds the Queen has pronounced sentence of death on him, which you will carry out this day, Husathirn Mueri."

His breath left him as though he had been punched.

"You will strike him to the heart when he comes forth to be acclaimed. And you, Chevkija Aim—you will strike down Taniane in the same moment."

It was impossible to believe that this little demon was only a boy of ten or twelve.

"On the reviewing stand?" Husathirn Mueri said, astounded.

"In full view of everyone, yes. It will be the signal. The people then will rise up and slay the rest of the highborn ones before they can comprehend what is happening to them. The entire ruling caste must go, all the oppressors, all the enemies of the Queen—Staip, Chomrik Hamadel, Puit Kjai, Nialli Apuilana, all of them. In one quick moment. You alone will remain of all the Presidium, Husathirn Mueri." Tikharein Tourb grinned savagely. "In the new order of things you will become Nest-king here. Chevkija Aim will be Nest-warden."

"Nest-king?" Husathirn Mueri repeated dully. "I'll become Nest-king?"

"That is how we will call the worldly ruler, yes. And his chief of staff will be the Nest-warden. And I," said Tikharein Tourb, "will be your Nest-thinker, the voice of the Queen in the city called Dawinno." He laughed. "In the new order of things. Which you two will serve to bring into being, this very day."

Husathirn Mueri said, as they left the chapel, "You go on ahead. I need to change into my official robes."

Chevkija Aim nodded. "I'll see you on the reviewing stand, then."

"Yes." Reaching out, Husathirn Mueri caught Chevkija by the wrist and held him a moment. "One thing. Despite what Tikharein Tourb said just now, I want you to understand this: Nialli Apuilana is to be spared."

"But Tikharein Tourb specifically wants—"

"I don't give a gorynth's toenail for what he specifically wants. The whole crew of them can be slaughtered, for all I care. I'll be glad to wield the knife myself. But she lives. Is that understood, Chevkija Aim? If she turns out to be difficult afterward, she can always be killed then. But she's not to be touched when the killing starts. Have your guardsmen protect her. Or, by the Five, I'll see to it that any harm that comes to her is repaid fifty times over. Is that understood, Chevkija Aim?"

It seemed to Thu-Kimnibol that the entire population of the city had turned out to greet his homecoming warriors. They had built a huge wooden stand right in front of Emakkis Gate, big enough to hold all the members of the Presidium and many others besides. And all around it were hundreds, thousands, of citizens, a gigantic horde of them, just about everyone in Dawinno who hadn't gone off to the war.

His hand tightened on Nialli Apuilana's arm. "There's Taniane up there, do you see? And Staip, and Chomrik Hamadel, and that's Puit Kjai, I suppose, in the enormous helmet—"

"Simthala Honginda and Catiriil, too, over there on the right, with Staip. And isn't that Husathirn Mueri? I can hardly make him out, with that guardsman blocking the view, but those bright white stripes, that black fur—it has to be him."

"So it is. I think he'll be wearing a long face today."

"Where's Boldirinthe? She's not there, is she?"

"We'd see her if she were. But it would be a job, hauling her up on top of that platform."

"If she's still alive at all."

"Do you think—"

"She was old. She was ill."

"I pray that it's not so," Thu-Kimnibol said. But in his heart he suspected that Nialli Apuilana was right. This had been a season for the falling away of the great old ones.

A helmeted figure on a noble-looking gray xlendi came riding out toward them now, carrying the banner of the city. Thu-Kimnibol recognized him after a moment as the young highborn warrior Pelithhrouk, Simthala Honginda's protégé, who had been in his entourage during the embassy to King Salaman, what seemed like a million years ago. The memory drifted back to him now of the time Dumanka had killed and roasted the caviandis, and Pelithhrouk had spoken out so idealistically on the theme of the oneness of all intelligent creatures. To have Pelithhrouk, one of those who had argued most strongly for peace, ride out now as the official bearer of welcome was a good sign for the reconciliation that must now be brought about.

Pelithhrouk dismounted and looked up toward them.

"The chieftain sends her greetings. She bids me to escort you to the place of honor."

Thu-Kimnibol nodded to Nialli Apuilana. Together they stepped down from their wagon. Pelithhrouk smiled and spread his arms wide, and solemnly embraced them, Thu-Kimnibol first, then Nialli Apuilana, in a formal gesture of salute.

"What a fine day this is," Thu-Kimnibol murmured, as they followed Pelithhrouk toward the reviewing stand. Guardsmen kept the crowds back on either side. Banners fluttered everywhere. The sun, bright and warm, was high overhead. As they started up the steps to the platform above Nialli Apuilana reached for Thu-Kimnibol's hand. They interlaced their fingers.

A row of guardsmen waited there. Behind them were Taniane and all the city's notables in formal array. Time had dealt with them in a heavy way. The chieftain seemed no more than a gray ember of herself now, and Staip looked withered and ancient beyond belief, and the others too had aged startlingly, Puit Kjai, Chomrik Hamadel, Lespar Thone. Thu-Kimnibol wondered how he must look to them, after the long months of marching through distant bleak lands, the battles, the wounds he had taken.

But his mood was buoyant despite all that. The battles were done for now; he was returning with victory. And more than that. Often in days gone by he had felt himself oppressed by the great weight of the world's past, the vastness of it. Now, though, what he sensed was the exhilarating vastness of the future: its infinite possibilities, more to come than lay behind, world without end, many difficulties, many triumphs, many wonders not yet dreamed of, never imagined even in the greatest eras of the past. The world might be ancient but also it was ever new and young. The best was still to come.

He reached the top of the platform and halted there, facing the great ones of the city.

There was a moment when everyone stood utterly still, frozen in a solemn ceremonial tableau. Thu-Kimnibol, still holding Nialli Apuilana's hand, bowed his head toward them all. Were they waiting for him to speak first? Surely the first word belonged to the chieftain. He remained silent. Taniane held the burnished, gleaming Mask of Koshmar in her hands. She appeared to be about to don it. No one else moved.

Finally Taniane began to speak, her voice faltering a little: "The gods have brought you safely home. We rejoice, Thu-Kimnibol, in your victorious—"

An eruption of frantic action then, sudden, bewildering. The figure of Husathirn Mueri burst into view, emerging from behind Taniane and rushing toward Thu-Kimnibol. A knife gleamed in his upraised left hand.

In that same moment Chevkija Aim, sprinting up the three steps that separated the lower platform from the one where the notables stood, came running toward Husathirn Mueri from the side. He too carried a drawn blade.

"Lady, watch out!" the guard-captain shouted. "He's a traitor!"

And an instant later Husathirn Mueri and Chevkija Aim were tangled up together in a desperate struggle at the center of the platform. Thu-Kimnibol, too astonished to move, saw weapons flashing in the sun. There was a grunting sound of pain. A startling gout of blood spurted from Chevkija Aim's chest and ran down over his thick golden Beng fur. The guard-captain lurched forward, his arms jerking convulsively, his knife skittering across the platform and landing practically at Taniane's feet as he fell. Husathirn Mueri, his face contorted and wild, swung around a second time toward Thu-Kimnibol. But Nialli Apuilana stepped swiftly between them just as Husathirn Mueri raised his blade.

He gaped at her, aghast, and checked his blow before it could strike her. His eyes glazed as though he had been smitten by the gods. Recoiling from her with a moaning outcry of despair, he lowered his arm and let his weapon drop from suddenly nerveless fingers. By now Thu-Kimnibol had managed to make his way around Nialli Apuilana in the confusion and started toward him. But Husathirn Mueri had already turned and was staggering crazily toward the rear of the platform, heading for Taniane, who had picked up Chevkija Aim's knife and was studying it in wonder.

"Lady—" he muttered thickly. "Lady—lady—forgive me, lady—"

Thu-Kimnibol reached for him. Taniane waved him back. She stared at Husathirn Mueri as though he were an apparition.

In a dark anguished voice he said, "Kundalimon's death was my doing. And Curabayn Bangkea's as well, and all the grief that followed."

With a desperate sob he threw himself upon her as if to embrace her. Unhesitatingly Taniane's arm came forward, rising swiftly toward Husathirn Mueri's rib cage in a single sharp jab. He stiffened and gasped. Clutching his middle, he took a couple of reeling steps back from her. For a moment he stood utterly motionless, rearing up on the tips of his toes. Blood trickled out over his lips. He took one tottering step toward Nialli Apuilana. Then he fell sprawling, landing beside the body of Chevkija Aim. He quivered once and was still.

"Guards! Guards!" Thu-Kimnibol roared.

Seizing Nialli Apuilana with one hand and Taniane with the other, he pulled them behind him and swung about to see what was happening below the platform. Some kind of disturbance was going on down there. The guardsmen were moving in to quell it. Further in the distance the warriors of Thu-Kimnibol's own army, aware now of the strange struggle on the platform, had left their wagons and were rushing forward. At the center of everything Thu-Kimnibol saw the figure of a bright-robed boy of ten or twelve years, holding his hands high in the midst of the crowd and screaming curses of some sort in a terrifying furious voice sharp as a dagger.

"Look," Nialli Apuilana said. "He has Kundalimon's Nest-guardian!

His Nest-bracelet, too!" Her eyes were gleaming as fiercely as the boy's. "By the gods, I'll deal with him! Leave him to me!"

The Barak Dayir was suddenly in her hand. Deftly she seized it with her sensing-organ. Thu-Kimnibol stared at her in bewilderment as the Wonderstone instantly worked some bizarre transformation on her: she seemed to grow in size, to turn into something huge and strange.

"I see the Queen within you," cried Nialli Apuilana in a dark frightful tone, looking down with blazing eyes at the boy in bright robes. "But I call Her out! I cast Her forth! Now! Now! Now! *Out!*"

For a moment all was silent. Time itself hung, frozen, still, suspended by a heartbeat.

Then the boy staggered as if he had been struck. He twisted about and made a dry chittering sound, a sound almost like one a hjjk would make, and his face turned gray and then black; and he fell forward and was lost to sight in the surging crowd.

Calmly Nialli Apuilana restored the Barak Dayir to its pouch.

"All's well now," she said, taking Thu-Kimnibol once more by the hand.

It was hours later, after general quiet had been restored. They were in the great chamber of the Presidium.

Taniane said, "So there is to be peace, of a sort. Out of the madness of the war comes a kind of victory. Or at any rate a truce. But what have we accomplished? At any time, at the Queen's mere whim, it could all begin again."

Thu-Kimnibol shook his head. "I think not, sister. The Queen knows better now what we're like, and what we're capable of doing. The world will be divided now. The hjjks will leave us alone, I promise you that. They'll keep to their present territory, and we to ours, and there'll be no more talk of Nest-thinkers setting up shop in our cities."

"And how will it be in territories that are neither theirs nor ours? That was what troubled Hresh so much, that the hjjks would keep us from the rest."

"The rest of the world will remain open, mother," said Nialli Apuilana. "We can explore it as we choose, whenever we're ready. And who knows what things we will find? There may be great cities of the People on the other continents. Or the humans themselves may have returned to the world from wherever it is they went when the Great World died, and are living there now, for all we know. Who can say? But we'll find out. We'll go wherever we want, and discover everything that is to be discovered, just as my father hoped we would. The Queen understands now that there'll be no penning us up in our little strip of coastline. If anyone has been penned up, it's the hjjks, in the godforsaken lands they've always inhabited."

"So it is a victory, then," Taniane said. "Of a kind." She did not sound jubilant.

"A victory, sister," said Thu-Kimnibol sternly. "Make no mistake about that. We'll be at peace. What else is that but victory?"

"Yes. Perhaps it is." After a moment Taniane said, "And Hresh? You were with him when he died, Thu-Kimnibol has told me. What was it like for him, at the end?"

"He was at peace," said Nialli Apuilana simply.

"I'll want you to tell me more about that later. Now we have other matters to deal with." Turning, she took the dark, gleaming Mask of Koshmar from the high table of the Presidium, where she had placed it when they entered. She held it forth. It was boldly carved: a powerful, indomitable face with strong full lips, a jutting jaw, wide flaring cheekbones. To Nialli Apuilana she said, "This was Koshmar, the greatest woman of our tribe. Without her vision and strength none of us would be here today. Without her we would have been nothing. Take her mask, Nialli."

"What am I to do with it, mother?"

"Put it on."

"Put it on?"

"It's the mask of chieftainship."

"I don't understand you."

"This is the last day of my forty years of rule. They've been telling me for a long while now that it's time I stepped aside, and they're right. Today I resign my office. Take the mask, Nialli."

Amazement and uncertainty flared in Nialli Apuilana's eyes.

"Mother, this can't be. My father has already named me chronicler. That's what I'll be now. Not chieftain."

Now it was Taniane's turn to look amazed.

"Chronicler?"

"So he told me, in his last moments. It was his special wish. I have the Wonderstone. I know how to use it."

Taniane was silent a long while, as if she had withdrawn into some distant world.

Then in a quiet voice she said, "If you are to be chronicler and not chieftain, then the old way is at its end. I felt that you were ready, that at last it would be possible for you to succeed me. But you will not have it; and there's no one else to whom I would give this mask. Very well. There will be no more chieftains among the People."

She looked away.

Thu-Kimnibol said, "Is there no way you could be chronicler and chieftain both, Nialli?"

"Both?"

"Why can't the titles be joined? You'd have the mask and the Barak

Dayir also. The mask makes you chieftain, the Wonderstone makes you chronicler. You'll hold both and you'll rule with both."

"But the chronicles—the work of the House of Knowledge—it's too much, Thu-Kimnibol."

"Chupitain Stuld can have charge of the House of Knowledge. She'll do the work, but she'll report to you."

"No," Nialli Apuilana said. "I see a different way. I'll keep the Wonderstone, yes, because my father intended it that way. But I'm not the one who should sit at the head of the Presidium. Mother, give him the mask. He's won the right to wear it."

Thu-Kimnibol laughed. "I, wear Koshmar's mask? Go before the Presidium in it, and call myself chieftain? This is a fine strong face, Nialli, but it's a woman's face!"

"Then make do without the mask," said Taniane suddenly. "And without the title, also. All things are new now. If you won't be chieftain, Thu-Kimnibol, call yourself king!"

"King?"

"Your father was a king in Yissou. You will be a king now too."

He stared at Taniane in wonder. "Do you mean this?"

"Yours was the victory. Yours is the right. You are of the same blood as Hresh; and Nialli Apuilana has chosen you to rule. Can you refuse?"

"There's never been a king over the Koshmar tribe."

"This is not the Koshmar tribe," said Taniane. "This is the City of Dawinno, and it'll be without a ruler after today. Will you be king here, or do you mean to leave us leaderless, Thu-Kimnibol?"

He paced back and forth before the high table. Then he halted and whirled and pointed at Nialli Apuilana.

"If I'm to be king, then you'll be queen!"

She looked at him in alarm. "Queen? What are you saying? Do you think I'm a hjjk, Thu-Kimnibol? They're the only ones who have queens."

Laughing, he said, "They have queens, yes, but why should that matter to us? In this city you are the king's mate; and what's the king's mate, if not a queen? So the hjjks will have their queen, and we'll have one too. Queen of Dawinno, you'll be. And when we go to the unknown lands, you'll be queen of those also, eh? Queen of everything that grows and flourishes on the face of this reborn world. The Queen of the New Springtime." He took her hand in his. "What do you say to that, Nialli? The Queen of Springtime!" His voice went booming through the great room with overwhelming exuberance. "And when that other and far less beautiful queen sends another ambassador to us, bringing some new and troublesome proposition, which she will surely do before we are old, why, you can reply to her as her equal, one queen to another! What do you say, Nialli? Queen Nialli, is it? And King Thu-Kimnibol?"

* * *

Nialli Apuilana sits quietly, staring at the blank page in front of her. Her fingers hover above it. Chronicler? Her? And queen, too? How strange that seems! But for the moment, chronicler only. She is in Hresh's study on the highest level of the House of Knowledge. All around her are Hresh's things, the treasures he collected. The past is everywhere in this room.

She must set it all down, these wondrous bewildering events. What shall she say? She can barely comprehend it. Is this where she has been heading all along, all through this difficult voyage of hers? What shall she say, what shall she say?

Lightly she touches the amulet at her breast. A flicker of faint warmth goes through her hand. And it seems to her that a slight ghostly figure has passed swiftly through the room at that moment, one who is lithe and wiry, with great dark eyes in which luminous intelligence blazes forth, and that in the moment of his passage he turned to her, and smiled, and nodded, and shaped the word "queen" with his lips. The Queen of Springtime, yes. Yes. To whom will fall the task her father had begun, of attempting to discover who we really are, and what it is we must do to fulfill the intentions of the gods, how it is that we are meant to conduct ourselves in the world into which we came forth when the Long Winter ended. She smiles. She puts her fingers to the page at last, and the letters begin to form. She is entering it in the chronicles, finally, on the topmost blank page, that on the day such-and-such in the year such-and-such of the Coming Forth great changes came about, for on that day the revered chieftain Taniane resigned her office and with her the chieftainship of ancient days at last was brought to an end for all time, and the first of the kings and queens of the city were chosen, who would preside over all that must be done in the aftermath of the great and terrible war with the hjjks. In which the People had acquitted themselves honorably and won a mighty victory.

She pauses. Looks up. Searches through the room by the faint glow of lamplight, seeking Hresh. But now she is alone. She glances back at what she has written. The chieftain, the king, the queen, the victory. She must say something about the change of chroniclers now, too. Another great change.

Many great changes, yes. With greater ones no doubt yet to come. For we are deep into the New Springtime now, and the springtime is the season of unfolding and growth. In springtime the world is born anew.